THE SYNNER

PATH OF THE WRAITHBORN

BOOK FOUR OF THE SYNNER SAGA

I0599433

NOOBURAI

PUBLISHED BY DRAFT2DIGITAL

ALSO BY NOOBURAI

DISCLAIMER

Many of the topics, verbal descriptions, and uses of language are NOT appropriate for children. If you have to ask whether your child should read this, the answer is *no*. In all honesty, if you've made it this far in the series, I shouldn't even have to tell you that, but here I am, beating a dead horse for the sake of those who haven't gotten that through their heads yet.

Seriously, do NOT let your children read this, unless you're one of those parents who doesn't give the slightest turtle shit. Just saying.

That said, any and all characters are merely created to serve a purpose, and are not intended to depict my personal views or feelings toward anything that could be (somehow, probably through *extreme* extrapolation) connected to the real world. Again, this is a *fantasy series,* meaning any similarities to real people, living or otherwise, is purely coincidental.

Reaching the start of the next trilogy in *The Synner Saga* is something I could have only imagined in my wildest dreams, and I know that I wouldn't have made it here without a few people:

First and foremost: Mom. At the time of writing this, it's been *three and a half* years since you left the Realm, and while I know that death is not the end of all things, I can only hope to hold my head up high, knowing I've done you proud.

Second: My siblings. If it weren't for their support, encouragement, and presence during my childhood, I don't think I would have been able to accurately portray a sense of *family* that these characters have. So, thanks for that, assholes. I love you all.

Third: Everyone else who's either read it, supported it, commented, or given their honest feedback. This kind of stuff has certainly helped me grow as an author, and we all know that a good author doesn't evolve or grow when placed inside of a bubble. Thank you.

Finally: The haters. I feed off your tears, jealousy, and whatever else you decide to throw at me, and will continue to stand by what I've been saying from the start...

Git gud... *fuckers.*

CONTENTS

PROLOGUE

SEALED

I woke to the sound of a knock on my door.

It's probably just the wind, I thought, rustling and turning in my bed to ignore whatever caused the sound.

It happened again, a much slower and deliberate rhythm this time, as if the patience of whoever was knocking was wearing thin. "Thoma, are you awake?" I heard a deep, muffled voice come from behind the thick wooden door. I recognized it as my father's voice, but knowing how late at night it was, I couldn't think of any reason why he'd want to talk to me.

As I looked out my small window, I could see the light of the full moon casting a silver glow on the gently swaying tree tops that surrounded our house. Judging by that alone, I knew that there were still more than a few hours until dawn, but that my mother likely wouldn't be home for *at least* another two days.

I remember they had a heated conversation earlier that week about a few-day mission she had to go on, but I couldn't immediately recall when she said she'd be home. What I *didn't* realize, however, was just how vital that information would have been.

I took a deep breath and sighed heavily, already fearing whatever would come of this late-night interaction, and got out of bed, rubbing my eyes with my knuckles. After lazily walking over to the door,

I opened my eyes only to find a bright lantern shining in my face, making me squint through my already heavy eyelids.

"What time is it? Is something wrong, Dad?" I asked, trying my best to shield my eyes from the bright light. "It's a little past midnight, and no, nothing's wrong. At least, it won't be for much longer," he said cryptically as I struggled to understand what he meant. "Come, there's something we need to do," he said as he pushed my door open and forced me away from it.

He briskly walked to where my cloak was hanging and grabbed it off the hook, wrapping it around my shoulders. "Can you at least tell me where we're going?" I asked bluntly as I felt my body jerk from his pulling the cloak's open seams across my chest as he clasped the small brooch near my clavicle. He squatted down to be at eye level with me and put his hands on my shoulders.

"I need you to listen to me very closely, Thoma," he began, staring into my eyes with an almost frightened look as the pendant around his neck glinted in the lantern's light. There was something about it that drew my attention, but whatever it was quickly vanished.

It wasn't like him to be fond of jewelry, although the green crystal inlaid in silver around his neck was a gift from my mother that he wore often. But, for whatever reason, I could almost *feel* something was different about it.

He wasn't a particularly kind man, at least not to me or my brother, but he wasn't one to scare easily either, and the look on his face was something I'd never seen, not even *once*. It was strange to see him in such a state, but I knew that I couldn't dwell on those thoughts for long, since he immediately lowered his head.

"There's something *wrong* with you, and we need to get you to a healer quickly before it gets any worse," he said, gripping my shoulders a little more tightly before looking back up at me. "What do you mean *something's wrong* with me? I feel fine, Dad, and if something's *really* wrong with me, then Mom can just fix it when she gets back," I shrugged, not knowing that my reply would cause him to react.

"You're a *fool* for thinking *she* could fix what's wrong, Thoma, but I know someone who can; someone *far* more powerful than she could ever hope to be," he replied bitterly in a tone of voice I'd never heard him use before. The pungent smell of wine on his breath made me wrinkle my nose a little, forcing me to try to back away a little, but he held me firmly in place.

He's going to force me to go with him to see this person, isn't he? I felt my stomach sink in realization immediately.

"Dad, I-I'm scared. Why can't we just have Mom do it? I'm sure she can fig-..." I cut myself off when my father's face twisted angrily for a brief moment, then quickly reverted to a pained smile as if he was suddenly back in control of himself. "There's no need to be afraid of him. I promise he's going to *help* you, but we need to move quickly if we're going to be on time to meet him," he said in a much calmer tone as he gestured to the door.

I knew I wasn't going to get any *truthful* answers out of him for the time being, so I nodded my understanding and followed his commands. As we walked down the stairs, I could see there was an empty bottle of wine on the table, and judging by what he'd said earlier, as well as the time of night when he decided to pull this little stunt, I could tell there was more going on than I realized.

As we approached the front door, I noticed the horse from the stables had already been prepared for what looked like a two-day trip, with only two small satchels attached to the saddle. I looked up at his face to see if there was any sort of answer I could get, but the strange smirk on his face told me everything I needed to know.

Nothing's wrong with me, *there's something wrong with* him. *I've never seen that look in his eyes before,* I noticed his plump cheeks bunching up near widened eyes as his fist slammed into the side of my head.

That was the last thing I remembered before darkness overcame me.

When I woke up, I found there were ropes tied around my hands and ankles, my shirt had been taken off, and there were candles at various points of strange markings in a pattern on the floor in front of me. I blinked a handful of times, already feeling the swelling begin to throb as I regained consciousness.

Where am I? I thought through blurry vision and a hazy presence of mind as I struggled to sit up.

With a small grunt of exertion, I managed to push myself up and sit upright, using my knees to try to rub my eyes in hopes of clearing my vision. Blinking another few times and trying to ignore the pain that riddled the side of my face, I did what I could to understand my surroundings.

The candles and strange lines on the ground were in a much more deliberate shape than I initially understood. Each one was placed at the apex of an octagonal ring, which I was right in the middle of. Above me, I could see hams of different meats and shelves of cheeses, though I had no idea what their purpose was.

Wherever this is, it looks more like a storage shed than anything else. Is this where the healer is supposed to be? I wondered, trying to figure out what was going on.

"*Ah*, you're finally awake. I was wondering how long it would take you to wake up," an unrecognizable voice came from behind me, making me flinch in surprise. I did what I could to face the source of my surprise, only to find a weathered old man sitting on a stool just a few meters behind me, with his calloused hands quickly raised in a placating gesture.

The top half of his face was covered by a sheet of cloth held by a thin leather band, with slits cut out for the pair of glowing, sickly-green eyes laced with black tendrils staring back at me. His beard was haggard and unkempt, and there was a considerable amount of dirt beneath his fingernails that I could see even from where I was sitting.

What surprised me the most, however, was that this old man was sitting with one leg loosely crossed over the other and leaning back, reminding me of the painting my father had of himself, which hung in our home.

"Wh-who are you? Why am I here?" I asked, trying to scoot as far away from him as I could. "Calm down, there's no need to fear me. I'm a friend of your father's, though I didn't expect him to bring you here in this state," the old man said with a voice that didn't match his features, revealing a set of rotten teeth as he grinned in an attempt to appear more *friendly*.

Needless to say, it didn't help.

"I apologize for startling you, as that was never my intention. I only meant to make you aware of my presence," he continued, getting up from his seat. I could hear the decades of wear on his joints crackle as he stood, but he showed no sign of being in any sort of pain as he walked over to the edge of the circle, where he got down on one, crackling knee.

Is he even human? I thought, as the sound reminded me of when I'd tear off a chicken leg at dinner.

"Can I have my shirt back? It's cold in here," I asked, trying to disguise the fear-filled chills running down my body as being cold. "We both know that's a lie, Thoma. Do you think it's *wise* to lie to your elders?" the old man asked, prompting me to shake my head in disagreement.

How does he know I lied? I wondered quietly.

"That's easy; I can read your thoughts," he answered the question I'd just asked myself, catching me entirely off guard. I felt my eyes widen in surprise and the realization that this person, whoever he was, was *much more* powerful than he was letting on.

"Now, I'm sure you're *very* confused by all of this, so I'll try to keep this simple," he said, rising from his kneeling position. As he entered the octagonal ring, the markings on the floor immediately responded to his presence, glowing the same sickly green color present in his eyes.

"Your father has told me a *lot* about you, but even with all of the information he's given me, there are still two more things I need *you* to confirm in his stead. Don't bother trying to hide it, as it won't work out well for you if you do. Do you understand?" he asked coldly as he sat on his heels, gazing into my eyes intently as he raised a pair of fingers.

I swallowed dryly and nodded my head, instinctively knowing that any other answer was likely to cause me *pain*. I don't know how I knew, but the feeling I had when looking at my father's pendant was present again. Even though he told me I didn't have to *fear* him, there was no other feeling I could comprehend in that moment, which sent another chill rolling down my spine.

"Good. The first question I'm going to ask you is a simple one: What do you see when you look into my eyes?" he asked, leaning in a little closer as the green color in his eyes flared. "I only see *green*, sir," I answered truthfully. For some reason, I was unable to see the black tendrils anymore, though he seemed satisfied enough with my answer, as the same, toothy grin reappeared beneath the cloth.

"Excellent, Thoma. I see you took my warning about answering truthfully to heart," he nodded slowly as he began to chuckle to himself. As he continued to laugh, I couldn't help but grow even *more confused* by this strange display.

"What about the second thing, sir?" I asked, hoping to get whatever this was over with as quickly as possible. His chuckling immediately halted, and I could tell he'd closed his eyes beneath the cloth. "The second question is: What about *now*?" he asked, suddenly grabbing the top of my hair and pulling my face towards his until I was at eye level with him.

The green color in his eyes immediately swarmed with the same black tendrils from before, only this time, they were much more pronounced. They flicked around violently, disrupting the glow in his eyes wherever they appeared like oil to water. Suddenly, the tendrils' sporadic movement quelled, and they began to swirl and flow counter to one another as if in a macabre dance.

"Tell me what you see," he said, still piercing my gaze with his own, prompting me to shut my eyes out of fear and shake my head. "Thoma, tell me what you see," he repeated more impatiently, but I held my eyes tightly shut and shook my head. "Tell me what you see!" he screamed in my face as he shook my head. A jolt of pain passed through my body like a saw tearing at every muscle, tendon, and bone in my body.

Why are you doing this? I thought, unable to vocally form a word since the pain was unbearable.

"Because you're not answering the simple question. The pain you're feeling will end when you tell me *what you see.* You're the master of your fate here, Thoma, and you can end this whenever you want to. I didn't want to have to resort to this, but you've left me no choice. Now, tell me what you see!" he shouted as he shook my head again, but the pain I felt from him nearly ripping out my hair was nothing compared to what was happening aside from that.

Through his shouting, I could hear what I thought was a stone being torn from the ground, and the light of the small candles around me began to grow more brightly as the air within the small shack began to tremble. The water from the nearby washing bowl splashed violently onto the floor, but whether that was my doing or *his,* I had no idea; however, I could *feel* it all happening.

The room continued to shake and tremble as my mind searched for a solution, *any* solution, to my current predicament, but nothing came. Nothing except the need to endure whatever this horrible test of his was.

I know I can't escape, but my only other option is to outlast this, I thought, not worrying about whether he could hear it.

"You can struggle all you want to, Thoma, but I *will* get an answer from you one way or another. If this continues much longer, you'll end up *dying*, or is death something you're starting to *welcome*?" he asked, but I didn't answer. My sole focus was to keep any other thoughts scattered and without order, so he wouldn't find the answer he was looking for.

Time seemed to come to a crawl as the pain riddled my body. There was little more I could do except try my best not to lose consciousness, but as my attention shifted back inwardly with another jolt of pain, I could feel that the pain had somewhat *lessened* when the room began to tremble. It was only after the pain had begun to subside that my jaw unclenched enough for me to speak the only words I knew would either put an end to it or *me*.

"W-Why do y-you need to know?" I barely managed to ask within the slight moment of clarity through gritted teeth, prompting him to suddenly release me from whatever it was he was doing to me and quickly get to his feet to leave the octagonal ring. As the pain receded, I was abruptly thrown into a fit of coughing, as blood poured from my nose and the corners of my mouth.

I coughed a few more times before I managed to look up at him, but the look on his face wasn't one I was prepared for. It wasn't fear, or anger, or any of the other expressions I could quickly recognize.

Instead, just behind the slits of cloth, there was *hope* in his eyes.

"Well done! Well done, indeed, Thoma," he said through an astounded chuckle as he began to clap. "I've been looking for someone like you for a *very* long time, you see, but I never would have thought you would have been right *here* all along. Your potential and levels of defiance are *exactly* the things I'm looking for," he spread his arms widely while I coughed up more blood, and spat whatever was in my mouth onto the ground as I began to double over.

"No, no, no! Don't do that. Your blood is much too precious to be wasted so frivolously. I apologize for your injuries, but your insubordination *was* the cause of them, after all," he said, moving forward to help me sit upright once more as a sickly-green glow emanated from the palm of his hand and into my chest. I could feel the exact opposite of whatever was happening to me before race through my body, as the same muscles and bones felt like they were being stitched back together.

"There, all better now," he said with another grin filled with rotting teeth as he removed his hand from my chest. I was still breathing heavily as a result of that experience, but I'd be lying if I said I wasn't grateful it was over.

Or, so I thought.

"Why did you do this to me? What kind of answers were you looking for?" I asked bluntly, not bothering to be polite to him anymore, but my question caused him to place a finger on his matted beard and twirl it loosely as he thought of an answer. After a few moments, he removed his hand and leaned in toward me once more.

"Because I needed to know if you would be of use to me. Your father made some bold claims about you, though I will say, I didn't expect them to be true," he said loosely, but no matter what tone of voice he used, I still felt apprehensive about him. There was something about his nature that was unpredictable, and I didn't like it at all.

"You want to *use me* for something?" I asked, trying to gain a better understanding of what he meant. "Not *use* you, *per se*, but form an alliance with you," he explained. "What's an *alliance*?" I asked, not knowing the meaning of the word. "Think of it like a *friendship*. You *do* have friends, don't you?" he asked, but I suppose the look on my face when he said the word *friends* told him everything he needed to know.

"*Ah*, well, I suppose we can't have *everything* in life," he said, backing away to sit on his heels once more. "How about *I* become your first friend?" he asked after a moment's pause, catching me by surprise. "Why would I want to be friends with *you*? You just hurt me," I sneered, but it had little effect on him.

"*That pain* was your own doing. I told you to answer me truthfully, but you refused to do so. You *forced* me to do that, you see. So, what do you say?" he asked with a nonchalant shrug, but I didn't immediately answer.

Everything about him was strange, and his unpredictable nature, like before, caused me a sense of unease that I didn't understand at the time. I didn't know what would happen if I flat-out refused, but I *also* knew that he wasn't going to let me walk away from this easily.

What should I do? I asked myself without voicing the words in my head.

"I'm waiting," he said in a sing-song voice as he tapped a dirty finger on his thigh, as his impatience began to grow again. The obvious choice would have been to accept and be done with this strange encounter, but after everything I'd heard, felt, and seen, I couldn't bring myself to trust him *at all*.

"I don't think it's a good idea for me to be your friend," I shook my head, mentally preparing myself for whatever came next. While I couldn't see his entire face, his body language told me he was disappointed in my answer as he let out a heavy sigh. "Then suffer the consequences," he said maliciously just before dashing forward and placing his palm on my chest again. There was a bright flash of the pale green light before I felt the same pain from before. This time, however, it was only focused on a single region of my chest, just below my heart.

I screamed in agony like before, but as the intensity of the pain grew, I tried to recall the same feeling I had from before to fight against it. The room trembled and the air swirled like before, and I could tell that whatever I was doing was working, because he began to grit his rotten teeth in exertion as well.

I did what I could to struggle against him for a few moments, but as the glow in my chest intensified, I looked into his eyes one last time. There was no hope in them, only a slight hint of *fear* over something I couldn't identify in the time I had before the energy between us exploded. I was sent flying backward into the far wall, and I saw he was knocked onto his back just before I blacked out.

I don't know how much time had passed, but it couldn't have been very long before I regained consciousness and noticed something was missing that I'd never realized I had before.

What just happened? I wondered, feeling incredibly weak as a sharp pain in my chest sped up my regaining of consciousness.

As I looked around the now-dilapidated storage room through teary eyes and listened through ringing ears, the pain became almost unbearable. I curled into a ball and began to sob uncontrollably, as I suddenly realized I wasn't able to fight against it like before. "Why? Why won't it work?" I hissed as a stringy wad of spit left my mouth in frustration.

Just then, I heard my father's muffled voice entering the room, but he didn't immediately rush to my aid. Instead, he was rapidly asking the old man a plethora of questions, but he only raised his grimy hand to stop him. "I've done enough for now. Your son will *never* be able to reach his full potential unless *I* allow it," the old man said, from what I could hear.

You bastard, I thought, knowing this was a part of his plan all along.

Even though the events were still exceedingly fresh in my mind, I dreaded the day I'd ever have to meet him again. If the only way to remove whatever he'd done to me were by *allying* with him, then I'd prefer to have lived with whatever he'd done with me and never see him again.

They must have realized I was awake because they immediately lowered their voices to a hush, preventing me from hearing anything further. At that point, I didn't want to anyway. I didn't care anymore, since whatever he did to me would likely be with me for the rest of my life, and I knew there was only *one way* out of it.

I stayed in the position I was in, focusing only on trying to survive the pain I was in. I could feel the tears streaming down my face and soaking into the wooden floorboards beneath me as they puddled beneath my cheek. The only thing left to do at the time was wait for it all to be over. I didn't know why my father had brought me to this person, but one thing I knew for sure was that whenever my mother got home, she wouldn't be happy to hear what had happened.

A few minutes later, my father came and untied the ropes around my hands and ankles, which left bright red marks due to my struggle against the old man. He held my face in my hands, but at this point,

I remember I was little more than catatonic, and entirely unable to give the slightest shit about whatever words left his mouth.

He helped me put my shirt back on and wrapped my cloak around me the same way he had before, then led me out to the horse, which carried more supplies now than the night we'd left. He helped me up onto the horse, probably knowing he didn't have to knock me out this time, and mounted just behind me.

As we turned to leave, the old man waved us off, but gave *me* a knowing look from beneath the cloth, sending what little contents I had in my stomach soaring from between my teeth. "It's alright, Thoma. You're all better now," my father said, patting me on the back as I spat the remaining bile.

Better? I thought, feeling a rage against him I didn't know I had in me.

Perhaps I *did* know, but this was the first time I ever dared to acknowledge it. I had no idea what he was thinking in putting me through that, but there was one thing I knew for sure: there was something about me that changed enough to satisfy him.

I don't know exactly how long we rode for, as all I could do was focus on not passing out from the pain accentuated by the horse's gait. I closed my eyes and focused inwardly, doing my best not to puke or fall off the horse. At some point, however, we finally made it home, and after helping me get down from the horse, my dad gave me a self-satisfied look that rubbed me the wrong way. I hardly had the strength to challenge it, and decided it was best to turn away and ignore whatever he was about to say.

"Where do you think you're going?" he asked as he watched me begin to walk toward the tree line, but I just ignored him. "I asked you a question, Thoma," he said, revealing a hint of annoyance in his tone, causing me to halt and turn to face him with a furrowed brow. "Does it matter?" I asked, not bothering to maintain any sort of pleasantries with him as my mental state finally recovered.

"How *dare you* speak to me in that tone?" he snarled, but it did nothing to me. There was nothing he could say that I cared for, and even less that I was going to obey at this point. I rolled my eyes and continued walking away, hearing him shout something I willingly ignored, though it was probably a string of insults and name-calling, judging by the pattern and tone of his voice.

As I moved through the trees, I found a spot I felt was far enough away from him to be outside of earshot. I slumped against the roots of a massive tree and gazed upward at the gently swaying branches.

Well, at least I can still smell the rain coming, I sighed as I looked off toward the distant rain clouds.

What's done is done. The only thing I can do now is live with whatever that old man did to me. If Mom were home, this wouldn't have happened, right? She would've probably killed that old man long before he laid a finger on me, I thought as I rested my head against the thick roots.

I didn't know what to do. Was there anything I *could've even done* about that situation? Not likely, but I figured I had to make the best of it while I still could. After a few hours, the smell of rain grew stronger, meaning it was time to head back home.

No, that's probably not a good idea right now, I thought, knowing my father was likely still angry at my behavior when we got home.

I sighed again, and as I let out the last bit of air in my lungs, the rain began to fall. The clouds above me were dark and gray, though the rain brought me a solace I didn't know I needed. I knew he wasn't going to come after me in the rain, so I decided to stay in the woods overnight.

If a creature wants a snack, I don't think I'm much of a meal, but I also wouldn't care if it did, I thought, letting my forehead rest on my knees as I bundled my cloak around me.

The following morning, the rain had subsided somewhat, though it was still drizzling, and I could feel my stomach rumbling from hunger.

Damn it, why now? I thought angrily at my body's inability to sustain me on nothing but rainwater and the handful of dried fruit I stole from the horse before I'd left.

I accepted my fate and decided it was time to head home, but I heard a rustling behind me. Initially, I thought it was just a wild animal, but when I turned to look, all I could see was a white piece of cloth hanging over a scraggly beard off in the distance.

Shit, did he follow us home? I thought, trying to feign that I hadn't seen him.

Whether he'd heard my thoughts was another story, but thankfully, nothing came of it, and I made my way back home without another instance of him appearing.

I snuck in from the back door, knowing my father seldom visited that area of the house, as he usually stayed in the living room during the early hours of the morning. I had no idea what time it was, but it was early enough that it was still the most likely place he'd be. But as I cracked open the door, I was surprised to hear not one, but *two* voices in the living room.

Mom? I thought, using my knowledge of the floorboards that creaked, and the ones that didn't, to get closer to hear their conversation from around the corner.

"I'm not going to ask you again. Where the *fuck* is my son?" she asked in a harsh tone of voice. "Siraye, I've already told you that I don't know. He went off into the woods and hasn't come back since yesterday evening," he said dismissively. "And why would he do that? What did you *do*?" she asked again, leaning in toward him. Her steel-colored hair was still matted from her journey home, and she was still wearing her armor.

It couldn't have been more than a few minutes that she's been back, I realized, immediately revealing myself.

"Mom, I'm right *here*," I said, stepping out from behind the corner of the short hallway that led to the pantry. "Thoma!" she said, rushing over to me and wrapping me in a tight, wet hug. Her armor still smelled of a creature's blood even though the rain had soaked through it. "I'm glad you're home safely. He didn't hurt you, did he?" she asked as she pulled back to give me a once-over with her eyes.

I glanced over at my father, who put a single finger to his lips and shook his head. I didn't have to be an adult to realize that if I'd said the truth right then, the next time she left, he was going to *hurt me*. "N-No, Mom. I'm okay," I said with as fake a smile as I could muster. She regarded me curiously for a moment, but her curiosity shifted into a bright, beaming smile, one that made me feel better *immediately*.

"I see. Gods above, you're soaking wet! Go upstairs, take a bath, and get into some warm clothes. I'll be up there shortly," she gave me a pat on the shoulder before I nodded my understanding and rushed upstairs. As I reached the last step where I could still see her from, I saw her fingers ball into a tightly clenched fist before she slowly made her way over to my father.

"Go upstairs, Thoma. Your Father and I need to have a conversation," she said, somehow knowing I was still watching. I swallowed dryly and did as she told me.

An hour later, the rain had gotten worse, and as I was just about to sit down on my bed, I heard the sound of a crashing glass and my mother's raised voice coming from below.

I know she told me to stay upstairs until she got here, but it's been an hour already, and they're still arguing? I should probably check on them, I thought, knowing it was something my older brother, Bernar, would have done.

But as I walked downstairs, I saw the front door wide open as the smell of the heavy rain began to fill the living room's air, and my mother standing in its doorway, with a tightly clenched fist around the hilt of an elegantly curved blade.

Is she leaving again? No, she just got home, so why...? I felt my stomach drop, and tears welled in my eyes as she took the first step out of the door, saying something I couldn't comprehend in my confusion.

CHAPTER 76
A TEST OF STRENGTH

"**B**rother, we need to talk," I said, already foreseeing how the next few weeks, if not *months,* were about to go.

Bernar looked at me with utter bewilderment, but lowered his sword when I gave him a nod of confirmation that it was fine to do so. "What the hell kind of sword *is that*, anyway? I didn't even hear you draw it," he glanced downward at my wrist as the *kataki* reformed into the bracelet.

"Like I said, this is Lady Kalia. She was my mentor during my time in the Underworld. She was also the one who gave me the blade," I said again, stepping aside with a wide grin to allow two of my favorite people in the Realm to interact *properly* this time. "*Ah,* well, I guess I should have asked before charging in like that," Bernar chuckled and scratched the back of his head.

"It's alright, Bernar. Thoma might not have known it, but he's all but warned me this could happen after *years* of hearing his stories about you," Kalia shrugged with an upturned lip, causing his eyes to widen. "*Years*? It's not even been a full month since you've been gone," he said without hiding the confusion rattling his mind, but that's when I stepped in.

"We were training inside a dome that used the density of dark mana to manipulate the flow of time even more than what the Underworld already does," I explained as loosely as I could, but it didn't seem to help. After a few pensive moments, he relented and let out a heavy sigh. "You're gonna have to explain that to me again later, but I have another question to ask: why are your eyes *red* like Ren's?" he leaned in to scrutinize me further.

Before I could answer, however, Ren stepped in and smacked him upside the head, surprising *everyone* present. "You didn't drink the vial I gave you either?" he asked frustratedly, but Bernar could only offer him a look of brief confusion, which quickly shifted back into realization. "*Oh*, hold on a minute. I think I know what you're talking about," he said, dashing over to his horse and pulling something from one of his satchels.

A few moments of frantic searching later, and some mild confusion from Leona, he returned with the flask Ren had given the two of us before we first came to Caegwen. "You mean this one? You never said what it was for, so I didn't bother to drink it," he shrugged as he held it in front of him. My mother and the others began moving toward us in the wake of the confusion he'd left behind, and I could already tell what was about to happen.

"I thought I told you two to drink it when you got here in the first place," Ren sighed as he pinched the bridge of his nose in a show of frustration I'd never seen come from him. In fact, it was rare to see him show any emotions *at all*. "You might have, sure, but with my mother's reunion with Thoma, it slipped my mind," Bernar chuckled nervously, while Leona and the group continued moving toward us.

"What's going on? Why did you suddenly atta-... wait, who is this?" Leona asked, halting her movement forward. "That's Lady

Kalia, the one I just told you about," my mother stepped in. "*Oh, I see. Well, it's a pleasure to make your acquaintance, and I apologize for his behavior,*" she said, jutting an elbow firmly into Bernar's side.

"It's an honor to meet you as well, Your Majesty," Kalia said with a bow, surprising Leona. "H-How did you...?" she stammered, but Kalia held up a hand. "Thoma filled me in as soon as you began to speak," she said plaintively, as if it were common knowledge that she and I could communicate non-verbally.

"But when could he have done that? It hasn't even been *a minute* since I laid eyes on you," Leona asked, regarding me curiously.

Shit. Ren, do you want to explain this to her? I sent him mentally, but he shook his head. *No, because I'm curious to hear your explanation. Also, she scares me,* he answered briefly, returning to his old ways more quickly than I'd expected. *Fine, I'll do it,* I gave a relenting sigh amid a mental chuckle.

"Leona, before anything else, I think we need to explain what *this* is," I accented the word as I snatched the vial out of my brother's hand and began to walk over to the small group that followed her. There were two new faces I didn't recognize immediately, but if they were here with her, I knew she trusted them with whatever took place.

Wait, did Erumon mention anything about revealing the Wraith realm to either of you? I sent Ysevel and Kalia before I began, but they both shook their heads. *He never mentioned it, but I don't know if it's a good idea to explain* everything *about it,* Kalia cautioned, which I took seriously. Knowing at least *some* of her past told me enough to know we had to be careful with what we revealed.

"This vial allows whoever drinks it access to a *different* kind of power," I said, avoiding using its real name. "A *different kind* of power? What do you mean?" she asked with unbridled curiosity. "Let's just say it lets you do something like *this*," I said as I produced a small scarlet dagger, which made everyone stare at me with widened eyes.

"I don't know how much detail I can go into right now, but if Lady Kalia and Ren deem it appropriate, I'll explain what I can," I said, turning to glance at them to get a nod of approval. *I've already given some to Siraye, so there's no real point in hiding it much more,* Ren sent as he nodded.

After acknowledging his words, I turned to look at Leona and the others, who were visibly struck with the same curiosity I had when I first met Kalia. "This vial allows one access to the Wraith realm. It's a different kind of mana that resides in the fine line between life and death," I began, getting a shocked look from the two newcomers more than anyone else.

"Those who drink the tincture Ren has developed and begin to wield the mana from the Wraith realm are known as *Wraithborn*; a much larger part of a whole, let's say. The abilities you can gain from wielding the mana can vary from person to person, but there are a few fundamentals that remain the same across the board," I explained as briefly as I could, though I was only met with confused stares.

Was I too brief? I sent Ren, but he gave me an approving gesture, likely noting that it was sufficient.

"Then what about *you*? Did you drink it while you were down there in the Underworld?" Bernar raised an eyebrow at me, as if he already knew I was hiding information. "I did, but I shared mine with

Ysevel, who drank the other half in hopes of understanding exactly what had happened to me," I shrugged, causing Bernar to glance over at her, mimicking my movement as well.

"What do you mean by that?" he asked curiously. "Well, drink half and see for yourself," I grinned, handing the vial back to him. He took it with a somewhat doubtful look on his face, but after a few silent urges from my mother and Ren, he did as I told him.

"*Oh*, you two might want to brace yourselves for this," I said, gesturing to a tall red-haired woman and a shorter man about my age with closely cut hair who were still blatantly staring at Kalia. *Snapping them out of their daze might have been a good call*, Ysevel chuckled, bringing a slight smile to my face before I turned to look at my brother's reaction.

"Okay, that was half, but I don't feel any different," he said with a blank look on his face, but my mother held an expectant smile. "*Juuuust* give it a minute," she grinned wolfishly as she gingerly took the vial from his hand.

As if the realm had heard her words, a massive burst of the Wraith realm's scarlet mana permeated the air, creating a dome much larger than I thought mine had and making everyone flinch.

Well, *almost* everyone.

"Wh-what the...? Ren, what the *fuck* was in that?" he asked as the density of scarlet mana began to dissipate. The others recovered from their guarded positions and stared at him cautiously in case of another blast. "Call it an *informal introduction* to being a Wraithborn," Ren said with what I could have sworn was a smile tugging at the corner of his mouth.

"*Informal introduction*? When do I get the real one?" Bernar asked bluntly. "Not yet, but we'll explain that later. You still have another half to give to someone," I noted as I gave Leona a knowing look, catching her by surprise. "Me? You want *me* to take the other half?" she asked breathlessly. "Well, you already understand *Ethereal* mana, so I don't see how understanding Wraith mana *wouldn't* be beneficial to you," I noted plainly, but whatever I'd said had nearly sent her into a state of shock that caused my brother to raise yet another eyebrow at me.

"Wh-what? Was it something I said?" I asked defensively. "How did you know she could use it? She's never said anything about it," the red-haired woman asked, taken aback, which made me chuckle. "Bernar just told me," I smiled, making him giggle and shake his head. "I never said *anything*," he shook his head with widened eyes. "You didn't have to," I smirked, knowing that the connection I had to his core was something he was yet to recognize.

After a few, silent heartbeats went by, I shifted my gaze back to Leona, who was seemingly lost in thought. "Well, it's no matter. I knew you would tell him *sooner* or later. But while I respect your suggestion, Thoma, I don't know what I would do with this power if I gained it," she admitted after a brief scowl at Bernar. However, I wasn't the one to answer her unasked question, as Kalia sent me a quick note that she wanted to help.

"Your Majesty, if I may," Kalia stepped out beside me, causing Leona to blink a handful of times, likely still getting used to a hegraphene being present.

"There is *much more* to being Wraithborn than fighting. *My* mentor, Sabura, who is considered what I believe you call a *sage* here in this realm, doesn't use it for combat. Rather, he uses it to *see* and understand things others can't, and has helped me grow into who I am today for a longer time than I care to admit," she continued with a light chuckle.

Leona was taken aback by the response, but Aurae, having learned about the *odoruki* technique from Ysevel, appeared beside her in a flash of movement. "It's alright to take it, Leona," she said in a soft, amicable tone that lessened the fright her sudden appearance gave Leona. "Queen Aurae," Leona said after taking a brief moment to compose herself.

"*Oh*, please. We do not need to use titles among friends," Aurae smiled brightly and gave a dismissive gesture, causing even the two newcomers to relax a little after having snapped to attention.

"In any case, what Kalia said is true, and I'd be more than willing to help guide you through the process of learning how it can be used to serve your people better," she continued light-heartedly as she placed a hand on Leona's shoulder, while Ysevel looked on proudly.

As she did so, I noticed Ren and Kalia had exchanged a glance before Kalia turned back to face Leona. "There is one thing that we must discuss *before* we give this to her," Kalia began with an air of caution, making everyone give her their undivided attention.

"Elves and hegraphenes are less affected by Wraith mana, given their naturally long lifespans. However, since she is purely *human*, wielding Wraith mana *will* extend her lifespan far beyond the capabilities of a normal human, though it will *not* make her impervious to *all* attacks," Kalia explained, getting a nod of understanding from Leona as she seemingly understood the gravity of what she was about to undertake.

The air hung heavily between us all as we waited for her reply. Leona was an intelligent woman I knew had studied many different cultures and concepts during her time in royal courts, but this decision was *also* one I knew she couldn't make lightly.

Any species that lived for more than a century knew the weight of living a long life, though it was more of an unspoken matter, as many painful memories were often borne of speaking about it. Having to watch friends and loved ones die, empires rise and fall, as well as the general passing of the world before your eyes, wasn't an easy price to pay, as some might have imagined.

Now that I think about it, not even *I* knew the true meaning of that yet.

Did you know? Bernar sent me as we all awaited her response. *Yes, but if I know her as well as I think I do, she'll make the choice that's best for her,* I sent back with a nod before he turned to look at Kalia and Ysevel, who also gave him the same. We remained silent for a few moments before she suddenly gave a sharp nod and a curt grunt as if to steel her will.

"I accept the offer, but I would like to spend some time here with Aurae to understand it better," she said in a much more sheepish tone than I'd ever heard her use. Surprisingly, I felt a sense of confidence coming from Kalia, who often talked about how much she hated what Nexis had become due to his greed.

"Wait, what about Coltend?" I asked, realizing that if she spent more time here, that meant more time away, leaving the rule over the city we'd fought so hard to protect unattended. "On the way back from Harut, we met with Gorm, whom I offered to be the vassal ruler in my stead since I knew we'd be spending a good amount of time here," Leona said with no small amount of pride in herself.

"Gorm? Wasn't he the guy who chased King Bash-...?" I began to ask, but after noticing the subtle shake of my brother's head, I gave up and dismissed my own question. "Yes, *that* Gorm. He's one I trust almost as much as Thorsen and Gwili," she nodded back toward them, who had flushed with her high praise as everyone burst into a fit of laughter after Bernar called Gwili out.

You can tell, too, can't you? I asked Kalia with a wry smile. *If it hadn't been for the information you've already given me about her, I might have objected, but she seems to have a* passable *presence of mind. Although I wonder what Erumon will have to say about all of this,* Kalia sent back in a similar tone.

"It's settled, then," Mom chirped, presenting the vial to Leona in a borderline sarcastic ceremony. Leona glanced at my brother, then to me and the others, before taking the vial in her delicate hands and drinking the remainder of its contents. Everyone seemed to hold their breath expectantly as we waited for the tincture to take effect.

"Is it working on her?" the one with the close-cut hair asked quietly. "Shut up, Neko," Gwili and Wyrran chided him simultaneously with an abrupt and unified smack upside the head, immediately reminding me of Irun and Athar, who were off training in the forest a reasonable distance from where we were.

In the moment that followed, however, Leona closed her eyes just before scarlet mana erupted from her petite frame, creating what I knew to be a decently large dome for someone who hadn't spent their life training with mana. "Not bad," I grinned, nudging Kalia with my elbow. "Not bad at all," Ysevel chimed in with a similar look in her eye.

As the mana dissipated, Leona immediately reopened her eyes in shock. "I don't like to use this language, but to quote Bernar: *What the fuck* was in that, Ren?" she asked, prompting my mother to burst out in a cackle. "I never thought I'd see the day when a *queen* swore in front of me. *Ah,* they grow up so fast, don't they, Aurae?" she said as she wiped away a joyful tear.

Aurae didn't verbally respond, but gave a soft chuckle and shook her head. "Well, then. Now that *that's* over with, I have another proposition to make, though I'd rather wait for the *other two* to be here for it," I said, butting into the situation, noticing the confused looks from everyone else. "What *other two*?" the red-haired woman asked.

"I'm sorry, I don't mean to be rude, but I never got your name," I said as politely as I could. "It's Marte, and you're not being rude, unlike *someone* I knew when we first met," she scowled at the one I assumed was called Neko. "Pleasure to meet you," I said with a nod. "And by *the other two*, I mean Irun and Athar," I said, almost forgetting that Bernar used to know Irun well.

Ah, shit, I thought, realizing I hadn't explained that part, nor anything regarding Ardrin to him yet.

"D-Did you just say *Irun's* here?" he asked more calmly than I'd expected him to, but I knew the only way to explain things was to rip the bandage off quickly. "Yes, he's here. Don't worry, we were *both* mistaken about him, but I'll let *someone else* explain that side of things," I said, careful not to use Ardrin or Erumon's names.

Bernar looked at me curiously, but after a few moments of scrutiny, he seemed to want to trust me.

"Well, where the hell are they, then?" he finally asked, crossing his arms. "They're training in the forest, but I'll go get them," I said, entering my fourth stage yet again and disappearing from their sight as I *leaned into the spaces between.*

Within a handful of dashes, I'd found them both on their backs and smoldering from what I could only guess was an intense training session. "Well, it looks like you guys had a good session," I chuckled, pushing the smoke and dust away from my face as much as I could. "We *were* until *this fucking moron* decided to try out a new spell in a *test of strength,* or so he called it," Athar groaned as he rolled over onto his belly to get back up.

"*Oi,* I told you I wanted to work on it in secret," Irun said in a pained voice. "Not my fault you let it get out of control," Athar groaned again as he rubbed his shoulder. "Work on *what* spell?" I asked, both amused and confused in equal parts at their discomfort. "Go ahead, *shit-ass,*" Athar's alternate voice spat the insult, causing Irun to sigh.

"I saw the move you did to end Nexis, and I've been trying to replicate something similar with my own mana the last few days. It was *impressive* to say the least, and I haven't been able to do it yet," Irun admitted bashfully. I raised my eyebrows in surprise at his honesty, but I'd never expected to see him try to *imitate* something I've done with a different source of mana.

"Well, maybe Bernar can teach you how to do it," I suggested lightly, trying to ease into the fact that he was already here. "*Pffft,* as if he'd ever look at me without trying to kill me," Irun waved dismissively. "At least it would be a quick death from what Thoma's told me of his skills," Athar chimed in with a shrug, making me snort a little.

"Well, it won't come to that. I've made sure of it," I said, getting a fearful look from Irun in return. "Fuck me. He's *here*, isn't he?" he asked with no small amount of genuine worry in his eyes. "Yeah, but we'd better get moving if we don't want his patience to run out," I said as lightly as I could. "I get to meet him, too?" Athar asked with more excitement than I expected.

"Yep, and I'm sure you'll love to get to know him and the others as well," I said cheerfully, but I could tell Irun was worried more Synners from Codrean were here as well. "Don't worry. It's just him for now. Let's get moving," I gestured, making sure they followed behind me back to the others.

Within a few minutes, we returned to the training ground, where Bernar still had his arms crossed. It was obvious that my Ysevel and Kalia were explaining things to him, but as soon as Irun broke through the treeline that marked the edge of the training ground, Bernar's eyes fixed on him immediately.

Like I said, give him a chance, I sent my brother, who didn't immediately respond. Instead, he just stood there holding the same expression as before until we reached him. I didn't have to read Irun's mind to know he was nervous, but I was definitely sure of Athar's excitement, as he rushed ahead to shake his hand.

"It's an honor to meet you, Bernar! Thoma's told me a lot about you," he said, tugging at my brother's arm and forcibly gripping his hand. "A pleasure to meet you, too," my brother said, giving me a befuddled glance. "Bernar, this is Athar Wishert. Bastard son of the late King Truls, and a member of *The Order of Nightfall's Blade*," I said with a gesture to help ease his confusion before moving on to Irun.

The fuck is The Order of Nightfall's Blade? *Is that some kind of cult?* Bernar sent Ysevel and I. *Not quite. It's something he came up with during our time in the Underworld that would give any concurrent missions we take on as a group a way to tell others who we are,* I explained as briefly as I could.

Is Kalia a member of this Order? Bernar asked bluntly. *Yes, and both your mother and I are* also *members of The Order,* Ysevel chimed in wryly. *It's even been made official by* my *mother as of two days ago, so I would recommend you take it at least* somewhat *seriously,* she continued, getting another raised eyebrow from him.

"Well, if that's the case," he said aloud with a slight sigh. "You already know *him*, so I don't think introductions need to be made, but for those of you who haven't met him, this is Irun Mothac, former Synner of Codrean and current member of The Order," I said, stepping aside to present Irun to the others.

Those who hadn't met him were only mildly taken aback at the daemonic arm that replaced his human one. "It's a pleasure to meet you all," he said humbly, performing a low bow. "Bernar, I know you and I have some issues to work out, but like with Thoma, I hope you and I can come to an understanding," he said without a single crack or show of nervousness.

Bernar took in a deep breath and walked over to him. "I only have *one* thing I feel I need to know," he said, his eyes glowing much more brightly than before. "Bernar, wait," I said, but he held up a hand to stop me, which he only ever did to me when he was in absolute control of the situation.

He continued moving toward him at a steady pace and came to a halt just in front of him. Irun, at this point, was nearly a head taller than he was, but in an actual fight, I *knew* Irun didn't stand a chance.

"I don't have to reiterate whatever Thoma has already said, as there'd be no point in that. The only thing I need to know is whether it was all worth it in the end," he said, immediately throwing a heavy punch aimed at Irun's stomach, who quickly moved to block the attack using his daemonic arm as a shield. A large cloud of dust kicked up from the resulting shockwave, but Irun skidded across the dirt floor of the training ground, never losing his footing.

"*Heh*, not bad, *shitling*," Bernar said with a wry grin. "That's all you needed to know?" I asked, hoping he wouldn't throw another one. "Well, I would've liked to pull his head out of his ass *myself*, but it seems you've already done that. I just wanted to know how much stronger he got *because* of it," he shrugged. "Fair enough," I said, knowing it was better than the *other* outcome of this encounter I'd imagined.

"How's the arm?" I asked sarcastically as Irun walked back up to the rest of us. "It's numb, but I'd gladly take *ten* of those hits over what happened in Pyrdredd," Irun shrugged, making me recall the spell from Nexis that he blocked to save Athar. "I think I'd rather deal with the spells," I chuckled nervously.

I'll explain later, I sent my brother, who nodded his understanding after giving me a confused stare.

"There *is* something I'd like to know, though," Bernar said after a moment's pause, prompting the rest of us to look at him. "Since

Leona will be training under Aurae's tutelage, what about me? Who am I supposed to train with while I'm here?" he asked bluntly, and I immediately felt Kalia's excitement bubbling through our connection.

"I'll train him," she immediately volunteered before I could even react to the sensation. Irun, Athar, Ysevel, and I all stared at her, knowing the kind of training he'd be subjected to. "He looks strong, but I'd first need to assess just *how* strong through a *Davo Dugo Guva*," she said in her native language. "A fucking *what* now?" he asked.

"It's like a trial by combat, but you're not allowed to use spells or mana of any kind, since it was created to be a coming-of-age event for the Iron Plume clan," I explained loosely, knowing it held much more to it than that, not to reveal anything about the Alternates just yet. "*Ah*, well. I'd love a good challenge. Have you ever lost one?" he asked Kalia, whose toothy grin began to show on her face.

I know that look all too well, I thought.

"*Nuh-uh*. Me first. I've been waiting for *days* for them to have recovered enough to *really* give me their all, and you just got back from Harut," my mother stepped in, matching Kalia's grin. "Fine, but I'll still have to be tested at *some* point," Bernar gave a relenting sigh as he raised his hands. "There will be time enough for us to test you *both*, but it's true that I owe Siraye a match first. Thoma, you can be the judge," Kalia said, prompting Ysevel and I to exchange a knowing glance.

Who do you think wins that *fight?* Ysevel asked me through our connection. *I genuinely have* no *clue, but I'm itching to find out,* I sent back with a pair of raised eyebrows as I followed both my mother and Kalia into the training ground.

Witness us, Battle-Brother, Kalia sent me briefly. *This is going to be fun,* my mother added to Kalia's statement through our connection, having heard the comment. *Of course,* I said, forming the *kataki* blade and drawing the one my mother gave me as they both got into their stances.

"Are both of you ready?" I asked, crossing the spines of the blades above my head. "Ready when you are, Kalia," my mother said with a wolfish grin, which Kalia only returned. I could feel, through the Wraith realm's connection, that they were both thinking I was already taking too long.

It made me chuckle.

"Begin!" I shouted, dragging the blades together as I swiped them downward to create a signaling sound for the duel to commence.

CHAPTER 77
UNFURLED CLUTCHES

As my swords reached the bottom of their arcs, the dust cloud my mother and Kalia kicked up with their dashes spread across the training ground.

My mother, unable to use any spells or augmentation due to the rules of the *Davo Dugo Guva*, surprised me with her natural speed. As she struck from above, Kalia was forced to deflect the blow to her left and attempted a pommel strike on my mother, who ducked under it. With a quick adjustment of her weight distribution, Mom managed to drop into a spinning motion, attempting to slice at Kalia's leg, but she was much faster than that.

Kalia leaped out of the way, only to land a few meters to her right and quickly dash in to try to strike my Mom's exposed side. Seeing this, I heard my mother click her tongue and promptly flip her sword around, so that the point was facing Kalia, creating some space. Seeing that there was a slight amount of hesitation suddenly present in Kalia's movements, Mom dashed in to take full advantage of the opportunity.

She struck repeatedly, aiming her strikes at Kalia's sides, chest, head, and neck at a speed that was difficult even for *me* to follow along with. Still, Kalia managed to deflect them all and eventually push her away for a counterattack.

This is about what I expected, but I never thought I'd be matched in speed, my mother sent me through our connection as she deflected another handful of strikes. *Yeah, she's pretty quick on her feet even without using her* odoruki *technique,* I added with a grin. *Whatever you do,* do not *let her get behind you,* Ysevel cautioned playfully.

No cheating, Kalia sent through a grunt of exertion as a heavy blow she intended to deflect caught her sword in a bind. They held it momentarily, and I could see they were enjoying this, even from where I stood. Not only that, but the sensation I was getting from *both* their cores told me everything else I needed to know.

"So, who's your money on? Mine's on Mom," Bernar said with an air of pride. "Mine would be, too, but I've been fighting Kalia for a *decade*. I know almost every one of her moves, but even so, I know there's still shit I haven't seen," I replied loosely, carefully observing the battle going on before me, as Mom leaped into the air and launched herself into a spinning attack aimed at Kalia's head.

"A full *decade*? Does that make you older than me now? Wait, before that, how the fuck were you down there for *so long*?" he asked, recalling what I'd loosely mentioned before. "Inside the training dome, a hegraphenian sage named Sabura used the properties of Dark mana to alter the flow of time using its density," I explained to refresh his memory, flinching as another cloud of dust blasted small rocks in our direction.

"I might be older than you in terms of *years*, but not in experience, *big brother*," I said warmly as I gave him a knowing look. "R-Right, yeah. I knew that," he stammered briefly as if in disbelief of my words. "Did you spend all that time in the dome with Irun and Athar?"

he asked, watching as Kalia dashed in for another barrage of strikes, forcing my mother to step back as she deflected the attacks.

"I did, and it took me a long time to be able to trust him again. If it hadn't been for Ysevel, Kalia, and even *Athar*, I might have never been able to do so," I admitted, scoffing at myself when I remembered how much I would have struggled fighting against him when we'd first arrived in the Underworld. I could feel him reading my thoughts as I recalled the situation of Ysevel holding us in place like separating two *children*, and I let the memory play out in my mind so he could see the whole story.

After showing him *nearly* everything right up until Kalia appeared, he seemingly understood a little more than before. The memory was cut short, however, as we noticed both Mom and Kalia preparing to launch another flurry of attacks. "*Oh*, I've seen *this* move before," Bernar said confidently, but as soon as I recognized Kalia's stance, *I knew* this would be an even match.

They dashed in and clashed in the center momentarily, before Mom broke the bind they were in and began a combination of blows I'd only ever seen her use *once*. Kalia deflected a thrust away from her, but as she did so, my mother used the momentum in her blade to spin it around quickly for another one in succession.

With each deflected thrust, my mom would use the momentum to reverse it into either a thrust or a slash. Kalia began to read her movements and started acting accordingly. I could tell she recognized some of the strikes my mother was doing from her fight with Gravar, but feeling them *for herself* was a completely different story.

As the two traded blows at matching speeds, I could see Bernar's expression shift from pure confidence in my mother's abilities to slight worry that he might have *lost* whatever bet he'd made with Gwili and Wyrran. It made me chuckle, but I knew that the duel was coming to a close as soon as I saw them back away from each other. "You're good. *Excellent*, in fact, Kalia," Mom said between breaths, getting a wry smile from Kalia, who was in a similar state.

"Likewise, Siraye, but I think it's about time we finish this up, as we have other matters to attend to," she replied with a single, firm nod. My mother responded with one of her own, and got into a high guard just like I had, and Taegin before me.

She already knows that move, I kept the thought to myself since Kalia had already scolded me for *cheating*.

However, the hegraphene surprised me when she entered a perfectly mirrored stance to that of my mother's. I felt both excitement and curiosity emanating from my mother, but a collected sense of confidence coming from Kalia. *I'm borrowing your move, Thoma. Sorry about this,* she sent me just before the two of them dashed in.

Oh, shit, I thought, recognizing the exact move she was talking about.

As my mother's blade came down, Kalia shifted her own from a high guard into an uppercut in less time than it took me to blink. My mother, somehow, managed to read and respond to it accordingly, and shifted the weight of her strike to match Kalia's. In the heartbeat before their swords clashed, I could feel a sense of both pride and fulfillment coming from them, as a much larger cloud of dust soared into the air.

"Mom! Kalia!" I shouted, immediately dashing in toward them, followed by Ysevel and Bernar. I knew they were still alive, but in *what state*, I didn't know. As I got closer, the density of the cloud diminished, and I could see both of their blades halted just before each other's necks, and bright smiles across both of their faces.

"It's a *draw!*" I shouted out to the others who were watching. The expressions on each of their faces differed, as Irun and Athar were pleasantly surprised, while Leona and her group were mainly shocked. My brother, however, simply chuckled in disbelief. "Well, then, Kalia. I'll certainly look forward to *our* match," he said, as the two of them pulled their swords away.

Kalia recalled her blade back into the rest of her armor, catching my mother by surprise. "So it wasn't just my imagination," Mom said as she watched the last portion of it be reabsorbed. "I thought I saw you *draw* your weapon from the sheath at your side, but I never would have imagined you'd *produced* something like that," she continued, immediately grabbing Kalia's armored forearm to inspect it.

"It's a little different than that, Siraye. The *kataki* we produce can take on all kinds of shapes, but it will shape itself following the bearer's *will*," she explained briefly, prompting my mother to immediately look down at my blade and chuckle to herself softly.

"Perhaps *one day* I will be worthy of the *kataki* myself. It's no wonder you were able to train them to such a high level," my mother gestured to Ysevel and I, who flushed at the compliment. "Well, to be honest, they're both incredible on their own, but I appreciate the compliment," Kalia said, giving us a knowing look.

"Thank you for the duel, and I accept the draw wholeheartedly," Mom said with complete honesty in her tone as she placed an open palm across her chest and gave her a bow. Kalia returned the gesture she'd learned from Ysevel and I, surprising Bernar the most.

"That was a truly magnificent fight, even though I could hardly follow along with it," Leona said as we returned to the edge of the training ground. "With time, you'll be able to see much more than with just your eyes, Your Majesty, though I'm sure you're already aware of this," Kalia said humbly, to which Leona raised a hand placatingly. "If Aurae doesn't want you to use titles with her, then I would *love it* if I could receive the same treatment," she smiled brightly, catching Kalia off-balance.

"O-Of course, Leona," she said bashfully as I felt a warm smile creep onto my face. "As for you four," Leona turned to face Ysevel, Irun, Athar, and I, causing my stomach to drop a little. "Were you training with her at that level the *entire time*?" she asked bluntly with a slight pursing of her lips that dug into the corner of her left cheek. "I wouldn't say the *entire time*, but yes," I answered loosely, but she continued to stare at me in disbelief. "Then how did you get so strong? What happened to you?" she asked. I didn't know how to respond immediately, but I was grateful when Ysevel stepped up to answer. "There was a seal placed on his core from a young age. When he arrived here in Caegwen, my mother and Siraye both undid whatever was sealing his core," she began, making Leona gasp in surprise.

"But who would *do* such a horrible thing to a *child*?" she asked, but as soon as I was about to answer, I heard Taegin's voice begin to speak. "I can answer that, but I'd rather not do it without some kind of protective measures in place," he said cryptically. He'd put his pendant back on to prevent even more of a shock from the others.

"Master," Leona gave him a curt bow of acknowledgement. "Please, if you'll all follow me, there is much to discuss about the recent events that have taken place," he returned the bow before gesturing for us to follow him back to the main palace.

There was a brief exchange of confused glances, but after some reassurance from Aurae and Siraye, the others followed ahead, while Leona, Bernar, and the other members of The Order trailed behind them. Ysevel and Leona seemed to get along well, likely exchanging stories about something I couldn't quite hear, but whatever it was, I could tell they were *both* enjoying the conversation along the way.

"So, you and Ysevel, *huh?*" Bernar asked smugly, yet quietly enough that they wouldn't hear it. "Yeah. It happened while we were staying in Deathwhisper Tavern," I replied with a nod, prompting him to raise a pair of eyebrows expectantly. "Gods, it was almost *painful* to see how slow he was to notice she liked him," Irun added, causing Bernar to chuckle. "Sounds about right," he said between laughs.

"You could tell back then?" I asked with a raised eyebrow. "Listen, I might be an idiot, but I'm not *stupid*. Anyone who leaps after you into a portal leading to *fuck knows where* with tears in their eyes doesn't strike me as someone who doesn't care at least *a little*," Irun scoffed and shook his head. "That's it? That's all it took for you to know?" I asked in disbelief, but he shook his head and laughed to himself.

We gave Bernar a few more details about the time we spent down there, mentioning Krozz and only *some* of what took place in Pyrdredd, so he wouldn't be caught by surprise when he heard the complete account in just a few moments. There were a few things he had questions about, but I didn't feel it was my place to explain them.

As we entered the main hall and took a left down one of the passageways, we arrived at a large meeting room. There was a large table borne from the roots that lay about the city, with a considerable variety of snacks and other such treats already laid out for us. However, what surprised me the most was that at the far end of the hall, Elhael was already waiting for us with Thorn, Anwill, and Nenvalur at his side.

The other members of my mother's team, Derion, Eirenne, Vyra, and Haldir, were off conducting a scouting mission that morning so that they wouldn't be back until at least the following day.

It's going to be a long one, isn't it? I sent my brother, who, judging by his expression, agreed with my assessment.

"Welcome, everyone. Please, take a seat where you see fit," Elhael's majestic voice rang out from across the room as he gestured toward the chairs. Aurae and Elhael sat at the head of the table with Nenvalur and Anwill standing behind them, while Taegin and my mother were across from each other beside the king and queen.

On my side of the table, we sat in the order of me, Ysevel, Kalia, Mom, Athar, Irun, Ren, and Thorn. On the other side were Bernar, Leona, Thorsen, Gwili, Wyrran, Neko, and Marte, with an empty seat beside Marte, and another at the far end of the table.

"I'm sure you're all wondering why there are still two who are not yet present, but they will be here shortly. Right now, I first wanted to formally thank the members of *Nightfall's Blade* for their accomplishments in the Underworld in putting a stop to the plans of one of our greatest enemies yet; Nexis Pelantyr," Elhael began, shocking Gwili and Wyrran more than others.

A few of the servants standing by stepped forward and immediately presented each of us who had fought Nexis with a metallic medallion that almost *hummed* with mana. Each one held the Caegweni Royal symbol engraved on the front, with an individual symbol on the back.

"This medallion will tell others across the Continent of your deeds, and will allow you greater privileges than nearly *anyone* in our kingdom," he said.

Mine also has my family's crest on the back, I caught myself smiling as Mom, Taegin, and Bernar each gave me a nod of approval.

"Thank you, Your Majesty," we said in unison, bowing as we could from our seats. I was grateful to see that Athar had adjusted his behavior accordingly, but, as *usual*, he remained *unpredictable*.

"It is *we* who should be thanking you. Your deeds have echoed *far beyond* the reaches of this kingdom already. However, there are some things regarding the thwarted return of Nexis Pelantyr that have been put into motion we need to address," he said, immediately shifting his gaze toward the door. "*Ah*, he's back. Good. Please, let him in," he signaled to the two guards by the double door.

As the door swung open, all eyes turned to see none other than Ardrin standing in the doorway. He'd since changed out of his robe into formal Caegweni attire, and while his hair and sideburns had been trimmed neatly, there was no denying that his presence filled those who didn't know he was here with a sense of *fear*.

As he entered the room, a handful of mages *drew a vast amount of mana* and summoned a sound-suppressing barrier around the room. Seeing this, Leona immediately shifted uncomfortably, but Bernar put a hand on hers to let her know it was alright. "He wouldn't be here if he weren't our ally, right?" she whispered cautiously, to which Bernar gave her a single nod, but also sent an uncertain glance my way.

As the silence from everyone present permeated the room, he glanced at each of us as if determining whom he knew. "I see there are a few faces I recognize, and more than a few I *don't*," he raised an eyebrow, then took a few steps forward, making Neko and Marte look at each other with apparent confusion.

"To those who don't know me, my name is Ardrin Pelantyr, but you may recognize me by the name *The Masked One*," he said, making Leona's eyes widen in both anger and fear. "Y-You? It was *you* who destroyed Coltend?" she asked in disbelief. "Hello, Leona. It's good to see you in good health, but yes, that was me; *in part*, anyway," he bowed, ignoring her seething anger momentarily.

"I-I can't believe it. Your Majesty, what is the meaning of this?" Leona asked Elhael directly. "He *slaughtered* my people and brought death and destruction, as well as a horde of creatures and corrupted members of the Church of Mideia, into my *home* that nearly wiped out the people of Coltend!" Leona raised her voice just enough to prompt Taegin to raise a hand.

But as he was about to speak, a portal appeared at the front of the still-opened door, causing everyone to shift their attention to it immediately. Those of us in *Nightfall's Blade* already knew who it was, but there were still more than a handful who didn't immediately recognize who could create a portal like that.

"I believe *I* should answer that question, Queen Leona," Erumon's voice and presence immediately permeated the barrier, forcing everyone to remain deathly still. As he crossed the door's threshold, he immediately reduced his presence drastically, but it was still enough to make Neko and Marte shudder in fear.

This is going to be interesting, I sent Ysevel, who silently nodded her agreement.

"I'm afraid *I* must be the one to apologize for the near-destruction of Coltend, as it was under my instruction that Ardrin was forced to do so," he began to explain, his voice resonating loudly through the room. "Lord Erumon, it's good to see you again," Taegin rose from his seat and bowed.

"*Ah*, Taegin. It's good to see you again, as well, though I don't believe that the pendant I gave you all those years ago is needed any longer," he said in a much more *amicable* tone than I was used to him using.

So they do *know each other. Just how deep does this all go?* I asked Ysevel and Kalia, but neither of them could give me an answer before *he* did. "An excellent question, Thoma. Though I will have much to explain here, as well as a mission for you and the other members of *Nightfall's Blade* in the coming months," he said, acknowledging me with a short nod. "Of course, Lord Erumon," I rose from my seat and bowed as Taegin had.

The look of surprise on his face wasn't anywhere *near* as strong as Bernar's, whose jaw might have dropped through the floor had it gone any further. Still, it made me feel like I finally knew something he didn't, *for once*. Leona, however, was just as confused as the rest of them, *including* my own mother.

Erumon and Ardrin took the last two remaining seats, with Ardrin sitting down next to Neko, while Erumon, who was almost *too* large for his seat, was at the end of the table opposite Elhael and Aurae.

"As I'm sure you all have many questions to ask about who I am, or why Ardrin was acting under my orders, I will explain what I can for now in as much detail as I dare, for there are still things even *I* don't fully understand yet," Erumon began to speak, creating a placating gesture with his hands.

Everyone listened intently, and even Leona's momentary outburst was quelled by the tone and smoothness of his voice.

"Allow me to begin with more *ancient* events, as they will help provide some context for things I will state later, including the invasion of Coltend Castle," he said, prompting Leona, Bernar, and Thorsen to immediately focus their attention on every word that left his mouth.

"Over a millennium ago, I came to the realm of *Kavrass*, which you all know as the *Between*, to find a former comrade of mine named *Mideia*," he began, but as he spoke the *true* name of the realm, there wasn't a single one among us who didn't feel like we just learned something we shouldn't have.

So that's *this realm's real name. I wonder if the others have their own as well,* I sent Ysevel. *I would assume they do, but I can't help but wonder whether knowing the true name of a realm is a good thing,* she cautioned.

"While we didn't know what he was up to at the time, it became apparent that the creatures that began to spawn and reside in this realm *didn't* belong here. The other Wardens and I, you may consider us *realm guardians* of a sort, knew that something was wrong and began to investigate the matter. However, what we found carved a deep wound in our ranks: Mideia had been corrupted and betrayed us," Erumon continued, his tone dropping in dejection as he spoke the last words.

While no one present knew of anything that could corrupt someone so powerful, we all immediately understood that his words carried a sense of *duty* behind them. As the heavy silence continued, no one felt they could say a word, as we all waited for him to continue.

"As a result of our investigation, we discovered that there was an elven mage, known as Nexis Pelantyr, who'd come into contact with him sometime *before* I arrived, but it was almost too late. Mideia's influence had already taken over him, promising him domination over Kavrass if he followed his orders," he continued, gauging everyone's reaction to his words.

"I've had to study the Coltendian archives countless times as a child, but there was never *any* mention of this *Nexis Pelantyr*," Leona began, still a little confused as to how her country played a role. "With all due respect to you and Lord Erumon, Your Majesty, I can help with that," Athar raised a hand. After a gesture from Erumon, it was evident, though his tone of voice, that he was in absolute control over his alternate's abhorrent personality.

Either that, or it was too scared of Erumon to dare show its face.

Athar retold the same story he'd told me and the others in the dome, about how Nexis stored a piece of himself inside the core of the then-king's unborn child, and that it was struck from all the records. When he finished his, thankfully *short*, retelling of the events leading up to our meeting in Kalia's homeland, those who didn't know the story were taken aback by the events that he'd been through.

"By the Graces, I had no idea he would have gone to such lengths," Leona put a hand to her mouth in shock. "I'm sorry you all had to go through that, but I'm glad you made it out alive. Rest assured that I will see you given a proper place in Coltend when this is all over," she continued, acknowledging his struggle like the others in the room did as well. "Thank you, Your Majesty," Athar blushed momentarily, but bowed his head in graceful acceptance.

"Thank *you* for that information, Athar. Those details will *also* help explain certain aspects of this situation we find ourselves in," Erumon gave him a nod of acknowledgement. "After his banishment to the Underworld, formally known as *Vareluth*, we placed a barrier around it to prevent Nexis from being able to leave, or even *draw* from other realms we knew he could, once we discovered what he was doing with the Gwynnleaf. Mideia, however, was interested in this work of his, knowing the potential that it contained, and sought to continue his alliance with Nexis by teaching him how to manipulate the Leech mana present within Pyrdredd; a power he's used on *countless* realms already," he continued, causing Kalia to shift uncomfortably this time.

"Does this have anything to do with the Great Partition and why Sabura and I were the only two Wraithborn in Vareluth, Lord Erumon?" she asked in an even tone, though I could feel her tension and worry seep through our connection.

"I'm sorry, Kerra Kalia, even though I know it *does*, I wasn't present, since I was off hunting down many of my former comrades during that time," he said solemnly, causing her to lower her head.

"Regarding the Great Partition, at least, it was a plan devised by *my* master to separate the hubs of mana that existed within Kavrass.

Nexis and Mideia's cooperation *was* one of the catalysts for it, though I don't know much more than that," Erumon admitted. However, Taegin, Kalia, and Ardrin were the only ones not surprised by that information.

"Was Pyrdredd one of those *hubs*?" I asked as much to myself as the others. "Indeed, Thoma, but like I said before, I don't know much else," Erumon said with a nod, causing Ysevel and I to share a glance, recalling the painting we saw in the dilapidated room.

"Nevertheless, after Nexis' banishment, Mideia went into hiding so deep that it even allowed him to evade my master's abilities. To draw him out of hiding and stop him once and for all, we had to devise a plan that would entice him enough to step forward," he continued, letting his words hang.

"Nexis still wanted the Gwynnleaf to appease Mideia, didn't he? That's why the attack happened in the first place," Leona realized, visibly distraught by memories of her citizens being slaughtered. "Unfortunately, yes," Ardrin began, knowing he would be the only one whose explanation she would accept.

"We knew Mideia had been keeping an eye on Nexis for a while using the *Realmwalker Blade*, which he'd corrupted beneath the barrier of Vareluth to avoid detection, but ended up *disabling* it as my brother realized when he retrieved it at Erumon's command," he continued, getting surprised looks from both me, Bernar, *and* my mother.

But why did he even need to corrupt the Realmwalker Blade? Was there anyone powerful enough at the time who could have used it? I asked Kalia, knowing she was there when Taegin was, but the response I got wasn't one I was expecting.

It must have been because of the Wraithborn. He must have feared them to the point where he had no choice but to stop them. It's the only thing that makes sense to me, Kalia acknowledged to those of us who shared a connection to her, as if a piece of the puzzle had just fallen into place for her. "What?" I asked breathlessly, but she shook her head, letting me know she would discuss that later.

"Granted, my brother had no idea *I* was involved in this plan, since we had to make the assault seem legitimate enough to lull Nexis *and* Mideia into a false sense of security. Erumon enlisted me to be a spy for him, and I was to act as though *I* was the only one behind the attacks, using only Vexing mana from Vareluth to make it more believable," Ardrin continued, getting a look of surprise from both Siraye and Bernar as a result.

"While the horde was the only thing I was *truly* in control of, the followers of the Church of Mideia acted of their own accord, regardless of my orders. Father Mourtis, the one you saw leading the attack, was *also* under Mideia's influence," he said with a finality that added real weight to his words.

Leona's expression was difficult to read, but there was a sense of both loss and understanding in the horrible situation she had gone through. "By the Graces, I never would have thought there was so much behind the lives we lost," she closed her eyes and shook her head. We allowed for a moment of silence to honor the fallen, both for the citizens of Coltend *and* Synners of Codrean alike.

She allowed herself a deep breath and let it out deliberately before she spoke. "I take it their sacrifices weren't *entirely* in vain, then?" she asked with only a hint of her remaining anger. "They weren't on a few accounts, but for now, I will only state the two that *matter*," Ardrin replied, holding up a pair of fingers.

"The first is that while we *did* manage to take a large portion of the Gwynnleaf, *none* of it went toward anything Nexis was after. I used it to augment several hegraphenes so that they could withstand his attacks in an eventual revolt. Kalia's daughter, Devyr, is one of those. However, she's still recovering from being forced to use too much of her *kataki* to create the portal he aimed to use to leave Vareluth," he began to explain as Leona nodded along with his explanation.

"The second was *Thoma*," he said bluntly, casting more than a few eyes in my direction. "Before the events that led to the attack, Erumon notified me that there was a possibility of a seal being put on a member of my family, and I knew instinctively it couldn't have been Taegin, nor Siraye. Still, after hearing Bernar had reached the fifth stage, I knew it had to be *you*," he said gravely, causing a handful of others who *didn't know* about it to widen their eyes in surprise.

Just how long has he been keeping an eye on us? Siraye sent me, but I could only shake my head in response. *Long enough for him to know Bernar had reached the fifth stage,* I returned with a shrug.

"I needed a spy of my own to determine whether my brother was going to make a move to save Coltend. That's when I discovered Irun and used his jealousy of Thoma to my advantage," he began to explain, as Bernar's eyes widened in surprise.

"Knowing Irun was close enough to Thoma, and yet not a direct member of Taegin's inner circle, allowed me to gain a lot of information regarding what moves they were going to make, but there was something I had yet to account for," continued, shifting his gaze toward me.

"You confirmed the seal on my core," I answered for the group, getting a shocked look from anyone who didn't yet know about it. "Precisely. I knew it had to have been placed there by someone powerful, but who *exactly*, I still didn't know at the time. That was until I told Erumon what I'd found, but he found it difficult to believe that someone could have done such a thing without the Realmwalkers noticing," he said gravely.

His last sentence struck me as strange. In my head, if the Realmwalkers and Wardens were able to see just about everything going on in a realm without a barrier, it made no sense that they *didn't* see what happened to me.

Or, someone *turned a blind eye to it,* I heard Erumon's voice in my head, shocking me that he didn't want to voice that aloud, even *with* a barrier around the room. *Are you saying there's a potential for there to be someone higher up who's been corrupted as well?* I asked, but the subtle shift of his features told me that he didn't know either.

"In any case, I sent a creature here to serve as my eyes and ears in Caegwen, and that was when I discovered that Queen Aurae and Siraye were able to undo the seal. It struck me as odd, but knowing about Her Majesty's *ambivalence*, I figured her Wraithborn abilities *must* have had something to do with it," Ardrin continued, getting a nod of agreement from Aurae.

"The moment the seal was released on his core, Erumon detected the presence of what is known as the *Autarchica Primaria*," he said, gesturing to Erumon to continue that side of the explanation, but as he did so, I felt a sinking feeling in my gut that I couldn't ignore entirely.

"The *Autarchica Primaria*, or as translated simply the *Authority,* isn't necessarily absolute control over mana, but rather the innate *understanding* of its primary functions," Erumon began to explain, prompting the others, including Ysevel, to regard me curiously. "How deep of an understanding are you talking about, Lord Erumon?" Thorsen asked in the others' stead, who were still too scared of him to ask.

"I believe Anwill would have a better way of explaining it in a way that you would understand," Erumon nodded toward Anwill as he stepped forward. "Thank you, Lord Erumon. Allow me to make a brief comparison here between our two newcomers and Taegin," he gestured toward Neko and Marte, who flushed the moment he gestured toward them.

"The two of them are still in the first stage of mana manipulation, while Taegin is in the fifth. The difference in their abilities isn't just how much mana they can output, but rather, their control and *understanding* of the mana," he began to explain, leveraging his hands in such a way to make it look like he was imitating a scale.

"Now, let's suppose that Neko was the one with the *Authority* for a moment. In theory, he would be able to reach Taegin's level of understanding within a few *years* as opposed to *decades'* worth of training," he said, evening out the *scale* he made with his hands.

"However, even if the two of them were in the same stages of mana manipulation, Neko's understanding of mana would be *much deeper* than Taegin's, even though he's had decades more experience with it," Anwill said, having inverted the scale entirely as he continued his explanation. "In essence, Neko's understanding of mana and *rate of growth* would be *exponentially* greater than Taegin's," he said.

However, before any other questions could be asked, Erumon took over the conversation once more.

"Anwill is correct, though there is something *else* that having innate *Authority* allows, though what I'm about to tell you absolutely *cannot* leave this room," he said gravely, glancing around to make sure everyone understood the severity of what he was about to say.

"Having this trait *naturally* allows whoever has it to *commune* with the realm's ruling powers. To our knowledge, the only ones who naturally have this ability are dragons, though there were cases of Wraithborn who were able to commune with the Wraith realm even without it," he let his words hang for a moment.

Is that what I was hearing when I fought Nexis? I thought momentarily, recalling the voices I'd heard during the battle. *You must have been able to commune with it out of necessity. I've also heard the realm speak to me, but I wasn't sure whether that was because I was around you and Kalia, or something else,* Ysevel sent me, catching me by surprise.

You've heard it? But how? Do you have Autarchica Primaria, too? I asked, but she shook her head subtly as if she didn't know either. *Well, I think we should ask Erumon sometime. Maybe he has an answer,* I said, putting a hand on hers gently and giving her a warm smile.

"I knew it! Dragons *are* real," I heard Marte whisper to Neko, who had a similar look of excitement in his eyes. "They are, indeed, Marte," Erumon began, fiddling with the bracelet on his wrist. "However, with what I've just told you about the *Authority*, you all need to know that the enemies we will likely be facing now that Nexis is dead have developed a *synthetic* version of it using the Gwynnleaf as its base," he continued, producing a large handful of pearls just like the ones he gave us.

"A-Are those...?" Taegin asked breathlessly, as if he knew what they were already. "These are synthetic *Authorities* that I've extracted from my fallen comrades who sided with Mideia," he said gravely. They were small in his large hand, but they glowed with an intensity similar to that of the tincture I drank when I was first introduced to the Ethereal.

"While not as powerful as having *innate Authority*, these will suffice to help you all grow enough to withstand the coming battles," he rose from his seat, handing each one a pearl to everyone who hadn't received one from him after the battle with Nexis. They all stared at them with unbridled curiosity, and even Leona was surprised she'd received one.

"Lord Erumon, I don't know what I did to deserve this, but I thank you," she said graciously. "If you're going to train with Aurae to protect your people, you will *need* this more than you realize," he said with a much warmer tone than his words conveyed. Her eyes widened for a moment, but thinned as she smiled when she understood his intent and bowed to show her gratitude.

After giving a pearl to everyone else, he returned to his seat and gestured for those of us who were present for the battle to produce our own. "Now that you all have them, I would recommend you take them in right now while I'm here, since I will be able to help reduce the intensity of their effects should anything go wrong," he began, but I looked at mine with mild hesitation.

"What is it, Thoma?" he asked, noticing my perplexion. "It's just that if I already have this *Authority*, what will happen to me if I take *this one*, too, Lord?" I asked, not bothering to hide my concern.

Everything regarding the *Authority* was still a bit of a mystery to me, even *after* Anwill's fantastic explanation. There was no way for me to know the answers on my own, and I knew that if I wanted to get any, I *had* to ask while I still could.

"While it won't give you something you already have, it will certainly *deepen* your own understanding of the *Authority* you already possess," he explained simply, but I still had no idea what that even meant. "You'll see," he smiled, knowing I was almost just as confused as before.

"Now, let's start with *you two*, since I know the others already have a much deeper understanding of mana manipulation; there is much *less* risk of something going wrong with them," he said, shifting his gaze from me to Neko and Marte, who grew pallid under the weight of his presence.

"O-Of course, Lord E-Erumon," Marte said shakily. I could tell from her build alone that she was likely from the same bloodline as Thorsen's, but to see someone of her stature tremble like that nearly made me giggle.

Don't you dare, Ysevel chided me playfully. *I wasn't going to, but I do find the irony of it rather funny,* I shrugged, giving her a wry smile. *I know, but think about the first time* we *met him. You nearly shit yourself,* she accented the word *shit* with a light elbow-jab to my ribcage. *Alright, alright! I get it!* I desperately held onto the laugh that was clawing at the back of my lips to escape.

Meanwhile, Marte was staring at the pearl with a mixture of curiosity and anxiety, but when she noticed Neko gently placing his hand on what I could only imagine was her arm, she immediately calmed down as she turned to see his supportive smile.

Aww, he likes her, Ysevel sent as she quickly tapped my hand. *How did you understand that so quickly?* Kalia asked, though I assumed it was because she was still trying to learn regular human expressions. *Look at his eyes; they're practically* glowing *with affection,* Ysevel sent, causing my Mom, of all people, to stifle a laugh at our light-hearted conversation.

It was abruptly brought to a halt when Ardrin scowled at us, forcing the four of us to quickly and non-verbally apologize.

After a nod of encouragement from Erumon, Marte consumed the pearl and washed it down with a few swigs of wine. We all held our breath to see what was going to happen, and like with the Wraith tincture, it took a few moments before her core began to glow brightly, then spread to the rest of her body.

The room was bathed in golden light for a few heartbeats before it slowly dimmed, returning her to her normal state. "How do you feel, Marte?" Thorsen asked, his concern for his subordinate obvious. "I-I can't explain it, but I can *feel* everyone's mana, almost as if I could reach out and touch it," she said breathlessly, causing Thorsen's, as well as everyone else's, eyes to widen.

"I'm glad to see it worked without a problem, then," Erumon said with visible satisfaction. I say visible, but in reality, it was only a slight shift in his eyes that told me he was. "Neko, please take yours as well," he directed. He followed the order promptly, probably excited to see what it would do to him after Marte's glowing display, and quickly washed it down with some wine.

Like Marte, his core and body began to glow, then dimmed a few moments after. "*Whoo*, what a rush!" he exclaimed, shaking his head as if he'd taken some kind of stimulant. "It would seem that the effects are different for each person," Ardrin noted to Erumon with a raised eyebrow.

As Erumon went around the table, each one had a different reaction. Gwili and Wyrran's were pretty similar, though Gwili's was more akin to Neko's than anything else. A bright smile showed on his face, but I could tell he was more than happy to take it. Wyrran, on the other hand, showed only graceful acceptance.

Thorsen had a similar reaction to Marte's, likely because they were descendants of the same line of giants. Still, his glow was *much* more orange and intense than hers, even making Erumon's placid expression shift into one of mild surprise. Leona was next, and while the amount of her glow was about the same as Neko's, it gave off a hint of scarlet and a secondary *pulse* before fading.

Why did that happen? Is it because she took the Wraith tincture from Ren? I sent Ysevel, but she could only shrug in response.

Bernar's expression didn't help answer my question, either, but since he was next, he gave me a knowing glance before consuming his pearl. "Time to catch back up, *little shit*," he grinned before his core began to glow similar to Leona's with a slightly scarlet hue interlaced with the gold. This was the first time anyone had seen one that bright outside of Thorsen's, although we all suspected it was due to his being a fifth-stage.

"I've always wondered what this might feel like," Taegin said idly as he carefully observed his own pearl before consuming it. He glowed brightly, but something happened that only I seemed to recognize.

His glow is the same as when we first met, I thought back to the fire-like tendrils of mana surrounding him as he argued with my father.

Nenvalur and Anwill had similar reactions to it. However, Nenvalur's was surprisingly brighter than Anwill's, making him puff out his chest victoriously. At the same time, Anwill pinched the bridge of his nose, knowing he would never hear the end of it.

Aurae and Elhael took theirs as well, and while Elhael's glow was slightly dimmer than Aurae's violet and scarlet, hers shifted and waved ever so slightly, prompting Erumon to raise an eyebrow, but he said nothing at the time. My mother then took hers, sharing a similar effect to Taegin's, nearly matching the brightness perfectly, with stronger hints of scarlet present than Bernar's.

Here we go, I sent Ysevel and Kalia before we took ours in unison. Like the others, our cores began to glow, but there was a sudden warmth that reached into me, one I welcomed like a long-lost friend. Ysevel glowed brightly, a beautiful mixture of violet and Scarlet, and I could have sworn her eyes were an even deeper color than before, though Kalia seemed to share a hue of scarlet around her like I did.

I couldn't tell whether Ysevel's eyes looked that way because of the effect the pearl had on her or the warm feeling I had earlier.

Erumon seemed to know exactly what had happened to me and put a heavy hand on my shoulder before moving on to the next two. Irun and Athar shared a glance, having formed a strong bond during our time in the dome, and took it together. Erumon watched Athar more closely than Irun, but when the violet glow from Athar's core seemed normal, we were relieved that nothing had gone wrong.

I did notice, however, that when Ren and Thorn took theirs, I could all but see Thorn's Rivet mana begin to resonate around him like Kalia's had, though it was much paler in color. Ren, however, had a similar effect to Kalia's.

"I'm surprised that it went as smoothly as it did," Ardrin noted to Erumon, who agreed with a nod. "Indeed. I was mildly concerned about Athar, but *nearly* everyone else was within my expectations," he said, giving a quick glance at Aurae before returning to his seat. "I must say, I didn't know Elves *could* possess *true* ambivalence, but it's certainly a nice surprise," he said, giving her a knowing nod which she returned in kind.

What was that all about? I asked Ysevel. *I'll explain it later, but you'll have to promise not to tell anyone else,* she said in an even tone, but I could tell it was something serious that she guarded carefully. *Of course,* I replied immediately, but as I did so, I caught Aurae regarding me with a warm smile, as if she already knew Ysevel was going to tell me.

I didn't know why, but I felt much more at ease about whatever Ysevel had to tell me than ever before. I trusted her with both my heart and my life, and I knew that if she'd held onto that information for as long as she had, it was because she wanted to *protect* her mother, and not because she didn't trust me.

Aurae's smile seemed to indicate all of my thoughts on the matter were correct, and the feeling I got from my connection to her core seemed to let me know Aurae trusted me enough to tell me, too.

It made me smile.

"Now that you've all had your shares of the synthetic *Authority*, there is something I would like to test," Erumon said, forcing my attention to shift to him immediately, as I felt something ominous emanating from him. "W-Wait, you don't mean to sh-...?" I cut myself off, as he spawned a blackened pearl, just like the one he'd created with Nexis' shattered core.

"What is this *malice*?" Elhael asked, genuinely surprised he hadn't felt it before, getting similar reactions from everyone else. I immediately felt a sense of dread, though it didn't overtake those of us who were Wraithborn as entirely as it had the others.

"As I said before, your understanding of mana will deepen, and continue to do so as you develop your skills. However, *this* mana can only be sensed by those who have either innate or synthetic *Authority* present within them," Erumon explained briefly. "It is what we Wardens call *Tyrant* mana, the direct counterpart to nearly *all* mana, save *one*. This is the very same mana that corrupted Nexis' core, although his wasn't quite enough to be detected, even by most Wardens, as it was secretly embedded into the curse we'd placed on him," he gave Kalia a knowing nod.

Her expression visibly shook me, and whatever emotions were swirling in her core nearly bled over to the rest of us as she began to speak. "Lord, are you saying that *this mana* is one of the reasons behind the near-extinction of the Wraithborn?" she asked the question that was burning in mine and Ysevel's minds as well. "I would say that it's a good starting point, at least. Tyrant mana can disrupt, corrupt, and counter nearly *all* mana except for that controlled by the Wraithborn," he began to explain as I felt Kalia's emotions surge.

"However, the mission I mentioned I had for you all earlier will require you to find more information on this matter. There are dwarven records on the Gramm Isles that will help you *all* to unfurl the clutches of Mideia in Kavrass. Go to the capital city of Narin; you'll find much of what you're looking for there," he said loosely.

"I hate to be the one to ask, Lord Erumon, but why can't *you* go?" my mother asked bluntly. Anyone could see that his expression shifted dourly at her question, but after a moment of consideration, he looked back up at us. "There are matters *beyond* this realm I must attend to, as it was *your son's* reasoning that is going to lead me down this path," he said, surprising us *both* with his answer.

What the fuck did you do? Mom sent me immediately with uncontrollable curiosity. *He might go looking for whoever put the seal on my core. Or, at the very least, someone who* knew *about it,* I reasoned, recalling what he said when he interrupted my line of thinking.

"Nevertheless, I hope that you all train hard and that you build the strength necessary for the war that I'm almost sure will reach your doorsteps," he said gravely, giving each one of us a stern look of determination as he rose from his seat. He moved over to my mother's side and handed her four more of the synthetic *Authority* pearls.

"These are for the other members of your team. I'm sure they will accept the *Authority* without much issue, but in the event something goes wrong, crush *this* one, and I will be here in the time it takes you to blink," he said, handing her a fifth one that was pure white.

"Th-thank you, Lord Erumon. I will be sure to pass it on to them," she bowed as graciously as she could. With a single nod to me, then another to Taegin, he left the room and summoned a similar portal to the one we'd used to get back from Vareluth, disappearing shortly after he stepped through.

There was a silence in the room that hung heavily, but none of us *truly* knew just how important what he gave us would be in the coming days. But as our meeting came to an end and everyone was leaving the room, I heard a voice I didn't expect to call out to me.

"Thoma, would you mind staying a moment longer?" Ardrin asked.

CHAPTER 78
MEMORY LANE

I turned to face Ardrin, who'd surprised me with his question just before I left the meeting room.

"What is it, *uncle*?" I asked with a small hint of sarcasm in my use of his title. I noticed he was accompanied by Kalia, Siraye, Ysevel, Aurae, and Taegin, although I couldn't understand why everyone else had been excluded from the conversation. "Shouldn't Bernar be here for this? I asked, confused as to why he'd continued walking with Leona.

"He has other things to worry about right now," Taegin said, waving a hand dismissively. "What do you mean?" I asked with visible confusion. "Didn't you notice what happened to her when she consumed the *Authority*?" Mom asked with a wry grin as if she already knew what was happening. "N-Not really?" I raised an eyebrow.

Mom chuckled briefly and shook her head. "Well, there's still a *lot* for you to learn. You might have spent a decade training with Kalia, but there's much about the world you've yet to see for yourself," she said cryptically. *What the fuck is* that *supposed to mean?* I sent her, but she'd blocked out my connection to her core momentarily to prevent me from digging around. "Fine. Fine! I'll just be in the dark *yet again*," I sighed as I rolled my eyes.

"So, what was it you wanted to talk about?" I asked Ardrin, who glanced at Taegin and my mother momentarily, to get an approving nod. "Thoma, there's something about the seal on your core that we believe not even Erumon was aware of," he began with a strange look of concern on his face, causing my stomach to drop.

"Was there anything you remember about that night that you noticed was *strange* about the man who did it?" he asked, though I couldn't determine why. I put a finger on my chin as I tried to recall the events of that fateful night. "He was old, weathered, and had a scraggly beard. His face was covered with a white sheet of cloth, though there were slits cut out for his eyes," I began to recall, causing Taegin and Mom to shift uncomfortably, but they didn't say anything.

"When I woke up, I was tied by my hands and feet, but there was something about the old man that didn't sit right with me. The way he moved was strange for such an old man, and the way he looked at me with those strange eyes didn't help ease my discomfort either. They were pale green with black tendrils swirling within them, not unlike the Tyrant mana Erumon just showed us," I explained, but as I did so, Ardrin was the one who seemed the most bothered by it.

"Then my suspicions have been confirmed," he said gravely. "Thoma, I think the person you met that night was under Mideia's influence, or worse, *possession*," he said gravely, making my stomach drop even more. "W-What?" I asked breathlessly. "It's true. The day I left you was to go hunt him down and kill him myself, but by the time I arrived, there was no sign of him present in the old man's eyes," Mom said, making me take a brief step back.

Wait, wait, wait. What? I thought, trying to understand what I was hearing.

"Do you remember the first expedition we took you on to Coltend Castle, and the old farmer we saved?" Taegin asked, making my eyes widen in realization. "N-No. That's impossible. *Jehn Boone*? The old farmer who was also sending ravens to the castle?" I recalled the name, to which he simply nodded.

"*He* was the one I found where your father told me he took you," my mother said dejectedly, shaking her head down and away from me. "So, you're saying Mideia might have *possessed* him to get to me? Why? Why go through the trouble of sealing my core like that?" I asked, but deep down, I felt I already knew the answer.

There were several things he said to me that night that started slowly coming back, but the memories were patchy at best. "I think it was more out of precaution than anything else," Kalia began, surprising everyone else present. "If what you're all saying is true, then it would make sense that he would do something like that," she said, taking a step toward me.

"If what Erumon said about the *Authority* and the slaughter of the Wraithborn is true, then it would make sense why he would want to *cripple* your potential, as a young Wraithborn who has the *Authority* would essentially be a *god-killer* in the making," she said gravely, putting a hand on my shoulder.

I didn't want to say or transmit anything just then, but I knew she was right, especially after everything that happened when I was fighting Nexis. If there was anything that made sense about my seal, it was that whoever ultimately did it wanted me *gone*, whether it *was* Mideia or not.

I could tell Ysevel noticed my inner turmoil when she gently tugged on our connection, as if trying to pull me out of my own head.

"S-Sorry, I'm just…" I trailed off, shaking my head and putting on a fake smile. "It's fine, Thoma," Ardrin began as he stepped toward me, prompting me to look up at him.

"We understand it's a lot to take in, but right now, we have our own missions to accomplish. Yours in the Gramm Isles, while Taegin and I will head to Valdis in search of answers, as I have *centuries'* worth of records untainted by royal families," he said with an obvious reference to Athar's story.

"I understand. I hope you can find what you're looking for," I said, giving him a short bow. "As do I, *nephew,*" he said with a grin tugging at the corner of his mouth before heading out of the room with Taegin. As I watched them leave, Ysevel came and put a hand on my shoulder. "Let's go check on Devyr. I've heard from Athar that she was doing much better the last time he saw her," she said warmly, hoping to take my mind off the conversation we'd just had.

"He's gone to see her? Not even *I* was allowed in when I asked to see her," Kalia snarled frustratedly. "That's because you didn't go with *me,*" Mom said playfully, taking Kalia's arm like they were about to walk into a formal gathering. "Come on. Let's go check on your daughter *together,*" she said with a warm smile.

After walking down several halls, getting more than a few stares due to my mother's playful demeanor with Kalia, we made it to the infirmary, where Devyr had been recovering since our return. The pair of guards that stood at the front snapped to attention as we rounded the corner, and I could tell immediately that they were being extremely cautious with the way they spoke to my mother.

"B-But Commander, she's not allowed inside due to the patien -…" the guard cut himself off when Mom's demeanor shifted from playful to authoritative in the blink of an eye. "*I'm* saying she may enter. It's her *daughter,* for fuck's sake. Now, stand aside," she said forcefully. I could tell the glow in her eyes had flared due to the slight reflection of them in the guardsman's helmet.

"O-Of course, Commander. A-As you wish," he stammered, obviously uneasy due to the sudden shift back into her playful demeanor. *See? I told you it would be alright,* Mom sent Kalia and the rest of us, causing Ysevel to stifle a laugh. She managed to keep herself under control, as she still greeted the guards cordially.

Nice save, I noted. *It would be unbecoming of me not to greet them with the respect they're due. Your mother just happens to have much more... How do I put this?* Presence *than I do,* she mentally chuckled. *Yeah, no denying that,* I grinned, giving her a gentle nudge with my shoulder.

"Do you two *always* have side conversations like that?" Mom asked over her shoulder as we continued down the hall that led to the main room. "Most of the time. Though we've gotten close enough not to have to speak, only reading whatever comes through our cores' connection," I noted briefly, since I knew she was still getting used to having a nearly-perpetual link to us.

"*Oh,* I'm not complaining. It's just nice to know you two have gotten along so well. Just so you know, Aurae and I *do* expect grandchildren someday," she said with a shit-eating grin on her face. "M-Mom!" I stammered, feeling my face turn a bright shade of red. Ysevel, however, only laughed and patted me on the shoulder. "Maybe when this is all over," she said smugly, knowing all too well that we were in *no* position to consider that right now. "I know. I know. Just so long as *you* know, is all," Mom snorted indelicately.

We rounded the corner and came to a large room full of beds neatly dressed in white linen, with an attendant at every bedside that held a patient. Each one had a cage of roots over it that served as a conduit for the attendants to push mana into, allowing the mana to flow over the patient as one, practically *engulfing* them in it.

As I watched a scout's broken leg mend itself together before my eyes, I realized this was a much more advanced form of mana than what we used in Codrean. To be fair, they *did* have hundreds, if not *thousands*, of years to perfect their craft. Needless to say, it was impressive to watch.

"*Egeshe marra!*" Kalia suddenly broke away from my mother when she spotted Devyr sitting up as we approached. She wrapped her in a tight embrace, and I could tell from our connection that she was both relieved and ecstatic to see her daughter recovering.

"*Mata dunin grusstek mireba, Murra,*" Devyr said with a sense of relief in her use of the hegraphenian word for *mother* that was slightly muffled by Kalia's shoulder. "It's good to see you too, Devyr," I said as Ysevel and I both greeted her with a balled fist across our chests and a light bow.

"I apologize for my use of my native language," Devyr said bashfully. "Don't worry about it. I think I'd even like to learn some since I'll be working with Kalia a lot more," Mom waved dismissively. "*Ah,* you must be Commander Siraye Fayren. Athar's told me a great deal about you already. It's an honor to meet you, though I must say he was incorrect about you being *terrifying,*" she said with visible confusion.

"Did he, now? What else did he say?" Mom's face shifted into a broken smile of desperate self-control. *Don't even think about it,* I sent her briefly with a chuckle. "That you were as kind as you were strong, but that for the most part, people tend to *fear* you when they first meet you," she said, putting a finger on her exposed chin. "I-I see. Well, he's not *entirely* wrong about that, but I'd like to prove otherwise and ask how you're doing," she said after clearing her throat.

Devyr paused for a moment as if considering how best to put it. Her violet eyes with golden tendrils shifted back and forth a few times as she put her thoughts together. "I feel *much* better than I did when I first woke up, though I'm not entirely sure how to describe *this*," she said, gesturing to the root-like cage around her lower body.

"When I first woke up, I was confused by where I was, or even who I was with. Once Athar came and managed to explain everything to me, I knew I was being well-cared for," she gave my mother a toothy grin, as her sharp fangs, like her mother's, protruded just a little. "I'm glad to hear you're doing better, *marra*. Did they say how much longer you had to stay here?" Kalia asked nervously.

"They said I should be cleared to leave by tomorrow, though I don't know my way around this place," she said, glancing around the infirmary as she lifted her hands in confusion. "Well, if you're up for it, we have a mission to go on soon. Do you think you'll be alright to go?" I asked. As I did so, her expression immediately brightened, and she nearly leaped from the bed as the last words reached her.

"*Egeshe krag!* Yes! I don't know how much longer I can sit here like this," she said excitedly. "*Marra*, you've only just healed. Are you sure about this?" Kalia asked calmly, though I could feel the concern behind her words through our connection. "Of course, *Murra*! Is...

Athar going?" Devyr asked sheepishly, causing Ysevel to snort and stifle a laugh at Kalia's expression.

"Yes, he's going, too. In fact, *every* member of *The Order* is going," I said with a bright smile, much to Kalia's chagrin. "*Murra*, I'm going. Freshly-healed or not," Devyr said with avid determination. Kalia sighed, but I could tell she was glad to see her daughter back to her former self. "You remind me a lot of Ysevel. Almost *too* much. Very well, then. We'll come get you in the morning," she relented. As soon as she did, Devyr quickly reached out and wrapped Kalia in a tight embrace.

"I guess we'll have to see Maikell about *another* set of armor," my mother said with a single chuckle through her nostrils. "Wait, you've already had them made? When did *that* happen?" I asked. "It was nearly a week ago, now. She thought it would be a good idea for Kalia, Irun, and Athar *also to* have armor that matched ours," Ysevel added with a knowing grin.

"You *do* realize that their bodies are *already* armored, right?" I asked my mom chidingly. "It's more of a disguise for Kalia and Irun, since I'm sure people would ask a lot of questions if they saw them outside of Caegwen. Come, Kalia. We'll need your help to measure out Devyr's armor as well," she replied, which caught me off guard.

Since I'd already grown so used to seeing Kalia and Irun, it never occurred to me that anyone *else* outside of our group was still entirely unaware that we had a hegraphene and a daemonically augmented human with us.

We bid Devyr goodbye, though Kalia said something to her in their native language that I didn't quite understand, but I *did* hear Athar's name mentioned, so I figured it wasn't any of my business. There *was* a strange mixture of frustration and happiness coming from her, which told me it couldn't have *all* been bad.

I think Kalia's still adjusting to the fact that her daughter's in love with Athar, Ysevel sent playfully. *It's been a few years since* that *reveal, though I suppose she's just being protective,* I shrugged. *Like your mother was when she read that letter She Who Shall Not Be Named sent?* Ysevel asked with a raised eyebrow. *I guess, but I don't know if Kalia realizes that yet,* I chuckled lightly.

We continued through the many halls of the palace, eventually meeting up with Irun and Athar, whom we led to Maikell's workshop. There was a mild tension in the air between Kalia and Athar, but it wasn't anything we hadn't dealt with before.

As we approached the workshop, I could see the smoke from his forge rising from the chimney that poked through the massive, root-like structure. However, there was a loud *crash* that sounded like a piece of armor being struck, so we quickened our pace to find out what happened. "Maikell, are you alright?" Mom called out from the large doorway, stopping at the threshold as she swung the door open.

"*Argh*, I can't figure it out, Siraye!" he shouted frustratedly, immediately confusing the rest of us. When I managed to get close enough to see what was going on, I realized he was doing a destruction test on *my* armor that Kalia had infused with her *kataki*.

"It just doesn't make any sense. How can this *kataki* be so *damned strong*? Here, look at this," he said, quickly grabbing the armor off the support he was using to hold it up, and another from the workbench. "See this? *This* is my armor. It's made of *twytanym,* which, to the uninitiated, is almost as tough as a *dragon's scales*. However, *this one* is my armor with that *kataki* stuff infused into it, and *look*! Not a single sign of damage to it whatsoever!" he thrust each one in my mother's face, respectively.

"I-It's incredible. I just don't know ho-..." he cut himself off when he saw Kalia standing next to me, his eyes growing wide in amazement. "By the First Flame, i-is that...?" he asked, nearly shoving my mother aside to get a better look at her, reaching for her armored hand. "I-I've never seen something so *beautiful,*" he said, his glowing eyes shining even more brightly against the light of the forge behind him.

I could tell Kalia wanted to pull away immediately, but at my mother's behest, she resisted the urge to do so. "Were *you* the one who did this to their armor?" he asked excitedly, twisting her hand this way and that, finding it difficult to decide which part of her to look at.

"Y-Yes, it was. His armor was slightly damaged during our training, so I used some of my *kataki* to mend and reinforce it," she said awkwardly, but his response to her words was one of pure befuddlement. "H-How? How did you do this, and with such high-quality craftsmanship?" he asked breathlessly.

She seemingly understood what he was asking for, though there was a slight hesitation present in her core that I felt I needed to gently encourage to be set aside. She sighed, but both she and Ysevel followed my lead to create our *kataki* blades, slowing the process enough so that he could see what was happening.

His eyes widened, and I could tell he was using as much mana as he could to better observe what he was looking at. After a brief explanation of what it was and how it worked, he nearly fell backward in shock, supporting himself on the stand he'd taken the armor from.

"I-I see. I'm astounded that such a thing even exists outside of legend. Even so, it was an incredible display of your talents, and I humbly ask you to do what you did to *their* armor to these pieces I've created for you," he said with a bow, then quickly turned to grab a handful of boxes.

There was one for each member of *Nightfall's Blade*, and one *extra* that struck my mother as odd.

"Who's that one for, *coal-eater*? Did you make one for yourself?" she said playfully. "No, you *brute*, this one's for someone named De-vyr," he said, prompting Kalia to freeze solid. "Who ordered *that*?" Mom asked with a raised eyebrow. "He did," he gestured to Athar standing behind me.

I could feel Kalia's displeasure at the knowledge, but knew there wasn't much I could do, since the damage had *already* been done.

"He found out you had put in the order, and even gave me all her measurements so there *shouldn't* be any adjustments that need to be made," he said, causing Kalia to shift from being frozen solid to a boiling pot of nearly unbridled rage.

"*Eg karaeda juka erugo*," she hissed, similarly to when she'd first found out Devyr's faceplate had retracted around him. "*Guto, Kalia*," I said, hoping to calm her down, while Maikell and my mother stared at the two of us in confusion. "It's fine. I'm fine," she said, raising both her armored hands as if surrendering.

Athar nearly died again, Ysevel chuckled, forcing me to beat down the shit-eating grin that was trying to surface.

Thankfully, Kalia sighed and unclenched her jaw as she did so. "I accept your earlier request, Maikell, and I will show you how *I* did it in full detail. Perhaps you might find a way of adding your *own* techniques into this," she said, begrudgingly taking a step forward to the sets of armor.

As she lifted the first lid to my mother's newest set of armor, we all gathered around her to see what she was doing. Maikell had moved up closer to her than I think she liked, but she ultimately knew he wasn't doing it to be weird.

At least, that's what *I* thought, anyway.

"Wait, what's that?" Mom asked, pointing to a trio of engravings near the top of the chestplate. "*Ah*, well, after the strange lad appeared, Aurae stopped by and asked me to add these to the armor, trusting me to put them in a place I felt they deserved to be," he said, gesturing to the engravings.

I leaned in closer to see what he was talking about, and on the left side of the breastplate, there was the Phrys family crest, as well as my own, though the third I didn't quite recognize.

"Athar, you son of a bitch," I grinned, looking over at him when I realized he'd designed a crest for *The Order*; an upward-facing sword backed by a crescent moon near its base, with seven stars arrayed near its point. While none of the crests had their words engraved, I shuddered to think about what he'd come up with.

"It's beautiful, and *very* fitting, Athar. Thank you," Ysevel said diplomatically. "I have to agree, it *is* beautiful, though I feel we may need to make more room for the stars once we acquire more members," Mom added with a light smile. "*Hush*, you two! Let her work!" Maikell snarled, more interested in whatever Kalia was doing than our idle conversation.

As she produced a decent amount of *kataki*, she slowed its movement down significantly, allowing him to inspect its flow as it wove itself into the fibers and metal of the armor, as if absorbing them. Maikell's eyes flared with mana once more, and he quietly observed its flow into the materials he'd used for the armor, making it a much darker green than before.

"Incredible," he said with a half-chuckle of disbelief. She continued to the following pieces, prompting him to watch just as intently as before. There was a slightly *warm* feeling coming from Kalia as she continued her work, though I couldn't place *exactly* what it meant.

Within a few minutes, she'd completed the sets of armor, including Devyr's, and let out a satisfied grunt. "I hope that was a sufficient demonstration of the technique for you. *Bear it and pass it on*," she said in a tone that matched the feeling in her core. "Th-thank you, Kalia. I will," he said, his eyes glistening with what I thought were tears.

What just happened? I asked my mother, whose eyes widened in surprise. *That phrase she just used was one his wife used to say to him before she passed over a century ago,* she explained briefly. I noticed Ysevel must have known her, too, since her expression shifted warmly.

I guess we all have our secrets, I thought idly.

"Please, do me the honor of trying them on. I-I know that you might not *need* the armor, Kalia, but I would hate to see you all leave here without that," he said, shaking his head briefly to refute the tears. Each of us did as he requested, and like the first set of armor he'd given me, it fit perfectly. Like before, every piece of the armor could be put on or taken off without assistance, making the entire process quick and painless.

The armor was very reminiscent of the one he'd made me before, though instead of being completely black, the dark shade of green seemed to indicate that Kalia was much more deliberate in her *kataki* infusion than the first time she'd done it.

It made me smile.

As we all lined up for inspection, I was reminded of my time in Codrean, where these sorts of things happened regularly. "I've made adjustments according to the young man's descriptions of your fighting styles. The armor seems to fit well enough, though I'm sorry about your attitude, Siraye. No amount of my smithing will fix *that*," he said, wrapping his knuckles on her breastplate with a grin. "And no amount of my *berating* will ever get you to treat me normally, but still, *thank you*, Maikell," she retorted kindly, causing him to snort and move on to Kalia, who was last to get into her armor.

"Is it comfortable, at least?" he asked, making sure she had adjusted the straps correctly. "Surprisingly so, though this *is* my first time wearing armor that I didn't produce *myself*," she added, causing his eyes to widen again. "You mean that tough exterior is something you produce *all the time*?" he asked. "Did you think only my face was what you might consider *normal*?" she returned his question with her own, surprising *everyone*.

"N-No, but... *Bah*, never mind," he said, redirecting his focus to the straps along her body. "Not bad for a first timer, though I would recommend keeping your waist strap a little tighter," he said, tugging on it and securing it into another notch for a closer fitting. It caused her to lurch forward momentarily, but she caught herself before accidentally bashing his face with her armor.

"Apologies," he said bashfully, but she did her best to present a warm smile to him, while the rest of us looked on with raised eyebrows. "Are you seeing what *I'm* seeing?" Athar whispered, but I had to quickly shut his mouth before he said anything that might get him killed, already finding it challenging to keep my *own* thoughts in check.

"*Oh*, one last thing, Thoma. This is for you, since I know you'll need one," he said, handing me a pendant similar to my brother's. "Well, go on then. Try it on," he said with an encouraging gesture. As soon as the chain settled around my neck, I could feel a subtle shift of mana surrounding my body. Glancing in the mirror he provided, it took me a moment to get used to the same brown hair I'd had for most of my life.

"Gods above, I almost don't even *recognize* you like that," Ysevel said jokingly. "She's right. Is that what you used to look like?" Kalia asked, inspecting my hair closely. "Yes. Yes, it was," I sighed as the two of them poked and prodded me. "Thank you, Maikell. You've done incredible work, yet again," I said, but all I got was a grunt in response.

After we left his workshop, Kalia noted that she wanted to see if it fit on Devyr before our journey the following day. We agreed, leaving Irun and Athar to their own devices, while Ysevel and I followed my mother to greet the rest of her team, to deliver the gifts Erumon had left behind, and to explain their purpose.

"Never thought I'd see you back in your original form," Vyra noted, tugging at a strand of my hair. "Well, I'm leaving tomorrow, but I can't walk around people who knew me like this with steel colored hair, can I?" I asked loosely, gently swatting her hand away. "No, I suppose you can't, but I'd still love to run an experiment on you *and* these strange pearls," Derion snickered.

"Absolutely not," my mother and I said in unison, getting a chuckle from Eirenne, Haldir, and Vyra as a result. They were grateful for the gifts, and as each one consumed their pearls, I was glad to see none of them had any adverse reaction to them. Derion was first, being no stranger to consuming unlikely things, while Haldir and Vyra took theirs after him.

"What the hell was *in those*?" Eirenne asked, looking down at her core's diminishing glow, having taken hers last. "It's called *Authority*, and it was a gift from Erumon," I said, giving them a brief explanation of what that meant. They struggled to understand the concept, but took it in stride, or at least that's what it *seemed* like.

"Well, if it means I can finally catch up to *you*, maybe it's not *all bad*," Eirenne said, giving my mother a wry smile. "I know I promised I'd help you reach the fifth stage, but as you know..." Mom trailed off. "*The mission takes priority*, as you've said more times than I'd care to count," Eirenne sighed with a wave of her hand.

"Speaking of which, we didn't find anything on *our* mission, but I suppose that might have been for the better, since we have to figure out whatever this *Authority* is," Haldir noted. "In that case, I suggest you train with the others, since they've also received this gift," Mom said, clasping his forearm tightly. "I'm looking forward to it. Good luck on your mission, Commander," he said with a warm smile, getting a nod from the others as well. We wished them the best of luck and returned to the palace to prepare for our journey.

The following morning, we were all dressed in our new sets of armor, though I wasn't *entirely* surprised to see Devyr's armor fit just as well as the rest of ours. The others, to include the group Bernar and Leona had arrived with, came out to see us off. Taegin and Ardrin had already left earlier that morning without much ceremony, though we all knew that their mission was *also* heavily time-dependent.

"Hey *shitbird*, don't go getting yourself trapped in another realm again, okay?" Bernar said, clapping me on the shoulder and giving me a shake. "*Oh,* come on! Like you wouldn't have fun chasing me down," I grinned, giving him a firm pat on the back. "I would, but Leona would *kill me* if I did," he said hushedly, jutting his thumb over his shoulder. "Just take care of yourself and mom while you're gone, alright? I hope you're ready for a little trip down memory lane," he said with earnest caution.

"Don't worry. We'll be alright," I said cheerfully. "Ysevel, you take care of him, too, okay?" he called out to her. "Why wouldn't I? I've only been doing that for a *decade*, after all," she quipped, causing him to chuckle. "It seems you're in good hands, then," Leona stepped forward, giving me a hug.

"As are you," I winked, bringing out that stunning smile of hers. "Indeed, I am. Be careful out there, and tell us all about it when you're back," she said with an almost *motherly* tone as I gave her a nod of understanding.

Ysevel and I knew Aurae would be keeping an eye on us through the Wraith realm, so there was no need for words to be exchanged between us, only a simple nod of acknowledgement.

As we left Caegwen, Mom and Kalia rode at the front, Ysevel and I just behind them, while Athar and Devyr rode side by side with Irun to their right. We left Myrdin's limits, holding idle conversation along the way, which mostly consisted of filling the gaps in Devyr's knowledge of what happened.

However, even through the intermittent idle conversation, I noticed that my mother and Kalia glanced back at me a few times, as if concerned about something.

Mom, what's wrong? I asked, unable to ignore the feeling any longer. *We'll come to you. This is something we must discuss as a group,* she replied in a tone that let me know she was serious. They slowed their horses down enough to allow the rest of us to catch up to them, and while the others had confused looks on their faces, I could already tell what she was about to say.

"Everyone, I have a bit of a favor to ask," she began solemnly as they shifted their attention to her. "Our path to the Gramm Isles will lead us right next to my old home in Coltend. After the meeting with Erumon, there's something I need to see for myself there, but it's a place with a lot of memories, and I don't want to make that decision on my own," she continued, glancing anxiously at the others.

"What kind of memories, Commander?" Devyr asked, still using her formal title. "Painful ones, but not just for me, for *Thoma* as well," she admitted. "He's told us about most of what happened there already, *and I can't wait to see the look on that fat fucker's face when The Order of Nightfall's Blade shows up together,*" Athar said, allowing his alternate's voice through freely, easing my mother's tension a little.

"It's true, we know almost as much as he was able to remember, but just know that we're with you," Irun said with a firm nod, which she returned in kind. "We'll be alright, Siraye, and we'll be there to catch *either* of you if you fall," Ysevel said supportively, giving me a warm smile. "And I will crush him into *zuresh* if he tries to lay a finger on you," Kalia chimed in, causing me to chuckle at her use of a term that could only be translated to *the shit beneath my heel*.

Thankfully, Mom didn't understand the term, but from her intonation, I think she *might have*, because she gave me a strange look as if to confirm what she'd heard. I could only give her a nod of reassurance to let her know it would be okay. "Thank you. *All* of you," she said with a humble bow.

We continued on our journey for the better part of two weeks, descending from the Rhydian Mountains through the pass and skirting west around Coltend before heading due north toward our old home.

Apparently, Kinth was a short distance away from a handful of farms that lay between it and Codrean. During our trip, my mother noted that it wasn't known for much other than being considered an *excellent place* for nobles who wanted to get away from Coltend to retire.

My father was the son of one such noble, and while it had been a long time since I'd last been there, I could still remember the sight of the nearby forest, the sounds of the songbirds, and the hill behind our house that marked the edge of his land.

As the path curved around a dense treeline, I saw the corner of our old house peeking out from around it. The two-story building was *much larger* than I remembered, with two peaks on the roof, a chimney poking out of the far end, and multiple windows along the front of it. The porch, however, was exactly as I remembered it, with the well-worn rocking chair gently moving with the breeze.

But as soon as we dismounted, it nearly made me puke to be back.

"Thoma? Are you alright?" Ysevel asked, noticing the shift in my complexion as the memories came rushing back. Not all of them were bad, she knew that, of course, but the ones I remembered the best *were*. "Yeah, I'm okay," I struggled to say as I argued with the boulder in my stomach. "Hey, I'm *right here*, okay?" she said, giving the others a nod of confirmation that I was, in fact, *not alright*.

"Son, you don't have to do this. I can go in alone," my mother said, putting a hand on my shoulder. "It's fine. I'm fine. Let's just get this over with," I said, shaking my head rapidly to clear it. I noticed she gave Ysevel a concerned look, but as I started moving toward the door, I heard the bolt unlatch before I could even reach to knock.

"T-Thoma? Siraye? Is that... Is that *really* you?" he shakily asked in his familiar baritone. He'd lost a lot of weight since I last saw him, making him look much younger and like the former self my mother must have fallen in love with all those years ago. "Hello, *Kayne*. Yes, it's us," she replied, causing my father, whose name I'd long-since forgotten, to shake not out of fear, but *joy*. "Gods above! I-I thought I'd never see you again," he said, darting forward and trying to give me a hug, which I backed away from, tilting my head downward as if preparing for an attack.

"*O-Oh*, I'm terribly sorry. It's just been so long since..." he trailed off, noticing Kalia's slight shift in her stance. "Since *what?*" I asked coldly, trying my best not to cut this man's head off. "S-Since *I lost you*," he said, his tone shifting into dejection. "You lost us the night you brought me to that *old bastard*," I spoke in my mother's stead.

"Thoma, wait. Kayne, we only came to grab something I left here that will be useful to us," she said, pushing her hand across my chest as she stepped forward, which caused his large, blue eyes to widen.

They were as clear as the sky above me, and I couldn't seem to sense anything strange about him, either. *I don't sense anything wrong with him. Do you?* Mom asked. *No, I don't, but I still don't trust him,* I replied coldly.

"Siraye, Thoma. I hope you find what you're looking for, but before that, I-I can explain everything, please. Step inside. Your, *uh,* friends are welcome, too," he said, taking a step back to open the door a little more for us to enter. The scent of the house was identical to what I remembered as the mahogany and cedarwood scent wafted into my nostrils. "*Nice place,*" I heard Athar mutter sarcastically, getting a strange glance from Kayne as he passed.

He gestured for the others to take their seats on the long couch in the middle of the living room as he fetched something from the kitchen. I looked around to see if anything had changed, but it felt like nothing *had.* The painting he had was still on the wall, though *he* was unrecognizable from that time. I scoffed as I stared at it, but when Ysevel cleared her throat to let me know he was coming back, I simply stepped aside and let him pass so he could serve them some dried meat and wine.

"I'm sorry that I don't have much else right now. I wasn't expecting any visitors," he said with a humility I hadn't expected. "This is fine, Kayne. Thank you," Ysevel said cordially, suggesting I take the single seat beside my mother. "Well, I suppose I should start talking about what I promised I would, shouldn't I?" he chuckled nervously, drinking a glass of *water* as opposed to wine.

"First, let me preface this with an apology," he began, fiddling with his hands. "Siraye, I-I know that you may never forgive me for what I did, and Thoma, I-I hope you know that I don't expect you to, either, but you've grown into a *fine young man*," he said shakily.

There was a gentle tug on my connection with Ysevel, telling me that I needed to be cordial if I was going to get any information out of him. "Thank you," I said dryly, tearing into a piece of meat without breaking eye contact.

"I-In any case, I want you all to know that I didn't do what I did with a *clear conscience*," he began. "Bullshit," I immediately spat. "Let him finish," my mother snarled.

"I-I'd met with the man once before, though I didn't think much of him at the time. He seemed a bit odd, sure, and his eyes seemed to glow much like Siraye's, but I figured he must have been a retired Synner then," he started nervously, fiddling with his hands more intensely this time.

"A few years before you were born, Thoma, was the first time I'd seen him since then, a-and he took a particular interest in the pendant your mother gave me. Not thinking much of it at the time, I handed it to him so he could see its beautiful details more closely. I didn't know it then, but he did *something* to it that took hold of me slowly, but surely," he continued, prompting Athar, of all people, to shift forward in his seat.

"You see, he disappeared again after that, and since that meeting, I didn't feel like I was fully in control of myself. I gained weight, drank and ate more than my fill, and by the time you were about four, he showed up again," he continued, lowering his head as if piecing it all together.

"He watched as you played in the forest for a few moments, before telling me there was something *wrong* with you, something not even *you* could fix," he nodded toward my mom, causing her eyes to widen. "Is *that* what he said?" she asked, but only got a nod in response.

"He said that I had to bring you to him so he could *fix it*, but didn't give me many details, other than I was to bring you when *she* wasn't around," he noted cautiously. "What led you to believe this man?" Kalia asked bluntly, catching him off-guard with the raspiness of her voice.

"I-I don't know how to explain it, but I was *compelled* to, in a way," he shook his head. "He also noticed that Siraye and I had grown *distant*, and offered to change his appearance permanently in addition to whatever he was going to do," he continued.

"For some reason, my anger toward Siraye reached a point of no return, and I accepted his offer, saying that I couldn't bear to look at him because he reminded me of *her* too much. Foolish, I know, but I now understand that I *wasn't myself*," he said, causing me to flinch and click my tongue.

"So everything that happened was because you were somehow under this person's *influence*? Awfully convenient excuse for an ambulatory piece of shit, don't you think?" I asked flatly, getting a look of embarrassment from Kayne as I got up from my seat and walked over to him.

"Listen to me, *Dad*," I emphasized the word with poignant sarcasm. "I only have one question for you, and if you don't answer it truthfully, *I'll know*," I said, momentarily flaring my eyes with Ethereal mana. "Thoma, what are you doing?" Mom asked cautiously. *I need an answer to something I heard that night, but he hasn't mentioned anything about it yet,* I sent her, while maintaining my glare.

"After my core was sealed, you walked in and saw me lying on the floor and bleeding from my nose and mouth. Instead of coming to help me, you started a conversation with him. I couldn't hear much, but I specifically recall him telling you something that you seemed relieved to hear. What *was* it?" I asked, getting a mix of emotions through the connection I had to the others.

There was a flash of *fear* in his eyes, as if whatever answer he was going to give me wasn't rehearsed like the rest of his explanation. After he searched my eyes for any hint of mercy and finding *none*, he gave a relenting sigh. "He said that he would continue to protect me from you, and that if you ever *did* come back, all I needed to do was break *this* to let him know you had," he presented a thin, unsuspecting wax disk that emitted a faint hint of mana from an octagonal pattern on it.

"Why didn't you, then?" I asked, quickly shifting my attention from the wax back to him. "Because whether you like it or not, you're still my *son*," he said firmly, which only made me scowl at his use of the term. "So is Bernar, but I don't see you trying to *rekindle* any sort of relationship with him," I snarled, frustratedly, prompting him to avert his gaze for little more than a heartbeat.

"Is that all, then?" I asked coldly. "No, it was also due to the letter I found on your pillow the night you were taken from me," he said, producing a worn-out page that looked like it had been read repeatedly.

I felt my Mom's emotions flare for a moment, as if she knew *exactly* what that was. "Here, take it. I've read it more times than I can count over the years, so I've already memorized it entirely," he slowly and cautiously moved it toward me. Hesitantly releasing my fourth stage, I took the letter and began to read it.

My dearest Thoma. You're probably wondering why I've had to leave you alone with him so often. I've been searching for an answer as to why he treats you and your brother the way he does, but I haven't found an answer yet. Please know that Mom is looking for one, and I hope to find it soon. Someone is coming to pick you up and bring you to a new home, and if you ever come back to this place, please try to forgive him. I know it won't be easy. It might be one of the most difficult things you've ever done, but I know you can do it. Never doubt how much I'll miss or love you, and know that when you're ready to find me, I'll show up to greet you with open arms. I love you, Thoma, I read silently, forcing myself to take a brief pause.

I didn't know how to feel about the letter, since I'd spent *decades* letting the thought of this moment burn in the back of my mind. I'd always wondered what it would be like to see him again, but never really thought I'd be in this position anytime soon. Regardless, I had a choice: Either succumb to my hatred of him or do as my mother asked.

There's a third choice, Ysevel sent me calmly, prompting me to look at her. *You know that these opportunities don't come often, so don't do anything you're going to regret,* she said with a slow nod.

I closed my eyes and sighed.

As I reopened them, I didn't see the face of the man I'd grown to hate, but rather one who'd *lost* everything. It wasn't hate or anger I was feeling, it was *pity*, I realized. I took a step back from him, unclenching the fist I was prepared to use to break his nose if he'd lied, and gave a relenting sigh.

"I don't forgive easily, but I know that what I'm about to say isn't just for *my* sake, but Mom's and Bernar's as well," I began, dropping my tone to let him know I was being honest, causing nearly everyone in the room to hold their breath. "I *don't* forgive you for the years of pain we went through, the trauma you gave me, the seal on my core, or the way you treated us," I began, getting a disappointed sigh from Ysevel and my mother.

"But I *can* forgive you for not knowing any better. I can't attribute to malice what I can tie onto the tail of ignorance, and *you* did something *really* fucking stupid," I said, immediately feeling both of them react to my words as I outstretched a hand to him. "Thoma, I..." he faltered, swallowing the lump I could tell was growing in his throat. "I-I'm sorry. I'm so sorry," he began to sob, taking my hand and squeezing it tightly.

"Saying you're *sorry* is like apologizing to a broken glass. Luckily for you, I'm not *made of glass*, but others might be," I said, regarding him without disdain or anger. I'd managed to push them down momentarily, but when he looked back up at me, I lowered my torso to be at eye level with him.

"Strive to be *better* than you were yesterday. You won't always get it right, but that's okay, just so long as you can show me you're trying, then I'll know you listened to me for once," I said with as warm a smile as I could muster, while he began to sob and shake uncontrollably, like a baby deer finding the ground beneath its feet for the first time.

I could feel the sense of relief pouring into me from Ysevel, Mom, and even Kalia, which somewhat surprised me. I allowed him a few moments to let my words sink in, knowing that this entire situation could have gone a different way entirely had I let my anger toward him take over.

"*Softy,*" I heard Athar's alternate voice mutter, nearly causing me to chuckle, just before I heard the sharp *crack* of Kalia's hand slap him upside the head. *Ignore him,* Kalia sent with a snarl while Athar gave a pained grunt. "Th-thank you, Thoma," Kayne said, wiping away a string of snot on his sleeve. "I thought you were going to *kill me,*" he said half-jokingly. "It wouldn't be the first time I've thought about it," I returned wryly, causing his eyes to widen.

"W-Well, if you *did*, then Siraye might have never found what she was looking for," he said, gesturing to a small box above the fireplace. "I've kept it there just in case you ever needed to go there again," he said, prompting her to get up and grab the box. As she lifted the lid, there was a golden insignia engraved in a shiny, black stone, right next to the necklace she'd given my father.

As I stared at it, I couldn't help but notice that much of its former color was gone as if it had been *drained* from the stone. My mother must have thought something similar, because she only took the black stone from the box. "It's been years since I've seen the necklace, but knowing what it represents..." she trailed off, picking the necklace up and turning it into *dust* as she infused a copious amount of mana into it.

The silver and green dust began to float into the air like ash in the wind, and it gave me a strange feeling I couldn't put my finger on. "There. You're *free* now," she smiled at my father warmly. While I didn't know exactly what she meant or *who* she was speaking to, I got a sense of both relief and *release* from her, as if she had just overcome some sort of trial, as well.

She quickly closed the box and handed it back to him, signaling it was time for us to leave. Kayne saw us to the door, and while he gave the others only a passing nod, his eyes fixed on me for much longer than I would've liked. "Will I ever see you again, Thoma?" he asked weakly, forcing me to pause and consider the possibility.

"Probably *not*, but if I ever come back here, I hope to see you doing better," I said, outstretching my hand yet again. He let out a short sigh and shook my hand with a small amount of determination and happiness in his once-dead eyes. "I promise," he said with a nod.

With that, we mounted our horses again and waved our farewells before beginning down the path that we'd come from earlier.

As we rode in contemplative silence, Mom gave me a warm smile, and the sense of pride I got from her told me everything I needed to know. "I thought you were going to cut his head off when he tried to hug you," Ysevel said jokingly. "I might have if he tried any harder," I scoffed, getting a light punch on my shoulder as a result. "Still, I'm proud of you. That wasn't easy, and I don't know if I'd have had the strength to do that," she said with a warm smile as she stared at her horse's nape.

"I *didn't*," I admitted, knowing it was what she'd said that allowed me to see the *third choice*. Her eyes widened in surprise, but she seemed to know what I meant.

After riding for another hour or so, we came to the fork where the paths split off; one to Hjalfar, and the other toward the Coltendian coast. As we turned down the path to our left, a sudden sense of unease overcame us all. "Do you feel that?" Devyr asked, catching most of us by surprise at her attunement to this realm.

"I do, but it's impossible; we *killed him*," Athar noted. As soon as the words left his mouth, I realized what he was talking about. "It's the same feeling I had when facing Nexis, but *why*?" I asked aloud, looking for any sign of danger. "Incoming!" Mom shouted, forcing all of us to split off the side of the path and out of the way of what looked to be a *portal* releasing a beam of pale green flame.

The earth erupted where it struck, knocking most of us off our horses from the size of the blast. Even though most of us were trained to fall from horseback, Kalia, Devyr, and Athar were *not*, causing them to hit the ground hard. "Are you guys alright?" I asked, having recovered from my own fall. Ysevel and my mother were also already on their feet, though I couldn't see Athar, Irun, Kalia, or Devyr.

"I wouldn't worry about *them*," a growling voice came from the dust-covered crater. *What the fuck is that?* I sent Kalia between coughs, hoping she would recognize the large silhouette that spawned from it. With a single swipe of its large axe, it separated the dust cloud, as if dismissing it from its sight, revealing the large Thran warrior.

"I'd be more worried about how you're going to *survive* an encounter with *me*," the Thran said with a snarl.

CHAPTER 79
BEGINNER'S LUCK

"**C**ome on, you can do better than that!" Gwili said playfully, dodging another strike from Thorsen.

"You're faster than you look, but not fast enough," he chuckled, deflecting a strike aimed at his torso and riposting with one of his own. Thorsen, growing mildly frustrated with his antics, lurched forward and grabbed his wrist and twisted his arm, using the pommel of his blade to pry the weapon out of Gwili's hand. "*Argh*, you..." Gwili cut off as the air left his lungs from a swift knee to the chest, causing him to slump to the ground in a heap.

"You talk too much, friend," Thorsen said with a chuckle as he watched the elf gasp for air. "Noted," Gwili wheezed through a cough. "I tried to tell him that when *we* used to train, but it seems that even after all these years, he hasn't learned his lesson," Bernar said, approaching the fallen elf to help him to his feet. "You alright?" he asked wryly.

"*Oh*, I'm fine. My stomach and my *pride*; not so much," Gwili managed, graciously accepting the extended hand, noticing Leona stifling a chuckle just behind Bernar as she trained with Aurae. "How's she handling her training now that she has the *Authority*?" Gwili nodded in her direction.

"Quite well, actually. It's obviously a challenge for her, but since Thoma and the others left nearly a week ago, she's been trying her best to grow so she can impress them when they get back," Bernar smiled proudly. "What about you? Have you and Ren figured anything out?" Thorsen asked, taking a step forward.

"Kalia, apparently, taught him a few things about Wraith mana that he's been trying to teach me. The *odoruki* technique, or at least that's what *she* called it, definitely isn't as easy as Thoma or Ysevel made it look. I've made some progress, but I haven't been able to reach their level with it yet," Bernar chuckled to himself.

"Well, there's no point in standing around here wasting time. We don't know when Erumon will be back with a mission for us, so we'd better make sure to use this time wisely," Thorsen gave him a supportive pat on the shoulder. "I know, I know," Bernar gave a wave of his hand. "Just make sure *he* doesn't bite his tongue, alright?" he continued, jutting his thumb toward Gwili. "No promises," Thorsen shrugged, causing Gwili to glare at him. "What's *that* supposed to mean?" he asked worriedly, raising both his eyebrows in concern, but Thorsen didn't verbally reply.

Just do your best not to talk, and you'll be fine, Bernar sent him with a wry smile. *I can't help it. He's too fun not to taunt,* Gwili replied in a similar tone with a mental shrug. *It's* your *funeral,* he replied, mimicking a gesture as if to show he was dusting off his hands before returning to Ren.

As he did so, Thorsen regarded him warmly, but it soon shifted into a look of concern as he recalled the events that took place in Harut. "What's on your mind?" Gwili asked, noticing something was wrong. "*Bah,* it's nothing," he waved a hand dismissively. "I know that look, *big man*. What is it?" Gwili prodded his elbow into Thorsen's side, urging him to speak his mind, which prompted him to give a relenting sigh.

"It's Unni. She's been on my mind lately, and I'm worried about Jashad being there with her," he admitted. "I wouldn't worry about them. The Mouth is there to help guide him, and I gave some of those *Elite* guards instructions to *take care of her* if she ever stepped out of line," Gwili said smugly, causing the giant to raise an eyebrow.

"You told them *what*?" he asked bluntly, not bothering to hide his concern. "It's fine! She helped us in the battle, sure, but until she can prove her worth to Jashad, she'll be watched closely," Gwili gave a dismissive wave. "I'm not sure I feel much better *at all* about that," Thorsen sighed, pinching the bridge of his nose.

"What are you so worried about? Anders and Trina are now in charge of Hjalfar. Didn't you tell me you trusted them with *your life*? There's no *way* they would let her even set foot in that country again," Gwili patted him on the shoulder. "I trust *Trina* with my life, since she's my cousin. Anders, however, is another story," Thorsen corrected him.

"*Meh*, same thing," the elf shrugged. "Come on. Let's see how far Bernar and Leona have come to take your mind off of things," Gwili suggested, trying to give the giant a shove in their direction, but nearly slipped on the loose dirt when Thorsen didn't budge.

As the two approached, they watched as Aurae gently guided Leona, who was sitting with her legs crossed in a meditative position. "Remember, you're not looking for perfection; you're just trying to create a more stable construct than you have before. Try it again,"

Aurae said gently, sitting directly across from her in a similar position.

Leona, who had her eyes closed, nodded a short response before *her consciousness entered the translucent Wraith realm. She couldn't help but marvel at its vastness and felt comforted that Aurae was already there waiting for her with a warm smile.*

They greeted each other with a wordless nod, as Aurae repeated the motion she had throughout the week. Gently and deliberately, she beckoned the scarlet mana down toward her, forming a small, elegant dagger in her hand before gesturing for Leona to do the same.

She did as directed and mimicked the smoothness of motion Aurae had to the best of her abilities, feeling the mana begin to flow from the large, swirling orb in the sky down to her hand. As it began to form the shape of a dagger, Leona suddenly felt a sense of unease, which caused the dagger to dissipate immediately as her consciousness returned.

"Damn it," she hissed frustratedly, seeing a few motes of scarlet mana rise from her hand. "I almost had it this time, but I still don't understand how this *Authority* is meant to help me," she admitted, causing Aurae to give her a warm smile as she placed a hand on her core. "It's only natural that you *still fear* the unknown," she began, causing Leona to look into her mismatched eyes.

"As Erumon explained, the *Authority* is meant to *help* you better understand the fundamentals of the mana you're using. Since Wraith mana resides between the realms of life and death, the *Authority* allows you to *see* that line more clearly, in a sense. However, rather than *fearing* it, you should *embrace it*," she explained, still holding the warm smile from before.

"But how can I *not fear* that line after already having come so close to it?" Leona asked after taking a moment to digest her words, but Aurae chuckled and shook her head. "That's where I think the problem is. You *fear* being close to that line, when in reality, it puts you in a better position to understand it than you realize," she began, causing Leona's eyes to widen.

"What you felt that day in Harut is no different than what you'll feel *now*, but since it's already known to you and you're in *control* of it, there's no *need* to fear it. I can only *guide you* toward it, but you have to be the one to *embrace* it," she continued with a slow nod.

It's so different from Ethereal mana. Just how the hell did Thoma reach such a high level with it? The Authority *has undoubtedly helped me reach the Wraith realm, but I feel like there's a difference in* experience *that's much larger than I anticipated,* Leona thought, furrowing her brow as she tried to wrap her head around the concept.

It's alright, Leona. I'll be right there with you, Aurae sent her, causing her to flinch in surprise. *You heard that? Could you* always *hear my thoughts?* Leona asked, getting a chuckle from Aurae. *Of course, but now's not the time for me to explain how it works. Right now, you have a task to complete, and I'll be here to help guide you through it,* she replied encouragingly.

Leona, still shaken by the realization that Aurae had been hearing her inner monologue the entire time she's been here, felt embarrassed at the fact, but did as Aurae instructed. She sent her *consciousness back into the Wraith realm and observed her instructor perform the same movement she had just moments before, creating the small dagger that rested gently in her hand.*

Knowing it was her turn, Leona beckoned the mana again and watched as the scarlet tendrils answered her call, forming a dagger similar to Aurae's in her hand. It was a bit less refined, but still a satisfactory result. As she stared at it momentarily, she noticed Aurae's presence grew more intense, feeling a warm sensation in her core, which she could only attribute to encouragement.

"I'm right here," Aurae's voice echoed throughout the translucent *valley they were in. Feeling more confident than before, Leona searched for the lines between the Wraith realm and Kavrass. As she searched, the familiar feeling of dread began to stew within her, but after a nod from Aurae's translucent form, she began to allow her consciousness and the mana she'd gathered to follow it* back into the Real.

Hearing the sounds of the birds chirping in the distance let Leona know she was, in fact, back in the Real, though there was something in her hand that wasn't there before. Cautiously glancing down at the strange weight in her hand, she could *feel* the dagger emanating wraith mana, as its phantasmal form had *mostly* solidified in her hand.

"I-I've done it!" Leona gasped as her eyes widened. She began to chuckle nervously, fearing she'd somehow lose her hold over it, but it remained present in her hand. "See? That wasn't *so bad,* was it?" Aurae smiled, closing Leona's fingers around the dagger.

"I don't know how to thank you, since I don't understand what you did," she blushed as Aurae patted her hand gently. "*I didn't do anything other than let you know that there's nothing to fear. You* did the rest," she said warmly before standing up.

"Bernar, Leona has something to sh-..." she paused, immediately conjuring a shield of violet and scarlet mana to protect against the incoming shockwave that resulted from his and Ren's training. Thorn, Nenvalur, Thorsen, and Gwili all stood by and watched, raising their hands up to their faces to shield them from the dust.

"You're still holding back, Ren. I *know* Kalia taught you more than *that*," Bernar chuckled as Ren, surprising everyone, held a subtle smile on his face. "You're right, she did," he replied, immediately vanishing from sight and appearing behind him in less time than it took to blink. Bernar nearly failed to react to the pommel strike aimed at the back of his head, feeling it graze the corner of his pointed ear as he got out of its way.

Grabbing Ren's wrist, he threw him over his shoulder and slammed him to the ground, causing Ren to cough and gasp for air. "You fight like Thoma, too. How the hell did you learn all that from them in just a few days?" Bernar asked, his eyes glowing a bright scarlet through the dust from the impact.

"How did *you* even react to that?" Ren sputtered as he struggled to get to his feet. Bernar outstretched his hand like he had to Gwili, but Ren gestured to let him know he was fine, and got back up on his own. "Beginner's luck, I guess? But you still didn't answer my question," Bernar shrugged, prompting Ren to scoff and shake his head.

"I don't think I'd call it that, but there's something I have to teach you before I explain *how* I learned all of that," he grinned, prompting Bernar to raise an eyebrow. "*Aaand* that would be?" he asked, rotating his wrist around as if hoping he would continue to speak. "Well, I think Leona should be present for that part, but to put it simply, I *read* the memories in their cores," Ren replied with a subtle smile, causing Bernar's eyes to widen in surprise.

"That was a good fight, Bernar. You've still got some fundamentals to work on as far as your Wraithborn abilities go, but from what *I* could see, that shouldn't take too long," Thorn began, interrupting Bernar before he could speak as he took a step forward. "Thanks, but I still can't quite get the hang of the *odoruki* technique. I feel like there's something I'm missing regarding it," he sighed.

"To be fair, I haven't quite gotten the hang of it either. While I don't need a dagger to pinpoint a location anymore, I still use that fundamental as a basis, but I'm not as fast as Ysevel," Ren admitted. "Looks like we'll have to figure that out together, then," Bernar grinned, but immediately noticed Aurae's scowl just over Nenvalur's shoulder. "What? Is there something on my face?" he asked with a raised eyebrow.

"Just the blissful ignorance of the *ass-chewing* I'm probably about to get," Bernar sighed, immediately moving over to where she was. "I take it you *enjoy* making it difficult for others to concentrate?" Aurae asked calmly as he approached. "No, that was ju-..." he cut himself off, noticing the scarlet dagger in Leona's hand and widening his eyes in both excitement and surprise.

"Holy shit, you *did it*!" he rushed over to her, being cautious not to touch it in case she lost control over the mana. "I did, but it's mostly thanks to Aurae's help," she said with a downtrodden smile that he immediately noticed. Before her head could fully tilt forward, he used a curled finger to pull her chin back up so she could look at him.

"It's incredible progress, my love. Please don't be so hard on yourself," he began softly. "You've only just recently come into this world of mana manipulation, and I'm so proud of you for coming as far as you have," he smiled, glancing down at the dagger momentarily before back at her. "Hard to believe that when your eyes are *scarlet* rather than *golden*," she chuckled weakly.

"You'll get there in *no time,* especially if Aurae's here to help teach you. She, *uh, has a way* with teaching that I *still* struggle to comprehend," he said, giving Aurae a knowing nod. *Thank you for not saying anything more than that,* she smiled, returning the nod. *It's not my place to,* he sent back.

"Even so, I still feel a bit at a loss for words with *this*," she said, holding up the scarlet dagger that was much more stable than the first time she'd managed to bring even a small orb into the Real. "*Progress is progress no matter how slow,*" Bernar said as if quoting something from a book, causing her to chuckle. "Where did you learn *that*? I didn't know you read books," she said playfully.

"It wasn't from a book. Well, it might have been, but *I* didn't read it; Thoma did," he said with an embarrassed smile as he scratched the back of his head. "It was something he used to say when I was teaching him how to create his own spell. Even with a sealed core, that *little shit* still managed to surprise me," he said warmly, as if recalling a distant memory.

"I'll remember that," Leona said, obviously considering her own situation. "And we'll be here to help you along the way. *Always*," Aurae chimed in warmly. "That is, of course, unless you don't want *me* to help you," she continued, noticing Anwill approaching the three of them. "I think you understand my position better," Leona replied quietly and nervously.

"I'm glad to see you've made some good progress, Leona," Anwill began, greeting her with a bow. "Thank you, Anwill. How are the others doing?" she asked, returning the gesture. "Thorsen and Gwili have asked Thorn and Nenvalur to help them reach the next stages of mana manipulation, though I don't suspect it will take as long now that they've taken the *Authority*," he replied briefly.

"That's good to hear," she said with a proud smile as she observed the two of them talking with Thorn. They seemed to be asking him all sorts of questions, though she couldn't hear what they were saying. "What of Neko and Marte?" she asked, looking back at Anwill.

"Those two are making *excellent* progress, though I feel Marte might reach the second stage before Neko. I swear, those two have been *constantly* in competition since I started training them," he sighed, pinching the bridge of his nose. "Reminding you of anyone?" Bernar asked wryly. "*Yes*, actually," he replied with a tilt of his head.

"Even so, I must admit, I never expected this gift Erumon gave us to be so effective. Even *Siraye's* team has been training in earnest since their return yesterday, and I suspect they'll be asking me to help them reach the *fifth* stage soon enough," he said almost tiredly, causing Bernar to reach out and pat him on the shoulder. "Don't worry, Thorn, Ren, Nenvalur, and I will be there to help soon," he said encouragingly.

"Not soon enough," Anwill scoffed, giving him a wry grin.

CHAPTER 80
OLD WOUNDS

As the dawning sun glistened off the peaks of the snow-capped Rhydian Mountains, Taegin and Ardrin continued their journey north toward Valdis.

"I still feel bad for leaving them without saying goodbye. It's already been two weeks since we left, but I still feel that way," Taegin said idly, pulling a piece of dried meat from his satchel. "I knew you would, but if Thoma and the others are going to focus on their mission, it *had* to be done this way," Ardrin scoffed, visibly annoyed by his twin's weakness.

"It doesn't *hurt* to be kind, you know," Taegin said wryly. "What kindness would there have been in *that*?" Ardrin snarled, causing his brother to chuckle. "I'm starting to think you've spent too much time alone in Valdis, *brother*," Taegin noted, causing a brief lull in their conversation.

"I wasn't *entirely* alone, you know. Athar, as much of an idiot as he was back then, was a *fine* source of entertainment and frustration," Ardrin continued after a brief pause. "So, you've grown to *care* for him? My, my. I never thought I'd see the day a *heart* grew in place of your pragmatism," Taegin added with unbridled sarcasm, prompting Ardrin to scowl at him.

"I said no such thing," he snarled. "But you *did* imply it. All that matters is that there's something *other* than your sense of duty that ties you to this world. I think it was awfully *noble* of you to bring him to Kalia back then," Taegin said smugly as his brother continued to hold his scowl. "You're *insufferable*," he replied with a shake of his head, allowing the conversation to lull yet again.

After a few moments, Ardrin gave a relenting sigh. "Finally going to admit that I was *right*?" Taegin chuckled smugly, causing him to scoff. "I only did what needed to be done in hopes of saving *everyone*," he said defensively. "Of course, but that doesn't change the fact that you still *helped* Athar to learn mana, or the fact that he *and* Irun have grown enough to reach the *fourth stage* because *you* brought him to Kalia," Taegin grinned, prompting his brother to give another groan in displeasure.

"Sometimes, *brother*, the ends *do* justify the means," Ardrin scowled. "*Oh*, I'm not saying they don't. If I had removed Thoma's seal earlier, he wouldn't have grown into the man he is today," Taegin nodded. "He likely wouldn't have grown *at all*, given everything Erumon's told me about Mideia," Ardrin retorted grimly, causing Taegin to regard him curiously.

"How long have you known about Mideia? From what it sounded like during that discussion with Erumon, it seems as if you've known for *centuries*," Taegin said, hoping to prod some more information out of his brother.

I suppose there's no point in hiding it anymore. It's not like it's going to open any old wounds worse than they already have been, Ardrin thought.

"It was a few years after I left. I was trying to find work as an Outcast, knowing it would help disguise any trails I'd left behind. During one of the missions I went on there in Hjalfar, I discovered there were several hybrid creatures far to the north near Valdis," he began to explain as his brother listened intently.

"As my team and I were sent to investigate, they were all wiped out by creatures known as the *Thran*," he said, causing Taegin to raise his eyebrows in surprise. "They were *already* here? But how is that even possible? I've heard of their battle prowess from Kalia, but I never suspected they'd made it here to Kavrass," he said, furrowing his brow as if there was a piece of information missing.

"They were, and their combat abilities are drastically *understated*. They wiped out my team, and just before I met my own end, Erumon showed up seemingly out of nowhere, killing them faster than I could follow along with. To say I was impressed would be a disservice to the truth," Ardrin said, his features gently twisting into one of sadness.

He cared about them, didn't he? Taegin thought as he understood the weight behind his brother's words.

"After that battle, I asked him if there was any way I could repay him, but he already knew I was a Pelantyr, and came to Kavrass looking for me to begin his plan of drawing out Mideia. It wasn't *purely* by chance that he showed up, but I knew that if I was going to help him, I had to keep *you* out of it," Ardrin said, getting a nod of understanding in return.

"I see. What of the Thran?" Taegin asked after a brief pause. "We spent the better part of a *year* hunting them down together. It was shortly after that I came into contact with Nexis after receiving guidance from Erumon," Ardrin noted.

"The summoning circle Athar mentioned," Taegin nodded, finally understanding how all the pieces fit together. "Precisely. It was designed only to allow *part* of him through, but Erumon kept a close eye on it in case he tried to alter it in any way," Ardrin added.

"I appreciate the explanation, brother. Let's just hope that we can find some more answers in Valdis, though I would like to pay a visit to Odensby. I feel it will help put Thorsen and Marte's minds at ease," Taegin suggested, prompting the two of them to pick up their pace.

The following day, they arrived at the gates of Odensby, only to be greeted by a sharp-looking young sergeant and a handful of guards who stood by. Some were leaning on the thick, stone walls, while others discussed which meal to have for lunch.

Only the young sergeant noticed the two riders approaching.

"Who goes there?" he asked, unable to identify the two riders as they came closer, prompting the other guards to stop whatever they were doing quickly. "We're emissaries from Caegwen, here to speak with the ruler of Odensby about some troubling news," Taegin replied briefly.

"*Caegwen?* That's at least a *two-week* trip. Couldn't you have sent a raven?" the sergeant asked, getting a chuckle from a few of the other guardsmen, though it wasn't meant to be a joke. "Listen, *boy*, I don't have time for these kinds of questions, and neither does *he*," Ardrin snarled, jutting his chin toward his brother. "Now, now. I'm sure we can resolve this matter *amiably*," Taegin scowled before dismounting his horse and approaching the young sergeant on foot.

"The news we bring is too vital to be sent by a raven, which is *why* we're here in the first place. Now, it's been a few centuries since I've been here, but I think we got off on the wrong side of the horse. I am the Master Synner of Codrean, here under King Elhael of Caegwen's orders to deliver a message to the current ruler of Odensby," he said calmly and with a confidence none of the soldiers had seen since Trina.

He's not lying, is he? Even his eyes are glowing, the sergeant realized as Taegin approached.

"No, I'm not, and *yes*, they are. Now, if you would be so kind as to open the gate for us and take us to whoever is in charge, I would be most grateful," he said with a grin as the sergeant's face paled. "O-Of course, Master Synner. I-I'll take you there myself. O-Open the gate!" the sergeant yelled with a heavy stutter as he snapped to attention. "See? That wasn't so hard, was it?" Taegin grinned over his shoulder at Ardrin, who merely huffed and turned his head away.

"What is your name, Sergeant?" Taegin asked, putting a hand on the young man's shoulder. "It's Bjorn Wien, Master," he replied with visible confusion at the sudden shift in tone. "*Wien*? You're not Ulfric's son by any chance, are you?" Taegin asked with visible surprise, though Wien only looked at him with pure befuddlement.

"I-I am, Master, though he died well over a *decade* ago," Wien replied solemnly. "*Ah*, I'm sorry to hear that. He was a good man and an *exceptional* warrior. You should be *proud* to carry his name," Taegin said, giving him another pat on the shoulder as they crossed the gate's threshold.

"I'm not sure I should be surprised you knew him, Master; given how long elves live and all. Even so, I thank you for the kind words, and welcome you to Odensby," he replied with a bow of his head as they walked together down the main path. "Of course, Sergeant. Though I would suggest the next time you meet *any* emissary, that you treat them with a little more respect," Taegin said wryly, getting several quick nods from the young man.

Ardrin reluctantly dismounted and began trailing behind the two who shared an idle conversation about days long past, observing the town and how prosperous it seemed to be. The thick stone walls echoed with the sounds of the market, as well as children playing entirely carefree on the streets.

"It's good to see so much has changed since I was last here. Don't you think so, too, *brother*?" Taegin asked over his shoulder. "I hardly even remember the last time I was here, so I can't say much about it," Ardrin grumbled, prompting his brother to chuckle and shake his head. "Then let *that* be a reminder of *why* we're here to begin with," Taegin gestured toward a group of children playing a game of tag along the side of the street.

As they made their way to the main fortress, Wien signaled to the other guardsmen, who stood at the entrance, to allow them to pass. They all regarded Taegin with a certain degree of curiosity, but fear overcame them when they noticed Ardrin's enlarged figure just behind him, with his arms clasped behind his back.

"Is the Commander here?" Wien asked after briefly introducing the two elves. "She's in a meeting with Lord Anders, but it should be over soon. These two can wait for her in the main hall with the others," one of the guardsmen said, signaling to the others to open the heavy, oaken doors.

We're wasting time. Haven't you seen enough already? Ardrin sent with a slight hint of frustration. *Confirming the wellness of the citizens is one thing, but I need to know whether this Anders is just going to be another thorn in this country's side, or if he's genuinely trying to make a difference,* Taegin replied as the hinges creaked under the weight of the massive doors.

While the main hall had remained generally the same, Anders' banner hung from the gaps between the large stone pillars in place of the former king's. Numerous others were waiting for the results of the meeting in the main hall, all fashionably dressed in the finest clothes Odensby had to offer.

These nobles make me sick, Ardrin snorted derisively after taking a moment to observe them. *We're not here for them, though I'm sure they plan an integral part in keeping this place as cheerful as we've seen it so far,* Taegin replied with a subtle shake of his head.

As soon as their brief exchange ended, the doors on the side of the hall opened, causing an immediate clamor amongst the nobles. "Lord Anders, what are your plans for the *sickness*?" one of them asked as soon as they entered the room. "Our cattle won't survive the winter at this rate. Please, you have to call for help!" another shouted, desperation evident in both his words and tone.

Sickness? What's this all about? Taegin asked. *I'm not sure, but whatever it is, it doesn't look like the peace outside will last for much longer,* Ardrin replied with a raised eyebrow, suggesting what Taegin was already beginning to fear.

"Everyone, please. We're doing what we can to find the best course of action," Anders raised his hands in a calming motion. "All we want are *answers*, Lord Anders. Why aren't you telling us what this is all about?" one of the ladies present asked bluntly, causing Trina to step in.

"Lords and Ladies, please. I'll answer what I can from what my troops have gathered about the situation. Honesty is the best policy right now, so I'll begi-..." she trailed off, noticing Ardrin's enlarged figure, and Taegin's glowing eyes right beside him. "T-Taegin? I-Is that you? Is that *really* you?" she asked with uncertainty as she squinted her eyes, immediately clearing a path through the crowd toward them.

"My apologies, Commander. It seems you've put me in a difficult spot, as I'm not sure I remember you," Taegin replied with her proper title after piecing together the information he got from Wien. However, it was apparent that he did so with visible confusion. "Of course, you wouldn't recognize me. I was only a young girl then, but I've never forgotten how you saved my home after your fight with the Mother Ochelon," she chuckled in disbelief, shaking her head.

"You were *there* for that?" Taegin asked as he rummaged through his memories. They were still clear, but he was struggling to put a name to a face. "My apologies, but what was your name again, Commander?" he finally relented after failing to recall it. "Trina. Trina Lande," she said with a bright smile and tears of hopeful joy in her eyes as the memory of the young girl visibly resurfaced in his mind.

"Of course! *Little Trina*, I believe your father used to call you. Though you're not so *little* now, it seems," he said, noticing she stood nearly as tall as Thorsen. He was both happy to see her again and relieved that he did, in fact, remember who she was. "That's right, he *did* call me that, but I hardly reached the height of your hips back then. Meanwhile, you haven't aged *a day*," she chuckled, while outstretching her hand to clasp his forearm.

"Clean living, you know," he smiled brightly as he took her arm in his after releasing his grip on her forearm. "My apologies for putting you on the spot like this, but we could really use your and your *companion's* help," Trina said, giving Ardrin a confused glance.

"*Brother*, actually, and we'd be *happy* to help, though there are other things we need to discuss," he said, raising a pair of eyebrows at Ardrin, whose expression was just as plain as before.

"I didn't know you had a brother," she said with a nervous laugh. "I didn't think I still *did* at the time, but this is Ardrin. I pray you'll treat him with the same respect as you would me," Taegin said with a gesture, prompting Trina to perform the same greeting as before.

Ardrin looked down at her outstretched hand, as if considering whether to take it for a moment, but after a subtle hint from his brother, he relented and did so anyway. "Pleasure to meet you," he said begrudgingly, getting a satisfied grin from Taegin.

"You as well. I hope that with your help, we'll be able to put an end to this sickness," she said with a firm nod. "Lords and Ladies, I apologize for the halt in regular proceedings, but these two gentlemen couldn't have come at a better time," she shouted, leading them through the crowd to the front of the throne.

Anders, gesturing for Trina to take over the conversation for a moment, gave a brief nod of acknowledgement to the two elves, though he was taken aback by Ardrin's hands when he turned around.

"I believe these two can help us solve the mystery of this sickness, but in the meantime, I'll need you *all* to be patient. I will take them to where our men have been investigating the matter, and with any luck, they'll be able to help us find an answer," she announced, getting more than a few murmurs from the crowd in response, prompting Ardrin to scowl at them.

"If you're done complaining, *leave*," he said roughly in a reactive response to the crowd before him. Some of them were appalled by his behavior, but others immediately cowered in fear. "*That* wasn't very polite, brother," Taegin whispered loudly enough for Trina and Anders to hear. "It worked, didn't it?" Ardrin raised an eyebrow, causing his brother to shake his head before Ardrin rose from his seat.

"While I can't *publicly* say that I'm grateful for your abrupt dismissal of them, I *was* rather tired of hearing their complaints," he admitted, outstretching his hand for Ardrin to take. "If you knew who I really was, I *doubt* you'd be shaking my hand," Ardrin scowled, prompting Anders and Trina to both look at him curiously.

"Well, if he's here alongside Taegin, I trust him; as should you, Anders," Trina gave him a firm nod after taking a moment to consider his words. "Thank you," Taegin added with a light bow. "However, I *am* curious as to where this *sickness* came from. Where did you last see it?" he asked.

Trina paused momentarily, as if trying to find the best answer to give him, but eventually shook her head. "I can't say for certain. It's been *everywhere* and *nowhere* at the same time," she said, causing Ardrin to raise an eyebrow. "What do you mean?" he asked, prompting her and Anders to exchange a glance.

"Listen, Trina and I are former Synners who have seen our fair share of creatures and spells. Whatever *this* is, it's different from anything I've ever seen before. It appears seemingly out of nowhere, and leaves little to no traces of mana behind whatsoever," Anders sighed defeatedly.

Do you think Mideia's making his move here in Hjalfar? Taegin sent his brother. *It seems likely, but to what end is another problem entirely,* Ardrin replied.

"Can you take us to the last place you saw it?" Ardrin asked, nearly making Trina flinch in surprise that *he* was the one to ask. "Y-Yes, I can. Rather, *we* can. It's not too far from here, though I can't guarantee we'll find anything of use to us," she admitted.

If these two can't figure it out, then we're in much deeper shit than I thought, she considered in the heartbeat between her statement and their nods of agreement.

"Good. I think it would be best if we left now. If this *sickness* is as you say, the longer we wait here, the less chance we'll have to discover its origins," Taegin suggested, getting a nod of agreement from Anders. "I won't be going with you, but I *do* wish you the best of luck," Anders said, giving the two elves a firm nod. "If things go the way I think they're about to, *you'll* need all the luck you can get," Ardrin said grimly, returning the nod before the three others left the main hall.

"Wien!" Trina called out loudly as she moved toward the large doors, followed closely behind by the two brothers. As soon as the word left her mouth, he poked his head out from around the corner of the large door. "Ma'am?" Wien asked cautiously. "Bring our horses. You're coming with us," she said as she continued to walk briskly. "W-Wait, what? I-I'm going *with you?*" he asked sheepishly, still a little afraid of Ardrin, but more afraid of whatever it was she had planned.

"Trina, I don't think it's a good idea for him to..." Taegin began, but immediately received a glance from her that prompted him to halt. "Master Taegin, while I'm well-aware how powerful you are, I can assure you that he will be a valuable asset to us," she began in a tone that exuded confidence, making Wien blush a little.

"He may be young and untrained in the ways of mana, but he knows the citizens better than I could ever hope to. If we're going to find this place, we're going to need his help," she continued proudly, prompting Ardrin to exchange a glance with his brother.

Do you really think it's a good idea to have him with us? He can't even wield mana, he sent briefly. *Neither could Athar, but he still proved helpful to you, did he not? Since this isn't familiar territory to me, or you, for that matter, I think it would be best to use all the help we can get,* Taegin sent back with a suggestive grin. *Fine, but you're protecting him if anything goes wrong,* Ardrin sent begrudgingly.

"I'll trust your judgment, Trina. Please, lead the way," Taegin nodded with a gesture for her to continue out of the hall, getting a bewildered look from Wien.

Why am I the only one who gets dragged into her weird plans? Wien mentally sighed, getting a slight chuckle from Ardrin who read his thoughts, which made him freeze after realizing that it wasn't just Taegin who could do that.

I'd better keep my thoughts to myself, then, he thought nervously as his eyes widened in surprise. *That's the best one you've had since I met you,* Ardrin sent, forcing his words into Wien's mind, causing him to shudder in a brief moment of embarrassment and fear.

Within the hour, the four of them departed Odensby and made their way northeast to the nearest town, as Wien and Trina led them to the last known location. Even though spring was just a few weeks away, there was still plenty of snow on the path, and icicles hanging from the trees' branches.

"So, what do you know about this so-called *sickness*?" Ardrin asked Trina who rode just ahead of him beside Wien. "Before I answer that: do you think it's *not* a sickness?" she asked with visible confusion. "No. I don't, but I want to hear your thoughts on it first, so I can have a better idea of what I'm looking for," Ardrin noted plaintively.

"*Ah*, I see. Well, the only things we seem to know about it is that whatever is causing it has seemingly *drained* the life out of anything it's come into contact with," she said grimly, causing both brothers to look at her with visible concern. "Sorry to interrupt, but we'll be arriving soon," Wien noted, pointing in the general direction of their destination. "Let's hurry," Taegin urged, digging his heels into his horse's sides to pick up his pace.

As they rounded the corner of the path, they found the remains of a small farmhouse that looked as though a loose boulder from the side of a mountain had crashed into it. "*Fy faen i Helvete!* What happened here?" Trina gasped, putting a hand to her mouth in shock. "The farmer who lived here said that it happened nearly two days ago. This is the most recent one we've heard of, but there's more to it than just the destruction of his home," Wien noted gravely as he and the others dismounted.

They approached the rubble cautiously, observing both the ground and the surrounding trees for any signs of damage. Ardrin put his hand to one of the trees and pushed mana into it, his eyes flaring with violet as the golden tendrils danced within his irises wildly.

Taegin similarly put his hand to the ground, feeling the response of the earth-attribute mana momentarily, before moving on to the rubble. He briefly closed his eyes, sensing the air around him as he bent it to his will. Trina and Wien did what they could to aid in the search for any signs that would indicate what had happened, but all they found were a handful of pig remains scattered about their pen.

"*Ugh*, I'm starting to see what you mean by it not being a sickness," Trina said, holding the back of her gauntlet up to her nose. "It both is and *isn't*," Taegin said, reopening his eyes. "What do you mean, Master?" Wien asked with visible disgust as he turned away from the gory pen. "It seems that our *visitor* brought something terrible along with him; something I'd rather hoped we wouldn't find here," Taegin continued, getting a nod of confirmation from his brother, noting he'd found the same.

"A *visitor*? You mean something, or *someone,* did *that*? I heard rumors that there was someone *powerful* wandering the northern lands, but *this* is something else," Trina said, gesturing to the caved-in side of the house. "Yes, though I thi-..." Taegin cut himself off, seeing the pig remains strewn across the pen.

"Did you find anything?" Ardrin asked, backing away from the trees and noticing his brother's look of confusion. He followed Taegin's gaze and immediately recognized what he was looking at. "*Thran*? But what are they doing here?" Ardrin asked hushedly, getting a glance from Taegin that suggested he didn't know either.

"Whatever they're doing, it *had* to be because someone *brought* them here," Taegin noted, putting a finger on his chin with a furrowed brow. Trina and Wien looked at him in confusion, but after a few silent moments, Ardrin spoke up. "I think I know how they got here," he said, observing the wreckage momentarily, prompting Taegin and the others to look at him.

"There are still traces of Leech mana present in the wreckage, but for whatever reason, those traces *also* contain Tyrant mana," he said gravely, prompting Taegin to nod in agreement with his assessment. "I thought so, too, but *why*? What purpose would they have here in Hjal-..." he trailed off as if suddenly realizing the obvious.

"*Leech* and *Tyrant* mana? Taegin, I know it's been a long time since I was an active Synner, but what the *fuck* is *that* supposed to mean?" Trina asked, moving toward him with Wien close behind, but Taegin held up a hand and shook his head. "I'm not going to ask you to come with us, but I'll have more time to explain on our way to Valdis. If you want answers, *that's* our best chance at finding them," he said urgently.

"We're with you, Taegin. I'd rather see this situation over with sooner rather than later. Wien, mount up. We're going with them to Valdis," she replied, getting a hesitant nod of confirmation from the young man.

"Looks like you're getting dragged around again, *boy*," Ardrin noted with a wry grin.

CHAPTER 81
THE BELURIAN CHANNEL

As more of the dust settled, I was grateful to see none of us, nor our horses, were hurt, but I *also* realized just how large the Thran *really* were.

This one in particular stood well over a head taller than Irun, with claws nearly as long as my forearm wrapped around the haft of a large, two-handed axe. The curved blade was brutish, almost like it had been forged by an inexperienced smith who lazily wrapped the haft in an unidentifiable leather. Judging by the size of the axe's head, it likely weighed at *least* over a hundred kilos, though it was probably about as much as a small horse.

I admit, I was impressed at the sheer strength it must take to wield such a weapon. However, there was something about the belt he wore that caught me off guard, as the dried half-skulls that were tied to it hung like trophies, though they made little to no noise whenever he moved.

That's because they're hunters and trappers by nature. If they wore anything that made a lot of noise, it would be an issue for them to capture their prey, Kalia sent me after sensing my mild confusion. *That makes sense. Buruz killed over twenty of them together the night we fought Nexis. But then, why is this one here alone?* I asked almost instantly. *Not sure, but don't worry, I'll handle it,* Kalia sent us all with a nod and a slight scrunching of her eye through the slit in her helmet.

Even after two weeks, I still hadn't gotten used to the fact that she willingly wore that armor.

"What is your name, Thran? I like to know who I'm dealing with before I kill them," Kalia said as she began to step toward the massive creature confidently, prompting the large beast to laugh. "*Hah!* I never thought I'd meet such a bold warrior in this Realm, but there's a small problem, you see," he began, swinging his axe to let it rest over his shoulder confidently. "And what problem is that?" Kalia asked, drawing the blade Maikell had made for her.

It was nearly identical to the one she could create with her *kataki*, though I could only attribute *how* he knew what that looked like because of Athar's descriptions.

"I was told that there was an *elf* here who would be the most likely to put up a good fight. I'll still end *you* quickly, but I'll only give *that one* my name," the creature said, pointing his axe toward my mother. *Don't take the bait, Siraye. This is how they operate,* Kalia sent with an air of caution. *I know. I started reading your memories the moment I didn't recognize the creature before me,* Mom sent back with a wry grin.

"Give us your name, then, *beast*," Mom said, not even drawing her weapon, causing the Thran to laugh heartily. "You're nearly as arrogant as she is!" he said between laughs in blatant disbelief. "My name is Gheraak Grayeater," he said proudly. *Grayeater? But I thought Buruz killed the last leader,* I sent Kalia quickly. *They take on the name of the clan when they become the next leader, though given his size, I'd say he should have been the leader from the start,* she explained briefly.

"But enough of this banter. I take pride in my skills and I wi-..." his words suddenly cut off as Kalia appeared behind him, already flicking the blood from her blade. I knew my mother was the most shocked at Kalia's display of skill, but the sense of *realization* that the hegraphene might be just as fast as her poured through our connection.

"Thank you for telling me your name, Gheraak," Kalia said over her shoulder as the enormous creature suddenly dropped the axe and slumped to its knees. Blood began to pour from wounds at Gheraak's wrists, armpits, groin, and crooks of his knees. "H-How did you...?" Gheraak snarled, obviously frustrated that he was no longer able to move however he wanted, as Kalia leaned in beside his ear.

"Do you have *any idea* how many of your kind I've killed, *Grayeater*?" she asked, moving in front of him and lifting her helmet just enough to reveal the marked eye socket of her faceplate. "*You*? What are you doing here? I wasn't told *Kalia the Annihilator* would be here," Gheraak said with fear widening his large, dark eyes. "So you *do* know who I am. Good, then this will be easier than I thought," Kalia said as she stood upright, lowering her helmet to cover her face again.

"You said you *weren't told* that I would be here, which means *someone* sent you here. Who was it?" she asked calmly as if she'd been doing this her entire life. *Now that I think about it, she probably* has *been,* Ysevel sent, having read my reaction to Kalia's calm demeanor, as the creature struggled against its own body.

"You're not getting any information out of me, *brak*," Gheraak said through bared teeth, prompting Kalia to tilt her head to the side as a child would to a curious object. "I don't think you understand the position you're in, *Grayeater*," she said, shaking her head momentarily before reaching for the axe at her feet.

Gheraak's eyes widened in realization, as if the stories of her exploits suddenly resurfaced in his mind. "N-No, wait, I can ex-..." his words halted and transformed into a wolfish yelp as the lower half of his arm was severed in a single swing of his axe. Blood began to pool just beneath the wound, but the Thran could do nothing to soothe the pain since the tendons in his other arm were also severed.

"Damn you, *Annihilator*!" he shouted between grunts of pain as he curled his abdomen inward, making him double over. "I'll ask a second time: *Who sent you*?" she asked in the same, calm tone. It was almost unnerving to hear her speak like that, but I knew that if I interrupted, it would have just dragged on longer.

Gheraak snarled with a defiant glare and spat a large wad of spit at her face, which she dodged with minimal movement. What little movement she *did* use, however, was seemingly transferred into the enormous axe, severing the other arm at the shoulder. Blood sprayed out in an upward arc following the massive axe head, and I knew that the next time she asked would *surely* be the last.

"Who. Sent. You?" she asked, pausing at each word as she put her face right next to his wolfish features. "I have asked you *thrice*, and I will not ask again. Tell me now, or your eventual replacement will have to suffer *even more* than what you've endured so far. Now, *speak*," she said without a single hint of a change in her tone. The creature stared into the slits of her helmet, but after a futile search for *any* sign of mercy, he lowered his head in dejection.

"L-Lord Mideia sent me here alone, but the rest of us will not let you live for long once they find out I'm dead. You've made a mistake in killing me, *Annihilator*, but I suppose you'll find out *why* soon enough," he muttered with a weak chuckle, his voice beginning to grow numb and distant from the blood loss.

"Thank you for the information. You may die knowing I will live up to my name when I find the rest of you," she said, swiftly lifting the axe above her head and burying it in the creature's hardened skull, nearly splitting it down the middle. The spurt of blood and brains that rose from the wound was primarily due to the impact, as the creature's heart had likely stopped beating just before the blow landed.

As the large body slumped backward, Kalia released the haft and used the base of her palm to wipe away a speck of blood that landed on her helmet. "We need to hurry. Where there's one, there are more, and I fear that if Mideia already knows we're on our way to the Gramm Isles, the people there *won't be safe* for long," she said, ignoring the fact that most of us had never seen her act the way she did.

Athar approached the body to burn it with mana, but Kalia held a hand up to stop him. "No. Leave his body here as a *message* to the others, who I'm sure will come looking for him," she said in the same, cold tone. "R-Right," Athar stammered, still visibly awestruck at her display of skill and strength. "Siraye, please continue to lead the way," she said, already mounting her horse as if nothing had happened. "Of course, Kalia, but I am curious about the name he called you," Mom said, hoping to get an answer to her unasked question.

"*Oh*, you mean *Annihilator*? Well, it's not without good cause. After all, I lost count after killing over a *million* of their kind," she said with a shrug, causing our eyes to widen in surprise.

While I *knew* their clans had been at war for a long time, I'd never suspected there were *that* many of them. It was apparent, however, that my mother was in a deep state of shock at the amount.

"I-Impressive," she said with an astonished look in her eye. "I'll have to take some lessons from you on how to deal with them," Mom continued in a half-chuckle to herself. "Of course, but that will have to wait. We still need to hurry," Kalia nodded, signaling for the rest of us to get moving.

Devyr probably has a kill count that high, too, I realized, recalling she hadn't flinched at the brutal sight of Kalia's interrogation. *It's very likely that she does, since much of their homeland was probably ravaged by these Grayeaters,* Ysevel noted. *That's fair, but how long do you think* that's *been going on for?* I asked, nodding my head back toward the carcass. *Probably long before she lost count. Although I will say, I feel bad for Athar if he ever breaks Devyr's heart,* Ysevel sent with a disbelieving chuckle as she nodded in his direction.

As I glanced at my friend, I could tell he was likely thinking the same thing, even though Irun tried to ease his mind. It never ceased to amaze me how both mature and childish she could be at times, but even after spending a decade with her, admittedly *fucked up*, sense of humor, it *always* made me smile.

As we continued down the path that would eventually lead us to the docks, there was a slight lull in our conversation. I could *sense that* there was something she wanted to ask me, but she was figuring out how to phrase her question most effectively.

"What's on your mind?" I asked, giving her a gentle nudge on the shoulder with my elbow. "Well, it's about what I promised I'd explain earlier, but I don't know how to ask the question properly," she said after a brief, pensive pause. "You know me almost as well as I know myself, but if you don't feel comfortable asking, then I won't prod any further," I said with a light-hearted shrug, causing her to glance at me and smile.

"I know, but I feel like I *have* to ask you, I just need to figure out *how*," she said, her smile weakening slightly as if she feared whatever answer I would give her. "Like you always tell me: *I'm right here*," I said, reaching for her hand to squeeze it gently as I did my best to be supportive.

Whether it was the gesture or the fact that I'd quoted her directly, I didn't know, but she gave herself a firm nod as I felt a wave of courage come through our connection. "What do you know about *dragons*?" she asked broadly, causing my Mom to turn around and look at her in surprise. I raised an eyebrow at both of them, but figured whatever meaning was behind the glance they shared was something I was probably about to find out on my own. "Not much, I suppose. I know they're ancient creatures, though no one has seen one for at least a thousand years," I shrugged with an upturned lip.

"I see," she said, closing her eyes momentarily as if comforted by my ignorance. "Well, I can tell you there's much more to them than you realize, but I'm glad to know you don't seem to have any prejudices toward them," she chuckled, leaving me a little confused. "H-How did this even come up?" I asked, blinking a few times and shaking my head.

"Well, do you remember what Erumon said about my mother's *ambivalence*?" she asked. "I do, but what does that have to do with dragons? Did your mom get that as a gift from them, or something?" I asked half-jokingly. "In a *sense*," she shrugged, but that only added to my confusion.

Before I could ask any more questions, my mother raised a hand and signaled for us to turn down the path to the left, which I could see would lead us to a sharp cliff. "We're nearing the docks. I think it would be best if that conversation didn't continue around people like this. Information is almost *too* freely shared around this place, so just be mindful of what you say or do," she said, glancing at the two of us.

Since this would be my first time anywhere near these kinds of people, I decided it was best to trust her judgment. *We'll have to talk about this again later,* Ysevel noted with a tone that let me know there were still things she had to tell me. *I'll be here when you're ready,* I smile warmly, though I couldn't help but wonder what *else* she wanted to say.

As we came to the cliff, I suddenly felt small. *Incredibly* small, as what I saw was like nothing I'd ever seen. A vast expanse of water as far as my eyes could see, that glistened in the late-afternoon sunlight. The blinding light vaguely reminded me of what it was like to be outside on a clear winter day, but the smell of salt carried on the breeze shattered that comparison immediately.

Off in the distance, just behind a layer of mist, I could vaguely make out the silhouette of an island, though any specific details were lost behind the fog. As I turned my gaze downward, I could see there were several large ships and a decently sized market that appeared to attend to whatever the sailors were unloading from the ships.

"*Ah, I love the smell of seal shit, syphilis, and fish guts,*" Athar's alternate voice said after inhaling deeply. "You can smell that from here? Better yet, *how* do you even know what that smells like?" Irun asked with a half-chuckle. "You *don't*?" Ysevel asked, scrunching her nostrils briefly. "No, I'm pretty sure my memory and sense of smell have gone to shit after being in the Unde-... *Vareluth* for so long," he corrected himself.

"I can smell just fine, and I've lived there *my entire life*," Devyr said playfully. It was the first real thing she'd said to anyone aside from Athar since leaving my old home, though I suspected it was just because he was constantly being asked questions about my past there. "I didn't mean it like *that*, Devyr," Irun waved a hand dismissively. "How *did* you mean it, then?" she asked with a wry chuckle.

"Irun, *don't* answer that," Mom turned to point a finger at him, causing him to raise his hands defensively. "I wasn't going to!" he shook his head quickly with widened eyes, causing the rest of us to chuckle. "Good. Let's get down there and onto a ship before nightfall. We still have to find one that'll take us over there," she said, gesturing for us to follow her down the steep path.

When we finally reached the bottom, we came to a small stable where we were instructed to leave our horses. I felt bad having to leave Celer behind yet again, but I could tell he would be in good hands. "Not as good as Caegweni stables, but they'll do. Don't kick anyone, and make sure they give you *lots* of apples, alright?" I muttered to him, gently patting his nape as he nuzzled my chest as if telling me to go.

"You speak to him like he *understands* you," Kalia said, following my lead as I tied the reins to the post. "They might not be able to answer verbally, but I'm sure they understand much more than we realize," I said, giving him a final few scratches on his forehead and nose. "I wonder what *mine* thinks of me," she said idly, similarly patting her horse's nape as I did mine. "She seems to appreciate you, though I'm not sure the same could be said for Athar's," I chuckled, noticing his horse was being rather stubborn when he tried to say goodbye.

As we left the stables, Ysevel said something in her native language to her horse, which caused it to bay weakly, as if it were sad she was going. "Don't worry, Elyna, we'll be back before you know it," she said comfortingly, putting her forehead to her horse's briefly before turning to join us. "She'll be alright," Mom said comfortingly, knowing just how much Ysevel cared for her horse.

Once, after a long training cycle in the dome, Ysevel told me how elves always gave their horses the same names. Not because it was due to a lack of creativity, but instead because they *felt* each one they chose held the same personality as the first. This, in turn, also meant that each was a small part of a greater whole.

Kind of like us, I thought idly as I watched Ysevel give her horse a gesture of farewell.

We continued through the market, observing all sorts of trinkets and foods from what I could only assume was the Gramm Isles. It vaguely reminded me of walking down the streets to Deathwhisper Tavern, but Krozz was, unfortunately, nowhere to be seen. "We never did say *goodbye* to him, did we?" I realized, suddenly fearing whatever anger that massive hegraphene had in store for us when we saw him again.

"No, you didn't. However, Buruz *did* tell him you wished him well at my command," Kalia said, trying her best to use a more *human* tone of voice, though she sounded more like my brother on a hungover morning. "Thank you, Kalia. It all seemed to happen so fast that I felt bad we didn't get to have one last meal with him," Ysevel noted with a feeling of regret. "You'll see him again, don't worry," Mom added over her shoulder with a comforting smile.

"I miss him, too, but I can't wait for this mission to be over to try more of *Lisai's* cooking," Irun chimed in with a thoughtful grin. "You know she's probably over *fifty* times your age, right?" I grinned, prompting him to scoff. "Like *that's* ever stopped *you*," he said with a smirk. "He's got a point, Thoma," Ysevel said, putting a finger to her chin pensively. "Are you on *his* side now?" I asked, feigning overt astonishment as I put a hand to my mouth.

"No, but I'm just saying that he spoke the truth. That doesn't mean I'm on his *side* or anything," she retorted wryly just before my mother held up a hand to signal for us to follow her into one of the taverns.

"This is probably our best bet at finding a sailor to take us," she noted in a hushed tone. *You mean one that's drunk enough to counter the ship's rocking?* I asked smugly, but she didn't reply with much more than a chuckle.

Once we entered the tavern, it was much different than what I expected it to be. The floorboards were surprisingly clean, the tables were neat and organized, and while there wasn't much in the way of debauchery, I could tell that there was an unspoken agreement not to cause a commotion. There were roughly thirty people in the tavern, each more weathered and worn than the last, but like the establishment they were in, they did their best to upkeep a *decent* appearance.

"Hello there," my mother began as she walked up to the bar. Just behind it, there was a large, bearded fellow who was probably well into his forties, though he kept a clean appearance with not a stain on his apron. "Hello to you too! What can I get you?" he said in an almost forced, cheerful voice.

Something's off, I sent Kalia and Ysevel quickly, though not outwardly showing my discomfort. "Seven ales and a platter of fish, please," Mom said, using a similar tone. "*Oh*, I'm sorry, but we're all out of fish today," he replied with a shake of his head. "I see. How about some stew and a loaf of bread?" she asked, keeping the same awkward tone.

"What's happening?" Athar asked me in a whisper, but I couldn't offer him any more than a shrug. "Sorry, we're all out of stew and bread as well," the bartender said, causing my mother to burst out into awkward laughter that the bartender mimicked. "*Oh*, what a shame! I have *all these Crescents* I've just been *dying* to spend on some food. I've heard this place had some of the *best* on this side of the docks," she said, clinking the bag of coins Aurae had sent her off with.

Immediately, a handful of the others on the far side of the tavern raced toward her, with bread, stew, fish, and precisely *seven* mugs of ale at the ready. "*Ah!* How wonderful!" she said in feigned surprise. "*Hmm*, there's still one thing I forgot to mention. You see, I need a *strong* and *brave* captain to take me and my companions across the Belurian Channel," she said, causing a few of them to step away cautiously and glance at each other nervously.

Dropping her little act, my mother immediately shifted into a much more hostile stance when she noticed none of the men who approached her were saying anything. "I see that the captain I'm looking for isn't among you. Those of you who are still here and wish to live to tell the tale, *leave*," she said coldly, as nearly everyone inside the tavern fled for their lives.

All except for the bartender and a thin man in the corner farthest from us.

"Good to see you, too, Siraye," he said tiredly, shifting his wide, leather hat and uncrossing his legs, bringing them down from the table. "Damien! What a *pleasant* surprise! Who knew I'd find *you* in here?" she said with an abhorrently sarcastic tone.

As the man stood up, I could see why everyone immediately fled. It wasn't because of my mother, though I suspect she had a *heavy* hand in that, but rather because of this thin man with scars all over his body. His clothes were relatively neat, though there were a few stitching marks present on his leather cloak, likely signifying he'd seen his fair share of action.

Is he the actual owner of this tavern? I wondered. *It makes sense to me, but what do you make of him?* Ysevel asked, glancing between him and my mother repeatedly. *Not sure yet. Let's see what happens,* I suggested, getting a subtle nod of confirmation from her.

His thick, leather boots clunked heavily against the hardwood floor, but there wasn't a speck of mud or dirt on them, just *decades* of use. "You coming back here doesn't bode well for anyone, *elf*. So tell me, why *are* you here? Don't you remember what happened last time you wanted to go *hunting*?" he asked in a tired, raspy voice as if he'd just woken from a nap.

"I do, but that's not why I'm here," she replied, giving him a proper greeting. "*Oh?* I'm all ears," he said, lifting his face from beneath the brim of his wide hat, revealing more scars on his face and a missing ear. His eyes were bloodshot and watery, though his dirty blonde hair and clean-shaven face told me there was a lot more to him than I realized.

"I'm calling in that favor you owe me," Mom said, immediately presenting the token she'd grabbed from the house. He glanced at it in astonishment for a moment, then rapidly shifted his gaze between her eyes and it. "You *can't* be serious," he scoffed. "After nearly *thirty* years, you finally decided to use *that* on me? That's *bullshit*," he said gruffly.

"Sorry, but it's urgent, *old friend*," she said firmly, making him sigh at the use of the term. After a few moments of consideration, he finally seemed to notice the rest of us. "Didn't think you'd bring your own *son* and her *Highness* with you. I can tell those two can handle themselves in a fight, but who are *these* two?" he asked, gesturing to Kalia and Devyr, who were still wearing their helmets.

"I'm more surprised you could tell who they were from a single glance," Mom chuckled as if she'd forgotten his personality. "These are Kalia and Devyr. They've taken a vow of silence until their enemy is killed. We've tracked him to the Isles, but we need *your* help to end this *duty* of theirs," she said almost mournfully.

He raised a scarred eyebrow at the concept, but after giving them another glance, he finally relented. "*Secrets within secrets*, right?" he scoffed and shook his head. "Fine. The tide's about to drop, so let's just get this over with," Damien sighed heavily, as he snatched the token out of my mom's hand with a speed I hadn't suspected he owned.

That makes a lot more sense, now, Kalia noted with a slight tinge of excitement. *I guess it does, but if he's* that *fast, then what could have given him all those scars?* Ysevel asked worriedly before we all followed him and my mother out of the tavern. Just before she crossed the threshold, she flicked a coin to the bartender and gave him a wink, though he offered a solemn bow in return.

He led us to his ship without a word. It was, like the tavern, clean and well-kept, but like his cloak, there were signs of more than just a *short skirmish* with a sea creature. *Sirens,* I realized, recognizing the tell-tale claw marks on the side of the ship from my studies in Codrean. *Whatever you do, don't say that name out loud unless you actually see or hear one, understood?* Mom sent with a strong, warranting feeling behind her words that I couldn't ignore.

"How much does *he* know about sea creatures?" I whispered to Irun, who was just behind me. "He knows more than you might think. He spent a lot of time in Ardrin's library and creature infirmary, but I can't confirm whether he knows about *those things*," Irun replied hushedly, causing my stomach to drop a little.

We'll be fine, but I'm more concerned about Kalia accidentally using her Wraith mana, Ysevel sent us, nearly making my mom stop mid-step. *She's right. We won't be able to use any of those abilities on the ship, since it would be too easy a target for Mideia to find. Which means that only you, Irun, and I will be able to defend the ship if we get attacked,* Mom said, her words laced with the memory of Gheraak and how he had come through the portal.

I realized that using dark mana, or *Vexing* mana as Ardrin had put it, was *also* out of the question, as it would cause much more suspicion among the crew than we needed.

As we stepped onto the wooden bridge, with planks laid out in even spaces to provide footholds, I looked down at the small waves that gently lapped against the edges of the stone dock and wooden ship. "First time on a ship, boy?" Damien asked, already at the far end of the bridge. "Yeah, something like that," I said, trying to hide my nervousness since it really *was* my first time.

Maybe it was the way I said it, but he began to chuckle and shake his head as he turned away and began to prepare the ship for our departure. The thick mooring lines were cast off, and the anchor was pulled from the seabed by the handful of large, weathered men employed to help control the large ship, and I could feel my stomach beginning to feel a little uneasy at the gentle sway on the waves.

"Never thought I'd be on one of these. Did you, Thoma?" Athar asked, approaching Ysevel and I, who were watching the sun begin to set on the distant horizon. "No, honestly," I chuckled, doing my best to keep what little food I had in my stomach where it belonged.

"How are Kalia and Devyr doing?" Ysevel asked, but he only shrugged. "*Meh*, about as well as one might expect. It's their first time seeing the sea, much less being on a *ship*. They're suffering from both excitement *and shitting through their teeth*," he said with a chuckle before leaning over the railing to watch the water splash beside the bow. "To be honest, it's my first time, too, but I'm too excited about it to feel whatever *they're* feeling," she said, turning to see both of the hegraphenes huddled together and holding their stomachs.

"*Oh*, I'm with them on that feeling, but I think we should get some rest, or at least *try* to," I suggested, noticing my mother's nod of approval from near where Damien was at the helm. "Let's at least finish watching the sunset, then we'll go," Ysevel said as she took my arm in hers, and spoke in a tone that didn't take much more convincing than that to get me to stay.

As we looked out to the horizon, the edge of the sun was just about to hide behind it when a subtle, yet noticeable, flash of green appeared where it had once been. Ysevel and I were immediately on guard, but once I heard my mother's and Damien's laughter at our reaction, we just glanced at each other with confused looks.

"That's not what you think it is, you two," Damien said between chuckles as he summoned us both to where he was. Not knowing what else to do, we followed his order and stood near the helm with him and my mother. "She told me everything while you were all *having a moment* with the sunset," he began, only increasing my confusion.

"That's comforting," I noted with a slight look of worry on my face. "So, what *was* that green flash, then?" Ysevel asked, more curious than worried, that my mother had just told him our real purpose for going to the Isles. "*Ah*, it's an old sailor legend that says that when the flash happens, someone's come back from the land of the dead," he said as if he didn't believe the legend himself.

"Is that true? I've always wondered what sort of stories were prevalent on the sea," Ysevel asked with childish interest, making Damien shrug. "Whether it's true or not, it doesn't matter, but it *does* give some sailors hope that friends and loved ones they've lost may return to them someday," he said distantly, causing my mom to look away uncomfortably.

"*Oh*, I see," Ysevel said, though not entirely unaffected by his words. "I've lived long enough to know that *hope* is something that can push people through difficult times, but *seeing* a small manifestation of it, even if it's just a legend, makes me happy," she said with a bright smile, causing Damien's eyes to widen and shift away briefly. "W-Well, I guess that's one way of looking at it," he said awkwardly.

She just hit a nerve, didn't she? I asked my mom, who nodded subtly. *He doesn't like to talk about it, but the last time I was here, I helped him and his wife stave off a Siren attack. He and I were the only two survivors that night, and as thanks for saving his life, he gave me that token in case I ever needed his help,* she explained, avoiding many of the details that I felt I didn't need to know, judging by the way she talked about it.

As the sky began to darken and our conversation with Damien waned, we left him and my mother alone on the deck while Ysevel and I joined the others below. There wasn't much in the way of accommodations, but there were a few nets strung up that were still available to sleep on.

"Maybe it helps with countering the ships' movement?" I asked Ysevel hushedly. "Only one way to find out. I'll see you in the morning," she said with an excited smile before giving me a quick kiss and getting into her net that was next to mine. Even as I lay there, I could feel Kalia's displeasure with the ship's movement, while Ysevel was already fast asleep. Mom, however, had a strange mix of emotions, which I could only identify as regret or sadness.

I did my best to dismiss the thoughts I had regarding what she'd told me about Damien and closed my eyes to sleep. The gentle swaying of the ship shifted from being annoying to rather soothing, as I felt like a small baby being rocked to bed.

I don't know how long I was asleep for, but I suddenly woke to the sound of a bell being rung.

That's not a good sign in the middle of the night. Ysevel, Kalia, get up, we've got to go up top! I sent them urgently. *What am I supposed to do?* Kalia asked, recalling the instructions my mother gave me. "Just defend Damien, and don't do anything fancy. Irun, with me!" I said aloud. I was grateful to see he hadn't forgotten *everything* about his time in Codrean, since he was already up and grabbing his blade.

As we hurried up the stairs, I heard the sound of ear-piercing screeches *somewhere* above me. "I can't see *shit* out here," Irun noted, which I didn't think would *actually* be a problem. The only available light we had was a handful of torches that lined the deck of the ship, but everything else around us was an eerie darkness that none of their light seemed to penetrate.

"I'm on it!" Mom shouted, already knowing what I was going to ask her. She cast a massive ball of light and stuck it to the top of the main mast, helping to illuminate the area immediately surrounding the ship in a white glow. As the area around us grew brighter, I saw a shadowy silhouette moving quickly along the edges of her spell's range.

Is that what I think it is? I thought, trying to figure out what other kind of creature it could possibly be.

"Starboard side!" Damien shouted, pointing a long spear in the direction I'd just seen it move. I wasn't sure how he was able to track it better than *I* was, but it was likely due to his having more experience with these creatures. The sound of beating wings and another screech came from almost precisely where the tip of his spear was pointed.

Kalia, I sent her, motioning for her to get up to the helm and guard him. Without another word or reaction, she quickly sprinted up the steps and drew the blade Maikell made for her. "I know you can't speak, but thank you," Damien said over his shoulder as the two of them stood back to back. Devyr and Athar suddenly joined us, though it was obvious that she was still feeling sick from the rocking of the boat.

"Thoma, Irun; Defend the sailors as best you can. I'll handle the ones up top," Mom said, immediately leaping to the crow's nest to get a better view of the battle. Just as she did so, one of the winged creatures' silhouettes flashed at the edge of her spell, and was quickly bathed in its light as it sped toward her.

It was easily the strangest creature I'd encountered so far.

Its body had scales and a tail like a fish, though beneath its long, clawed arms were thin membranes of skin that I could only guess were its wings. What *really* surprised me was the fact that its face had a nearly unmatched beauty, though its long, sharp teeth broke that illusion quickly.

"Sirens!" my mother shouted, severing the head in a single strike from her incoming attacker before it could do any damage to her or the top of the mast. As the head rolled onto the deck, a handful of the crew did their best to steady themselves, but the sirens moved with such speed that it was likely impossible for them to keep up with them.

"Get below the deck and to safety. We'll handle things up here!" I shouted to them. "*Hah*, you think this is our first time dealing with them?" one of the larger crewmen said. His tree-trunk arms held several strange tattoos, though many of them were ruined by the scars they held. As Irun and I could only glance at each other and shrug, knowing there was little more to be said, we got into positions at opposite ends of the ship. I was near the bow, while Irun stayed in the middle of the deck, and Kalia was near Damien at the helm. I'd waited for another to appear, but in the time it took me to blink, one of the sailors was pulled over the edge with a blood-curdling scream.

"They're in the water!" Damien shouted, prompting his men to step away from the edges. I heard the sound of beating wings coming from my left, and in the short heartbeat I had to react, one of the sirens came at me at full speed, claws and teeth ready to get at my throat.

My heart was racing, but I did what I could to maintain my composure as I swung my sword upward and sidestepped out of the way. The fish-like humanoid corpse slammed against the far side of the deck in a fleshy heap, but before I could even acknowledge what I'd just done, another two came at me.

It's not that they're hard to kill individually, but if they're in a swarm, they can pose a problem, I sent Ysevel, who'd made her way up to defend the second mast, which was a little lower than the one my mom was on. *They're even harder to fight with one hand,* she sent with a grunt of exertion, as another pair of heads rolled near my feet.

Another trio came at me, each one swinging with the speed and accuracy of a trained killer, forcing me to backstep a little to avoid getting hit by the barrage of attacks. It was challenging to manage, as there were still the sailors behind me I had to account for. "A little *help* would be nice!" I shouted to Irun, but he, too, was being swarmed in a similar manner. "Would if I could, *lanky*," he snapped back, trapping one of their wings beneath his elbow and tearing it in two with his free hand.

Athar and Devyr did their best to hold their own, and even though she was still feeling sick, I could tell she was still doing reasonably well to defend herself. Kalia and Damien were also surrounded, though I could sense she was growing tired of being unable to use her Wraith mana to dispose of them quickly.

Thoma, on me! Ysevel sent, her eyes flaring with violet light. *What's the plan?* I asked, severing two out of the three sirens' heads before ducking beneath the third's strike aimed at my face. *I have a plan, but you're not going to like it,* she said. *I'll take whatever you've got in mind,* I sent back, already running out of ideas of what to do.

Meet me where Siraye is, she sent just before leaping from her position up to where my mother was. I followed her lead and hopped onto the cargo net, praying the rope would take the force of the jump I was about to do to get up there quickly. *Pushing mana into my legs,* I pushed off the small square of net my foot was in and soared through the air to reach the crow's nest.

"What's the plan?" I asked, doing my best to deflect a strike aimed at my back as I hung over the side. "Siraye, you're the only one with enough mana to do this, but get up there as high as you can, and cast as large an *Inar* spell as you can," Ysevel pointed to the top of the mast just a few meters above us.

Without another word, my mother did as instructed, but just before she cast, Ysevel extended her hand out to me. "Trust me on this," she said with a determined look in her eye. "When have I not?" I grinned wolfishly, already starting to piece together her plan.

I felt the mana around us swell far beyond the reaches of the light, engulfing everything above the surface of the water. I could feel that my mom was taking extra care to wrap her mana far away from the thick, wooden masts that held the sails, demonstrating her near-absolute control over mana.

Even as I marveled at her level of control, I felt a tendril of mana wrap around my waist, prompting me to look at Ysevel with mild confusion. "As if I wasn't sick enough," I chuckled and shook my head. "Sorry, love," she smiled, just before my mom pulled the flying creatures toward us with her spell. I jumped back, fully trusting Ysevel to keep me from falling onto the deck below, and readied both my blades.

As I felt her begin to swing me around like a rock on a string, the airborne sirens were quickly around us in a sphere-like formation, being held in place by my mother's mana. "Now!" she shouted, prompting Ysevel to launch me higher into the air in a rapid spinning motion. I did what I could to hold onto my blades as each of them quickly became drenched in gore, turning me into little more than a vortex of *death*.

As their heads and wings were severed, I could hardly hear the sounds of their corpses slamming into the sea below over the cacophony of death *I* was, quite literally, flung into. Ysevel's *leash*, for lack of a better word, was taut and guiding me along in a sequence of circular patterns as my blades dug into their flesh.

As I felt the last bite of cartilage and scales on my blades, she let me down to the deck, though my dizziness, coupled with the rocking motion of the ship, caused me to stumble and fall flat on my face in a puddle of siren blood.

"What the ever-living *fuck* was that, Siraye?" Damien shouted. While I couldn't see his face, I could tell from his tone that he was both impressed and *horrified* at the sight before him. "It wasn't *my* plan," she said as she dropped from the crow's nest onto the deck, nearly breaking one of the boards beneath her feet.

Thankfully, Ysevel landed with a little more grace beside me and helped me to my feet. "I think I'm go-... *hurrok*... I think I'm gonna be sick," I said weakly as the sea, ship, and lights spun around me uncontrollably. "I'd be more concerned if you *weren't*," she said with a chuckle, carrying me over to the port side of the ship so I could shit through my teeth. "It's not the *first* time I've seen you like this," she said playfully, gently patting my back. "*That* was... *hurrok*... different," I spat the last remnants of dinner out before swishing a mouthful of water.

"True, but still, thank you for trusting me," she said warmly, though I could only return a weak, pallid smile. "You two weren't half-bad up there, though I wasn't expecting it to rain *siren parts* today," Damien said with a chuckle as he approached us with my mother and the others.

"Well, if it hadn't been for her quick thinking and, arguably, *gory*, adaptation of my *Whip of Doom* technique, that fight would have lasted a lot longer," I managed weakly, jutting my thumb in her direction. "I-I see. Thank you, Your Highness," he said, offering her a proper gesture. "Just *Ysevel*, and of course! I couldn't just stand there and wait for more of your men to die. Plus, if it hadn't been for Siraye's control over mana, that plan might not have worked," she shrugged, causing him to chuckle.

"You speak *far* too casually for someone in such a high position," he said in disbelief. "Still, thank you, Ysevel," he said, using just her name this time.

After allowing me a few minutes to recover, we helped the crew clean the ship of the severed body parts and blood to the best of our abilities, though no matter what we did, it didn't seem to be enough to meet *his* standards. "It will have to do for now, but you're going to end up owing *me* for the cost of the cleaning crew I'll have to hire," Damien said, jokingly elbowing my mother in the ribs.

"Fine, but you still owe me a good meal when we get back from *there*," she retorted, pointing out to where the silhouette of the Gramm Isles was just beginning to come into view in the early hours of the morning. "*Those* are the Gramm Isles?" I asked, as I observed the titanic cliffside and distant mountains begin to grow exponentially larger.

I couldn't see much in the way of details, but I was sure that what I *could* see was nearly as large as the Rhydian Mountains, perhaps even *larger*. I felt my nervousness begin to turn in my stomach, not fully knowing what this place would be like, but Ysevel took my hand in hers and gave me a knowing nod.

Whatever happens there, we'll go through it like we always have; together, she sent me and the others as we watched the cliffside, still hidden by the fog, begin to grow even larger than initially expected.

I know. Let's see what this place holds, I smiled back, squeezing her hand a little more tightly.

CHAPTER 82
STUNNED

We drew closer to the docks, and I noticed I could finally see some more details about the land just behind them.

There was a range of mountains that extended about as far as my eyes could see, while the waves crashed against the sharp rocks and steep cliff face where it met the sea. The docks, now only a few hundred meters from us, stood much taller than the ones back in Coltend, though I still had no idea just *how much* taller.

"Have you ever been to the Isles before?" Damien called out to Ysevel and I as we looked through the fog, prompting us to move toward the helm and stand beside him. "Can't say that I have. Is there anything I should be on the lookout for while I'm there?" I asked loosely, but what I *really* wanted was more recent information than whatever my mother might have had.

"Well, the food's decent, but I'd be careful with whatever drinks they offer you. Dwarves have come up with some interesting ways of creating alcohol, and much of it will be stronger than anything I think *you've* had," he chuckled, realizing that kind of answer wasn't what I was looking for when he noticed my raised eyebrow aimed at him.

"You're just like your mother in some ways, you know that?" he scoffed and shook his head. "I don't think that's a bad thing," I shrugged and upturned my lip. "No, it's not, but would it kill you to relax a little? They've cut themselves off from most outside interactions, even going so far as not allowing foreigners to stay here without consent from the Lord of Narin," he said with a distant stare.

"You mean only dwarves are allowed to live here? What about traders or sailors who come here to exchange goods?" I asked with visible curiosity. "They're forced to stay in a designated area a fair distance away from the capital. As for *why* that is, I have no idea," he said indifferently.

He must not know about the Great Partition, then, Ysevel sent me briefly, as if letting me know to watch what I would say next. *That would make sense. What* doesn't *make sense is the fact that people are still allowed to trade with them. What could they possibly gain from not allowing foreigners to live there?* I sent back, but Ysevel didn't seem to know the answer either.

"Either way, I'd be careful if I were you. They don't tend to like Elves, and I'm not sure how useful that little *pendant* of yours will be here," he cautioned with a nodding gesture to the pendant that was dangling openly around my neck. Heeding his advice, I tucked it away behind the opening around my neck and patted it gently to make sure it wasn't twisted.

"Good thinking. *Oh,* one last piece of advice," he began, turning the handles of the large, wooden wheel which guided the ship before leaning toward Ysevel and I. "Whatever your goal is here, *don't say it directly,*" he said hushedly, shifting his gaze between the two of us before barking orders out to the crew to prepare for our arrival.

I wonder why he told us that, I sent Ysevel with an upturned lip. *When we arrive, let* me *do the talking. Dwarves can be fickle bastards, and are more hard-headed than anyone* you *know,* Mom sent with a knowing look.

I didn't have much of a choice but to trust her, after all, this *was* still unfamiliar territory. As we drew closer to the dock, which had somehow grown in size exponentially during our brief conversation, I suddenly realized that there were a lot of large metal parts that seemed to move on their own.

Or I thought they did, at least.

Near the base of one of these structures was a person, or *dwarf,* I reminded myself, with a pair of odd-looking sticks in his hands that seemed to control its movement. "Fascinating," I said, still awestruck by the absolute control he had over the massive device. "What do you even call something like that?" I asked, nudging my mom with an elbow.

"They call it a *lifter.* Pretty simple name, but that's precisely what it does. It just lifts things from the ship's deck onto the dock itself. Instead of taking multiple trips and risking whatever it is falling into the sea below," she said with a genuinely proud smile on her face.

Whether that was because she knew what it was, or she had some *hand* in creating it, I didn't know.

"What's that thing over there?" Ysevel asked, pointing to a large building. Upon closer inspection, I could see that it wasn't just the building, but the docks seemed to have the same, glowing stones, for lack of a better word, embedded into their structures. "That's one of the places we need to go before we set off to Narin. It's where they keep track of everything and *everyone* who comes through these docks," she said, though her tone suggested she didn't want to go there either.

"Is it like a bureaucratic department?" Ysevel asked, visibly disappointed in my mom's answer. "Unfortunately, yes," Mom sighed heavily. "Quiet. Don't let them hear you talking badly about them," Damien hissed, prompting Mom to roll her eyes. "They'll survive a little bit of shit being thrown at them," she scoffed and shook her head.

Don't talk shit, and don't tell them you're an elf. Interesting set of rules, wouldn't you say? I sent Ysevel wryly, making her stifle a chuckle.

As the ship slowed its pace to the dock, I could see there were a handful of dwarves already preparing to grab the mooring lines and secure us to the docks. When we got close enough, I was finally able to make out some of the details of what they were wearing.

Their short and stocky bodies were made doubly so by the thick garments they wore. The shirts were open at the necks, revealing a dense tuft of hair just beneath them, while their sleeves were rolled up to the height of their elbows. They each had a pair of devices on their heads, loosely reminding me of the *eyes* we Synners wore, but theirs were made of stone, with thin, transparent glass where the device would meet their eyes.

That could protect their eyes from harmful substances, right? Ysevel sent with visible curiosity, as if she wanted to try them on. *Maybe from the sun, too, but I guess they don't need them today because of the fog,* I sent back with an upturned lip.

As the crewmen let down the mooring lines, our ship gently drifted and then came to a sudden stop with a slight nudge, indicating it was securely fastened to the dock. The bridge we'd used to go onto the ship was lowered, but at the same time, the large metallic *lifter* began working its way over to us on thick metal pegs that moved like an insect's legs. They moved to a set of holes in the stone dock and locked into place, letting the others know it was prepared to be used.

"I've never seen anything like *that*," Ysevel said, still in awe at the strange device. I couldn't say anything in return, but it was safe to say that my surprise was evident. Kalia and the others came up to the deck as Ysevel, Damien, my mother, and I left the helm. "*Glad we made it the rest of the way in one piece,*" Athar's alternate groaned as he cracked his neck and shook his head.

"Not sure I could say the same for these two, though," he continued in a normal voice, jutting his thumb over to Kalia and Devyr. While I couldn't see their faces, Kalia's scowl spilled over to me through our connection, nearly making me laugh. "Are you two alright?" I asked.

"I think my organs might have gotten rearranged from how much I *puked*, as Athar called it," Devyr whispered tiredly, hoping Damien hadn't just heard her speak after we told him they took a vow of silence. "I'm glad *that* was the only reason they did," I said in a similar voice playfully, giving Athar a knowing look and trying to lighten the mood just before I received a smack on my shoulder and a look of shock from Ysevel.

Whaaat? I thought it was funny, I sent, stifling a laugh. *It was, but someone has to tell you that it was inappropriate,* she said, jutting her head subtly to Kalia, who was, thankfully, turned away. *What was inappropriate?* Kalia asked without looking. *Nothing,* I sent back much more quickly than I intended.

I was grateful for the interruption by the lifter's arm that came down from above to grab a pallet of barrels and wooden chests the crewmen had prepared for it during our conversation. As it came down, I noticed the same glowing stones were embedded in the device along its length, though upon closer inspection, they radiated *mana*.

"H-How did they manage to do that?" Athar asked, seemingly the most shocked out of all of us. "Even Ardrin couldn't come up with something like *that*," he continued after a brief pause, causing Kalia to scoff. "You're not impressed?" he asked with genuine surprise. *It's primitive at best, though it* does *remind me of some of the devices we have at Tason'Gareshe Numa,* she sent Ysevel and I, but only shook her head at Athar to maintain her act.

"Come on, it's about time we got them off the ship before they expel *anything else* from their stomachs," Damien gestured for us to follow him from the top of the bridge with a raised eyebrow. Following his command, we made our way down the wooden bridge onto the stone docks.

There are guards on their way to inspect us. Don't answer any of their questions, just let me do the talking, Mom sent us all just before she made her way down the bridge. *Got it,* I sent back quickly.

They were a little slippery from the sea's waves beating against the rocks, though Athar was the only one who nearly lost his footing. "Careful now; wouldn't want you to slip and fall into the sea, would we?" one of the approaching dwarves asked in a thick accent. As I turned to look at the group that approached us, I was surprised to see that they weren't *as short* as I had initially been led to believe.

For the most part, they were only about a head and a half shorter than I was, though the tallest of them, whom *I* pinned as being the most likely captain of their guard, stood nearly as tall as Ysevel. Their thick leather armor had fur poking out from behind multiple, strategically placed metal plates with traditional markings etched into every piece.

However, the one who spoke first wore a different attire altogether. It was a fine, turquoise robe laden with golden details and thick golden rings on each finger. His long beard, which nearly reached the apex of his obtuse stomach, was neatly braided and adorned with a single golden clasp to hold it all together.

As he continued approaching us, I could hardly see his bright blue eyes that hid behind the dark, bushy eyebrows.

"So, tell me: What brings *you* here?" he asked, gesturing to the rest of us. "Greetings, Mayor Lokren," my mother said as she stepped forward to present a balled fist that she pounded twice against her chestplate. "*Oh*, fuck me. What are *you* doing here? Shouldn't you be back in your homeland, sipping on some tea you milked from a pine tree's teat?" he said gruffly, visibly annoyed by her mere presence.

"Trees don't *have* tits, though if they did, I'm sure more people would try and *not* chop them all down for *fuel*," she retorted quickly. "*Bah*, you know what I meant, *elf*," he waved a hand in front of him dismissively. "But go on, then, tell us why you're here," he continued, regarding the rest of us curiously for a moment.

"I'm here to see *him*, of course," she replied, taking a step toward Lokren, whose hidden eyes suddenly widened, prompting his guardsmen to close in around him with their shields that were nearly as tall as they were. "N-Now, now, Siraye. Let's not cause a scene here," Lokren raised his hands placatingly, prompting her to halt.

"Do you think I *want* to cause a scene? I'm just here to see *him*, though whether you help me *willingly* is entirely up to you," she said in a calm, even tone that would send chills down *anyone's* spine. The guards, I noticed, even shared a few glances as if unsure they would be enough to stop her if she *did* do something.

"*I* wasn't the one who blew a massive crater into sacred ground after your last fight here. We're grateful for what you did in saving Narin, sure, but we've *also* grown wary of *your kind*," he said shakily, causing my mother to click her tongue. "Then what do you want to do, Lokren? I don't have a lot of time, and I *am* going to see him, whether you take us there personally or not," she said, spreading her arms a little.

"You want *me* to be your escort? *Hah!* That's a good one, Siraye! Rich, even!" he said in blatant disbelief at her request, which my mother began to chuckle along with as well. "Want to know an even *better* one? I *could* put a crater *twice* the size right where your fancy building is if you keep this up, Lokren," she said between laughs, immediately causing him to halt and give her a questioning look to see if she meant it. "I'm not saying *I will*, but it *is* an option. You know me well enough for that," she shrugged.

"R-Right. Of course, you wouldn't do that," he chuckled nervously as he quietly signaled for his guardsmen to back away. "I'll take you there, just, *uh*, give me a moment to prepare the transport," he said with a false smile.

"See? That wasn't so hard to negotiate, was it?" she asked playfully. "N-Not at all! You *were* a little rude about it, but I'm glad we could come to an agreement, Siraye," he said shakily, pounding his fist against his chest twice the same way my mother had before quickly walking away.

"Remember how I said *not to* tell them you're an elf?" Damien whispered, leaning his face between Ysevel and I from just behind us.

"Makes sense," Ysevel replied with a chuckle. "Just how *sacred* was that place, anyway?" I asked, but Damien scoffed through his nostrils and walked away without giving me an answer. *Guess we'll just have to find out,* Ysevel sent me with a knowing look.

Within a few minutes, I heard the sound of what *I* thought was a growling beast, but quickly discovered that it was another contraption the dwarves had come up with. It looked like a carriage, but it wasn't made of wood or drawn by horses. Instead, there was another glowing stone that radiated strong earth-attribute mana.

As Lokren approached us in the strange form of transport, I realized that the growling sound I'd heard was actually the earth *beneath* the metallic carriage shifting to provide movement. "Here we are," he said in a much more cheerful tone than he had initially approached us with. "Your, *uh*, companions can ride in the back, though I *was* instructed to keep a close eye on you, Siraye," he said with a grunt as he dismounted. "*Yes!*" I heard Athar's alternate voice hiss just beside me.

"That's fine by me. We *do* have a lot of catching up to do, and I'm sure the journey there will be the best time to do that," she said with a smile that sent shivers down his spine. "I-I'd love that. Please, allow me," he said nervously. Just before he stomped his foot, I could feel a surge of earth attribute mana being pushed into the floor to make a set of earthen steps for her to climb up.

Whether *he* could draw mana or it had something to do with those glowing stones, I couldn't tell in my state of amazement.

Is this where she learned that trick? I wondered, thinking back to the first time I'd seen her use the steps to attack me during a training session, though she'd adapted it into platforms she could move to without me being able to reach her. She looked over her shoulder and grinned at me before stepping up to the first available seat.

"I can't *wait* to ride this... *thing*!" Athar said excitedly, doing his utmost best to keep it under control. "I'm with Athar on this one. I've never seen anything like it," Irun chimed in with widened eyes as if Athar's excitement rubbed off on him. I smiled, knowing it was almost *rare* to see Irun excited about anything, but I didn't add much else to it.

I helped Ysevel onto the transport, but as soon as it was my turn to step up onto the small earthy platforms Lokren had created for us, I felt a gentle pulse of mana from somewhere just beyond the cliff's ridge.

"Did you feel that?" I whispered to the others, who were looking at me with concerned glances. "I did, but it was so faint, I thought it was the *wind*," Ysevel noted as I took the seat beside her. *It could have been another portal,* Kalia sent with a worried sensation. *It's pretty likely, but we would have heard another blast, right?* I asked, but she shook her head to let me know she didn't seem to know the answer either.

When she did so, I could feel the gentle acceleration of the transport and the *less-gentle* rumbling of the earth-moved mana beneath us. "Well, whatever it was, I think we'll find out soon enough," Irun said, but something was going on with Athar that I couldn't quite identify at that moment.

We continued in silence, though it was only a better part of an *hour* later that we felt a much *stronger* pulse. "Fuck me, there it is *again*," Irun said as he pushed open one of the square windows along the walls of the transport to look out of. "That one was *much* stronger than the last. Probably means we're getting closer to whatever's causing it," I added, opening the window just behind my head as well, though I was only met with the cliff face.

"I didn't like the feeling of that *at all*. Whatever it was, I was instantly reminded of Pyrdredd, though," Athar shuddered as his eyes widened. I'd only ever seen him fearful of a few things since meeting him, but this was the first time I'd ever actually seen him *genuinely* uncomfortable.

As I digested his words, I noticed his fingers were flexing back and forth across his skin, as if his alternate was trying to get away from whatever it was that caused it. "It's alright, Athar. We're right here with you," Ysevel said, putting a hand on his to prevent him from scratching himself a new wound. Devyr put a hand on his, as well, and gave him a wordless nod of reassurance.

"Don't go freaking out on us again, alright?" Irun said hushedly, but in a tone that suggested he knew how to handle whatever was trying to get out. "You've seen this before?" Ysevel asked for the rest of us. "Yeah. Scared the shit out of me the first time, too. He went missing for a few days in Valdis, and I had to go find him," Irun said, putting a hand on Athar's shoulder firmly.

As Athar looked at Irun's warm, yet knowing, smile, his trembling and scratching began to slow to a halt. "I'm fine. I'm alright," he said softly with a few rapid nods and a shake of his head. I noticed he'd swallowed dryly, likely trying to hold back whatever threatened to exit his stomach.

By this point, I hadn't even noticed that the metal carriage had begun moving, and that we were nearly to the top of the steep mountain that overlooked the docks. "How fast does this thing even go?" I asked, leaning over to Lokren and my mother, who hadn't noticed Athar freaking out. "We should reach Narin by noon, if all goes smoothly," he said, muttering the last few words out of the corner of his mouth.

"What do you mean *if it goes smoothly?*" I raised an eyebrow. He and my mother exchanged a glance momentarily before he finally gave a relenting sigh. "We've had strange creatures roaming about the last few weeks, though no one seems to know where they come from," Lokren said with a shake of his head, but I could already feel Kalia, Ysevel, and Mom's reaction to it seeping through our connection.

Before anyone could answer, however, there was another pulse that passed through us. "W-What was that?" Lokren asked, though we all knew this one was much stronger than the last, if *even he* noticed it. "Lokren, I need you to get us over this mountain. I think whatever's causing it is just on the other side," Mom said with a stern glare.

"You're not going to blow another crater in the ground, are you?" he asked nervously. "I'll tear down entire *mountainsides* if I have to, though I'd rather see what's happening first so I can get a better idea of what's going on. Thoma, let the others know," she motioned to me before turning to look ahead. I could feel the mana in her eyes grow more intense as she enhanced her vision, but I did as instructed.

"Get ready for another fight, though I suspect Kalia won't be able to do this one on her own," I said, giving her a knowing nod. *I could, you know. If those are more members of the Grayeater clan, I'll be sure to do my part to eliminate them,* she sent back with a wolfish grin in her tone. "Athar, are you going to be alright?" I asked, noticing

Devyr was still sitting right next to him and making sure he wasn't scratching at himself.

"Y-Yeah, I'll be fine. I just... tough memories, you know?" he said with a weak chuckle. "Hey, those are all in the past now. Shit happens, but the members of *Nightfall's Blade* always get back up on their feet, right?" I said with a grin as he looked into my eyes. He gave me a nod of understanding and clapped both his hands against his cheeks as if to wake himself up from a long nap.

"You're right, Thoma. *Time to pull my head out of my ass,*" his alternate voice came through, letting me know that they were finally in agreement with one another. "Then let's get to work. Whatever it is should be just over the pass. Irun, I'll need you to stick with Athar just in case," I said, getting a nod of understanding from him.

"Devyr, Kalia. Since you two have more experience with them, give us a quick overview of what we're getting into," I said, knowing they weren't going to say anything verbally that would ruin their disguise. Ysevel and I both felt a strong pulse coming from Kalia, though there were memories within that belonged to Devyr. *Is that a hegraphene thing like what you had with Lord Gravar?* I asked loosely. *Yes. In fact, family members can share specific insights at a much faster pace since we're blood-related,* Kalia sent back with a sense of pride.

Glad to have her with us, then, I gave Devyr a knowing nod that she returned promptly before turning back toward the front of the carriage to see what was coming. We'd already reached the top of the pass and were now overlooking the vastness of the Gramm Isles.

It was hilly primarily, though there was a range of tall mountains in the distance that indicated there was much more to this land than I realized. The dirt below us had changed from a sandy brown to a near tar-black and held plenty of short vegetation beneath large, healthy trees.

"A real shift from the shoreline, isn't it?" Lokren asked over his shoulder when he noticed the look of both surprise and amazement on my face. "There are a lot of active volcanoes in this land, but the last eruption was well over a thousand years ago. It's what caused this dirt to be as dark as it is," he said, pointing toward one of the distant peaks.

"I've never heard of a volcano. What is that?" I asked. "*Hah*, well, think of it like when you need to have a good *shite*, but instead of *you* having a good one, the *ground* is," he said with a chuckle. "That didn't help much at all, but I'll take your word for it," I said, still scouring the treetops for any signs of the Grayeaters' presence.

As we descended the other side of the pass, the trees along our path began to grow increasingly dense, reducing our overall visibility of the surrounding land. "Do you feel anything, Thoma?" Mom asked as our view of the land between us and Narin disappeared behind the canopy. "Nothing yet. Maybe that wa-..." I halted, immediately sensing something to my right that I couldn't ignore.

I was glad to see my mother had felt it, too, because we immediately leaped off and drew our blades, while I sent Kalia and Ysevel what I'd felt, prompting the others to do the same. "Go on ahead. We'll be fine," Mom shouted to Lokren, who stared at us with widened, fearful eyes.

"They're here," Kalia said quietly, drawing her blade at her hip instead of reforming her *kataki*. "How far do you think they are?" I whispered. "There are no traps on the roads yet, so either they've just arrived, or they just haven't found this one yet," she muttered, scanning the treeline with a fierce gaze that showed even through the slits in her helmet.

"Irun, Athar; you're with me. Thoma, Ysevel; you know my methods. Take Siraye and Devyr with you. I'll let you know if I spot them first," Kalia said in a tone that reminded me a lot of my mother when we first found Irun in the forest.

With a wordless nod, we fanned out along the treeline, making sure to stay within visible reach as we quickly and quietly made our way through the dense trees. I realized, and *very quickly* at that, there were several plants I couldn't recognize or tell whether they were poisonous, but I was glad my armor did a fine job of protecting me against them.

That means they must not know either, giving us the advantage, Mom sent with a wry grin as she leaped silently over a fallen log and continued her sprint as if nothing had interrupted it. *I know it's not really Kalia's style, but I'd wager a few of these plants would fuck them up pretty badly if we ever needed to take care of a lot of them at once,* she continued, though I could only offer her a quiet scoff.

It's not exactly your style *either,* Ysevel added proddingly. *Fair enough, but where* are *these bastards, anyway?* Mom sent back. I could tell she was unwilling to use her mana in case they sensed it, meaning we were forced to rely on our eyesight to find them.

Over here, Kalia sent from what I could tell was a reasonable distance away to the west of where we were. *Stick to the eastern side of my position and only move in when I tell you to,* she continued, letting us all know she already had a plan in place that *we* simply had to execute.

We sent her an acknowledging pulse before veering off to our right slightly to maintain the directional instructions she had given us. As we drew closer to the Thran, Kalia sent us constant pulses to let her know our location and the direction *we* needed to take.

After a few more minutes of following her commands, we came to a gentle slope that overlooked a brand new camp these Thran had made. It was brutish in nature, just like their personalities and clothing choices seemed to be, but it was efficient nonetheless. They couldn't have been there very long, since there were still a number of them who appeared to be unloading equipment and other supplies needed for the camp.

I count forty, but that doesn't mean there aren't more spread out somewhere else, I sent Kalia, but I could feel that I was wrong through our connection. *No, this is just a scouting party. They're too prideful to set up guards like the elves would,* she sent back, though I could tell there was something in the tone she used that suggested things might be different.

I've done plenty of ambushes in my time, but I'm still a little unfamiliar with these creatures. Anything I should know? Mom sent the rest of us, though I could tell, both through our connection and the look she had in her eyes, that she was itching for a fight. *Nothing you probably don't know already, but beware the smaller ones; they're faster than they appear,* Kalia cautioned us.

Wanna see who's faster? Mom sent me directly with a wolfish grin. *I can't keep up with you when using Ethereal mana, but if I could use my Wraith mana, I'd leave you in the dust,* I grinned back, but she shook her head. *Somehow, I still doubt that, since you've never seen me really try,* she chuckled through her nose quietly.

Before I could even understand what she meant by that, Kalia gave us a signal letting us know she was ready, though her version of being prepared was *not* something I was ready for.

Why is Irun just walking up to the front gate of their abatis? Ysevel asked me directly. *I'm just as confused as you are, but let's see how this goes,* I sent back with a shrug, still keeping an eye on him as he approached the felled and sharpened trees. They were tied together tightly, though each of their sharp ends was pointed outward to stave off potential intruders.

"Hello there," Irun called out in a friendly voice, startling a few of the Thran as if they hadn't heard him coming at all. "Who's this? Did lunch just walk into our laps?" one of the Thran asked. "*Oh*, no, no, no. I would *hardly* make a mouthful for you," Irun chuckled, raising his hands placatingly as he continued to move inside their camp.

"Then what makes you think you can simply walk into our camp? You wouldn't do that if you didn't know what, or *who* we are," one of the larger ones stepped out from behind a freshly pitched tent.

He was at least a head taller than most of the others present, which, given my limited experience with them so far, likely meant he was the leader. His waist and shoulders were adorned with dried skulls, while whatever armor he wore beneath was dyed a deep blood red. The bracers he wore were wrapped in thick chains with a pair of half-skulls embedded within them.

What is he? A captain of some sort? I asked, trying to figure out why his clothes were dyed and adorned with so many skulls. *He's one of the Bloodmauls, but they're sworn enemies of the Grayeaters,* Kalia sent with evident confusion. I could tell she immediately felt more uncomfortable about sending Irun in alone. *He'll be alright. He's not* that *much of an idiot, you know?* I sent back with a slight lack of confidence.

"*Ah*, well, you're right about that. I *don't* know who you are, but even if I did, it wouldn't matter, since you're going to tell me one way or *another*," Irun chuckled, making the large Thran snarl in both anger and confusion. "You might not know our ways, but do you not know who we are?" he asked, taking a few steps forward until he was face-to-face with Irun.

"Go on, then. I'm sure you're just *dying* to tell me," Irun said flatly, as if already bored by the situation. "You insolent little *iskarin*. I will make sure you suffer horribly for your disrespect, on my honor as Grond Bloodmaul the Untouchable," Grond snarled with visible strings of drool dripping out of the sides of his wolf-like features. "*Oh, you're* Grond the Untouchable?" Irun asked with feigned surprise that the creature *clearly* didn't pick up on.

There's that dry sarcasm of his, I sighed.

"You *have* heard of me, then, which means you should *also* know we don't take prisoners," Grond said, staring down at Irun imperiously. "No, I haven't, but I'll gladly take *you* as one only if you decide not to fight," he shrugged as if he weren't standing in front of someone who could crush his head with a single hand.

Grond laughed loudly, though it came out more like a *dog's bark* than anything else as his voice reverberated through the forest. "I'm going to have a lot of fun wi-..." Grond cut himself off, as a head rolled between his legs. "What's the matter? *Oh*, look at that; It's a head," Irun said, bending over to grab it from the floor and flip it around in his hand like a child would a ball.

"You *dare* to use such tactics on us *and* defile our dead?" Grond asked as he watched Irun gingerly put his index finger on the lifeless muzzle as blood began to pool beside his feet. "Like I said, I'll gladly take *you* prisoner if you decide not to fight," Irun reiterated, but his words only managed to piss the enormous Bloodmaul off even more.

Just as Grond raised his fist to strike, I felt Kalia give us the signal to push in and attack. Mom was quick on the uptake as she dashed in, severing Grond's arm at the elbow, while the resulting *boom* from her blade striking the air nearly knocked Irun unconscious. Ysevel, Devyr, and I moved in after her, slaughtering a handful that were still trying to grasp what was happening the moment we leaped over the abatis. As their heads rolled, we split up and began moving onto another group to our right.

A group of three Bloodmauls came at me, each with a weapon well over a few meters long. I was forced to dodge the sword strike aimed at my clavicle, while the second Thran moved behind the first with an axe, hoping to catch me on the far end. I was lucky I saw it coming, because it gave me just enough time to push mana into the earth beneath me and create a barrier between us.

The third came from above with a powerful downward thrust of a spear, but was only met with a deflected blow that slid off my sword to my left, giving me an opening to slice its head cleanly from its shoulders. The first Thran snarled and tried to cut my torso in half with his oversized sword, but I could feel it coming through the slight shift in the wind's mana.

Pushing off a small, earthen platform with my foot, I slid under the massive blade and severed the Thran's wrist, sending the large weapon and all of its momentum barreling into the one I'd split off with my impromptu earth wall. The blade spun a few times, leaving an arc of blood from the still-attached claw as it dug itself into the unsuspecting Thran's thigh.

Between the roars of pain from each of them, I thrust my blade up beneath the chin of the first, soaking my gauntlets in blood and brain matter, and pulled outward to sever its face in half before dashing in toward the other, who was pulling the blade out of its tree-trunk thigh. Just as he did so, he looked up, only to find the edge of my blade glinting at the height of his eyes before slicing his head in half. As the top half of his head fell, I *pushed more mana* into my eyes to get a much broader view of our battlefield.

Athar was doing *surprisingly* well, severing a few limbs from a pair of Bloodmauls that came for him before burning their bodies from the inside out with mana. I was glad to see he and Irun were closer together now, as I wasn't sure how much *real* battle experience Athar had.

Ysevel, on the other hand, was in almost perfect synchrony with Devyr, as their fighting styles complemented each other beautifully to leave behind a trail of corpses and gore in their wake. Limbs, heads, and gore soared through the air wherever they went, though they managed to avoid getting any of it on them as they moved about the battlefield.

Meanwhile, Mom was creating ripples in the air with every strike, discombobulating any enemies in her immediate vicinity for a moment, before striking them down with a wolfish grin accented by the blood all over her face. "Four at once? Is that a new record or something?" I shouted over to her. It wasn't because I couldn't communicate with her, but I knew her tactics often involved confusing or frightening the enemy with *every strike.*

Just as the words left my mouth, I felt Grond's remaining fist soaring through the air and aimed at my head through the mana between us. His eyes were widened with rage, and the knuckles on his claw-like hand were pale with tension. It didn't take an expert to understand that he was hoping to *behead* or turn my head into a pie filling with it, but I stood my ground until I was sure he was fully committed.

I was hoping you'd do that, I thought, pushing an obscene amount of mana into my legs, arms, and the earth beneath my feet.

I could hear the ground beneath my feet crush gravel into dust as I pushed off at a diagonal angle to the right, avoiding the left-handed punch entirely and trailing my blade to sever his arm at the shoulder. The shift in his overall mass caused him to lose his footing and land face-first into the dirt.

You were counting on that, weren't you? Ysevel asked wryly. *I might have,* I shrugged as I watched Grond struggle to use what was left of his remaining arm to get into a kneeling position. *Well played. For a heartbeat, I thought he had you,* Mom sent with a sense of both pride and relief.

"*Argh,* damn you, *iskarin*! You'll pay for that!" he snarled as he turned to face me with blood pouring from his face and an empty shoulder socket. "*You* shouldn't have fallen for it, *Untouchable,*" I replied with a scoff and began walking toward him, as the last remaining members of the Bloodmaul scouting party were being wiped out.

"You should have listened to my friend over there," I said, pointing over my shoulder to Irun, who was just ripping his blade out of his enemy's throat. "But now, what to do with *you*?" I asked aloud, watching his dark eyes grow wide in fear, allowing me to see Kalia with a gore-ridden sword in their reflection, standing just beside me.

Take his head. We'll use it as a bargaining token for the rulers of this land, she sent coldly. *Don't we want to try to get information out of him?* I asked quickly. *No point, no time, and just knowing the Bloodmauls are working alongside the Grayeaters tells me everything I need to know*, she sent with a shake of her head.

Before the creature could even realize she and I had some kind of exchange, I did as she instructed and severed his head in one, clean strike, cauterizing the wound at its base with a *Pyrus* spell. "Here, put it in this. We don't want to frighten any of the locals, knowing these kinds of creatures are in their land," she said, handing me a thick leather bag that was crudely sewn together.

"Anything else?" I asked as I gripped the thick fur on top of Grond's head and stuffed the head into the bag. "Athar's already collecting their right ears, but we should move soon. They have an incredible sense of smell, and with all this blood spilled, it's just a matter of time before reinforcements arrive," she said, already glancing around at the treeline for any signs of movement.

After giving her a nod of understanding, we did everything she instructed us to do regarding the disposal of their bodies in hopes of hiding the scent. Mom piled them all together into a giant sphere of gore and death, pulling the mass of bodies deep beneath the earth to bury them.

"That should buy us plenty of time, but they're going to be looking for them regardless," she said, giving Kalia a nod, which she returned. "Also, it wasn't *four* at once. It was *six*, but the other two were almost hitting the floor," she said with a wry grin, but I heard Kalia's harsh chuckle echo within her helmet. "Not bad for your first *real* fight with them, but let me know when you hit *twenty* at once," she said between laughs, giving Mom a hefty pat on the shoulder.

Needless to say, we were all in shock while she just walked off as if she hadn't just dropped a meteor on us.

By mid-afternoon, we'd finally caught up to Lokren, though we were forced to handrail the path on the way there in case any more Bloodmauls or Grayeaters were setting up camp. I think Athar was the most grateful we didn't find any more, because I could hear his stomach growling as we went the rest of the way.

To be entirely fair, we were *all* hungry.

As we approached the city of Narin, I could tell at a glance that this place was far more technologically advanced than any city I'd ever heard of, much less *dreamed* of. The high, stone walls were covered in runic symbols that glowed with the same sort of stones Lokren used to power his transport. Twin banners flowed gently in the breeze above the titanic stone doors, with Narin's symbol sewn into them: a massive hammer with swirls of mana wrapping around its handle, backed by a deep, green cloth.

The guards atop the walls and those who stood before the massive stone gate wore similar armor to the others who'd first greeted us, though theirs seemed much more polished and refined. Meanwhile, Lokren stood by the entrance, fiddling with something anxiously as he waited for our return.

"Glad you made it safely," Mom said from a distance with a wave, prompting him to glance at us with widened eyes. "That wasn't a *stone* that just fell in your pants, was it?" she asked when she saw his look of pure astonishment. "It might have been a nice clump of *shite* to throw at you, but I'm glad you're alive!" he said, immediately putting away whatever it was he was fiddling with.

"*Aaand* covered in *something's* entrails. What the hells happened back there?" he asked, putting a hand to his nose when we got closer. "To make a long story short, we found something we think *he* will be interested in," she said, gesturing to the crude leather bags Athar and I were holding.

His thick eyebrows rose even further in surprise, but he shook his head to get rid of whatever thoughts he had. "I've learned not to question *whatever* it is you do when you're here, but I've already let the guards know that you'd be coming, as well as the new Lord of Narin, Calduran Lytehammer," he said, gesturing to the handful of them that looked at her, then *us* with suspicion.

"For the sake of simplicity, *I'll* be the one escorting you," he said, shifting his gaze toward the large doors that began to rumble as he spoke. There were no commands shouted, nor any sign of guards exerting themselves to swing the massive doors open.

Whatever's opening the doors, it has to be *extremely powerful,* I sent Ysevel, who gave me an excited nod.

As the seam of the twin doors widened, we caught our first glimpse of the city behind the stone walls. Each street was carefully planned and aligned to extreme levels of accuracy, while the sides of the roads held the glowing mana stones along their edges. I assumed it would be more efficient than lighting torches, but it looked so unfamiliar that even *that* concept seemed beyond me.

Each building, house, or establishment was built similarly to that of Lokren's, but like the guards' armor, these were *much more* refined and pristine. "It's incredible," I muttered almost breathlessly, as I noticed there were a few buildings that had the mana stones embedded into their edges. "She's a real *beauty*, isn't she? Took my people nearly *two thousand* years to complete, but it's withstood the test of time like *no other*," Lokren said proudly as we made our way through the dwarven city.

I was so *stunned* that I couldn't help but blink when he said that, but I knew that the time for asking questions would come eventually. The streets were lively enough to take my mind off things, as children played with strange, mechanical toys that seemingly moved on their own, or merchants who sold appendages made from metal and the glowing stones to imitate a lost limb.

No matter where I looked, I had *far more* questions than I could ever hope to have answers for.

As we approached the steps leading to the palace entrance, I realized that its construction seemed relatively similar to that of Myrdin's. However, it was built more like a *military fortress* than a royal palace, with its mana stones embedded in the darker, more polished ones.

Lokren briefly greeted the guards before we entered the already-opened doors, and I could tell that *something* was already happening on the inside, as there were a handful of dwarves shouting and pumping their fists in the air angrily.

What the hell happened here? I sent Mom with a raised eyebrow. *Must be about the Thran, or worse, the pulses we've been feeling since we got here,* she replied with a furrowed brow as she looked to the far side of the hall. *That would make the most sense. I'm sure they're all frightened by whatever's causing them,* Ysevel added. *Only one way to find out,* I said, giving my mom and Ysevel a nod as we began to approach the rabble of dwarves.

As I loosely took in the details of everything around me, I kept focused on the task at hand, since I knew we were likely going to be staying here for a reasonable amount of time. However, just as we got closer to the rabble, I couldn't help but feel an odd sensation in my core coming from Ysevel.

What is it? Are you alright? I asked, unable to sense any sort of danger around us. *I'm fine, but I can't shake this strange feeling like I've somehow been* here *before,* she sent back, furrowing her brow. I turned and reached over to her, grabbing her hand and giving it a gentle squeeze before she gave me a nod of reassurance that she was alright.

"Thoma?" I thought I heard a familiar voice call out from over the tops of the angry dwarven shouts that died down immediately. Unsure of what I'd heard, I turned to look in the direction I *thought* the voice was coming from, only to be met by two familiar faces.

"Holy shit, it *is you*! Gods above, it feels like forever since I've seen you!" Ed's familiar smile brightened, but while I wanted to run over to my best friend and hug him, I forced myself *not to*, because the second face wasn't one I was prepared to see with her arm locked with his.

Is that who I think it is? Kalia sent a probing look from beneath her helm, but I could already feel her rage and anger reaching a boiling point. Mom and Ysevel shared similar reactions, though they kept their thoughts to themselves.

Yeah, that's Meliss, I said, already struggling to push down the memories that flooded in, feeling my *own* anger beginning to flare.

CHAPTER 83

RESENTMENT

As my connection to the others began to flare with rage, I realized that it was affecting me more deeply than I would have liked.

Ed was wearing armor that resembled the guardsmen's quite closely, though his had to be modified to match his height and build. Meliss wore similar armor, though hers had a breastplate of a strange metal with numerous engravings etched into it. What those engravings meant was something I couldn't understand if I tried.

"Are you alright?" Athar asked hushedly over my shoulder. "I'm *fine*, it's just... been a while," I replied with a subtle nod just before I noticed Ed and Meliss pushing their way through the crowd. "It's good to see you again, Thoma! How long has it been? A little over a year, right?" Ed asked, letting go of Meliss's arm to wrap me in a tight hug.

"Yeah, something like that," I chuckled loosely as I patted him on the back. "Damn, did you finally put on some weight?" he asked with a chuckle, leaning back to look me over and grabbing my shoulders. *I'm not sure how to answer this,* I sent mom and Ysevel, who seemingly understood what I meant. "Hello there, Edryd. I believe *I'm* the cause of that," Mom said as she stepped forward, causing his eyes to widen.

"H-Hello," he said, almost fearfully at her presence, causing him to blink a few times. "Sorry. I just haven't seen any other elves aside from Ren, Thorn, and Nenvalur. Although it's been a few months since I last saw them," he noted with a slight, pensive pause. "*Ah*, well, that's alright. I think anyone would be surprised to see *me* here," Mom waved dismissively before glancing around the room at the handful of guards who were watching her closely.

"I'm glad to know he was in good hands, then," Ed said with a smile that fell immediately when he noticed Irun standing a few meters behind me. His eyes flared with third-stage mana momentarily, and I could tell from our years together that he was probably going to attack him.

"What the *fuck* is *he* doing here? Better yet, what are *you* doing standing next to him?" Ed snarled, prompting a few of the remaining dwarves around him to take a few steps back. "Ed, calm down. We're not here to start a fight. This is neither the time nor the place to do that, and if you let me, I'll explain everything," I said, raising my hands to try and stop whatever he was thinking.

"That *sack of shit* got Batch killed, or did you forget that already while you were over there in Caegwen?" he hissed through gritted teeth, prompting me to put a hand on his shoulder and do my best to de-escalate the situation.

"No, I didn't *forget about* that, but like I said, I'll explain everything later. You *also* have some shit to explain, so don't think that you're the only one who's got some questions to ask, alright?" I said, dropping my tone just enough to let him know I was serious. Ed looked at me with both anger and confusion, but after glancing at the others, who all held similar glares, he finally relented with a heavy sigh.

"Fine, but you'd better have a *really* good reason for this," he said hushedly while glaring at me from beneath a furrowed brow. "A *part* of that reason is *why* we're here in Narin to begin with," I said, holding up the leather bag. He looked at it curiously for a moment, and once I held it out for him to take, he cautiously looked inside to find Grond's severed head. "W-What the *fuck*?" he asked with widened eyes.

"Like I was trying to say, we're not here to pick a fight. We need to speak to whoever the ruler of Narin is, or someone with enough influence to give us the attention these creatures deserve," I said calmly with a slow nod, hoping it would let him know that there were much larger things at stake here.

"I guess introductions to the others will have to wait, for now," Ed replied, understanding my intent. "Come on, I'll introduce you to someone I know can help," he said, gesturing for the others and I to follow him down one of the side halls. I could see that Meliss was staring at me out of the corner of my eye, but I could only offer her a slight, greeting nod.

So she's *the zuresh that broke your heart all those years ago?* Kalia asked as she passed by her without indicating she'd just inspected nearly every part of her. *It might have been over a decade for us, but it hasn't even been a few* months *for her,* I replied, not wanting to give that much more thought than it needed right then.

Regardless, I think you handled that *and Ed's anger rather well,* Ysevel added. *Well, I'm just glad to know I wasn't the only one caught off guard by it,* I sent with a slight chuckle after recalling the emotions they'd fed me through our connection.

Ed led us down several hallways that had each corner lined with more of the glowing mana stones. There were many trophies, weapons, and other advanced mechanical devices that I couldn't identify along the walls and in trophy-like cases. Still, no matter where I looked, I could hardly understand what they'd be *used* for, let alone how they were made.

"Where are you taking us?" I asked, still trying to understand even *half* of what I was looking at. "To make a long, and rather *convoluted* story short: I'm taking you to see Balgrim. He's the head Druid of this place. If anyone would know what to do about those creatures, it'll be *him*," Ed replied over his shoulder as we walked, causing my Mom to chuckle through her nostrils subtly.

This should be fun, she sent with a wry tone. *Is he the one you were looking for?* Ysevel asked with a raised eyebrow. *Yep, and if that* fuck knuckle *has risen to the ranks of Head Druid, this meeting is* not *going to go smoothly,* Mom sent back with a heavy sigh, letting us all know the two of them had history.

Ed led us to a large, double doorway with various runes etched into the stonework that lit up as we approached. "Listen, he's old, cranky, and doesn't get along well with people, so just try to be patient with him," he cautioned just before opening the door. "I think we'll be alright," Mom grinned, gesturing for him to push the doors open.

As we entered, we found an incredible amount of equipment strewn about the large room. In the center, there was a vast table with more equipment and a handful of scrolls messily laid about, while many of the glass phials contained strange, fuming liquids. The room, only illuminated by the glowing mana stones embedded in the walls, felt much *smaller* than it appeared.

"Balgrim, are you in here?" Ed called out, but as soon as he did, we heard a rustling of metallic parts and a grunt of pain. "Damn you, Edryd. How many times do I have to tell you not to come in if the runes on the door light up?" Balgrim's grouchy voice snarled from beneath a pile of metallic arms.

"Well, you have visitors, so get out here already, you cranky old *bastard*," Mom called out, bringing an immediate halt to the rustling. "*Oh,* fuck no. No, no, no. It can't be..." Balgrim muttered in a panic, immediately revealing himself from beneath the pile.

He was covered in a slick, dark substance from head to toe, though his thick forearms and hands held scars that could be seen even beneath the dim light of the laboratory. *He doesn't look like a druid,* I sent Mom with an awkward glance. *Dwarves have a different use for the word, but he's still extremely powerful when it comes to mana manipulation, so don't underestimate him,* she replied, still observing the grimy old dwarf as he tried to compose himself.

"Hello, Balgrim. It's been a while," she said pleasantly, trying to maintain some form of diplomacy. "Not long enough for the likes of you, but I know you wouldn't come back here without a good reason, much less drag around companions that haven't seen too many winters. So, go on then; out with it," he huffed, causing her to chuckle at his frustration.

"I suppose I should have *expected* that kind of welcome, but as you wish. We're here to warn you that creatures are invading your lands, unlike any you've ever seen," she began, gesturing for me to approach with Grond's head. "*The fuck* you mean I've never seen these creatures before? Do you have any idea how ma-..." he trailed off as soon as I unfurled the bag's brim to reveal the head.

"By the earth between my toes, what the fuck are you doing walking around with *that*? Better yet, *how* are you walking around with that?" Balgrim asked with visible astonishment. "So, you *don't* know what they are," I said, raising an eyebrow at him. "N-No, lad. Well, at least, not really," he stammered after blinking a handful of times. Ed moved beside me after noticing Balgrim's reaction to the head I presented to him, and I could tell he was just as stumped as the grouchy dwarf.

"D-Did *you* kill that thing?" he asked, darting his eyes between me and the head. "Not this one, but there are likely hundreds, if not *thousands*, more on the way. We found a scouting party on our way here, but we suspect that wasn't the only one," I said, shifting my gaze from Ed to Balgrim to see if he knew more than he was letting on.

Mom must have seen what I was trying to do and stepped forward to get his attention again. "Balgrim, we need to know if you've seen anything *strange* happening here on the Isles. It could help us *save* your people," she said, using a much more pleading tone than before. "You said that *last time*, Siraye," he scoffed. "I promise, *this time* will be different," she continued in a similar tone as before. "You said *that* last time, too," he sighed and shook his head.

There was a silence between us as he paused to consider her offer. He ran his thick fingers through his beard in an upward direction to scruff it up, then patted it back down quickly before turning to look at the rest of us. "You swear on Taegin's life?" he asked, making me blanche at his casual use of the name. Ed looked at me with visible confusion, almost as if he suspected I already knew who that was.

"I do, and you know I wouldn't do that if I didn't mean it," she nodded gravely, prompting him to sigh and scratch the back of his head. "I know, and *that's* what worries me. Fine. Get some rest; you've done enough in killing that scouting party, but *I* still need to think about how I'm going to present this to the king. Ed, take them to the guest rooms. We'll discuss this later," he said with a dismissive wave.

"*Oh*, and leave those bags, will you? I don't need you *terrorizing* the place with them. Your presence *alone* would be enough to do that," he called out as we turned to leave. Athar and I brought the bags over to him as requested, but I noticed something was different about him than it had been just a few moments ago.

"Here you are," I said with a warm smile, doing my best not to wear my thoughts on my face. "Thank ye, lad," he said in a much more casual tone as he snatched the bags out of our hands.

As we turned to walk away, I felt a cold chill go down my spine that I couldn't explain, but I knew I wasn't the only one who felt that. "*Something's off*," Athar's alternate whispered while he gave me a serious glance. I gave him a nod to let him know that I'd noticed it, too, but I knew that it wasn't the right time to talk about it.

"Come on, Thoma. I'll lead you guys to where you'll be staying," Ed said, gesturing for us to follow him again. We went down the same halls as before, but instead of going to the main hall again, we turned right and then took another turn, and went up a wide set of stairs.

Just beyond the handrails, I could see countless paintings of both dwarves and strange mechanisms that I couldn't identify. I slowed my ascent just enough to look at one of the paintings, thinking the face was somewhat similar to Meliss.

"*Ah*, there's a pretty good story about that," Ed patted me on the shoulder, gesturing to the painting shortly after. "Yeah, I bet there is," I scoffed in disbelief, trying to figure it out on my own. *You know she's been staring at you this whole time, right?* Ysevel sent with a loose chuckle. *She can stare all she wants,* I sent back with a mental chuckle and a careless tone.

I know, but just remember: you're going to have to talk to her at some point about what happened. If not for your sake, then for hers, Ysevel said. I was grateful she could read every emotion in my core, and that I could read hers, because I knew that we were both confident enough in our relationship to allow that conversation to happen.

She didn't think about my sake *when she sent that letter, did she?* I sent half-jokingly, causing her to chuckle. *No, I guess she didn't,* she sent with a hint of bitterness. It was the first time I'd ever *actually* felt her feel any sort of resentment toward Meliss, but I kept it to myself.

I still want that zuresh *to pay for what she did to you,* Kalia jumped into the conversation, getting a sense of agreement from my mother. *She wouldn't last the time it took me to* blink *if* you *were the one to do it. Besides, Ed seems happy with her,* I sent back, doing my best not to show the grin trying to creep onto my face.

As we continued down the hall at the top of the stairway, Ed showed Mom and the others to their rooms, though he gave Irun a distrustful look when he passed. Irun didn't seem to pay it much mind, but I could tell *that* would be an interesting conversation to have.

Finally, Ed and Meliss led Ysevel and I to our room, which had a large bed big enough for the two of us, and a vast window that overlooked the glowing city below. The bed was furnished with a fine set of dark, turquoise covers and sheets that complemented the light from the large mana stone in the ceiling.

"You have to turn this little thing to turn it off," he said, twisting a small, circular device on the wall that immediately dimmed the light. "It's like an oversized lantern," I chuckled, staring up at the ceiling as the room darkened.

There was a pause between us, and I knew Ed had a lot of questions to ask me, but then again, so did *I*. "So, *uh*, I guess we'll see you tomorrow?" Ed asked awkwardly. "Sit down, Ed. If I know you, you're not going to rest until you get rid of that question that's been dragging your tongue out of your mouth," I smiled, gesturing to a long sofa near the foot of the bed.

"H-How did you know?" he asked nervously, scratching the back of his head. "It was a lucky guess," I shrugged, gesturing for him to sit. "You too, Meliss," Ysevel added warmly, though I could tell Meliss was nervous about being in her presence. Seeing the two of them sitting side by side made me realize just how much more beautiful Ysevel was, but, obviously, I wasn't about to say that *aloud*.

"So, h-how was Caegwen?" Ed asked awkwardly, rubbing his hands together. "It was *interesting*, to say the least, but why are you acting all weird?" I asked, punching him in the shoulder with a chuckle. "Well, it's just. *Ah*, I can't explain it. You seem *different*, somehow," he said with a furrowed brow. "I mean, we *did* go through quite a bit," I shrugged, nodding toward Ysevel.

"S-Sorry, I've just realized I never introduced myself. I'm Edryd Baelis, Thoma's former roommate in Codrean," he said, performing a proper elven greeting he must have learned from Thorn and Ren, since Nenvalur wasn't one for formalities. "Ysevel Phrys, Thoma's *current* roommate," she chuckled, prompting both him *and* Meliss to widen their eyes.

"P-Phrys? Like, *Elven King Elhael Phrys*?" Ed asked as the blood drained from his face. "*Mh-hmm!*" she replied with a cheerful nod. Ed slumped in his seat, scoffed, and shook his head. "What, and I cannot stress this enough, *the fuck*?" he said between chuckles. "I apologize for my demeanor, Your Highness, but it's just not every day I have to interact with royalty," Ed said dejectedly.

"*Oh*, it's alright. I've had to deal with Athar and Irun for a long time now, so I'm used to it. Besides, I don't like formalities *either*," she said, giving him a warm smile. "I was going to ask about that, actually. Why the *fuck* is Irun with you?" he asked, turning to face me. "It's kind of a long story," I said, averting my eyes and scratching the back of my head with a chuckle. "Good thing I've got *plenty* of time, then," he said.

I gave Ysevel a quick glance to ask whether I should tell him everything or just enough to satisfy him for now, to which I got a response in my core to the latter. *You already know that won't be enough,* I sent with a mental chuckle. *You're right, but we don't know how much we can say right now, especially not after that chill down your spine when we were with Balgrim,* she cautioned, but I knew she was right.

I went on to loosely explain how it all happened, leaving out the part of my unsealed core, our training with Kalia, and the fact that the Undergod was actually my ancestor. I also left out the fact that Ardrin was my uncle, but I already knew that questions about my family would come up sooner or later.

As I told the two of them our story, Ysevel chimed in with bits of information as well, causing Ed and Meliss to stare at us in both awe and a slight hint of worry. "We're fine, now, of course, but it *definitely* wasn't easy," I said, finishing our recapitulation with a shrug.

"Gods above and below, I had no idea things were that intense, but I guess that explains the changes in your behavior," Ed said, slumping back into his portion of the sofa. "To an extent, yeah. What about you two? How did *that* happen?" I asked, gesturing between him and Meliss, who lowered her head just subtly enough for me to notice.

"W-Well, after you left, the Master told Thorn, Ren, and I to help train her. We spent a lot of time together, and... well, I think I should let *her* explain the rest," he said, gesturing for Meliss to continue.

She looked at me, then Ysevel, and immediately lowered her head for a moment as if she were embarrassed by whatever she was about to say. "It's alright, Meliss. Go ahead," Ysevel said, placing a hand on her shoulder gently. "It's *not*, but thank ye," Meliss replied with a weak smile that immediately faded as she shifted into a pensive stare.

"After you left, I spent a lot of time asking Ren and Thorn everything they knew about dwarves, but even *their* knowledge was somewhat limited. I knew that if I was going to find out the truth of why I was in Coltend to begin with, I had to come *here*," she gestured around the room momentarily before chuckling to herself.

"I didn't know it at the time, but according to a few of the records here, my father was, in fact, a *very* influential person here. I knew Ma was human, but I never would have expected her to have fallen in love with a dwarf," she scoffed and shook her head. "What do you mean?" I asked, raising an eyebrow.

"See, dwarves aren't allowed to marry humans; it's got something to do with keeping the purity of their bloodlines, but I never really understood why until I came here. Their rulers have to be of direct dwarven descent, but it's not only restricted to royal bloodlines," she began, getting up from her seat and walking toward the window.

"Which means *anyone* could potentially become the ruler?" I asked, making sure I'd understood that correctly. "Yes. I didn't know it back then, but my grandfather was the ruler at the time, and when he found out Pa had fallen in love with her, they were forced to flee the Isles," she continued without turning around.

"What happened to them? They must have made it off the Isles, right?" I asked, but only got a shake of her head in response. "Not quite. You see, Pa was a druid, much like Balgrim, though arguably *more likable*, which meant he was constantly being watched to make sure he didn't try to destroy the country. Ma was a trader who'd often have tomes to sell him whenever she came to the Isles," she continued, turning to face us again with tears welling in her eyes.

"When they tried to leave on her ship, the guards at the docks recognized him and forced him to stay behind, telling her never to come back," she said, using the back of her hand to wipe away a tear as she sat back down. "I thought you said he *died*," I noted, but instead of disagreeing, she nodded in agreement.

"He did, but not when I thought. He was sent on a mission to investigate some strange sources of mana that had begun spawning around the Isles," she said, catching me off balance. "Wait, when did *that* happen?" I asked, giving Ysevel a knowing look. "It was about a week before we arrived," Meliss said, confirming my suspicions.

Which means that happened roughly around the time we were dragged down to Vareluth with Irun, I realized, but there was still a piece of the puzzle that didn't make sense to me. *What if Mideia thought Nexis was going to win and began his invasion early?* Ysevel asked. *It seems likely, but would someone that powerful* really *make that kind of mistake?* I sent back, but she didn't seem to have an answer either.

"Damn it. I'm sorry, Meliss. I had no idea," I said, trying my best to be empathetic. "It's fine. I just wish I could've gotten to know him before the end, but I suppose I can't miss what I've never had. I was just glad to have Ed with me when I was going through that," she continued, giving him a warm smile.

When I saw him return the smile, a part of me was still shocked to see them together, but now that I'd heard her explanation, I realized it wasn't much different from my own with Ysevel. It also made me realize that the resentment I had felt when I first saw them together was *only slightly* misplaced.

"Well, I'm glad you had each other," Ysevel said, having understood the same thing I had. "Thank ye," she replied solemnly, letting the conversation hang for a few moments.

"Have there been any other instances of those sources showing up lately?" I asked, breaking the silence. "Some of the other druids here are going to investigate another one tomorrow. Since you guys are here, I think it might be good to have you go with them in case more of those creatures show up," Ed replied, but seemingly held back something else he wanted to say.

"Go on, spit it out," I groaned, knowing he liked to ask as many questions as I did. "Well, speaking of the others, who's the other elf with you guys?" he asked bashfully, prompting me to chuckle. "Why? Did you think she was *pretty*?" I asked sarcastically, prompting him to blush.

"I-I didn't mean it like *that*," he raised his hands placatingly, more to prevent Meliss's wrath than anything else. "She's the commander of the Caegweni guard. She came instead of Bernar, who's still helping with some stuff over there," I said loosely, carefully dancing around the fact that she was my mother. "*Ah*, I see. What of the other two? The ones with the full sets of armor," he said, putting a finger on his chin.

"They're elves as well, but they've taken a vow of silence until their mission is completed," I said tactfully, nearly getting a chuckle out of Ysevel as a result. "Well, if they're the kinds of people you've been training with, I'd love to see how strong you've gotten lately," he said with a wry grin. "If we go on that mission with the rest of the druids tomorrow, hopefully you'll catch a glimpse," I said, returning the smirk and clasping his forearm.

"Well, I think that's enough for one day. You guys must be tired, right?" Meliss asked, getting a nod from Ysevel and I in return. "I see. Well, the shower's over there and there are fresh clothes laid out for you on the countertop," she gestured toward the bathroom, prompting Ysevel to grow restless at the thought of being clean again.

"It was nice to catch up for a bit. I guess we'll see you tomorrow, then?" Ed asked, giving Ysevel a proper bow as he rose from his seat and prompting Meliss to do the same. "See you tomorrow," we said graciously, returning the bow, causing Ed to give me an awkward glance before turning to leave.

I think Ed's a nice person, Ysevel sent as they waved at us from the door. *Yeah, and if she hurts him, I might just let Kalia and Mom have a go at her,* I returned with a chuckle, getting an elbow to the ribs in response. *As much as I don't want to agree with you, I don't think*

I would even try to stop them at that point, she relented with a sigh before making her way to the bathroom.

"Coming?" she asked playfully, unlacing the tops of her armor and letting them drop to the floor. "Absolutely," I replied, almost before she could even finish her question.

CHAPTER 84
BETWEEN THE LINES

In the Erebor forest training ground just outside of Myrdin, Nenvalur's eyes widened as he was forced to sidestep away from Thorsen's blade aimed at the crown of his head.

"You're getting faster," he noted with a wry grin before kicking the giant's legs and sending him crashing into the ground. As Thorsen landed, Gwili moved in for a strike of his own, but the force of his blade was met with the immovable object that was Nenvalur's blade. The shockwave that their blades produced sent bits of the training ground soaring away from the spherical wave.

"And *you're* getting stronger," Nenvalur noted with a cheeky grin as Gwili was seemingly suspended in mid-air. "You can thank Lord Erumon for that," Gwili noted wryly before pushing off the blade to regain his footing, which allowed Thorsen a moment to get to his feet. "I still don't understand how your minds can keep up with that kind of speed," he noted as he dusted himself off, causing Nenvalur to chuckle.

"That's because you're still *thinking* about what your body is doing," he noted, prompting both Gwili and Thorsen to tilt their heads. "When you've trained enough, eventually the only things you'll think about are the best ways to exploit your enemies' weaknesses, rather than what attack you should do," Nenvalur explained.

"Not *everyone* gets to live as long as an elf," Thorsen shook his head disappointedly. "That's fair, but giants still live a long time, right? It might not take as long as you think, since you've been training for most of your life," Nenvalur said with a nod. Thorsen acknowledged his words with a similar nod.

I'll probably never reach his *level, though,* he thought momentarily.

"Still, those pearls Lord Erumon gave us really *are* something, aren't they?" Gwili said in an attempt to change the subject after noticing his friend's dour expression. "They're impressive, that much is certain. I wonder if this is how Thoma felt during his training when he was younger," Thorsen added. "Not quite," Bernar said from a short distance as he approached with Anwill and Leona.

"What do you mean by that?" Thorsen asked with a raised eyebrow. "Thoma had a seal placed on his core when he was younger. He spent most of his life until coming here to train being severely handicapped. It's a wonder he made it as far as he had, to be honest," Bernar shrugged, causing Thorsen and Gwili to glance at each other with concerned looks.

"Even with the seal, however, he always seemed to have a way with mana that even *I* had a hard time comprehending, but with Kalia's training, I'm sure he's almost as strong as I am now," he continued with a chuckle.

"After your displays in Harut, I find that hard to believe," Leona chuckled, prompting Bernar to smile nervously and rub the back of his head. "Well, about that..." he trailed off, causing Nenvalur to raise an eyebrow. "What kind of *display*?" he asked with visible curiosity.

"I fought over two hundred of Harut's finest; made quite the mess, too," Bernar grinned. "*Oh*, and *I* wasn't invited? That was rude, *cousin*," Nenvalur huffed, prompting the others to chuckle.

Cousin? Leona's eyes widened, glancing back and forth between them. *Distantly related, but yes, Nenvalur, Thorn, and Ren are my cousins,* Bernar sent back immediately, making Leona blink a handful of times. *I-I had no idea your family roots ran that deeply,* she sent with mild shock in her tone.

"Not many do, but since you're Bernar's lover, that makes *us* practically family, too," Nenvalur said with a brighter smile than he'd ever shown before.

"I feel left out," Gwili sighed quietly, leaning in toward Thorsen, who simply nodded his head. "You've known me since I was young, you're like an older brother to me," Bernar said placatingly, tilting his head as he shrugged. "Doesn't count when you were basically *forced* to come here," Gwili pouted.

"There, there, friend," Thorsen began, placing his large hand on Gwili's shoulder. "We're brothers in arms, and that's all that matters to me," he said, giving the much smaller elf a shake. "Thank you, Thorsen," Gwili said with a half-chuckle and a nod. "In any case, we need to get back to training. Ren said he was going to teach me something, but it seems he's running late," Leona glanced around the training area for any sign of him.

"No, I'm not," Ren said from just behind her as she reeled in surprise. "What the...? How did you get here so fast?" she asked, placing a hand to her chest to still her racing heart. "It's a technique I learned from Kalia. Apparently, Thoma and Ysevel have already mastered it, but I'm still getting the hang of it," he said with a small amount of dejection.

"They've *already mastered* it? But how is that even possible when you've only just learned it?" Leona asked, glancing at the others for an answer. Anwill and Bernar exchanged a momentary glance as if deciding whether to explain what they'd learned from Thoma.

"The only way that I can explain this to where it makes any sense, since even *I* still have a hard time understanding how it worked, is that the hegraphenian sage known as Sabura created a dome that altered the flow of time for them," Anwill began, pinching the bridge of his nose as if it pained him to even think about it.

"W-What?" Leona asked breathlessly. "Wait, that would mean..." she trailed off, considering the ramifications of what she'd just heard. "What he's trying to say is that Thoma, Ysevel, Irun, and Athar spent roughly *ten years* training with Kalia," Bernar said bluntly, knowing it would be much easier to tell her directly.

Her eyes widened in surprise as she took a few steps back and shook her head. "N-No, that's not..." she muttered. "Unfortunately for *both of us*, it is. While he's *technically* older than I am now, he doesn't have as much life experience," Bernar chuckled, but between him and the others, only Nenvalur laughed. "I thought he looked a lot stronger than last time," he said playfully as he shook his head.

"R-Right, he certainly looked and *moved* differently than before, but I had no idea that he'd undergone such intense training," Leona said nervously. "All the more reason *we* need to catch up to them," Ren suggested playfully, getting a nod from Leona as a result, though it was clear she was still in shock.

I think she handled that rather well, don't you? Anwill sent Bernar as Ren led Leona a short distance away from the group and began to explain what he wanted her to do. *It's not every day you find out someone's aged a decade in roughly two months, but yeah, I think she did,* Bernar shrugged, still observing her to make sure she was following Ren's directions properly.

Ren and Leona moved to the middle of the training ground, where Thorsen, Gwili, and Nenvalur's fight had just taken place, and signaled for Anwill to create the targets they would use for their exercise. With a wave of his hand, the mana flowed out from him into the nearby trees and ground, spawning wooden, humanoid targets firmly secured by the mana-packed earth at their bases.

"Alright, like I said, you have to hit at least *one* target from behind, one from the side, and one from above," Ren raised a hand and gestured to each one he wanted her to hit. "But I've only just been able to make a dagger recently. I don't know if I can do that," she said with a slight worry in her tone. "I know, but Kalia gave me some instructions after having taught Thoma and Ysevel," he said with a wry grin.

He got direct instruction from her? I wonder if they were always in communication somehow, Leona wondered momentarily. "No, but like other Wraithborn, we can share our experiences through our cores, allowing us greater insight into our abilities much more quickly," Ren said with a chuckle. "*Huh,* I guess that explains how the two of them were able to master that ability so quickly," she replied, putting a single finger to her chin pensively.

"I wouldn't be too sure about that, since according to Thoma, she prefers a much more *practical* approach to training," he said, prompting her to raise an eyebrow. "So, she wanted them to figure out the power for themselves, correct?" she asked, getting a nod of agreement from Ren. "Then why did she share it with you so freely?" she asked. "She didn't, initially, but just before she and the others left, she allowed me only a small *hint* of what I would need to learn the *odoruki* technique, as she called it," he replied with a shrug.

I guess that hint alone was enough, Leona thought, immediately recalling the surprised gasp she gave when he appeared behind her.

"But enough about that. You've had some lessons with Aurae, but I'm here to help you refine any mistakes you make. Go on then, give it a try," Ren said encouragingly, gesturing to the humanoid targets a few dozen meters away.

Leona planted her feet just as Gwili and Thorsen had taught her to when she first began to use Ethereal mana and *sent her consciousness to draw from the Wraith Realm*. Within a few moments, the familiar scarlet mana began to envelop her hand in the real, forming an imperfect, but solid dagger. "Excellent, now, try to hit that one on the right," Ren said encouragingly, but could see Leona's face visibly twisting to maintain her concentration.

She raised her arm over her shoulder and threw it with as much force as she could muster. The dagger soared through the air momentarily, but fizzled out into a small cloud of mana a few meters away from her, prompting her to click her tongue frustratedly.

"It's the same thing every time. Every time I've tried to throw it, it disappears into thin air like it never existed in the first place," she said with a heavy sigh. "I still don't understand what I'm doing wrong," she continued, but noticed Ren was regarding her curiously.

"I think I might know who can help explain my thoughts a little better," he said, closing his eyes for a moment, as though he were trying to communicate with someone.

What is he doing? Leona thought, observing him curiously as she felt the Wraith mana permeating the air around them. A few minutes of silence went by, but during that time, Ren repeatedly nodded his head in understanding, eventually reopening his eyes to look at Leona with satisfaction. "What did you do?" she asked expectantly. "I asked Thoma and Ysevel for help," he grinned wryly, prompting her to raise an eyebrow in surprise.

I've never seen him smile before, she realized.

"Y-You did? But they should be on the Gramm Isles by now," she asked, astonishedly. "When you reach a higher stage of mana, you'll be able to as well," he smiled thinly. "Well, what did they say?" she asked, growing anxious to hear her new set of instructions.

"You've been close to dying before, right?" Ren asked bluntly, causing her to blink a few times in surprise. "Y-Yes? Most recently in Harut when I got stabbed in the back," she replied with no small amount of confusion in her tone and features. "Do you remember what it felt like?" he asked. "Aurae's already asked me that question, but yes," she replied again, still unsure of where Ren was taking the conversation.

"Good. Then this will be easy. Thorn!" he called out over his shoulder, lacing his voice with mana. "He's back at the palace," Gwili replied, but quickly ate his words when a spark of gray mana suddenly appeared before him, and with it, Thorn, which caused Gwili to fall flat on his ass.

"W-What the *fuck*? A little warning would have been nice," Gwili shouted frustratedly as he rubbed his backside. "He gave you one when he called my name," Thorn said cheekily, but it was clear that this was the first time anyone else had ever seen him do that.

Leona, of course, was the most surprised that he could do that from such a distance. "H-How?" she asked, struggling to find any other words. "My apologies for startling you, Leona, but that ability is something Ren and I have developed over the last century together. The time it would take me to explain it would force us to be here well into the late hours of the night," Thorn said with a bright smile.

"So, you need my help? You've already asked the others, right?" Thorn directed the question to Ren. "I did, but both Thoma and Ysevel think it would be easier to explain if you *showed* her," he replied with a shrug. "*Ah,* I see. Very well then. Leona, please produce another dagger like the one you just had, but don't throw it yet," he said, earning him a confused look.

"Trust us," Ren said warmly, putting a hand on her shoulder and giving her a nod of confidence. She did as instructed and produced yet another imperfect dagger, causing Thorn to lean in and inspect it closely. "*Ah,* I see the problem here," he said after a few moments, leaving Leona that much more confused. "What do you mean? Are you able to wield Wraith mana, as well?" she asked, trying to figure out what was happening.

"It wouldn't matter if I did. I've spent most of my life honing my skills in Rivet mana, but the principles for one type of mana are similar to the others," he began, conjuring a small dagger of his own. It was a smooth, gray dagger of pure rivet mana identical to the one Leona had in her hand, though it lacked any sort of imperfection.

"Watch carefully," he said, bringing his dagger near hers, causing the emanating Wraith mana to begin pulling toward his dagger gently. Her eyes widened in astonishment as she observed the scarlet tendrils starting to flow toward his dagger. "How is this possible?" she asked, feeling the weapon in her hand begin to be drawn toward it once the other tendrils had fully enveloped his dagger.

"All mana, regardless of what realm you draw it from, links to one another. It's how a fourth-stage Ethereal user can wield other types of mana to the same degree. However, Wraith mana is slightly different in that it resides in the spaces between life and death, as I'm sure you've already heard explained to you," Thorn began, glancing at her to make sure she was following along.

"But what does this have to do with controlling it at a distance?" she asked, causing Thorn to chuckle lightly as her dagger dissipated. "Have you ever considered that those lines between life and death don't *only* exist in your immediate vicinity?" he asked with a raised eyebrow. "*You* saw that my dagger was drawing tendrils of *your* mana toward it. What *I* saw was your mana *reaching out* to mine," he said with a smile.

"Look for the lines between you and your target. It was created with mana, after all, and if Gwili and Thorsen have taught you how to use Ethereal mana correctly, you'd know that *all things* have mana in them. The target Anwill has so graciously created should allow you to see it *much more* clearly," he continued, holding the same expression as he gestured toward the one on the right.

As she turned to look in the indicated direction, she sighed curtly and began to chuckle in disbelief. "Focus, love," Bernar said, having approached during Thorn's explanation. "I know you can do it," he said encouragingly, standing a few meters away from her, accompanied by Anwill and the others just behind him. "No pressure," she chuckled, but did as Bernar instructed.

She closed her eyes again and *drew once more from the Wraith realm, pulling the mana to her between the lines of life and death.* When she reopened her eyes, she found the dagger was emanating the excess mana just as before. "Remember the feeling from Harut, and look *between* the lines," Ren reminded her gently as he took a step back.

How am I supposed to feel that again? Leona asked herself briefly.

She thought back on the fight between her and Zari, and did her best to recall the memories with as much detail as she could. Without realizing it, her heart began to race as the final moments of the battle took place in her mind. As the memories ran through her mind, her vision began to blur like it had in the moments after she'd been stabbed.

Wait, something is *different,* she noticed, seeing the world around her blur momentarily as it would in the Wraith realm.

Focusing on that sensation, she *drew more mana from the realm and* pushed it into her dagger, causing the tendrils to flare, and the lines between her and her target to become more pronounced. "I-I can see them," she said, disbelieving her own eyes. "Ren, give her a hand, would you?" Thorn asked with a wry grin, prompting the dark-haired elf to step behind her and put his hand in the middle of her back to align himself with her core.

"This is going to feel weird, but it will help," he said softly before pushing his mana into her core, allowing her to see his memories and those from Thoma and Ysevel when they were learning this process from Kalia. As the flood of information entered her mind, her breath faltered momentarily, causing Bernar to take a step forward. "I'm alright," she said, holding up a hand to stop him. "It's just... a lot," she shook her head in a desperate attempt to regain her concentration.

"Try to align what you're seeing in their memories to what you're seeing in front of you," Ren said calmly, maintaining his flow of mana. "It's a bit hard to focus," she admitted. "I know, but that's the point," he replied light-heartedly.

Taking a deep breath and doing her best to compartmentalize what she was seeing both in her mind and in front of her, the lines between her and her target steadily grew stronger. "They're growing thicker," she noted, getting a wordless nod from Ren that she felt pass through this newfound connection. She gripped the dagger a little more tightly and prepared to throw it.

Her shoulder muscles tensed as her dagger began to cut through the air, eventually relaxing when it was released along one of the lines leading to the target. The imperfect dagger soared through the air, following the path she'd sent it on in her mind, and as it struck the target, it embedded itself firmly within what would be its ribcage.

"I-It didn't disappear this time?" she asked as much to herself as the others. "No. No, it didn't," Bernar said with an air of pride in his voice when she turned to look at him, causing her to burst out laughing in excitement at her accomplishment. "I'm so proud of you!" he said, rushing over to her and wrapping his arms around her, which, given her lack of focus, caused the dagger to disappear.

"Well done, Leona," Thorn said proudly over cheers and *whoops* from Gwili and Thorsen. "I couldn't have done it without your help. *Both* of your help, actually," she gave Ren a respectful bow. "I'm sorry that I almost made you lose focus, but Thorn's always been a good instructor, so I trusted his judgment when he asked me to give you a hand," Ren returned the bow, feeling the blood rush a little to his face.

When she noticed he was doing his best to remain humble, she leaned over and kissed him on the cheek, forcing him to blush an even brighter shade of red. "Thank you, Ren. I hope Bernar and I can learn much more from you and Aurae in the days to come," she said with a beaming smile that all but forced him to avert his gaze. "I-I... I just did what I could," he allowed a small smile to creep onto his face.

Oooh, he's going to remember that one, Bernar sent her jokingly, nearly causing her to giggle.

"You two won't be the only ones training. I still have to bring *these two* up to *at least* the fourth stage before Lord Erumon returns," Anwill said, jutting his thumbs out to Thorsen and Gwili, who immediately halted their cheering. "Wait, *you're* going to teach us?" Gwili asked, immediately going pale. "It's been a long time since I've had you as my pupil, Gwili. I just hope you can keep up this time," Anwill said with a wolfish grin.

"Well, then. I suppose we should keep going. We don't want to disappoint him when he returns, do we?" Leona said playfully, getting a nod of agreement from everyone except Gwili, who was still in shock at the prospect of being Anwill's pupil once more.

As the others turned to get into their positions, Leona felt a warm sensation emanating from her core. *Well done, Leona. See me when you're finished with Ren. I have something I want to teach you,* Aurae's voice resounded in her mind. *Of course, Aurae, but what do you want to teach me?* Leona asked.

Why would I spoil the surprise? Aurae asked playfully.

CHAPTER 85

HOMECOMING

As Taegin, Ardrin, Trina, and Wien made their way along the dirt path toward Valdis, Trina anxiously fidgeted with her reins as she rode beside Taegin.

You know she has a lot of questions that you're going to have to answer, right? Ardrin sent his brother with a heavy mental sigh. *Of course I do, I'm just trying to figure out the best way to present the information,* Taegin sent back immediately, prompting Ardrin to raise an eyebrow. *Don't you trust her?* Ardrin asked loosely. *I do, but whether she's ready for that information is another story entirely,* Taegin sighed, glancing at Trina momentarily as she tightened her grip around the leather reins.

"Alright then, out with it, already," Ardrin said tiredly, aiming a tired gaze at Trina, whose eyes widened in surprise. "I-I wasn't going to say anything," she stammered. "No? Then why are you constantly fidgeting? The sound is annoying, and I'd rather not be bothered with the sounds of your gauntlets constantly rattling, so say your piece and be done with it," he groaned, causing Trina's brow to furrow in concentration.

"That was a bit rude, brother," Taegin muttered, prompting Ardrin to shrug. "I just want to move things along so we don't have to have a drawn-out discussion when we reach Valdis," he said with an upturned lip as if he'd done nothing wrong. "It's fine, Taegin. I hate to admit it, but he's right," Trina replied defeatedly.

"Well, go on then. What questions do you have?" Taegin asked, allowing a thin smile to show. "For starters, where in *helvete* have you been all this time?" she asked, briefly glancing at Ardrin to see whether he was going to make another snide remark. "In Codrean. I've been the Master Synner there for quite some time, now," Taegin replied loosely.

"Were you the Master when you came to help us?" she asked. "I was, yes, but my helping your village was more of a side-quest that I just happened to be involved with," he replied with a shrug. "Then what *were* you doing here?" she raised an eyebrow in confusion. "I'd received a letter from someone in Caegwen that there were signs of one of the gifts from the gods in Hjalfar, but the trail of information I was following died out before I made any real headway," he replied dejectedly.

"What? One of the artifacts was *here*? I've only heard stories about them from Trina," Wien chimed in with visible excitement. "Yes, and *I* had it," Ardrin replied, causing the two of them to widen their eyes in astonishment. "*You* had it? W-What was it? Better yet, *where* is it now?" Trina asked, leaning forward in her seat.

"It was *taken* from me," Ardrin replied loosely. "*Ah*, that's a shame. I would have loved to see it," Trina said with visible disappointment that Wien mirrored. "I-If you don't mind me asking, sir, but which one was it?" she asked skittishly. "It was the *Nethersong Mask*," he replied coldly, causing Trina's eyes to widen once more. "That would mean..." she trailed off. "Yes, I *was* the rumored *Masked One*," Ardrin replied, maintaining his tone.

This can't be possible. I'd heard he was a cold-blooded murderer, Trina thought idly.

"That *was* his intention, you know," Taegin chimed in, catching Trina by surprise. "Don't worry, I felt the same way when he did it to me earlier," Wien muttered in support of his commanding officer. "*Oh*, I-I see," she said, letting the weight of Taegin's response hang for a moment.

"In any case, he played his role well. Almost *too well*, I might add," Taegin said with a wry grin. "Yes, but even the Undergod kept secrets from *me*. If it hadn't been for *his* guidance, we might have never made it as far as we have," Ardrin replied gravely, prompting Trina and Wien to glance at each other in confusion.

"Were these *Tyrant* and *Leech* mana types part of those secrets?" Trina asked cautiously. "Yes," Taegin replied with a grave tone, averting his gaze momentarily. "It should also go without saying that the utilization of these two types of mana is still relatively undiscovered by us, so we must proceed with caution once we reach Valdis," he continued, receiving a nod of understanding from Trina and Wien as they spurred their horses onward.

As they moved along the trail that led deep into the mountains, they discovered several more traces of the strange mana, prompting Ardrin and Taegin's concerns to become more solidified. After nearly a week of traveling, the four arrived at the entrance to the valley that would ultimately lead to Valdis.

The snow-capped mountains of the frigid north made it difficult for the trail to be followed, but Ardrin knew his way around the region even better than local hunters. The Rhydian Pass was well known to be perilous, but it was also home to rare species of animals that hunters found great value in using their materials for weapons, armor, or making money off the sales of their hides or scales.

Only the most adventurous of these hunters would ever dare tread foot in the region, and not all of them would make it out alive.

"We're nearly there. Once we round this boulder, I'll lower the protective barrier I put up so we can cross without much issue," Ardrin noted, pointing with a free hand to a massive boulder that nearly blocked the entirety of the Pass. "Thank the gods. I can't feel my fingers. It will be nice to be out of this damned wind for once," Wien muttered to himself.

Brother, up ahead, Taegin sent Ardrin after sensing a trace of Leech mana present in the wind, prompting his brother to enhance his senses even further. "That's..." Ardrin trailed off, urging his horse to break into a gallop toward the boulder. "What's the matter?" Trina asked, urging Wien to spur his horse to follow the twins. "It seems the barrier has been breached," Taegin said over his shoulder, causing Trina and Wien to begin worrying.

As they circumvented the boulder, the dark citadel could be seen just a few kilometers ahead, nestled deep within a valley. Its violet glow seemed dim and wavering, much unlike how Ardrin had initially left it. "That's not a good sign, is it?" Wien noted, seeing the fluctuation of violet light emanating from the highest tower of the citadel. "No, it's not. We need to hurry," Ardrin urged, spurring his horse once more.

As they approached, they noticed there were signs of a battle near the bridge's entrance, with hundreds, if not *thousands*, of bodies all mangled and torn. The smell was almost enough to make Wien vomit, but Trina could only put a gauntlet up to her nose in a feeble attempt to block out the stench.

"*Fy faen i helvete,* what happened here?" she spat, struggling to keep what little food she had in her stomach where it belonged. "*They were here,*" Ardrin told Taegin, who nodded in confirmation upon examining a pile of bodies. "It seems many of these creatures were closer to being *butchered* rather than simply slaughtered," Taegin noted, realizing many of the fallen creatures were primarily missing their legs.

"Wait, you're saying this place was attacked by a creature intelligent enough to do that? What sort of madness is this?" Trina asked with natural disbelief. "Yes, but they're not native to this realm," Ardrin said, standing imperiously near a pile of bodies. Noticing a head that hadn't belonged to his former horde, he severed it from its enlarged body and held it aloft for the others to see.

"These creatures are known as Thran. They're hunters by nature and have a lot of pride in what they can accomplish with just a few traps. They *also* love eating other creatures they deem weaker than they are," Ardrin explained, though Wien was unable to keep his lunch in any longer when he saw the head's rotten cheek slide off its face.

Ardrin discarded the head back into the pile of corpses and began making his way across the bridge with Taegin. Trina and Wien, not knowing what else to do, followed quickly behind. "Here, clean yourself up," she said, handing her sergeant a small handkerchief. "Thank you," he managed weakly, doing his best to keep up with the others.

While there were more bodies scattered along the bridge of glicks, daemons, trolls, and other such creatures, it was what they saw when the great black doors opened that surprised them the most. At the far end of the hall, Karak lay motionless with a spear far too large for him to wield stuck in his gut, pinning him to the stairs before an empty throne.

"Karak!" Ardrin called out, surprising the others. "I-Is that what I think it is?" Trina asked quietly, as she and the others followed behind Ardrin. "That's a story for another time, but yes," Taegin replied, nearly vanishing from sight with how quickly he moved toward his brother's side.

"M-My lord, you've returned..." Karak managed weakly, coughing up a mouthful of blackened blood that dripped down the sides of his grotesque features. "Hush now, old friend. I'm going to help you, but I need to remove this spear first," Ardrin said, grabbing the haft of the large spear. "I'll help with that; you focus on closing the wound when it's out. Ready?" Taegin said urgently, creating a large, smoky hand that hardly reflected the citadel's violet hue.

He wrapped the fingers of this hand around the haft of the spear and nodded to his brother that he was ready to remove it. Wordlessly, Ardrin replied, and within the time it took to blink, the spear was pulled from Karak's torso and clattered to the ground like the sound of a fallen, young tree. Ardrin immediately poured a vast amount of Vexing mana into the wound, doing his best to seal it shut.

As Trina and Wien watched with unabated curiosity, the wound sewed itself shut, and the life in Karak's dark eyes returned with a deep gasp of air. "T-Thank you, my lord," Karak said, still weak from the ordeal as he tried to sit up. "There's no need to greet me formally, just tell me what happened here," Ardrin said urgently.

If my master brought them here with him, then I suppose I shouldn't be wary of them, Karak thought momentarily as he glanced at the other three. "Of course, my lord. The Thran rained down from the heavens shortly after you left Valdis. I never would have thought *any* magic would make it through your barrier. Still, by the time I noticed them, they'd already numbered in the hundreds. They even tried to control *me* with a strange device that reminded me of the one we used to control the horde," Karak began, doing his best to recount the situation, but Ardrin's look of surprise wasn't one he'd ever seen before.

"M-My lord?" Karak asked when he noticed a blank and frightened stare on Ardrin's face. "That *bastard,*" Ardrin seethed, causing everyone, save Taegin, to become even more confused than before. "He made his move the second he believed the others were trapped, but how could he have known?" Taegin asked, breeding even more confusion amongst the others.

"What's even more concerning to *me* is that we don't know how far this invasion reaches. As for how he knew, the Thran must have noticed Thoma and the others' arrival. That's the best explanation I have. But to think they were in direct contact with *him*..." Ardrin trailed off as he shook his head dejectedly.

"I'm sorry to have left you so defenseless, old friend," he continued, turning back to Karak and helping him to his clawed feet. "I was just doing my duty, my lord, but it seems I might have failed in keeping the citadel safe," Karak wheezed, placing a claw to where the spear once was. "What do you mean?" Taegin asked with visible concern.

Karak cracked his neck and forced his body to move as he began to proceed down one of the halls, signaling for the others to follow. As they followed the daemon down the dark halls, Trina and Wien couldn't help but marvel at the construction of the citadel. "How long has this been here?" Trina wondered, running her hand along the cold, metallic wall. "Since long before the Great Partition," Ardrin noted distantly, making her jaw drop a little before wordlessly following the others.

They eventually made their way to the library, where many of the books and scrolls were scattered around the room in a disorganized manner. Some were torn, while others had little more than scraps of paper left within their bindings. Ardrin traced his eyes loosely over the room, taking in all the devastation those creatures had left in their wake.

As he lowered his head, his aura of violet mana began to surge violently, as his elongated fingernails dug deeply into the palm of his hand. "*Centuries* of knowledge; gone by the whims of these barbaric creatures," he seethed as blood from the fresh wounds began to splatter on the floor.

"Brother, what's done is done," Taegin said in a calming tone, enveloping his hand in Ethereal mana to place it on his brother's shoulder. "You don't understand. I've never cared for riches, but these books and scrolls *were* my riches. Now they've been turned into little more than *scraps* by the whims of those barbaric creatures," Ardrin snapped angrily, prompting Taegin to breathe a heavy sigh.

"I *do* understand, brother, and you *will* have your revenge on them. I promise," Taegin said with a single nod, but Ardrin could only glare at him. "Mark my words, brother; these creatures will not feel their souls leaving their bodies peacefully," Ardrin said coldly, to which Taegin could only give another nod.

"I believe you, and they *will* suffer in time, but that time is not right now. We came here for information, and we cannot maintain the upper hand without it. Is there *any* other place you can think of that might have what we came here for?" Taegin asked, glancing between his brother and Karak.

A few pensive moments of silence came over them as Ardrin paced around the disheveled library and struggled to get the torrent of emotions within him under control. "There may be *one* place I can think of, but I don't guarantee we'll find anything useful down there," Ardrin finally said. "*Down there*? What do you mean by that?" Trina asked, prompting him to turn and face her and Wien.

"Trina, I'm sure you're already aware, but the Underworld, or *Vareluth*, as it's formally known, was where the citadel once known as Pyrdredd was brought, and with it, all the knowledge it once held. Whether that knowledge still exists is something I can only hope the Undergod *hasn't* destroyed," Ardrin began, causing her to raise her eyebrows in surprise.

"You can't be suggesting we *go* there, can you?" Wien asked nervously. "Look around you, boy. Does it look like we have any other choice?" Ardrin snarled, spreading his arms widely to gesture to the disaster beneath their feet. "We've already lost a great portion of our advantage, and it would be wise of us not to let any more of it slip away," he continued, glaring at Wien, who felt a chill run down his spine.

"What *advantage* are you talking about?" Trina asked after stepping in front of Wien. "You've heard of the Church of Mideia, correct?" Taegin began, receiving a nod in response. "*That's* who we're up against; the one who did all of *this*," he gestured around the room. "The *Church* did that?" she asked with a raised eyebrow.

"*Mideia* did. He brought these creatures *from* Vareluth to do his bidding. We still haven't fully figured out what it is he wants, but we are a step ahead of him if we can gather whatever information he's looking for before his minions do," he continued gravely.

"You're saying that Mideia is *evil*? Why do we have a church based in his name, then?" she asked with visible confusion written on her face. "Because, like most other things in this realm, Trina, much of our information on what happened *before* the Great Partition has been lost. People will believe just about anything if you say it loudly and often enough," Ardrin chimed in with a scoff.

"So what? This *Mideia* is actually a god who's trying to wipe this realm from existence?" Wien asked after taking a moment to muster the courage to do so. "We're still not entirely sure of *what* he wants, but that's a good place to start," Taegin added, causing Wien to whistle critically.

"If that's the case, then we really don't have any other choice but to go see this Pyrdredd, do we?" Trina said with no small amount of worry in her tone. "Not if we want to survive the coming war," Ardrin lowered his head and tone, causing her to raise her eyebrows in shock when his aura of mana dissipated.

As soon as she understood the gravity of what he meant, she walked over to him and placed a hand on his shoulder, prompting him to look up at her. "Well then, we'd better get going. I don't want to fight in a war I know nothing about, and even less so one that I don't have any say in," she said with a single nod. "The question is:

How do we get there?" she asked, looking around the library for a device that might allow them to do so.

"Like this," Ardrin said, raising a fistful of mana and slamming it into the ground beneath the five of them, creating a swirling, violet portal that swallowed them whole.

Wien and Trina both let out screeches of fear, though it was difficult to tell which was which, since both were roughly the same pitch.

While they were falling, Trina and Wien observed their surroundings. The twilight sky filled with infinite pathways leading to unknown realms was unlike anything they'd ever seen. Her eyes began to well with tears at the beauty, while Wien's were merely filled with awe. As their bodies raced toward Vareluth, Ardrin turned to face the two of them.

"Since this is your first time leaving your realm, I must warn you: This one is nothing like anything you've seen before, and I would advise caution when dealing with the locals," he said cryptically, causing the two of them to exchange a confused look. "You're going to see a lot that you don't understand, but I promise, it will make sense in time," Taegin added, already knowing the shock the two were undergoing, as well as their most likely reactions to what was coming.

The two of them nodded in agreement, and at Ardrin's signal, they braced for impact. The five of them slammed into the ashen ground at the same time, though Ardrin, Taegin, and Karak were well prepared to land in such a brusque manner.

Both Trina and Wien landed face-first in the ashen wasteland and had the wind knocked from their lungs. "A little more warning would have been nice," Trina said, accepting the hand Taegin presented to help her to her feet. Wien, on the other hand, paused before reaching for Karak's outstretched hand. "If I wanted to *eat you*, I would have done so already," he said in a tone that might have suggested otherwise. "T-Thanks," Wien said, gingerly taking the clawed hand and allowing it to pull him to his feet quickly.

Is he reconsidering what he just said? Wien thought, realizing Karak had looked him up and down more than once.

"I'm merely checking to see if you have any other injuries," Karak said, likely knowing what the man was thinking. "R-Right. O-Of course," Wien chuckled nervously before observing his surroundings. The vast wasteland of dead trees and ashen ground held little more life to it than a burned field, but there were signs that life *was* returning to the realm.

The vast sky above them, much less gloomy than before, still held the swirling orb of pure Vexing mana, though the clouds that once surrounded it were replaced with a bright, starry sky. "I've never seen anything quite like that," Wien said breathlessly.

"After the defeat of the Undergod, the barrier that was once placed on the world was removed, allowing life to return to it. It's a slow process, but with time, this realm will return to its former glory," Ardrin noted, while Trina raised an eyebrow. "I'm just glad that the smell is gone, at least," Taegin added with a wry grin. "What happened here? Is this realm like this because of the Great Partition?" Trina asked, trying her best to understand her surroundings.

"Partly, yes, though it's primarily due to Mideia's influence. If he succeeds in his plan, you can expect *our* realm to turn out much like this one," Taegin chimed in, glancing up at the sphere of mana far above him. "With the portal we used, it should have alerted the hegraphenes that we're here," Ardrin noted, turning to his brother.

"Who would come to meet us out here?" he asked, glancing around to see if he could spot any of them from a distance. "Buruz and Krozz should be joining us soon, though they already know where we're going, given the instructions I sent along with the portal," Ardrin explained.

"What do you mean by *instructions*?" Trina asked, not bothering to hide her confusion. "When Lord Erumon, a warden of the realms, allowed us to travel freely between this realm and our own, he developed a way to send instructions to certain personnel before we even arrived. This way, it will be easier to tell who is a friend and who is here for more *nefarious* reasons," Ardrin explained, forcing Wien to shake his head in confusion.

"That was a lot of information for my uninitiated mind, but I'll take your word for it," he said, visibly trying to comprehend what he'd just heard. "Lord Erumon is much like Mideia, though he's on *our side*, if that makes it easier to understand," Ardrin said, staring down at Wien imperiously.

"So, he's a god?" he asked. "Compared to *you*, yes. In any case, we'd better get moving. I've had to create the portal out here so that *this one* would have time to get used to the Leech mana still permeating the air around the citadel," Ardrin replied with a light scoff before turning to lead the others toward Pyrdredd.

The rest of the group followed him, though Taegin and Karak were the only two who seemed genuinely unaffected by the realm.

It's been a long time since I've been here, Taegin sent his brother. *So much has changed, and yet much remains the same, it seems,* he continued, kicking up a small cloud of ashen dust beneath his feet. *With Nexis gone, this realm will begin to heal again, though I don't know how much it will be able to, given that Pyrdredd is still heavily infused with Mideia's mana,* Ardrin sent with a mental sigh.

Before Taegin could reply, Trina noticed a group of dark figures moving in the distance, silhouetted by a sickly, green glow. "Wh-What is that?" she asked Taegin, pointing in the direction of what she saw. "*That* is Pyrdredd, and if you're wondering who those figures were, I would recommend that you keep any thoughts regarding their appearances to yourselves," he replied, already able to see who was coming to greet them.

Buruz, Krozz, and Niashin approached them rapidly, though Wien could hardly believe his eyes at their speed.

I think they might rival Trina in speed, but how is the largest one moving that quickly? Wien thought, heeding Taegin's warning as best he could, since they reached them within mere moments.

"Lord Ardrin, it is good to see you well," Buruz said with a deep bow. "You as well, friend. How are things here?" Ardrin asked with a slight hint of joy hidden within the thin-lipped grin. "About as well as you might expect. Now that Nexis is dead and the barrier is gone, the realm seems to be healing, though it still has a long way to go," Buruz replied, then immediately shifted his gaze to the others he didn't recognize.

After glancing at them, he pulled Ardrin aside to discuss something briefly, while Niashin and Krozz stepped forward.

"You brought allies, Karak. Who are they?" Niashin asked flatly. "These are Lord Ardrin's allies: Trina, Wien, and Taegin," the daemon replied, gesturing to each of them. Niashin's eyes widened when they fell on Taegin. "*Egeshe krag*, is that really you? The legendary swordsman who gave *Kerre Kalia* the cut in her *kataki*?" he asked, taking a few, obviously *anxious* steps forward.

"It is, indeed," Taegin replied humbly, giving the hegraphene a low bow. "*Ah*, you don't need to bow to us. Not after what Thoma and the others did," Krozz said, taking a few steps forward and outstretched his tree-trunk-sized arm for Taegin to clasp.

"I thought that was you, Krozz. It's been so long that I hardly recognized you," Taegin said with a grin, clutching the large forearm.

"Thoma and Ysevel wouldn't shut up about you, and while they haven't been able to return, they send their regards," he continued warmly. "*Bah*, I knew they'd be too busy to come and see me, but I hope you'll remind them they're always welcome at Deathwhisper Tavern," Krozz replied. The faceplate still covered most of his features, but it was evident he was smiling brightly from the wrinkled skin near his eyes.

"I'll be sure to let them know," Taegin replied. "Come now, we've got a lot of ground to cover, though I do hope these two will quit being so shy and introduce themselves properly," Krozz said with a tilt of his head toward Trina and Wien, who were visibly astonished by the two's friendly interactions.

Th-this is fine, right? Wien asked himself before clasping the oversized forearm, trying his best to imitate Taegin and Trina's greeting.

After a brief exchange of greetings and introductions, they quickly followed behind Buruz and Ardrin. Wien, of course, struggled to keep up with the rest of them, but he was grateful the others had slowed their pace enough for him to follow.

"Do you need me to carry you?" Krozz offered in as warm a tone as he could muster. "N-No, I'll be alright. Thanks," Wien replied nervously. "Time is of the essence, Wien. Let him carry you the rest of the way so we can move more quickly," Taegin said, getting a stifled chuckle from Trina and a defeated sigh from Wien in response. "Very well, then. I apologize for the inconvenience," Wien said.

Krozz scooped him up like an adult would a small child and placed him atop his broad shoulders. "Hold on tight," Krozz said, creating two handholds just off to the side of his plume for Wien to grab onto.

This is ludicrous, he chuckled to himself before Krozz immediately picked up the pace to match Buruz's speed.

Within the hour, they'd made their way to Pyrdredd's great hall. Signs of Thoma's battle with Nexis were still visible in its thick pillars and shattered ground, though Trina could only guess as to what *truly* happened there. "I'll have to tell you the story someday. It's quite impressive what they were able to accomplish here," Niashin said, noticing her concerned look.

"I'd love to hear about it," Trina said, shaking herself out of her thoughts momentarily before following the others into the depths of the halls. "We should split up here. It will be more effective if we search for any scrolls, though, since Wien isn't allowed to use mana, I suggest he stay with Krozz," Taegin suggested with a wry grin before splitting off from the group to explore the citadel.

I'd recommend you start in his room, Ardrin noted, spawning a small orb of mana for Taegin to follow. *I appreciate the help, since I don't know my way around,* Taegin sent back, immediately turning to follow the violet orb down the halls.

Within a few moments, Taegin reached the upper levels of the citadel, doing his best to ignore the many distractions still hanging on the walls as he made his way to the room.

The small orb flashed before the large doorway that indicated he'd reached his destination, but his eyes widened when he laid his eyes on the state of the room.

It looks well lived in, but just how long has this all been here? Taegin thought, taking in even the most minor details he could observe.

His heart nearly stopped when he laid eyes on the fractured painting of Nexis. Taking a few steps forward, he looked over it carefully.

No matter how long it's been since he was cursed, I suppose his looks have *carried through his bloodline, haven't they? I wonder what Thoma must have thought when he saw this*, he asked, closing his eyes momentarily.

When he reopened them, he turned away from the painting and resumed his search for whatever notes he could find. Realizing he needed to see more than with just his eyes, he cast a spell that coated the entirety of the room in mana.

Within moments, his spell indicated that he should move toward the bedside, where a small nightstand held a drawer that was locked with a mana ward. Pushing a counterspell into it, the octagonal rings undid themselves, spinning counter to each other before finally disappearing. He pulled on the small, metallic ring, and the drawer creaked open, producing a small cloud of ashen dust as it slid on its mechanism.

Within the drawer was a miniature painting of a set of octagonal rings lined with runes, a dried-up inkwell, and a leather-bound book with silver inlaid into the ancient Elven script on its cover. "There you are," he muttered, pulling the book out and blowing on it lightly to get rid of the light coating of dust that had accumulated over the years.

He gingerly opened the book, doing his best not to damage the spine, and began to read the content written on the pages. As he flipped through each one, he spotted numerous diagrams for different spells, portal formations, as well as a handful of other instructions written in a language he couldn't understand.

This must be the Wardens' native tongue, but why would Nexis have something like this? It could be something Mideia might have left behind for him to study, he surmised, flipping through a handful of other pages before concluding that he couldn't read the language.

Ardrin, I've found something I think you might want to see, he sent his brother. *Continue searching for any additional information you believe may be useful. We'll meet back at the main hall later,* Ardrin returned curtly. *As you wish, dearest brother,* Taegin replied smugly.

He continued to skim through the pages to see if he could find anything else he knew how to read, but only found a detached note and another miniature painting that slid out of the book and onto the floor. As he lifted the two pieces of parchment and flipped them over, he realized that the painting depicted a man with elegant silver hair that reached beyond his shoulders, a square jaw, and a pair of differently colored eyes; one red and one violet.

He couldn't have known him *back then, could he?* Taegin asked himself, quickly shifting his attention to the note, which was also written in a similar language to that of the book.

"Damn it, no answers there, either," he grunted, placing the two pieces of parchment back where they belonged before returning to his search.

CHAPTER 86
NOTHING VENTURED

The morning following our conversation with Ed and Meliss, we donned our armor and waited for the others in the main hall.

Of course, Mom, Devyr, and Kalia were already waiting for us with Athar and Irun, though the other two were nowhere to be found.

"*Someone* stayed up too late. It's about time you got here," Mom said with a wry grin the moment she saw us. "*Oh*, come on. We're not even late yet!" I sighed heavily. "*Riiiiight*," Athar's alternate voice chimed in with a shit-eating grin smeared across his face, wrinkling the bags beneath his eyes. "You look like a bag of smashed assholes. What happened to you?" I asked, noticing his eyes were much more tired than usual.

"*Eh*, I just couldn't sleep last night," he said, fighting back a yawn, prompting me to raise an eyebrow and lean in toward him. "Because of Balgrim?" I asked hushedly, to which he returned a barely noticeable nod. "I tried to work it out in my head last night, but I can't figure out what's wrong with him," he replied, getting a raised eyebrow from mom this time, too.

"I've known Balgrim for nearly a *century* now, but I didn't notice anything so different about him. Then again, he's *always* been grouchy with me, given my history here," she said, averting her gaze and scratching her cheek. "That doesn't surprise me, but you've got to believe me when I say something just *isn't right* with him," Athar said with a furrowed brow.

"Mom, I think we should listen to Athar. After all, he's been dealing with his alternate's personality for a decade. If anyone's going to know the signs, it's him," I said, giving my mom a solemn nod to know I meant every word. "Alright, alright. Let's suppose something *is* wrong with him; what the hell are we supposed to do about it right now?" Irun asked, keeping his voice low. "Not much we *can* do, except watch what we say or do around him until we find out more," I replied, getting a nod of agreement from the others.

Before anyone else could pitch a theory, Ed, Meliss, Balgrim, and a score of guardsmen walked through the doors. "*Oh*, I didn't expect you all to be here early. I take it this means you're ready to go?" Balgrim asked, giving us all a once-over with his eyes as if inspecting our equipment. "We were told to be here at first light, so we came as instructed," Mom said as if stating the obvious.

Will you be alright if she comes along? Kalia asked me with a slight air of concern. *I'll be okay, don't worry,* I sent back with a thin-lipped grin.

"Of course, I should have expected as much from *you*," he said with a half-chuckle. "Follow me, then. We'll be heading this way," he continued with a gesture. *Do you think he's in league with the other corrupted wardens?* Kalia asked us. *If he is, then that just means we'll have to feign* a little *ignorance in the event he asks us questions about whatever we find,* Ysevel replied, causing Mom to raise an eyebrow.

I could feel Kalia's concern about Balgrim begin to grow through our connection, but we didn't continue that portion of the conversation. Instead, we simply followed the dwarves, Meliss, and Ed down the numerous streets to where our transport was waiting for us.

It was much larger than the carriage-like vehicle we'd ridden in the day prior, including thick metal panels that covered the backside of it entirely. The dwarves entered first, filling in the far side of it first, allowing the rest of us to sit near the large door.

"I apologize for the rush, but time is of the essence here," Balgrim began after pushing a small glowing stone embedded in the metal plate next to him. "It's fine. Just tell us what we might be up against," Mom said, raising a hand dismissively. "Of course. After what you brought me last night, I figured that it couldn't have been a coincidence," he began, regarding each of us seriously.

"A few months ago, we noticed a burst of strange mana that caused several creatures to awaken. As a result, we've sent out numerous scouting parties to discover its origin, but only a handful have ever come back alive. The survivors spoke of large, dark creatures; ones they had never encountered or even *read* about before," he continued, prompting Kalia to tilt her head slightly.

"Those bursts came to a halt until about two months ago, when they showed up again. One of our head scholars, Markus, died on that expedition, and when we retrieved his body, we noticed there were strange markings all over him. However, we couldn't identify if it had been one of the creatures or the *mana* that had done that to him," Balgrim explained carefully.

He's trying to be honest about the situation, but not go into too much detail to cause Meliss any further pain, I realized, seeing her expression sour a little at the mention of Markus' name.

"So, what's *our* job here?" Mom asked pragmatically. "Since your arrival, there have been several bursts of this strange mana, and our scouts seem to have found a potential origin point. Your job will be to help us investigate this potential source and take care of any resistance we may meet," he explained.

Kalia immediately sent the others and I a flood of information compiled from hers and Devyr's combined knowledge of the creatures from Vareluth. I could hardly think straight with the sheer quantity of possibilities of creatures that could be drawn to such a source, but until now, we'd only seen the Thran present on the Isles. *Do you think it's any of those we* haven't *seen yet?* I asked Kalia, who cocked her head slightly, as if to tell me it was likely.

"Sounds like a trap," Irun muttered to no one in particular with raised eyebrows. "One, you probably laid *yourself*," Ed scoffed and shook his head.

Ah, shit. Here we go, I sent the others with a mental sigh.

"Ed, I'm fully aware you still don't trust me, but I did what I *had* to do, and I'm sorry that it had to go as far as it did," Irun said with a sigh, surprising *Meliss* most of all, while Ed, naturally, didn't believe a word he said. "While I can't speak for Edryd, I do hope that your remorse is truthful. After all, it wasn't *just* him who was affected by your and the Masked One's actions," she said calmly, but I could see it in her eyes that those memories were still *very much* at the forefront of her mind.

As soon as the words left her mouth, there was a unified surge of disgust in my core coming from both my mother and Kalia. *The sheer audacity of her to say something like that about being remorseful. I wonder if she was sorry for the way she treated* you, *Thoma,* Kalia sent, hardly able to contain her spite.

Deep down, I knew Irun's betrayal couldn't compare to what she did to me. After all, *I* was the only one truly affected by it back then, but I'd had more than enough time to get over it. To her and Ed, however, Irun's betrayal was still pretty fresh in their minds, *and* they didn't know what *I* did about why he did it to begin with.

"It is, Meliss. I'm well aware of the consequences of what we did. I know Ed won't believe a word I say, but *I am* sorry about how it all happened," Irun said, offering her a slight bow of his head, interrupting my thoughts. As I regained awareness of the others around me, I noticed Athar was beginning to grow uneasy with something.

"Hey, Athar. You alright?" I asked, leaning forward to get a better look at him. His teeth were bared, and while I couldn't exactly tell what he was going through, it *looked like* he was in pain. "T-They're… here," he barely managed, causing the rest of us to become alarmed immediately. "Thoma, do you feel that?" Mom asked me urgently.

As soon as the question registered in my mind, I began to feel something strange in the air. Ysevel and Irun noticed it as well, immediately clutching their swords like the rest of us. "We're under atta-…" the driver called out, but was cut off just before the armored carriage flipped over.

In the heartbeat that it took for us to realize the situation we were in, we braced ourselves with mana, adding barriers to the dwarves as well. Ed braced for impact with Meliss, and I admit I was glad to see his quick reaction to shield them both from the damage that was sure to come.

The carriage came down with a heavy crash, and I knew that it was improbable that the driver had survived, since his voice had cut out just before we were flipped. "Fuck! Is everyone alright?" I asked, quickly glancing at the others who were still recovering from being flipped on their heads. "We're fine, but we're sitting glicks in here. We need to get out *now*!" Mom commanded, springing the rest of us into immediate action as she blew open the back end of the carriage.

One of the dwarves sitting next to it hopped out first and was quickly met with an axe to the face. "*Oooh*, I like the way these small ones *bleed*," a snarling voice came from just beyond the threshold as the gigantic axe was pulled from the dwarf's parted skull. "Tough little bastards, aren't they?" the voice said again, getting a few howling cackles in response.

They're close. I'll handle them, Kalia sent us. *No, we can't risk using Wraith mana here,* Mom urged, *drawing a massive amount* of mana to her before bolting out the back. As I heard a few slashes and *whelps* come from just outside, alongside various deafening *booms* from her blade, I knew we had to move.

"Get the fuck out, now!" I belted, following behind Ysevel and Kalia, who were already out the door. I helped Ed and Meliss to their feet and gestured for them and some of the other dwarves to wait a moment. "You guys will come out last," I urged, nodding to Balgrim as well. "We can handle ourselves," Ed said, almost as if he were disappointed in my distrust of his and the dwarves' abilities.

"I know, but that's exactly why I don't want you going out there to fight them right now. You have no experience with them, especially *you*," I glared at Meliss, who lowered her head in understanding as the battle raged on outside. "Fine. Have it your way, but how am I supposed to get experience with them if I'm stuck here?" Ed asked, frustratedly.

"You'll have your moment, trust me. These fuckers don't show up in small numbers, and they're at least *twice* as strong as an ochelon," I noted as I moved toward the back of the overturned carriage. Peeking outside, I could see a few heads already severed, along with massive weapons and pooling blood beneath those corpses.

"We're clear, but stay close to the carriage. If shit goes to *fuck*, at least you'll have quick cover to hide behind," I said, drawing my blade from its scabbard. As I stepped outside, I realized the trail before us was riddled with almost as many traps as there were bodies, but they were well hidden beneath the dirt.

How long do you think they've been here? I asked Kalia. *At least a week, maybe two. It takes time to set these traps up, and there are* a lot *of them,* she replied, dismembering a pair of Thran who hardly knew what hit them.

"I'll handle the traps," Mom called out, waving her hand for the others to take a few steps back. "*Ooooh* no. No, no, no!" Balgrim's voice rose behind me, as if he already knew what to expect. I could feel the surge of mana rippling through the air, as a massive wave careened along the path, exploding and triggering well over a hundred traps along its trajectory.

"F-Fucking hells," Ed gasped, watching the golden wave carve out chunks of the mountainside as well. "They don't call her *Commander* for nothing, it seems," he said through a nervous chuckle. "*Noooope,*" I grinned proudly. "I know I should have asked this before, but who are the other two?" Meliss asked, gesturing to Kalia and

Devyr, who were making quick work of the Thran who'd survived Mom's blast, while the others kept an eye out for any movement.

I'm just glad Athar is still able to fight in his condition, I thought idly as he severed the head of one of the Thran crawling away from him.

"Those two are Kalia and Devyr. They're elves, under Mo-... Siraye's command," I caught myself, but got a suspicious glance from Ed regardless. "They're incredibly efficient," Meliss said, observing their movements closely as if she were trying to learn something from them. "You should see them when they're genuinely *trying*," I chuckled, giving the area a quick look.

We were somewhere to the north of Narin, that much I knew, but since the entire Island was covered in mountains and cliffs, it was difficult to know *precisely* where. Thankfully, we were still just below the snow line, so there was only a bit of mud on the path.

Well, that and a score of severed limbs.

"Are you three alright?" Ysevel asked the others just behind me. "We're fine, but are these the same kind of creatures you guys found on your way to Narin?" Ed asked, his eyes widening at the realization of just how formidable these creatures were. "Yes, though this may not have been *all* of them," Mom added, flicking the blood from her blade in a swift arc as she came toward us.

She's right. Reinforcements are likely to come soon after she destroyed the traps. Be ready, Kalia sent us, which I passed on to Irun and Athar with a knowing glance.

"We're gonna have to flip the carriage if we want to make it back before nightfall. It might be too dangerous to continue this mission," Balgrim noted, already working out the logistics of how to flip the massive, plated carriage in his mind. "*Oh*, we're just getting started," Mom said, causing him to flinch at her words. "W-We are?" he asked shakily.

Thoma, tell this idiot that we didn't come all this way just to be thwarted by zuresh, Kalia sent, mimicking fake hand signals to not rouse suspicion regarding how we were able to communicate. "Kalia's right. We have to keep going. There will be more coming, and these bastards need to *die* if you want to protect Narin from a full-force invasion," I said, loosely translating what she said so it was a little more digestible.

Balgrim's glance darted between us for a moment, but said nothing at the exchange. "F-Fine. But how are *we* supposed to fi-..." he cut himself off as a small rock clattered off the side of the carriage, prompting the rest of us to glance upward. "They're above us, aren't they?" Meliss muttered, her eyes widening at the prospect of there being more of the titanic beasts.

"Yep, and here they come," Irun snarled, *drawing a large quantity* of Vexing mana as well as over a hundred Thran prepared to slide or jump down from the cliff face.

How many do you think I can kill before they land? Mom asked with a wolfish grin. *At least ten, maybe twenty?* I replied, matching her grin and gripping my blade tightly. Without another word between us, I entered my fourth stage, while Ysevel, Devyr, and Kalia, who had realized our intentions, readied their weapons as well.

"Ed, Irun, Athar; protect Meliss the dwarves," I said, my now-golden eyes flaring brightly with mana. "*F-Fourth* stage?" he muttered before flinching away from the clumps of bloodied mud I left in my wake.

I tried my best to catch up to Mom as she dashed up the cliff face, but she was far too quick for me to do so. Instead, Ysevel, Devyr, and I peeled off to the left, while Kalia and Mom veered off to the right.

The Thran commander, wielding a pair of sharpened metal slabs for swords and a deep-set scar cutting diagonally across his wolfish face, roared for the others to attack us. I couldn't see his face, but I could almost *feel* Ed's surprise at our coordination and movements.

The first few Thran carreened toward us, howling and snarling as they descended the cliff, bounding from boulder to boulder, while the others and I did the same. However, Mom was already three steps ahead of the rest of us, painting a canvas of blood and limbs along her path toward the leader, while Kalia took on a score for her own.

I could *see* the excitement in his eyes as he watched her move toward him, but I don't think he fully knew what he was getting into.

However, I had *my own* problems to deal with, as the first Thran lunged at me spear-first. I summoned a blade of wind to sever the haft, which ended up taking a quarter of its forearm with it. It *roared* in agony, but still tried to take my head off with its massive remaining claw. I responded accordingly by bringing my blade up in time to catch it, splitting it along its length like cutting a cucumber in half.

The creature, fully off balance, hit the ground below with a squelching *thud*. I heard it, but I was already busy fighting the next pair that came at me. The first swung his axe at my neck, which I only narrowly avoided, but used the momentum to cut deeply into its torso, spilling its guts onto the boulder beneath my feet.

The other came barrelling down with twin dagger-like blades swung over its shoulder, then arced them to send its body into a spiral. Unsure of what else to do, I slammed the ball of my foot into the cliff face to send a few spikes of stone to see if it would stop it, but the blades were so sharp and heavy that the Thran sliced right through them with minimal effort.

Shit, that's not good, I thought, weighing my options in the few heartbeats I had left.

As the spiraling creature came for me, I realized there was something I hadn't used in a long time.

Just like old times, right Ed? I thought, preparing my *Whip of Doom* technique, he'd so adequately named all those years ago. I flicked my free hand back, infusing my self-made spell with *far more* mana than I really needed for it, and launched it at the creature, catching a handful of others as it chained from creature to creature. I was grateful to see that my improved *Whip* had halted the creature's spinning, but the sheer look of befuddlement and fear on its face was priceless.

Instead of flicking my finger to ignite the whip, I infused it with flame attribute mana, allowing it to race along the length of the *Whip* and compress it as much as I could. With a quick release of the pressurized mana, it turned those who were caught in my spell into little more than pink, fuzzy mist. "*Heh*, not bad," I muttered, racing toward another set of creatures that had come over the edge.

On my way up, I'd noticed that only a few had managed to slip past us, but I was confident Irun and Athar would be more than sufficient to take care of them. Ysevel and Devyr, once again, were almost *dancing* with each other along the cliff. The two of them were little more than streaks of violet mana as each one's strikes complemented the other's, raining blood and entrails along their combined paths.

As I was reaching my next foothold, I felt the entire mountainside shaking along with an explosion of mana that couldn't have come from anyone else, other than Mom.

Having fun up there? I sent with a mental chuckle. *Abso-fuck-ing-lutely. This guy's a real treat to fight,* she said, her tone almost ravenous. I could tell by her tone that she was merely toying with him to gauge these creatures' strength for herself. Still, we had a job to do, and that job was to protect the ones below us.

Don't take too long. A pair of them have already gotten by, I sent, severing the legs off another creature, causing it to plummet to the ground head-first. *What? Devyr, pick up the pace,* Kalia sent sternly, already having killed roughly *thirty* herself, judging by the amount of corpses splattered on the ground below.

Without another word, Devyr immediately followed the command, prompting Ysevel to increase her speed to match the hegraphene's. I realized I needed to do the same, but one of them managed to get by me in my rush to keep up with the others.

"Ed! Look out!" I shouted, prompting him to glance up and prepare for the large creature's arrival. It landed with a heavy thud, but I didn't have time to watch his fight, since I had several Thran who'd now turned their focus onto me.

"Let's dance, *fuckers*," I muttered, forming my Kataki blade upside down so I had more variety for my attacks. As each one came, I did what Mom and Kalia taught me to do best: keep them guessing. With each of their strikes fueled by their rage, it was challenging to keep a solid footing without pushing mana into the boulders around me.

Each one had enough force to carve a wide gash wherever I once stood, but using the boulders to my advantage, I severed the head of the first, split the second in half, and used its entrails to conceal my waist-height assault on the third. The fourth aimed a spear at my back, but I'd accounted for it and deflected the blow with my reversed *kataki* blade, allowing it to glance off my blade without much issue.

I jammed my elven sword in the flesh beneath its jaw and raised my other blade to sever its head from its shoulders. The fifth, wielding a pair of blades similar to the commander's, tried to crush me beneath their weight, but I managed to create an extension of the boulder beneath my feet just in time and side-stepped it deftly.

Its twin blades nearly carved the boulder from the cliff, but I took the opportunity to create a pair of wind-blades beneath it, while I swung mine from above its haunched back, splitting it into four, thick sections that fell toward the path in multiple heaps.

My eyes followed the pieces down to where Ed was still battling his Thran, while Irun and Athar battled another handful that had gotten by to protect the dwarves, though a few of them had died due to the sheer force of the shockwaves from the Thrans' strikes.

He's doing well, don't you think? Kalia sent, having only briefly glanced in his direction. *He's always been a good sword-caster, but it seems all the training with Ren, Thorn, and Nenvalur is paying off,* I noted with a bit of pride. *He might even rival* me *now,* I continued, watching him between killing another Thran and checking on the others.

Not likely, Ysevel added with a warm tone that, if any *sane* person had heard, would likely have sent a shiver down their spine at her efficient brutality. *Let's finish this up and help the others, shall we?* Kalia added, to which we all agreed.

Just as we did so, however, the leader at the top of the cliff leaped off the side, bounding from one boulder to the next, leaving a clear trail of blood in his wake. "Come here, *weasel shit*! I'm not done with you, yet," Mom shouted before she broke out into an almost untrackable dash toward it, shaking the entire cliffside and knocking a cluster of boulders loose in her wake.

Damn it, she's gonna bring down the entire cliff *at this rate,* I thought, realizing no others had come down from the ledge they were fighting on. *If you're done up here, go down and check on the others,* Kalia commanded firmly, finishing up what I realized was likely her *fiftieth* kill.

Ysevel, Devyr, and I finished off any stragglers that were sprawled across the boulders as we made our way back down to Ed and the others. Thankfully, Irun and Athar had subdued the other creatures that managed to escape us, while Ed was hunched over the corpse of his first Thran kill. His shoulders were rising and falling rapidly, and I could tell at a glance that it had taken him nearly everything he had to kill it.

"Not bad for your first one," I said from a distance, flicking the blood off my elven sword while reforming my *kataki* one. "You weren't kidding; these guys are *tough*," he chuckled tiredly. "Can't say I didn't warn you, but I'm glad you're alright," I smiled, patting him on the back briefly before turning to the others.

"Are you alright?" I asked the group of dwarves who'd huddled inside the overturned carriage. "Y-Yes," one of them answered, bug-eyed and breathing shallowly as he peered out of the ruined doorway. "That *damned elf*. Where the hell is she?" Balgrim asked, stepping out from behind the others. "She's chasing the commander down for *sport*," I said lightly, causing the others to glance at me with confused looks.

Hey, I found something. Meet me around the bend, I heard Mom's voice echo through our connection. "It seems she's found something," I said, not explaining how I knew that information, prompting Ed to raise an eyebrow. "I-I'm going with you!" Balgrim stammered gruffly. "I'm counting on it," I nodded, motioning for the others to follow along.

As we neared Mom's location, I could tell Athar was struggling to keep it together now that his focus was solely on whatever this source of mana was. "Anyone care to explain what *that* is? He wouldn't talk," Mom asked as she kicked the corpse beneath her, pointing out a large sphere of Leech mana burying itself in the ground a reasonable distance away.

"Anvil's recoil, what *is* that?" one of the dwarves asked. "Something none of you here are prepared to deal with," Balgrim said to the other dwarves idly, causing Athar to look at him with slight confusion. "So, you *do* know what *Leech* mana is," he spat, ignoring his own trauma as he walked toward the druid.

"I-I only know what Markus was able to discover, but I never knew its name," Balgrim stammered, raising his hands defensively. "*He's fucking lying,*" Athar's alternate voice seethed through gritted teeth. "We don't know that yet, Athar," Mom said, stepping down from atop the fallen commander's head.

"*Maybe not, but I still don't trust him,*" Athar continued, glaring at the dwarf he towered over. *Thoma, I've got this,* Irun sent me, regardless of his personal feelings towards sending telepathic communications. Given the gravity of Athar's accusations, however, he must have deemed it necessary.

"Hey, it's like Siraye said: we don't know enough yet, but he *does* have some explaining to do," Irun said, placing a hand on Athar's shoulder, while giving Balgrim a curious stare. "I-I'll explain what I know, I swear!" the dwarf replied quickly.

It made perfect sense for him to be afraid of us at that point, but there was something off in the distance that caught my eye. "The land around it is... *dying*. Look," I gestured toward the base of the sphere, which was currently killing all the nearby vegetation.

Just as I did so, the sphere began to swell to nearly four times its original size. "Get back!" Mom shouted, putting up a barrier to protect us. Kalia and Devyr did the same, while the others in *Nightfall's Blade* and I did the same as a secondary level of protection against whatever came next.

The orb of Leech mana exploded, voraciously devouring all the vegetation in its wake, leaving behind nothing but ash and brightly colored *sand*. The wave of mana reached our barriers, and while it hardly did any damage to them, we could tell that anything within its range was either horribly disfigured or *dead*. Athar's face blanched, but whether it was from shock or pain, I couldn't tell.

"That was too close for comfort," Mom said, slowly lowering her barrier, as the others and I followed her lead. *If this is what the corrupted Wardens are capable of, then this will not be an easy war to wage,* Kalia noted, giving voice to our unsaid concerns.

Hearing Kalia's words, Mom immediately turned to face Balgrim, who, based on the expression he wore, nearly had a brown river running down the back of his leg under the weight of her glare.

"Athar, I'm sorry I couldn't fully protect you," she said, never once averting her gaze from the druid. "I-It's alright, Siraye. I'm actually feeling a lot *better* now that it's gone," he said, allowing himself a sigh to regain his composure. "If that's what we're going to be up against while we're here, we're going to need a *damned good* explanation, Balgrim," she said coldly.

"O-Of course. I'll give you whatever information I have if it helps us to protect the Isles. *N-Nothing ventured; nothing gained*, right?" the dwarf stammered, still heavily shaken by my mother's piercing gaze. Mom could only offer a tilt of her head in response.

Shiiiit, I know that look on your mom's face. I can tell she knows he's hiding something, *but* I can't tell what, *exactly,* Ysevel sent me, causing me to raise an eyebrow. *I guess we'll find out soon enough,* I sent back, inhaling deeply as I readied myself for another plunge into the abyss of knowledge.

CHAPTER 87

A SILVER LINING

We made our way back to the overturned carriage, and with a bit of earth and wind mana, we flipped it back over. Still, the back end of it was bent outward after Mom destroyed it, but with a bit of mana, Balgrim was able to reform it.

"It's not as strong as it was *before* the brute blasted it open, but it'll have to do for now," he said with a heavy sigh. "It's still better than having mud and rocks kicked up in our faces on our way back," Irun shrugged, getting a few nods of agreement from some of the other dwarves. One of them, however, had gone over to the one who'd first fallen and pried the axe from stiff, dead hands.

"What's he doing *that* for?" Athar asked hushedly. "If a dwarven guard dies in battle, we bring his weapon home to the family since, for the most part, their children will carry that same weapon in the future," Meliss explained solemnly. As we watched the dwarf say a silent prayer for his fallen comrade, I couldn't help but feel bad that we weren't able to protect him.

"I see. I still don't know much about customs in other countries, but if there's any way that I can pay my respects to his family, I would like to do so," Athar said, receiving a weak smile from her. "That won't be necessary, but thank you for your offer," Balgrim added while we watched the dwarf finish his prayer and climb into the backside of the carriage.

"We should hurry back to Narin. Our work here is done," he continued, gesturing for us to get on. As the other dwarves got in first, Irun sighed and shook his head as Balgrim gestured for him to get on, then proceeded to the front of the carriage with Mom. "What's your deal, huh?" Ed asked as Irun sat down, prompting the rest of us to pay attention to whatever this exchange was about.

"What do you mean?" Irun asked without meeting his eye as he checked his blade for any damage he'd have to repair. "I know you guys don't trust him, but why are *you*, of all people, giving him nasty looks?" Ed asked with a raised eyebrow, which made Irun pause for a moment.

He's trying to get a rise out of you, I sent quickly, but didn't receive a reply.

Instead, he rested the weapon on his lap and let out a soft sigh. "I'm just worried that, if what *I think* is happening is true, then he might be messing with forces he doesn't understand. People tend to do that for their own gain, after all," Irun explained, but it was evident by Ed's tongue click that he wasn't satisfied with the answer.

"*Oh*, I'm sure you'd know *all about that*. After all, your decisions were part of what got Batch, and *fuck* knows how many others, killed," he spat, but Irun only shook his head. "What are you trying to get at here, Ed? Are you looking for revenge?" Irun asked flatly. "I *dunno*. Maybe I'll just take your head off your shoulders, but I don't think that would be enough to compensate for Batch's death. Thoma, how the *hells* did you ever become his ally, *huh*?" Ed asked, turning his anger toward *me* now.

"I already explained how that happened last night, Ed. What more do you want me to say?" I asked, but even though I knew he believed me, *accepting* it was a different story entirely. "I don't *know*," Ed snapped, and immediately lowered his head. "I-I don't... know," his voice softened, his fingers curling into tightened fists as his knuckles blanched.

There was a moment of silence in the air that everyone, including the dwarves, who were so awkwardly placed in this situation, knew he needed. We let the air hang for a few moments, but Ysevel and I both knew that we'd have to tell him the *whole* truth at some point, if he was ever going to get past his anger.

Strangely enough, it was Athar who moved first and put a hand on his shoulder. "Edryd, or *Ed*, I'm not sure which to call you, since we've only just met; can I tell you something?" he began, getting a silent nod from him in response. "Y-You don't have to believe what I'm going to say, but since you're attacking your *friends*, I think a more neutral stance might be needed here," Athar began, glancing back at me as if wanting my approval.

I gave him a few subtle nods to let him know it would be alright. After all, Ed *had been* my best friend for most of my life. Athar seemingly understood what I meant and turned to face him again, though his grown-out hair hid his face.

"I've been with Irun for quite some time now. I know you've known him longer than I have, but I promise you, *he does* feel remorseful. Granted, I've had to dig that information out of him, *stubborn fuck-ass that he is*," Athar winced after realizing his alternate's voice had come out.

"But even so, I know he played a vital role in getting us to where we are today. In fact, if it weren't for him, we'd probably be in a much *worse* situation than we are now," he continued, prompting Ed to look up at him finally.

His eyes were bloodshot, and it was clear to see he was fighting back a waterfall of tears not borne from sadness, but *frustration* and *anger*. "Trust me when I say that Thoma didn't decide to trust him lightly," Athar chuckled loosely, while Ed swallowed the lump in his throat.

"D-Did he try to kill him?" he asked expectantly. "Yeah, twice," Irun scoffed with a chuckle, shaking his head. "*Oh*. R-Right," Ed muttered, averting his gaze. "Even so, they still came to terms with what happened, and look at them now, working together to help *save* this land. I know that, to you, they should have no reason to be allies, but I think you'll *also* come to understand it, in time," Athar said, giving him as warm a smile as he felt appropriate.

He's right, you know, Kalia sent Ed *and* the rest of us to make sure she wasn't going to say anything wrong. His eyes widened in surprise when he heard her voice in his head, and he began looking around for whoever had said that. Ysevel and I had refrained from reading his thoughts, since we didn't want to reveal that we could do that in the first place, so Kalia took it upon herself to send *us* whatever he said.

W-Who said that? Ed asked in his mind, while Kalia sent us, and Mom, whatever he said. *I did, though I do apologize for the intrusion,* Kalia said, offering him a subtle bow of her head. *I thought you took a vow of silence,* Ed replied nervously, getting a shrug from her. *Silence of the mind, and silence of the* mouth *are two different things, Edryd,* she sent him with a chuckle, hoping to ease his nervousness a little.

C-Can the others do that? What about Commander Siraye? Ed asked nervously. *I'm here, too,* Mom said loosely, making him blanche. *F-Fuck. This is,* uh, *awkward,* he chuckled nervously, rubbing the back of his neck.

Be that as it may, what Athar said is true. It takes time to understand why others do things to us, Kalia began, pulling his attention back to the matter at hand. *For example, Commander Siraye killed my mate, Lord Gravar, just before Irun brought Thoma to the Underworld,* she continued, making his eyes widen in surprise.

But like you with Irun, it took me time to understand that there's no way she could have known the ramifications of her actions entirely. No one can, after all, she said, shrugging again. *But regardless of whether she knew, the fact remains that it* happened. *Nothing is going to change that, sure, but we can* always *choose our way forward. There is* always *a silver lining, no matter how dark the cycle may seem,* she said, allowing her words to hang between them for a brief pause.

Mine, as difficult as it was in the beginning, was to train Thoma enough that we could defeat the Undergod, she said, making his eyebrows raise as high as his skin would allow. *Y-You trained him?* Ed asked, giving me a surprised glance.

I wasn't the only one, but yes. It was the way I found *to get through my pain. Still, I would be lying if I said that he and Ysevel didn't play a significant role in my getting over it, much like Irun and Athar played their own roles,* she replied, making him lean back in his seat, trying to understand what he was hearing.

I understand the loss of your friend, and believe me when I say that you're not the only one *who suffered from it. Thoma, too, had his own reservations about Irun, but with time and understanding, we've come to where we are now. I hope* you *can do the same, someday,* she said warmly, offering him another nod, but I could tell she was smiling in a way that matched her tone through our connection.

Whatever walls Ed had built up began to crumble as he slowly digested what he was being told. After a few moments of consideration, he finally nodded in agreement, but turned to look at Irun again. "I still want that duel, by the way. I want to know how much stronger than me you *really* are," Ed said, using the back of his gauntlet to wipe away a stray tear.

"We can have it once we're done with all this bullshit. I *promise,* but it can't be to the death," Irun replied, extending his non-daemonic arm out toward him. Ed paused and considered whether to take it for a moment, but ultimately gave in. "F-Fine, but don't expect me to go lightly on you," he said as he gripped Irun's hand firmly.

Athar, however, returned to his seat beside Devyr and let out a sigh of relief as he slumped into it. "*Fucking finally,*" his alternate voice muttered, getting a chuckle from Ysevel and I in response.

As we continued on our way toward Narin, I was glad to see Ed beginning to come to terms with what happened, even going so far as to strike up a loose conversation regarding Irun's arm. The others in the carriage were *also* visibly relieved that the awkward situation was finally over. Still, they merely exchanged glances and silent sighs of relief that they weren't going to be caught up in a battle in the back of the carriage.

Of course, it had only been a momentary distraction from the losses they'd suffered.

We reached Narin within a few hours, but when we arrived, there were a handful of dwarven families anxiously awaiting news of the expedition. Tears welled in their eyes when the weapons and armor of the fallen were brought out, but the sight that hit *me* hardest was that of a young girl realizing her father wasn't coming home as a guard kneeled before her, presenting the weapon.

"I'm sorry, little one. He fought bravely, and..." I heard the guardsman's voice trail off as we continued toward the main palace. I did my best to maintain my composure, but the sight of the girl slowly realizing it wasn't some sick joke was etched into my memory. "Damn it," I hissed silently, balling my fist and feeling the tensed gauntlet tighten around my knuckles.

While the mission wasn't a *complete* failure, the look on her face sure made it *feel* like one.

"We should head to the palace and wash up. I hear the Lord of Narin would like to have a few words with you all," Balgrim said, interrupting my thoughts after discussing something with a group of servants. "The *Lord of Narin*?" I asked, realizing we'd yet to meet this figure. "Calduran Lytehammer," he reminded me with a furrowed brow. "Why haven't we met him yet?" I asked, trying to figure out *who* was actually in charge of this place.

"Because while I deal with anomalies across the country, *he* deals with the industry owners and mayors, such as Lokren, which often keeps him away. Edryd has been a great help to me in managing my time so I can work on upcoming technologies, but even *he's* been overwhelmed with everything that's been happening here," he explained loosely.

That's rather unusual, Ysevel sent, having overheard the conversation. *There's nothing* usual *about anything he's told us so far, but*

I think we should play along for now until we find out how much he knows about Leech mana, Mom added, regarding him warily.

"I see. I suppose it would be best not to waste his precious time, then," I said as diplomatically as I could. "Indeed. Meet us at the Great Hall in two hours. The banquet should be prepared by then, and I'll be expecting you *not to* look like you've just crawled out of a Thran's ass," he said, aiming the final part of his comment at my mother. "Such a large mouth for such a *little man*," she muttered sardonically, giving him a chagrined smile.

We followed him into the palace and split off to our rooms. I was wondering how we were supposed to dress for the occasion, but I was surprised to see a set of formal attire already laid out for us. After a quick wash, Ysevel and I tried to figure out the proper way to wear the clothes we were offered, but after a few minutes, we'd finally figured it out.

It was a loose-fitting, dark-gray tunic accented by turquoise strips that lined the outer edges. The waist strap had small metallic plates engraved with geometric designs near each end that clasped together with a satisfying *click*, while our boots were tightened by similar mechanisms, lined with more turquoise designs.

"Heavy thing, isn't it?" Ysevel asked idly, rolling her shoulders once or twice to adjust the weight balance better. "Compared to Caegweni tunics, yeah," I realized, mimicking the same motion she'd made. "I wonder how Devyr and Kalia are going to show up," I said, tugging on the V-shaped opening near my clavicle. Ysevel's eyes widened, but immediately thinned as she stifled a giggle.

"I have *no* idea how this is going to work for them, given they've likely never been in *this* kind of situation before," she said, immediately sending a pulse to Kalia to check on her.

I... need help, Kalia replied defeatedly within a heartbeat, prompting the two of us to come to her aid just a short way down the hall. When we entered the room, we found that they, too, had figured out how to wear the heavy tunic, but there was something else bothering her that we hadn't accounted for.

As it turned out, Kalia's hair was cut short on the sides, while the top was combed forward to where there was an elegant arc in the strands that favored the scarred side of her face. Devyr had a similar hairstyle, though she seemed to prefer hers neatly slicked back.

"I-Is this the way I should wear my hair? *Oh,* and what do I do about these?" Kalia asked bashfully, turning to us and gesturing to the slits near her temples. Ysevel's eyes widened in delightful surprise before she immediately rushed forward. "*Oh,* my. I've just realized I've never seen you two without a helmet," Ysevel said, putting her hands up to Kalia's cheeks and manipulating her head to inspect her hair.

"Y-Yes, that's because I've never been told I *couldn't* wear it," Kalia said with visible frustration. "Who told you *that*?" I wondered with genuine surprise that *anyone* could tell her to do *anything*. "Your *mother*, actually, though I suppose she hadn't accounted for the fact that our faces are *much* different than an elf's," she sighed.

We considered the ramifications of this for a moment before Ysevel snapped her fingers and laughed victoriously, as if she'd just defeated her greatest opponent in a children's game. "I think I know how to fix that. Can you make your *kataki* look like *hair*?" she asked, bringing her face right in front of Kalia's with expectant eyes.

"I-I think so? I've never *had* to do that before, but I'll try," Kalia said awkwardly, closing her eyes for a moment as she focused on her task. Just as I expected, her control over her *kataki* was absolute, and within a few moments, thin strands of it began to grow from the sides of her head. "Keep going. I have an idea," Ysevel said, watching as more strands caused her hair to reach the middle of her shoulders.

"Is this enough?" Kalia asked with a raised eyebrow, visibly uncomfortable at having her hair longer than it likely ever had been. "That's perfect. Devyr, you do the same. I'll braid it for you, Kalia, so don't worry about the styling. Thoma, would you mind helping her?" Ysevel jutted her head to Devyr, who was already growing out her own strands of *kataki*.

I obliged, of course, and I was grateful to have spent all those years with her in the Dome to have learned how to braid hair properly. "If you'll excuse me, Devyr," I said with a light chuckle, which she matched, then turned to allow me to braid it.

"D-Do you think Athar will like it?" she asked when I'd reached the halfway point of her hair, causing me to freeze solid under the weight of Kalia's glare. "I-I think so, y-yes," I replied nervously, quickening my braiding pace so I could avoid any further questions. Ysevel handed me a thin, leather strip, which I tied to the end of the braid to secure it.

Devyr inspected herself for a few moments in the mirror and smiled brightly. "It's... *perfect*. Where did you learn to do that?" she asked, still maintaining her smile. "When you spend *ten years* with someone who *loves* keeping their hair braided, you learn a thing or two," I shrugged, getting a giggle from Ysevel.

"Come on, then. We should get going or we'll be late," Ysevel said, taking Kalia's arm in hers. "Let's see what Athar thinks, shall we?" I whispered, offering Devyr my arm with a wry grin. "I heard that," Kalia growled, causing both of us to chuckle.

When we arrived at the Great Hall, a long table spanned nearly the entire length of it, lined with numerous different haunches of meat, bread, fruits, and a score of barrels containing an unidentified liquid. I soon discovered that it was, in fact, *alcohol* of some sort, since Mom was already acting like she was back in Caegwen, with her arm wrapped around an unsuspecting Athar.

What, and I cannot stress this enough, the fuck? I sighed, pinching the bridge of my nose as she tried to force him to drink more. "*Ah,* there you are!" Mom said, noticing we were in the doorway. Her face went from a bright red to pale white when she saw the disgruntled look on Kalia's face.

"*Shhhhiiiiiiittt,* she must be mad at me for telling her *not to* wear her helmet," I heard her mutter to Athar, who was paying her *zero* mind, since his focus was on Devyr.

To be entirely honest, she *was* beautiful, though he was evidently *far more* smitten with her than I even thought was possible. Noticing his expression, I quietly nudged her in his direction, and she took her seat by his side, while Ysevel and I sat with Kalia beside my mother.

"What took you so long? The Commander's nearly drunk an *entire barrel* on her own," Ed chuckled, passing me a mug of the strange liquid. It was dark and turbid, but try as I might, I couldn't identify *what* it was. All I knew was that it smelled like a mixture of powerful, fermented herbs.

"I don't want to be rude, but what *is* this stuff?" I asked him with a raised eyebrow. Ysevel, not bothering to wait for Ed to answer, took a large swig of it, but the look on her face made it obvious that it was *delicious*. "It's called *Murt na Maidne*, which roughly translates to *The Morning's Bane*, though what it's *made of* is something those who make it keep closely guarded," Meliss answered in his stead, raising a mug of her own.

"I can't *imagine* why it would be called *that*," I muttered, already imagining the potential hangover this would give me. Still, I did my best not to be rude and took a drink of the turbid alcohol. To my surprise, it was strong, but not strong enough to burn the back of my throat.

"I retract my previous statement," I said with an upturned lip, realizing just how easily one could get drunk off it. Ed and Meliss *clinked* their mugs together and drank after crossing their arms, but I couldn't help but feel something was off.

I bet fifty crescents she'll come to talk to you about what happened, Ysevel sent with a mental chuckle, wanting to do the same as they had. *That's it?* Hah, *I bet a hundred,* I replied, locking my arm around hers and taking a massive swig of my *Murt na Maidne*.

Just out of the corner of my eye, I could see Meliss' expression shift slightly, before changing back into a thin-lipped smile as she turned to look at the others. I knew she wanted to talk to me, but I wasn't going to be the one to initiate *that* conversation.

Ed, Ysevel, and I held an idle conversation, with the occasional interruption from my mother, of course, but overall, the dinner was going smoothly. We talked about what it was like in Caegwen and how different everything was here. Naturally, we couldn't compare *everything*, but what we could, we did.

"So, wait, does that mean you're never going back to Coltend?" Ed finally asked after I'd told him I still had more training to do there. "Not for another few years, at least. I've only just broken into the fourth stage, after all," I lied, taking another swig of *Murt* and waving my hand dismissively.

"*Nah,* I get it. I'd want to do everything I could to get stronger while I had the chance, especially after what I saw today. You've made incredible progress, so I'm not surprised by your answer," he said, not-so-subtly tilting his head in Ysevel's direction, to which I chuckled through my nose and shook my head.

"Well, it hasn't been easy. Breaking through the third stage was... *difficult,* but the fourth nearly killed me," I said, taking a bite of food that had gotten a little cold during our conversation. "It *nearly killed* you?" Ed asked, pausing his chewing momentarily. "Yeah. If it hadn't been for Ysevel, I might have, honestly," I said, putting my hand on hers and squeezing gently.

Ed forcibly blinked a few times, but Meliss' expression told me everything I needed to know. *Here it comes. Are you ready for this?* Ysevel asked, earning me curious stares from everyone who shared our connection. *Nothing to be ready* for, *but I'll let you guys hear whatever she has to say,* I sent with a mental sigh.

"T-Thoma, rather, *Ysevel*," Meliss began skittishly, getting a look from Ed as he took another bite of food and washed it down with more *Murt*. "Do you mind if I speak with Thoma for a few moments?" she asked, nervously fidgeting with her fork.

You can still say no, *you know that, right?* Ysevel sent with a raised eyebrow. *I know, but I'd rather rip the bandage off before she makes things even* more *awkward,* I mentally sighed.

"Of course, Meliss. Just bring him back in one piece. That's all I ask," she replied with an unmistakable undertone of a *threat*, not because she was jealous, but rather because she wanted Meliss to know *she knew* the extent of what happened better than anyone. "O-Of course," Meliss replied cautiously.

I rose from my seat and followed her out of the hall toward the balcony that overlooked the city of Narin. Its turquoise glow created a gentle gradient of color against the star-filled sky, and the gentle breeze in the air was warmer than usual, given that spring was just around the corner.

"So, what did you want to talk about?" I asked, leaning on the stone railing, folding my hands together as I sent every word to the others, who were not-so-subtly staring at us.

"I'm sure you can guess," she said as she walked up next to me, keeping half an arm's length between us and leaning on the railing. "I *could*, but what would be the point of my doing so if you were the one who asked to speak with me?" I chuckled, trying to ease the *obvious* tension.

A gentle wave of the breeze rolled between us, causing her hair to flow gently along with it. She caught a few of the floating strands and tucked them behind her ear, gazing down at the city below.

"I just wanted to say that I'm sorry," she began, still fidgeting nervously with her interlocked fingers. "*Sorry* for what?" I asked with a scoff. "I-I'm sorry that I... hurt you, and especially for the way I did it. I don't think I *could have* if it had been face-to-face, but I *needed* to find out more about my past, and I didn't want to drag you through its mud. I even had to ask Ed to help me write it in a way that would have hurt you the least," she said, struggling to voice whatever was going on in her head.

"*The way that would have hurt the least?*" I asked, finally turning to face her. Her eyes widened and began to well with tears, likely fearing whatever rageful, *spiteful* comments that *could* have come out of my mouth. "I don't know how else to explain it," she admitted, lowering her head a little.

I could feel my buried emotions beginning to swell as the memories of that fateful evening flooded back, but reliving those memories, even for a fraction of a second, nearly prompted Mom and Kalia to rush toward us. Thankfully, I saw Ysevel raising a hand out of the corner of my eye to stop them.

I closed my eyes and took a deep breath, desperately trying to avoid lashing out.

No. Fuck that. I'm allowed this. I'm allowed to say what it really did to me, but how do I tell her? I asked myself, glancing over at Ysevel once more, who gave me a reassuring nod. I returned the nod and took another deep breath, turning to lean back on the railing.

"I know there's no way for you to know *what* I felt that night, but I'll try to explain it as best I can. I think I'm owed at least *that much*," I began, pausing to gather my thoughts and organize them accordingly. I could hear her swallowing a dry ball of spit as she waited for me to speak again.

"You know, I've thought about what I would say to you if I ever saw you again, but I don't even know if that person *exists* anymore,"

I began, causing her to look up at me expectantly. "What do you mean?" she asked nervously.

"*That* Thoma cried and puked himself out of my body and onto the floor of his bathroom in Myrdin. His heart ached like it had been stabbed, and his entire being shook down to its core as he pounded his head against the wall; wondering, rather *idiotically*, I might add, whether he did something wrong, or if he simply *wasn't good enough* for you," I began, keeping my gaze fixed on a distant point on the far side of the glowing city.

I forced my thoughts to catch up to what I was saying with a brief pause. In that moment, I saw a tear race down her cheek out of the corner of my eye, but I didn't acknowledge it.

"However, even as emotionally *mangled* as I was, I was *lucky* to have had people I care about close to me, pulling me off the ledge before I could even get near it. *Heh*, it's almost funny to think about how *miserable* I must have looked when they came to find me," I chuckled dryly and shook my head.

I noticed a slight shift in her movements out of the corner of my eye. A slight tensing of her hands together, followed by a rapid sucking of air through tightly clenched teeth.

I knew all too well what that feeling was like.

"It wasn't a *total* disaster, but I'm *also* not saying that it couldn't have gotten any *worse*," I said, finally turning to look at her.

When I did, I realized tears were streaming freely down her face, and her lower lip quivered, but at that moment, I felt nothing but *pity*. Pity for the girl who'd shattered the love I once had for her with a simple letter because she thought she needed to. She was lost in her own trauma, but I knew if there was anyone who was going to guide her back home, it was *me*.

"I-I'm sorry, Thoma," she said hoarsely, using the back of her sleeve to wipe away most of the tears. "It's fine. I'm not saying that I *agree* with your methods, but I *do* understand them," I began, causing her expression to shift into one of utter confusion. "H-How could you *possibly* understand that? I thought you would have *hated* me for what I did to you," she said, swallowing another lump in her throat.

"That's the thing: I *wanted to* hate you. On the surface, I wanted to hate everything about your existence that could bring back memories of the time we shared. I wanted to bury you so deeply that not even the most voracious *earthworm* could ever find you," I sighed, feeling a weight I didn't know was still present, beginning to lift.

"Gods, I thought I'd *die* with all the anger flowing through my veins over how *selfish* I thought you were," I said, my voice lowering to little more than a whisper. I saw her face pale, her shoulders slightly trembling at the tone of my voice, and the leaden weight of my words.

"But, not unlike your situation with Ed, *someone* was there to keep me from doing just that," I looked over through the glass to see Ysevel smiling warmly as she and the others had returned to their seats, likely laughing at something my mother had done.

Her gaze shifted over to where I was looking, then closed with a sudden understanding. "*She* saved you, didn't she?" Meliss asked, shifting her gaze from Ysevel back over to me. "She did. She was there to help me not only pick up the pieces but put them back together into something *much* stronger. Granted, it took time and an incredible amount of patience on her part, but whatever she did *worked*," I said with a light chuckle, but my mention of *time* seemed to confuse her slightly.

"But, even going through all that, there is something I feel it's my *duty* to tell you," I began in a more serious tone, hoping she would take whatever I had to say to heart. "What might that be?" she asked with slight apprehension.

"Ed's a good guy, and I've known him for most of my life. I'm genuinely *glad* you two have gotten together, but if you want to be happy with him, I need you to promise me something: Don't bleed on someone that didn't cut you," I said softly, giving her a look that was sure to let her know I was serious, but her eyes only began to well with more tears.

"No matter how fucked up your past is, that doesn't give you the right to decide whether someone, who genuinely cares about you, can stay in your life because *they* are free to decide to bear that burden *with* you, too," I said, causing her eyes to widen in surprise, then shift away from me as she buried her face in her hands.

I let her sob for a few moments, placing a friendly hand on her shoulder, because I felt she needed to know that it was okay, but also that I didn't want her to make the same mistakes she had made with *me*.

"When did *you* get so wise?" she asked after a few moments, turning her face up to the sky as she tried to stop herself from crying, but I could only chuckle at the notion of her calling me *wise*. Of course, I couldn't tell her it had taken me a few *years* to get to this point, but that was neither here nor there.

"Promise me, Meliss. Promise me that you won't give up on *him* like you did me," I said, placing my other hand on her shoulder to

stare into her dark green eyes intently. A few, silent heartbeats passed
between us, her eyes shifting to each of mine searchingly as her small
frame quivered. "I-I promise, Thoma," she finally said with a few,
quick nods of agreement as I felt a warm smile beginning to grow.

"I'm glad to hear you say it aloud, because if not, I don't think
I would have been able to keep the *others* at bay for much longer,"
I chuckled, but this only made her stare at me in mild confusion.
"N-Nevermind," I waved a hand dismissively and shook my head.

I pulled a handkerchief Ysevel had knowingly prepared for this
moment from my tunic and handed it to her. "Here you go. Can't go
back to a party looking like *that*, can we?" I said lightly, causing her
to mildly scoff and rip it from my hands. "It's your fault I look like
this," she said, wiping her cheek. "Technically, it's *yours*, but who's
counting?" I continued in the same tone with a shrug.

"Ready to head back inside?" I asked, realizing she was done cleaning herself up as she inhaled deeply and shook her head. "Not really,
but... thank you, Thoma," she said, giving me a tear-stained smile.
Not knowing what else to say, I returned the smile and led us back
into the Great Hall.

That was beautifully executed, Ysevel sent with a nod and a warm
smile toward us. *Thanks. I just hope she learned something from that,*
I said, returning to my seat beside her and receiving a handful of nods
from the others. *I still want to* crush *her, but I have to agree with
Ysevel,* Kalia sent with a raised mug of *Murt. Maybe I* should *let you
two duel so she knows what's coming if she slips up with Ed,* I sent with
a chuckle.

"Ladies and Gentlemen," a heraldic dwarf began, drawing our
attention to him immediately as we rose from our seats. "Please,

welcome Lord Calduran Lytehammer, Lord of Narin," he said with a grandiose gesture to a doorway on his right. A roar of cheers rose from the dwarves who welcomed the stocky, white-bearded dwarf.

His hands were old and calloused, likely from tinkering with their strange technology for many years, but his bright, green eyes were sharp and calculating. His clothes looked much like the tunics we were wearing, though he was garnished with bits of rare metals I struggled to identify.

As we watched him enter, followed by Balgrim close behind, he raised his hand to settle the others down. "Druid Balgrim has told me of an expertly handled situation earlier today," he began in a wizened, yet abnormally strong voice for someone his age.

"As this feast is in recognition of their accomplishments, and in honor of our fallen brothers, I would like you *all* to welcome the members of *The Order of Nightfall's Blade*," he gestured toward our section of the long table.

Athaaaaar, I mentally sighed, earning me a nervous look from my companion.

Another roar of support came from the dwarves in response, but I could tell he wasn't exactly happy to see my mother sitting right beside me. "As is tradition here in Narin, those who have valiantly fought to protect our homeland are offered a boon of their choosing. Please, let us know what we can do for you," he said, immediately snapping Mom out of her slight daze.

Thoma, I'm too drunk to ask him coherently, but we need to get to the library, she sent, though even her thoughts seemed slurred. *That's fine, but I think Ysevel should be the one to ask since she's more formally trained than I could ever hope to be,* I said, giving her a nod of confidence. *That just means I need to train you harder,* she sent wryly as she stood up.

"Great Calduran, it is an honor to be standing here before you," she greeted him formally, causing him to raise his thick eyebrows in surprise. "Princess Ysevel Phrys, the honor is *mine*, as it's a pleasure to finally meet you in person. But what could elven royalty possibly request from this *old dwarf*?" he asked, giving her a slight bow in acknowledgement of her status. "*Oh,* come now. You don't look a day over *fifty,*" she said lightly, making more than a few of the dwarves stare at her beauty.

Can't blame them for that, I chuckled inwardly.

"However, if it is within your power to do so, we would like to request access to the *Tasglann Arsaidh,*" she said in *flawless* dwarven, causing his eyes to widen even further. A hush fell over the dwarves that forced them to hold their breath under the weight of her request, but it was Balgrim's face that set alarm bells off in my head.

His face twisted from one of surprise into one of deep contemplation before he spoke. "What knowledge could *we* possess that Myrdin doesn't?" he asked cautiously. "That's precisely what we're hoping to find out, Great Calduran," she replied humbly. "I see," he said, running his fingers through his thick beard momentarily and starting to pace across the platform before his throne.

We all held our breath, hoping we hadn't just offended the only person who *could* grant us access.

After a few tense moments, he finally halted and stomped his heavy, booted foot on the platform, and I could feel his mana permeating the ground and up through my legs to wrap around my core.

"Do you understand the *gravity* of what you're asking?" he asked, his voice much more palpable than before.

"We do, Great Calduran," she replied without flinching or stuttering. He inhaled through his nose deeply and raised his foot to dispel the mana he'd imbued into us. "I find no lie in their words or intent, merely a deeply rooted curiosity. I will grant you access to the *Tasglann Arsaidh*, but only under the condition that Druid Balgrim and I accompany you," he said, allowing the rest of us to breathe normally.

"*Moran taing* for this historic opportunity, Great Calduran," Ysevel bowed humbly, prompting the rest of us to do the same. "Of course. It's been nearly a *century* since it was last opened, but I sincerely hope you find what you're looking for," he said in a much warmer tone than a moment ago. "We shall reconvene here in the morn, though tonight, I hope you will enjoy the rest of this feast," he said, raising both his arms in a gesture that caused the others to cheer.

Now that *was beautifully executed,* I sent her with a look of genuine pride.

CHAPTER 88
A Humble Request

"I request an audience," Erumon said sternly, gazing at what appeared to be a portal, bright and swirling, but he knew all too well what it *really was*.

As his words traveled through and across the innumerable paths in the realm between realms, the portal's swirling intensified against the backdrop of the eternal twilight. His strong jaw set and his fist clenched when he could see what lay beyond the portal.

The portal stabilized with a thin sheen of mana racing across the tear in the realms it created, allowing him to step through. The bright sun, illuminating the sky with a bluish tinge, shone off the tower peaks at the far end of a long, glistening road.

Each portion of the palace before him had various thin, open arches that allowed for as much sunlight to enter the palace as possible. The ground, inlaid with intricate golden designs that spanned across the white marble flooring, gently shone in the morning light, though it never ceased to amaze him.

How long has it been since I last set foot in these halls? He wondered, breathing in the air deeply.

"Welcome home, *Warden* Erumon," a female voice came from his right with a fair amount of sarcasm in its tone. The fact that he was welcomed didn't catch him off guard by any means, though the owner of the voice was someone he hadn't expected. "Vauv? What are *you* doing here?" he asked the woman who stood nearly at eye level with him.

Vauv was clad in armor made of pure mana that radiated a variety of colors from just beneath its borders. She had an exceptionally athletic build that beguiled most who looked at her porcelain features, though there *was* a hint at her true strength for anyone who knew to look for it.

"I see you've managed to hide them even better than the last time I saw you," he said, his mouth slightly twitching into a thoughtful smile. "It's not fair that you know they're there to begin with, but I suppose I should thank you for the compliment," she said, raising a hand near her pinkish, blonde hair, tucking a loose strand behind her ear that had thin, but noticeable striations to it that crossed in an angled pattern.

"It's not like they're *marks of shame*, but you still haven't answered my question: What's a warrior of your calibre doing out here?" Erumon said with a shrug, continuing to walk toward the palace. Vauv's bright blue eyes, with deep shades of orange near her slitted irises, widened with his comment, but she didn't immediately reply. Instead, the striations became slightly more visible near her temples.

"I-I was informed you were coming, and wanted to be the one to welcome you back. After all, it's been quite a while since you were last here," she stammered, feeling her cheeks beginning to grow hotter the more she spoke.

I don't think I should tell her I saw her blushing. That would only make matters worse, he felt from behind the barrier he'd placed around his mind.

"I see," Erumon said, allowing much more of a smile to come through. "It's... good to see you again, Vauv. Truly," he shifted his gaze from the multiple distant towers to her. Once again, she found it difficult to hide her flushed features, but she turned away and cleared her throat. "You too, Erumon," she replied in little more than a whisper.

The pair of them continued walking in a slightly awkward silence, though it was evident they were happy to be in each other's company. "So, tell me: how is the *old bastard*?" Vauv asked wryly. "I assume you mean *Ardrin*? He's done an excellent job in releasing Vareluth from Nexis's clutches, but there is still much work to be done regarding the protection of Kavrass," Erumon shrugged, but she could only offer him a suspicious look.

"You're hiding things again," she said wryly, prompting him to chuckle. "Not *hiding*; *reserving*. It's different," he said with a subtle wink as they approached the main gate. Before them stood a massive row of these pillars, and upon closer inspection, it was evident that the spaces between them were filled with mana barriers that gently shimmered as the mana passed from pillar to pillar.

High above the gate stood a pair of wings raised high into the air, with a large, pale stone at their center. On the ramparts of the gate, there were a handful of watchtowers suspended about halfway up the gate's height, and Erumon could *feel* their eyes on him.

"What's going on? Do they think I'm some kind of traitor?" he asked Vauv under his breath. "Not at all. Their glares are merely *precautions*. There have been some strange rumors going about, so Lady Sildyr requested more vigilance to uproot them," Vauv replied, sending the other guards a telepathic command to allow them passage.

"That's strange. I've never known her to be fond of politics," he said distantly, but Vauv shook her head. "Not *those* kinds of rumors. Although I will admit, she's terribly curious about the ongoings within the kingdom," she said, greeting the guard as they passed.

Erumon performed the same gesture: a flattened hand covering his heart and a slight bow, which was oddly reminiscent of a Caegweni greeting to him. "You've spent too much time with them, it seems," Vauv said jokingly, prompting him to chuckle through his nostrils. "Perhaps I *have*, though I'm not sure I appreciate you *seeing* me like that," he raised an eyebrow slightly.

"I *didn't*. It was the thoughtful look on your face that told me everything I needed to know," she grinned proudly. "If you say so," Erumon shook his head. "Speaking of Lady Sildyr, where is she?" he asked, glancing around the palace grounds, hoping she would be in her frequent spot tending to the Borumi flowers.

He cast his gaze toward where she would have been, but she was nowhere to be seen among the hedges of multi-colored, rose-like flowers that easily spanned over a meter in width. "*Hmm.* Well, if she's not here, then she must already be with Lord Karthus," Vauv surmised, prompting Erumon's features to shift into those of mild concern.

"He's *here?*" he asked, eyebrows slightly raised. "Like me, he *also* heard you were coming," Vauv shrugged idly, but Erumon's jaw set.

If he's here, that can only mean something truly terrible has happened, he thought privately as a pair of guardsmen allowed them passage into the tower.

It wasn't so much a tower as it was an illusory external construct. Inside this tower, however, was an entire *human castle's* worth of space. "Spatial spells will never cease to amaze me. Perhaps I might spend a century or two to learn it," Vauv said, staring up at the high, luminous ceiling in awe.

"You're already more adept at them than *I am*. What more could there be for you to learn?" Erumon scoffed. "True, but you can always stand to learn new things, can't you?" she asked with a wry grin, poking his broad shoulder playfully. "Perhaps," he admitted, before they continued down the main path that would eventually lead to the throne.

As they made their approach, there was a heavy sensation of mana that permeated the entire inside of the tower that could easily crush anyone who wasn't strong enough to withstand it. "He's here," Vauv said excitedly, hardly even fazed by the extreme pressure bearing down on her.

"Lord Karthus, it's an honor to see you again," Erumon bowed immediately, prompting Vauv to do the same. "Rise, Erumon. You already know that I'm not overly fond of formalities between us," he replied with a slight sigh, his voice reverberating throughout the tower like a distant rolling thunder.

Erumon did as instructed and raised his eyes to lay them on the one before him. The tell-tale blood-red hair and eyes like the purest flame *saw* him. His long silver robes, lined with strips of mana that flowed like the barriers, swayed gently as he raised his arms in a welcoming gesture.

"It's been too long, *pupil*. Tell me, how are our friends in Kavrass? I've heard you've finally met the man who is *one with death*," Karthus said cryptically, getting a confused look from Vauv as she tried to decipher its meaning. "I have, indeed. Although I must admit, I never expected him to be so *young*," Erumon admitted, getting a slight chuckle from Karthus in response.

"That's because *everyone* there is considered *young* to us, but I digress. I know you didn't *only* come to visit your old master and his *daughter*," he said, subtly raising an eyebrow at Vauv, who blushed slightly. "If only things were that simple. I have some rather disturbing news from Kavrass, but before that, I have a question of my own," Erumon sighed as a gentle frown began to grow.

"You may ask him anything you like, and if he doesn't answer, *I'll* tell you what I know," another female voice appeared seemingly out of thin air. "Lady Sildyr," Erumon bowed again as she walked out from behind Karthus. Her pure, pearlescent hair glistened in the morning rays, though her robes were much darker than those of her husband's.

"Welcome home, Erumon. It's good to see you again," she said with a smile that could have charmed a rabid ochelon. As he gazed into her gentle, sapphire blue eyes, he closed his own for a moment to bask in the mana that permeated his entire being.

"You as well, Sildyr, but unfortunately, my question will likely not be easy to answer," Erumon replied, reopening his eyes and doing his best to maintain eye contact with her. "I've noticed you had the guards intensify their vigilance, but what is the meaning of this?" he asked, causing the two elder beings to break eye contact momentarily.

It was hardly noticeable, but a thin barrier of mana erupted around the four of them before they spoke. "It seems my *daughter* has a way of loosening her tongue when she's around you," Sildyr sighed, causing Vauv to give her a nervous grin. "I'm also sure that you felt like you were being looked at as a *traitor* when you made your approach, but that was intentional. We simply don't know who we can trust here in Polarion," she replied with a dour expression.

"W-What? How can that be?" Erumon asked with genuine astonishment. "It seems we were careless. Mideia's corruption and reach might have even extended to some of the *dukes*, but we can't be certain at the moment," Karthus replied solemnly. "Then, allow me to investigate in your stead. If you're seen to be making a move like that, it could spell trouble for *all* of us," Erumon cautioned, spreading his arms pleadingly.

"No. Your work in Kavrass isn't finished yet, and it's impera-..." Karthus halted and snapped his head to the right with a furrowed brow. His eyes flared in ire, and his teeth bared toward whatever he was looking at.

What in the realms could dare to risk the ire of Lord Karthus? Erumon questioned with widened eyes as the pressure from before returned in full force.

"Erumon, I know this reunion was short-lived, but there is something I must see to immediately," he said in a darkened tone. "You must return to Kavrass and continue your work there. Vauv, please stay here with your mother. I'll handle this," he said, opening a trio of portals without so much as flexing his finger.

"O-Of course, Father," she replied, watching as his mana circulated throughout his body at an alarming rate before moving through the portal before him. "Stay safe, Vauv. Lady Sildyr," Erumon said with a bow, knowing full well there was no time for an emotional farewell.

"Y-You, too," Vauv replied, almost reaching for him, but she knew what had to be done.

Erumon stepped through the portal and realized he was already back in Myrdin's training area, where Bernar and a handful of others were already training.

His way of teleportation is still so far beyond my comprehension, he sighed, but felt a tinge of worry for his former master.

"*Fuck,* that scared me," Gwili said, having flinched away from the sudden appearance of the titanic warden. "Greetings, Gwili," Erumon said as the portal quickly shut behind him. "G-Greetings, Lord Erumon. *Uhhh,* w-where did you come from?" Gwili asked, having caught only a small *glimpse* of the world beyond the portal before it shut.

"From my master's home," Erumon said plaintively, glancing at the others, who were conducting a training session a short distance from where he stood. "Why aren't you training with the others?" Erumon asked flatly with a slightly raised eyebrow. "I-I was on my way to get some water, but as soon as I'd made it here, a surge of mana presented itself, and, well, I think you can understand the rest," Gwili said with a nervous chuckle.

I suppose he is *telling the truth,* Erumon thought, glancing down at the empty water skin in the elf's hand.

"Here, I'll save you the time. I need to speak with the others," Erumon said, lifting a single finger and pouring water attribute mana into it, nearly causing the water skin to overflow. "O-Oh, thank you, Lord Erumon. Forgive me for asking, but is something the matter?" Gwili asked, noticing the Warden's expression was furrowed just enough to be noticeable.

"My master gave me some troubling news just before he opened the portal for me to return here. He didn't specify what was going on, so I need to make sure you're properly preparing for the coming war," Erumon replied with a sigh, prompting Gwili to blink a few times as if he were struggling to understand what he'd just heard as he walked behind the warden.

Within a few moments, they reached the others, who were firing off spell after spell at Anwill's command. Even Leona, Marte, and Neko were partaking in this training and doing their best to attack Anwill's targets. "Impressive progress, isn't it? I'd like to say it's only thanks to those pearls you gave us, but they've all been working extremely hard since the last time you were here," Gwili said proudly.

"*Oh*, Lord Erumon. Good to see you again," Bernar said, having heard Gwili's voice over the deafening sounds of their spells. "You as well, Bernar. I came here to check on all of you, but it seems Gwili was correct in his earlier statement," Erumon replied, closing his eyes and allowing a slight smile to show.

"*Weeeeell*, yes, but I feel like there's still so much more that we're missing to truly take advantage of the *Authority*," Bernar said, rubbing the back of his neck, as the others took notice of the Warden's presence. "Welcome back to Myrdin, Lord Erumon," Anwill said with a bow, prompting the others to follow suit.

"It's good to be back, though there are a few faces that are still missing. In the meantime, Bernar tells me that you're having difficulty understanding the *Authority*," Erumon said, glancing at the others momentarily and greeting them accordingly.

"It's not that we don't *understand* it, but it feels like it's *out of our reach*, even though we've made incredible progress already," Anwill said with a shrug as he gestured out toward the destroyed targets.

"I see. Which one of you is struggling the most?" Erumon asked, prompting Leona, Neko, and Marte to raise their hands bashfully. "I'm having trouble fully comprehending the depths of mana, but that's mostly because I wasn't exposed much to it when I was younger, Lord Erumon," Neko explained, getting a nod of agreement from Marte as well.

"And you, Leona?" Erumon asked, though it was evident she was struggling for words. "Even having broken through to the second stage, thanks to Anwill and Bernar's help, I still find it difficult to direct longer ranged spells the way I want to," she admitted, prompting the Warden to place a hand on his chin.

"Very well, then. You three, come here. I want to try something with you," he said, gesturing to the ground in front of him. Hurriedly, the trio made their way to him and stood as straight as a flagpole, though they tried to hide their nervousness at being so close to him.

Let's hope Vauv has some insight I can pass on to them, he thought, digging into the depths of his memories of their time spent training together.

It had been nearly half a millennium since they last trained together, but he was able to recall a few bits of information. "Perhaps this will prove useful to you. Neko, please step forward," he said, raising his arm out in front of him with his palm facing downward. "W-What do you need me to do, Lord?" he asked nervously, realizing the Warden's other hand was being placed near his core.

"It's a technique an old... *friend* taught me. I hope it will work for you, too," Erumon said nostalgically, as he began to pour mana that ran through Neko's head, and met the other flow near his core. "Stay still, it's going to feel strange at first, but you're going to have to trust me," Erumon said, closing his eyes for a moment to precisely control the flow of mana.

Within a few moments, Neko's eyes shone brightly, as if he, *too*, had reached a new height in his mana manipulation. The others, who regarded whatever Erumon was doing curiously, felt almost *drawn* to this strange method.

"W-What's happening to him?" Marte whispered to Leona, who could only shrug and shake her head, but quickly returned to observe them, as an aura of mana began to envelop Neko. Just as suddenly as it appeared, it raced back into his body, and his eyes ceased their bright glow.

"*Whoa*," Neko said, taking a near-stumbling step back, flexing his hands once or twice as if to touch a tangible level of power in his palms. "What was that?" Anwill asked, taking a few steps toward the young half-elf to inspect him and make sure he was alright.

"Where I'm from, we have a way of sharing insight, much like the hegraphenes do. However, since our methods aren't bound by blood, we can share information freely if we choose to. I couldn't share *much*, given his current stage of mana manipulation, but I hope it will help. Go on then, fire off a spell for us," Erumon gestured to the training yard behind them.

"W-Which one do you want me to use, Lord?" Neko asked, his voice a mixture of nervousness and excitement. "Whichever you feel you know how to use best," Erumon replied with a single nod. Neko turned around excitedly, flexing his fingers once more as he looked at them with newfound interest.

He approached the firing line and began to *draw Ethereal mana*, though this time, it was evident that he was able to draw much *more* than before. A small orb of ice appeared in his hand, though when he raised it above his head, it moved away and began to grow, going into a spin that gradually increased its speed.

"Careful, now, Neko. You've only just learned that one," Anwill warned, tilting his head to the side. Neko gave him a single nod and returned to focusing on his spell. As the orb rotated more quickly, spikes of ice came out and began to form along the outer wall of it. With a grunt of exertion, he used his other hand to start firing off the spikes of ice, each one reaching its target with incredible speed and accuracy, shattering them and the earth beneath them with ease.

Sharing insight wasn't the only thing he did, was it? Bernar sent Anwill with raised eyebrows. *Perhaps not, though I wonder how it's even possible for him to share insight to begin with,* Anwill replied with a curled eyebrow, still observing Neko's spell until all the targets were defeated.

"Consider me impressed, Neko. Even *I've* never learned to do that spell with such accuracy and power," Thorsen said, clapping his large hands together. "With time, your spells will begin to grow even stronger, so I would recommend you continue training hard to reach new heights. Now, it's your turn," Erumon said, looking at Marte.

The process was much the same for her, though she chose to use an array of flaming spears that arced over her head. The renewed targets were quickly transformed into little more than steam, but now, it was Leona's turn.

Erumon placed his hand atop her head and the other near her core, but as he began to pour mana into her, he forcibly stopped himself and took a step back to look at her intently, just as Thorn and Ren made their approach.

"I-Is something the matter, Lord?" Leona asked with a slight tone of worry, but he shook his head. "N-No, nothing's *wrong*," he said, deflecting her question lightly. *I've just realized something vitally important, though it is beyond my skill to use for* your *situation,* Erumon sent her, placing a barrier on their thoughts so that it remained private.

Ah. It's because of that, *isn't it? I understand,* she said with gracious dejection. *I'm sorry, but that's beyond my skills to use that technique with confidence. If I mismatched the output, even by a* little, *it could cause you significant harm,* he cautioned her with a silent, solemn nod as Bernar looked on in confusion.

I'm sure there's a good reason he didn't say it aloud, Bernar realized, not wanting to pry any further.

"Lord Erumon, we heard you'd arrived and came to greet you," Thorn said with a humble greeting. "Greetings, Thorn and Rennyr. How are our friends in the Gramm Isles?" he asked, turning to face them.

"I've been keeping in contact with Thoma and the others, though it seems they've run into more of those Thran creatures over there, as well as the presence of a Leech mana sphere that nearly wiped them out. They're on their way back to Narin as we speak, but I hope we'll have more information soon," Ren said, offering him a formal greeting.

"I see. What of Ardrin and Taegin?" Erumon asked. "They should be arriving shortly, though I haven't heard much about their progress in the north," Thorn replied with a light shrug. Just as he did so, a violet portal opened up a short distance away from the growing group, and out of it came the subjects in question.

With them were two others they hadn't expected.

"I.. *hurrok*...I *hate* portals," Trina stumbled, covering her mouth. "I can't say I... *hurrok*... disagree with you, Commander," Wien said, doing his best to stay out of Taegin and Ardin's way as they remained unfazed by the portal's effects.

As Trina and Wien gathered information about their surroundings, they were met with a score of eyes regarding them curiously, and even more confusion at the tall forest that surrounded them. Their biggest surprise, however, was the fact that Erumon stood well over a head taller than even Ardrin.

"*Whaaaat* the fuck?" Wien muttered, getting a slight smack on the head from Trina when she noticed Taegin and Ardrin bowing to the giant. "Lord Erumon, we apologize for our tardiness," Taegin said, glancing at the other two from beneath his bow to make sure they were doing the same.

"Greetings, Taegin. I take it you've gone on quite the journey if you've had to use *that* portal," Erumon noted, having recognized the mana signature of the portal that originated in Pyrdredd. "We have, indeed, but we found something there we need your assistance with," he said, producing the book from within a small waist pouch and handing it to him.

Erumon's eyes widened the moment he read the first page, shifting his attention between it and Taegin rapidly. "W-Where did you get this?" he asked. It was the first time *anyone* had seen him have any expression that wasn't minimal, let alone the two newcomers, who had *no idea* who he was.

"It was in Nexis' room in Pyrdredd. I can't read the writing, but I assume it's of *your people*," Taegin replied with a solemn nod. "I-I see. I'll have to bring this up with my master to determine whether it can still be translated, but from the little I *can* read, it will prove to be *crucial* in the days to come," Erumon said, offering him a gesture of gratitude.

As he rose from his short bow, a surge of Leech mana permeated the air, causing everyone nearby to flinch in response to it.

Trina seems more affected by whatever this is than I am. Is that because she can use mana? Wien thought, noticing her worried expression.

"That's *Leech* mana," Ardrin noted, staring off in the same direction. "It's not *just* Leech mana. I sense *Tyrant* mana as well," Erumon said to the others as he stared off in its direction. "You there," he said, casting his gaze toward Wien, who flinched in surprise. "Y-Y-Yes, L-Lord?" he stammered under the weight of the Warden's gaze.

"You can't use mana, can you? I suggest you stay here with the others until we return. Leona, stay behind with Thorsen, Marte, Neko, and the other newcomer. I'll go with the others to investigate this source of mana," Erumon commanded sternly, as Trina finally realized Thorsen was standing right beside him with a stunned look on his face.

"O-Of course, Lord Erumon. We'll be here awaiting your return," Leona replied with a bow, leading the others back toward the palace.

What new devilry is he conjuring now? Erumon thought as he, Taegin, Ardrin, Thorn, Ren, and Anwill began to move toward the forest at an astounding speed.

CHAPTER 89
CONSUMED

The morning after the banquet, we met with Calduran and Balgrim as instructed.

There wasn't a single one among us, including the two dwarven leaders, who wasn't at least *slightly* hungover from all the *Murt* we drank the previous night. Still, it was a wonder we'd all made it on time to our meeting, but to our benefit, Balgrim had accounted for that.

"Here, drink this. You won't feel like you've got a buffalo sitting on your head," the druid said, handing the others and I a small flask of some unidentifiable liquid. *At least it's not as murky as the stuff last night,* Ysevel sent with a wry grin before taking a sip. *I don't think Meliss was joking when she said it was called* Morning's Bane. *I haven't felt like this since the* first *time I got drunk,* I mentally groaned, as a simple task, such as thinking, made my head pound.

I was grateful for the *elixir*, as Athar called it, but had no idea how it worked. My stomach felt better within a few seconds of taking the first sip, and my head cleared shortly after, though I could have sworn I still had some residual phantom pain. As each of us drank it, we could physically see the results that removed the dark bags and redness from our eyes.

Even Kalia's posture has improved, I noted, unable to see her face beneath her helm.

"Now that I can see some life in your eyes, most of you, anyway, I think it's time we went to the *Tasglann Arsaidh,* don't you?" Calduran asked in a much more chipper tone than I'd expected him to. "Of course, Great Calduran," Mom replied, getting a bright smile from him, and a scowl of disapproval from Balgrim.

As we followed their lead down the many, luminous halls, I couldn't help but wonder what sort of relationship she'd had with the dwarves. It was clear Balgrim disapproved of her being there, but Calduran had a much more light-hearted disposition toward her.

That's because I saved his daughter the last time I was here. Had to destroy an ancient burial ground to do it, since she was kidnapped and brought there for some sacrificial ritual, Mom said, having read my thoughts through our connection. I couldn't help but be surprised she even told me the story, but I felt there was still a lot missing.

Would the ritual have worked if you hadn't *been there to stop it?* Kalia asked, coupling her question with my own curiosity. *I wasn't about to risk it, if that's what you're asking. Additionally, there were stories about a creature residing in that region that allegedly fed on human souls. I couldn't risk a beast like that to be left alone, so I destroyed everything in the area to make sure it had no chance of survival,* Mom shrugged.

Before we could ask any further questions, however, we turned a corner and came to a large stone door that was locked in place with a dozen thick chains. It was obvious to us all that they were reinforced with whatever mana resided within an octagonal seal at the door's center.

"I understand you keep the secrets here closely guarded, but how could you expect any normal person to get in there?" Mom asked Balgrim jokingly, but he could only offer her a defeated sigh. "It's not meant for keeping mere *mortals* out," he began to speak as Calduran moved toward the door. "Wait, are you saying that this was meant to keep *something else* out?" I asked, getting a curled eyebrow from him.

"As you'll come to see here shortly, there are many *other* beings who would easily *kill* for the chance to see what we've kept hidden here. That's not to say there haven't been attempts in the past, but none have succeeded thus far," Balgrim replied.

He's dancing around the answer. Mideia probably tried to enter this place at some point during the Great Partition, I sent Ysevel, who nodded in agreement. *I think we should be grateful he hasn't succeeded yet, then,* she replied. *Not that we know of, at least,* Kalia sent with an air of caution.

It made perfect sense, but I couldn't afford to dwell on that for too long, since Calduran had muttered something in his native tongue and cut a slit across his hand. A few droplets of blood sank into the geometric design carved into the floor beneath his feet and began to move toward the door.

It seemed like the mana from the door was *pulling* his blood toward it, but that wasn't the only thing I noticed. *His mana is radiating through the floor and into the lock,* I realized, wondering just how much control he had over his mana. *It must be a three-part locking system. Blood, mana, and the correct heritage must be the keys to this place,* Mom sent back, having observed the same thing I had.

For a heartbeat, I recalled her story of the ritual she'd stopped. *What if that sacrifice was meant to open something to allow the crea-*

ture out? I asked loosely, but quickly realized it must have held more truth than I understood at the time. *Now that's a theory I'd also come to, but since I destroyed the area, I never got the chance to see if I was right,* Mom replied regretfully.

The lock came undone with a heavy *clunk*, and I could hear some form of machinery within the walls retracting the chains in response, leaving the large, stone door open to us. "Follow me, then," Calduran said, pouring mana into his palm to seal the wound.

The doors opened to a deep stairway that could have easily taken us *hundreds* of meters underground. As we crossed the threshold, the mana stones embedded in the walls responded to our presence, illuminating our path as we made our way downward.

"How far do you think this goes?" Athar whispered, squinting his eyes to see if he could see the end. "Your guess is as good as mine, but I suspect the deeper it is, the more well insulated it would be against superficial attacks against the city," Ed surmised, getting nods from the rest of us. "And you'd be right, Edryd," Balgrim said over his shoulder with a prideful look.

"Narin has faced many trials and tribulations over the years, though each time, the *Tasglann Arsaidh* has remained unblemished," he continued with obvious, prideful satisfaction. We unanimously wondered what he meant by that, though we didn't have time to answer, as the end of the stairway appeared before us.

We've been walking down the stairs for the better part of twenty minutes. It's about time we see something at the end of this hall, Ysevel sent with a bit of satisfaction, which I agreed with wholeheartedly. *Coming back up these stairs is going to suck, isn't it?* I returned with a slight frown, knowing it wasn't likely for there to be some way to transport us back to the surface.

The end was in sight, and we all held our collective breaths when we crossed the final threshold. Before us was an incredibly vast room, filled to the brim with countless bookshelves, scrolls, tomes, and artifacts that my mind had a hard time comprehending.

Each one spanned from the floor to the high ceiling, with each section lit adequately by more of the mana stones.

"Welcome to *Tasglann Arsaidh*," Calduran said, raising his arms as if to welcome an invisible flood of knowledge. "Let's make this a little easier to read in, shall we?" he asked over his shoulder just before flooding the room with mana, causing the lighting to change from turquoise to a bright yellow that could have easily been mistaken for daylight.

The ceiling responded to his command and projected the morning sky onto every open space of wall that wasn't covered by the bookshelves or artifact housings. "This is incredible," I thought aloud, hardly bothering to hide my amazement. "That's not even half of it. Observe," Calduran said with a wry grin, moving to a thin pillar of stone that rose from the ground at his command.

Pressing a stone button that presented itself, a panel of light presented itself before him, with a runic language written on it. I couldn't help but wonder what other sorts of technological advancements they'd made since the Great Partition, though I knew no amount of time here could ever reveal them all.

"So, what is it you *truly* came here to learn about?" he turned to face us with a bright smile. After exchanging a few knowing looks, we all agreed on what we had to ask for. "*Ah*, Your Highness," he chirped when she stepped up. "We'd like to learn about the Great Partition and other known sources of mana. Given our encounter yesterday, I think it would be wise to learn as much about it as we can," she said, matching his bright smile.

It nearly faded when Balgrim's eyes met hers, but she managed to maintain her composure.

"*Oooh*, a warrior princess *and* a scholar, are we? Very well, then," Calduran replied, stroking his beard in amusement. He turned to face the panel once more and spoke in a language *no one* immediately recognized.

Well, no one except *Kalia*, anyway.

This is the language of the Wardens, she said in utter astonishment. *What? But that should be impossible for him to know,* Mom sent with genuine surprise. *I'm sure of it. I recall hearing a similar language when my people were slaughtered,* Kalia replied with a hint of sadness in her tone.

What's really going on here, then? I wondered, observing the two elder dwarves. Balgrim's eyes widened in surprise, as if not even *he* was privy to the fact that it was a language from otherworldly beings. What his honest thoughts were, however, I couldn't tell, but Athar's expression reminded me of what had happened the day prior.

As the archive responded to his commands, a number of the titanic bookshelves moved aside, making way for those that came from the far end of the room. "That's a time saver if I've ever seen one," Ed muttered beside me, his eyes widening just as much as mine.

A large bookshelf halted just before us, with books and scrolls that seemed to have not been touched since they were first placed there. Thankfully, the mana barrier surrounding the bookshelf helped to preserve them, but I could tell at a glance that these books were going to change my view of everything I, and the others knew forever.

My palms began to sweat as Calduran spoke a spell to undo the barrier, then another to bring out the shelves dedicated to the topics we wanted. "Here you are. Please, take your time in reading them. I will answer any questions regarding what you find that I can," he said, spreading his arms out beside him as the shelves moved to his left and right, spawning legs out from underneath them like tables.

"Thank you, Great Calduran. I hope we can find the answers we're looking for here," Mom said with a gracious gesture. "Of course, Siraye," he said, returning the greeting. "I'd suggest you start with this one and move along them carefully, as they're all laid out in chronological order. Just make sure to put them back where you found them," he continued, gesturing to a large, black book at the end of the table shelf nearest to us.

"Ready to find out the answers to all those questions you used to have?" Ed asked me with a wry grin. "You have *no idea*," I chuckled, feeling my pulse beginning to race as we all started to move toward the books.

I picked up the first one and gingerly opened it, unsure of how secure its bindings were, only to find that I couldn't quite read the language. "*Ah*, right. I'd forgotten about that. Perhaps *this* will help," Calduran said after noticing my confusion.

A panel of the same light appeared along the page, and extracted the information on it, translating it into Common or whichever language it seemed to know we were most comfortable with. Balgrim's eyes widened when he glanced at Kalia and Devyr's book, written in strange, runic symbols, but he said nothing.

Probably because she'd kill him without a second thought, Ysevel chuckled, but I did my best to avoid letting him know we'd seen his surprise.

Hours passed as I read through the first book that told the same tale Taegin had reminded me of all those years ago, when I'd accidentally scorched my blanket with a failed *Pyrus* spell. However, my eyes widened when I noticed something *hadn't* lined up exactly.

"Ed, look at this," I said, leaning over to him while the others pored over their own books. "What is it?" he asked, leaning sideways to inspect where my finger was pointing. "Wait, so they *didn't* just come here to give us the artifacts to give us the power to protect ourselves from monsters?" he asked, to which I nodded my head.

"It seems their giving the artifacts had some hidden agenda behind it, but it doesn't clearly state what. Here, let's see about this one," I said, putting the book back in its place as I grabbed another one and began reading. "This one says that a certain *Nexis Pelantyr* placed a curse on the king, but he was banished before he could complete his full goal. Something about *carrying his essence far beyond a single life,*" Edryd said, turning to look at me with a raised eyebrow.

"*Oh*, we already knew that. I'm that *same king's* descendant, after all," Athar said matter-of-factly, but anyone who *didn't* know that was severely taken aback. "*What? How else did you think I ended up splitting my mind with this dumbass?*" Athar's alternate voice asked, stunning the others yet again.

"You've *got* to tell me the story behind that someday," Ed muttered under his breath. "When this is all over, I'll tell you whatever you want to know," I chuckled.

Continuing in my book that was merely a retelling of what came after the Wardens had left, I found that there were a few names I couldn't place *anywhere* in my knowledge, though I still wasn't sure if they were the names of spells or *beings* that we'd simply lost the knowledge of. I committed them to memory and moved on to the next book.

"*The Great Partition*," I heard Ysevel say, almost to herself, prompting everyone to look at her. *Be careful how you word what you read. If there's something you already know, try to act surprised,* I reminded her. "What's that supposed to be?" Ed asked. "It's one of the things we came here to look for," Mom replied, giving Ysevel a nod to begin reading.

"It says here that beings known as *Wardens* sought to wield a power reserved only for the most powerful of beings: Dragons," she said with *genuine* surprise as everyone looked at her in awe. "I knew it! I *fucking knew* they were real!" Ed said, grabbing my shoulders and shaking me excitedly. "H-Hold on, Ed! I don't want to tip over," I chuckled, freeing myself from his grasp before she continued.

"It says here that the *Blasphemers*, as they're called here, wanted to wield a sort of culmination of *all* powers, though the Dragons couldn't allow that, since it would destroy the balance between the realms. As their greed steadily increased, it spawned *another* strain of power known as *Tyrant* mana; one designed to disrupt all other sources except *one* they couldn't control," she said, but I already knew the answer to that.

Wraith mana, I thought silently, giving her a nod to continue.

"It goes on to state there are *six* primary powers: Ethereal, Vexing, Leech, Rivet, Shifting, and Wraith. Each of these has its own realm, and while most of them were deemed *good*, the Blasphemers sought to use them to take control of the citadels that housed them in this realm," she continued, lifting her eyes momentarily to see the expressions of the others.

Judging by their expressions, Calduran and Balgrim seemed to know this already, but I couldn't help but wonder *to what extent*.

"How did these Dragons respond to that sort of rebellion? Were these *Blasphemers* successful in any way?" Ed asked, putting a pair of fingers to his temples and rubbing them gently. "To an extent, yes, but it says here the Dragons played a role in thwarting their plans," she said, skipping through a few pages. "What about their enemies?" Meliss asked cautiously.

"It seems the Blasphemers weren't happy about that at all, as they've tried countless ways to continue their original mission. They nearly..." Ysevel trailed off, swallowing a dry ball of spit and glancing at us worriedly for a moment before continuing. "N-Nearly wiped out a race of powerful creatures known as *hegraphenes*, the only ones stated here that knew how to wield Wraith mana, when they refused to give it up," she read with difficulty, feeling a surge of emotions beginning to well in our cores.

I didn't know how to frame my emotions at that moment, but I knew that we needed to find out the truth, even if it pained us to learn it.

"However, that wasn't without the help of *other creatures* known as the *Alternates*. It says that the Blasphemers *banished* those who couldn't wield Wraith mana to a realm known as *Vareluth*, the Underworld; using the Alternates as a means of controlling the hegraphenes there," Ysevel said.

She did her best to read it as a matter of *fact*, and not reveal the fact that a piece of Kalia's life, once shrouded in mystery, had just fallen into our laps.

"T-That's *horrible*. Those poor creatures must have suffered so much pain," Meliss said, putting a hand to her mouth in shock, but the rest of us, those who'd come to know Kalia and her clan, felt an almost unbearable weight in our cores.

Ysevel did her best to fight back tears, blinking a few times and shaking her head as all the emotions rushed through our connections with Kalia. *It's alright, Ysevel. Please, keep reading,* our mentor said in as soothing a voice as she could muster.

She subtly nodded and cleared her throat, reading a few lines of the book to find where she'd left off.

"When the slaugh-... *deaths* of these hegraphenes were discovered, the Dragons used their might to *remove* the remaining Alternates from the land, stripping them of their cores to walk as little more than empty husks of their former selves. They even went as far as removing half the citadels that served as hubs of these powers from the realm, though it doesn't say where they put them," she said, finding it difficult to read through blurry eyes.

"That's probably for the best. If one of these *Blasphemers* ever managed to get in here, that'd be the first information they'd search for," Ed said, considering the possibilities, but *we* knew the answers to at *least* two of them: Valdis and Pyrdredd.

"Indeed, though it also says that there were *scars left upon the land* as a result. I wonder what they mean by that," she muttered the last half almost to herself. "I believe *I* can answer that quite simply: The Rhydian Mountains, Harut, and the ground beneath your feet, the

Gramm Isles," Calduran said gravely, causing Irun to flinch at his words. "Y-You're saying *Harut* is one of these scars, Great Calduran?" he asked, trying to hide his genuine surprise.

"Not the country, but the *desert* that remains. Have you ever wondered *why* it's so perilous to traverse it without a special compass? The actions taken by the Dragons when the Great Partition occurred *caused* the once-fertile land to become that way. However, Caegwen was spared much of the damage due to the *Hynafol Arboraneth* in Myrdin," the old dwarf replied, raising more than a few eyebrows in response.

Ysevel flipped through a few more pages to see if that was correct, and her eyes widened when she found her answer. "He's right. It says here that the land was once as lush as Caegwen, though the land became barren and scarred, as it was the epicenter for the Blasphemer's attacks on the hegraphenes," Ysevel continued, prompting Irun to blink several times in shock.

That explains why Irun noted their architecture was so similar, I realized, getting a nod from mom and the others who shared that thought.

"What of the Isles, then? How are *they* a scar?" Meliss asked, but Balgrim was the one to answer. "That's because once our forefathers discovered what had happened, they thought it would be better to remove themselves from the equation entirely and *begged* the Dragons to separate them from the mainland," he said with no small amount of embarrassment.

"*Cowards*," Athar's alternate spat, but neither Balgrim nor Calduran could say anything against it. "It's true. They *were* cowards for leaving the Continent to fend for itself. Technology might have even progressed much further had it not been for their decision and upholding of traditions to keep our history safe," Calduran replied solemnly, shocking Athar that he'd actually been right in his assessment.

Ysevel closed the book and her eyes simultaneously. "Everything that follows is history we already know, for the most part, but I think we've found *enough* of the answers we were looking for," she said, still feeling Kalia and Devyr's emotions just as strongly as before.

We all knew there was more to the story of the Great Partition, but there were still questions that couldn't be answered by what the dwarves had kept locked away for nearly a thousand years. As we left the archive, I was grateful to see there was a way for us to return to the surface quickly. A mechanical cart powered by mana stones that was only revealed by a hidden space in the hall we'd walked down by activating it with mana.

As it turned out, it was only accessible on the way back up, but that was neither here nor there.

There were, of course, many questions that burned in my mind.

Why the Wraithborn? Was it just because Tyrant mana couldn't control them, or was there something more? Is finding the other citadels part of Mideia's plan? I asked myself after we bid Balgrim and Calduran thanks and farewell for the day.

I couldn't put my finger on it, no matter what I tried, but I knew there *had to be* a reason for that small piece of information to be there. We walked silently alongside Kalia, Devyr, and my mother, trying to absorb all the information we'd just received.

"Kalia, I... I'm sorry," Ysevel said, knowing she wouldn't answer aloud. "It's alright," Kalia whispered, placing a hand on her shoulder.

"At least we know what we're up against now, right?" she continued hushedly after realizing there wasn't anyone within audible distance.

Ysevel paused momentarily, but nodded her head in understanding. "We'll make them pay for what they did to your family," she said sternly and in a tone I hadn't seen her use before. "Yes, we will," Mom added.

They didn't need me to chime in, already knowing my thoughts on the matter, but I did anyway. "We're with you, *battle-sister;* in both victory and defeat," I said, quoting an excerpt of the vow we all made. Kalia gave me a firm nod and bid us farewell, leaving with Mom and Devyr.

After saying goodnight to the others, Ysevel and I returned to our room, but before we could even unclasp our armor, there was a knock on the door. We both looked at each other with pure befuddlement, but to our surprise, we found Athar waiting just outside our door.

"Thoma, we need to go, *right now.* Ysevel, you come too," he said urgently. "What's going on? Did something happen?" I asked seriously. "On my way back to my quarters, I overheard one of the maids talking about some *massive beast* to the north, and that they were going to send some scouts to investigate it," he replied hushedly.

"You think Balgrim will be going along with them?" Ysevel asked, getting a nod of confirmation from him. "Do we tell the others?" I asked, but Athar shook his head. "If we're spotted, it might add tension between Siraye and Balgrim, even more than there already is," he said, tilting his head slightly as he shifted his gaze away from us.

"Fair enough. Let's get moving," I said, following Athar down the halls. I was grateful he had such a good memory, since he perfectly retraced our steps back outside while still avoiding many of the guardsmen, who were likely to report whatever it was we were doing.

We made our way outside the main palace and over the tall wall that surrounded the illuminated city, narrowly avoiding the guardsmen on watch on the ramparts. "I think we're in the clear," he said, looking over one of the boulders we hid behind. "Look, over there," Ysevel hissed, pointing in the general direction of a handful of dimmed mana lanterns to our north.

We gave each other a silent nod of understanding, moving from boulder to boulder and tree to tree as we did our best to get closer. We followed them for the better part of *two hours* before they came to a halt, but when they did, it was near the edge of a cliff that overlooked a small, grassy valley, brightly lit by the full moon's light that came up over the distant ridgeline.

As we scaled a nearby boulder to get a better look, we realized they'd done something similar. "That must be where the creature is going to show up, but how could they know its precise location?" I asked the others, but neither of them could answer that question. Still, we waited to see what would happen, and within a few minutes, we felt it.

"That's *Leech* mana," we almost said in perfect unison, scooting up a bit more to have a clearer view of the valley below. Within moments of doing so, a large orb of sickly green mana appeared. However, having obtained the *Authority* from Erumon, we were able to see what the dwarves likely *couldn't*.

"Not just that, but I can see streaks of *Tyrant* mana present as well," Ysevel noted. Her eyesight was *far* better than mine, after all, but I could feel it swirling through the currents of mana that permeated the area. "Wait, what's that over there?" Athar asked quietly, but we realized the dwarves, too, had seen it.

They quickly hid behind some boulders, slamming their backs against them and nearly spotting *us* in the process. It forced us to duck, but since we were much higher up than they were, we could still keep a good eye on the creature that presented itself.

It was, undoubtedly, *massive*. A hunking, lumbering beast that looked like molten shadows as it moved. Its arms were roughly the thickness of a Caegweni tree, though the maw that opened from the front of its body did so at the height of its stomach. Its mouth glowed and let out a bellow that trembled the boulder we used for cover.

"What, and I cannot stress this enough, the *fuck* is *that*?" Athar asked us with widened eyes, still staring at the creature. "I-I've never seen anything like it. Has Kalia ever mentioned anything of the sort?" Ysevel asked, but I couldn't fathom a beast like that residing in Vareluth. "I don't know if she's ever mentioned a *shadow titan* before," I said, giving the *twenty-meter* beast as good a name as any at that point.

We observed it for a few heartbeats before it began to move toward the growing orb of Leech and Tyrant mana. It gradually picked up speed and started to race toward it like a hungry dog to a slab of meat. Its gigantic maw began *consuming* the orb, pulling the tendrils into its mouth and causing the shadow titan to *glow* with a sickly green light.

"D-Did it just *eat* it? It moved like it was being *controlled* by something, right?" Athar asked shakily, as we could now see the finer details of the creature, now that more information began to appear. "I think you might be right," I muttered, knowing he had experience in what that would feel like, but none of us could take our eyes off the shadow titan.

The Leech mana seeped through its skin in vein-like striations along its body that radiated from its maw to its extremities. A pair of these veins wrapped around its body and moved straight upward toward its head.

The veins ran up the back of its neck, over the top of its head, and filled the once-empty eye sockets with the sickly light. "That's a lot like the technique Sabura used for his eyes," I muttered, getting a nod of agreement from Ysevel.

"You there, what the *fuck* are you doing here?" a familiar voice came from below our boulder.

Shit, we've been had, I mentally sighed before peeking over the edge of our boulder.

"Druid Balgrim?" I asked, feigning surprise. "Get your asses down here before it sees you," he hissed, pointing to the ground beneath him. Ysevel and Athar moved first, but I wanted to get one last look at the titan from my vantage point.

It loomed like a menacing *mountain* of shadow and mana. It raised its head to the sky, almost as if reveling in its newfound power, but within a few heartbeats, it suddenly snapped its head in my direction.

Fuck! Did it see me? I wondered, risking a final look over the edge of my boulder.

Its maw was… *smiling* in my direction, but it didn't come toward us. Instead, it turned and left the way it came, moving at nearly twice the speed it had when it arrived.

"Are you as insane as your mother? What the hell were you idiots thinking?" Balgrim asked grouchily. "That's my fault," Athar said, stepping in front of Ysevel and I with his arms spread widely. "I'd overheard some of the maids mentioning a creature, but *you already knew about it, didn't you?*" Athar's voice shifted into his alternate's, causing Balgrim to flinch at first, but it suddenly turned into a wolfish grin.

"I did. I've been hoping to find one for quite some time, and I've spent the last *few years* working towards this goal. Now that I have, will you help us defeat it? I've seen the way you all fight, and I'd be willing to bet you *could*. Am I correct in my assumption?" he asked us, but his tone was *not* one I felt comfortable with.

I don't think there's any way out of this one. If he tells Calduran we were out here, we might be in trouble, I sent the two of them. *I hate to admit it, but I think you're right. I'm sorry, guys,* Athar sent back with a mental sigh, to which Ysevel put a hand on his shoulder and nodded in solidarity.

"I don't know *how* we'd fight something like that, but I think it's best we warn the others and formulate some kind of plan. The three of us probably won't be enough to take it down by ourselves," I shrugged.

It was a *half-truth*, but since we didn't know its full capabilities, it would be reckless to rush in unprepared. But no matter what kind of creature it was, I knew there *had to be* a way to kill it. "*Whether it breathes mana, air, or shadow, it can die,*" Athar's alternate said, revealing a wolfish grin.

"Right then. Let's head back for now. Tomorrow, we'll come up with a plan to defeat it," Balgrim said, beating his fist twice across his chest as if to swear an oath to his words.

We had no choice but to agree to his wishes, and we were aware of it.

CHAPTER 90
OLD FRIEND

E rumon led the others through Erebos forest at breakneck speed, their shadows flickering amongst those of the leaves far above them in the afternoon sun.

While they didn't have much difficulty keeping up with him, it was evident to *everyone* that he was holding back quite a bit. Even so, they followed him through the dense, titanic trees as best they could.

"We're nearing the source. I suggest you all prepare yourselves, but we must maintain whatever element of surprise we can," Erumon said over his shoulder, getting silent nods of confirmation from the others.

We're nearing the communion chamber Siraye made use of to speak with Thoma. Do you think the Guardians are in danger? Ren sent Thorn with a concerned look. *We'd better hope not. I don't want to fight them if I don't have to,* he replied, exhaling strongly through his nostrils.

Within half an hour, they reached the chamber and hid behind multiple trees, spreading out in an arc that allowed them to see as much of the surrounding area as possible. Even at that distance, the palpable aura of Leech and Tyrant mana could be felt weighing down on them.

Erumon signaled for the others to move in slowly and quietly with a single hand gesture, and the others followed his command to better see through the trees.

What they found was a large, ravenous orb of mana seemingly drawing the life out of the surrounding area. One of the chamber guardians moved toward it, its upper body *lurching* toward it like an unstoppable force was sucking it in.

What is it doing? Ren wondered, but before he could even get an answer, Erumon stepped in and cast a barrier of pure, white mana around the orb, halting the Dericoed in its tracks and stopping the orb from drawing more of the surrounding mana to it.

The tall, tree-like creature quickly turned to the barrier's owner with a rageful screech. Erumon signaled for the others not to attack the creature and took a few steps toward it, spreading his muscular arms widely.

"Be at peace, *old friend*," he said in a voice much louder than he had ever used within the confines of Myrdin's limits. "We would not bring harm to an honored guardian of the realm," he continued, causing the Dericoed to flinch and twitch like it had just been struck by surprising news.

"There are *descendants* among you. How can I be sure you do not aim to bring me harm?" the creature asked, its deep, crackling voice resonating through the ground beneath the others' feet. "*Nexis Pelantyr* is no more. He has been defeated by one of his descendants, and will never be able to harm you again," Erumon replied, lowering his arms and prompting the guardian to regard him curiously.

"How do you know this?" the creature asked, glancing around for any other potential intruders momentarily. "I was *there* to see his end," Erumon responded, producing the black pearl from the bracelet on his wrist and holding it out for the creature to see clearly.

It took a halting step backward, almost as if it were reeling in *disgust*. "That... cannot be," it said after a few heartbeats, shaking its head in confusion. "But it is, *old friend*. What reason would I have to lie to you?" the warden asked, returning the pearl to his bracelet. "You would not be the first to lead us astray, but *why* do you call me an *old friend*? Have we met before?" the creature asked with a snarl.

"You don't remember me or my kind? That's a shame. It must have been difficult, living all these long years without knowing who brought you here in the first place. I'm sorry," Erumon said gravely, though the others who'd come with him to stare at him in utter shock and confusion.

"The *other* said something similar, and we believed his words wholeheartedly, but he led one of our own to wander the wilds without conscious purpose," it said, prompting Erumon to become surprised this time as it pointed to the still-growing Dericoed embedded in the chamber's outer wall.

"*The Other?* What other?" he asked urgently. "*The Scourge of the Twilight Sea*, he called himself. We did not know or understand his purpose here, but we've since sworn a vow to Siraye Fayren to guard this place with our lives as payment for saving our fallen brother," it said, putting a hand across its chest and performing an elven sign of respect.

If it remembers its oath, then it must remember us, *right?* Ren sent Thorn with raised eyebrows. *It might, but I don't know if we should interfere, here,* Thorn cautioned, but Ren shook his head. *It might be a way to make him warm up to us and get us the answers we need,*

Ren replied with a shrug, causing Thorn to sigh. *If you say so, I'll let Erumon know you're coming,* he said, his eyes glowing immediately to form a link to the Warden.

Erumon looked back at them with visible surprise, giving them a curt nod of understanding and motioning for them to step forward. "What are you doing?" Ardrin hissed, but Ren held up a hand to keep him from asking more questions.

The creature spotted the two who were there that day, with Nenvalur close behind them. He'd hardly said a word the entire time, but Thorn had signaled for him to approach as well.

"Guardian, it's been some time, hasn't it?" Ren asked, also spreading his arms widely, prompting the Dericoed to raise what would be its eyebrows in genuine surprise. "*Little Rennyr,* I hadn't sensed you were here. How and *why* did you hide your presence from me?" the creature said in a more light-hearted tone than he'd used with Erumon.

"My apologies, Guardian. Old habits," Ren shrugged. "I see the one we left in your care is doing well," he continued, gesturing to the half-grown creature. "It was thanks to you and the others that he returned home. Lord Warden, I apologize for my attitude toward you. I didn't realize you were with *them*," the Dericoed said, gesturing to the others.

If a creature such as this could be flustered, it likely would have been.

"All is forgiven, Guardian. But tell me, what do you know of this orb?" Erumon asked, nodding his head in its direction. "It only recently appeared here. It was small, at first, but it began to grow at an alarming rate just before you arrived. I moved toward it because it *called to me*, almost as if I had no control over myself," the Dericoed replied with a slight hint of confusion in its tone.

"It *called* to you? Do you recognize the mana still permeating the air?" Erumon asked, but the creature shook its head. "I have only ever felt it once before, but that was when the world was still cracked and splintered," it said, gazing back at the sealed orb.

The Great Partition, Taegin sent Ardrin, who nodded in agreement alongside Anwill from behind their massive tree.

"When I realized that no *drake* would come to our aid, I understood that the mana wanted me to sacrifice myself to absorb it, leaving me with no control over my will. I am... *indebted* to you, Warden, just as I am to the *little one* and Siraye Fayren," it gave another elven bow.

Erumon paused, placing a finger to his chin pensively, crossing his other arm, and tucking it into the crook of his elbow. "This is ill news indeed. Perhaps this *orb* and so-called *Scourge* wanted to draw *him* out," he began, almost speaking to himself. "You three, come out here. There is something we must discuss," he called out over his shoulder, prompting Taegin, Ardrin, and Anwill to step forward.

"Whither my roots, I was right. There *were* two more descendants with you," the Dericoed said, its brow furrowing slightly as the dark, hollow ovals it had in the place of eyes turned to them. "Indeed, Guardian. I am known as Taegin, Siraye's father, and this is my brother, Ardrin. It is an honor to meet you," Taegin bowed, prompting Ardrin, however reluctantly, to do the same.

They introduced Anwill briefly, with Bernar following close behind, exchanging pleasantries and helping the guardian to understand the current situation of the realm he'd long-since been isolated from.

"So, this realm is under threat yet again. Perhaps it *was* he who called himself the *Scourge*," the creature said pensively. "There is a good chance it was, but an even *better chance* that it *wasn't*," Erumon noted. The Dericoed's blackened eyes widened. "You mean to say there is another? *He* has not yet arrived?" it asked with genuine surprise.

"Not yet, but *that* is a clear sign he is making his move," Erumon pointed to the sealed orb, which began to diminish in size under the weight of his sealing spell. "Then you will have no choice but to *wake him* if this realm wishes to survive the coming war. We Guardians are too few and too vulnerable to fight an all-out war, but we *will* protect the land with which we were entrusted," it said, prompting looks of pure befuddlement on everyone's faces.

Well, everyone except Erumon's, that is.

"Are you sure about this? Even if we *do* wake him, it will not be easy to convince him of our need, as he's long-since shut himself off from the ongoings of the realm, from what I've heard," Erumon protested, spreading his folded arms out beside him, but the creature let out a rhythmic sound that could only have been a chuckle.

"You see much, know much, and are capable of much, Warden, but if you want to protect the realm you *swore* to keep watch of, then your best chances lie with *him* and the *ones who walk with death*," it said, tilting its head toward Ren with what might have been a grin on its face, sending a slight chill down the small elf's spine.

"The Wraithborn," Anwill muttered, finally understanding a piece of a puzzle that had long-since turned in the corners of his mind, getting a nod from the creature in response.

"Very well, Guardian. I will gather our allies. In the meantime, I trust you will continue to guard this land to the best of your abilities," Erumon said, looking up at the massive creature with a tinge of hope written in his expression. "Such is my purpose, Warden. See to it that you do not defeat *your own*," the Dericoed said, offering him a deep, respectful bow.

Before they left, Erumon condensed the orb down into another pearl and placed it in the hidden space in his bracelet. They bid the creature farewell and made their way back to Myrdin in contemplative silence.

When they arrived, they were met by the others with expectant, fearful looks on their faces. "W-What was it, Lord Erumon?" Leona asked, followed by the others who stayed as well as Aurae, who greeted him with a bow. "An orb of Leech and Tyrant mana nearly wiped out the guardians near your *communion chamber*, I believe Ren called it," he replied gravely, causing the others to be taken aback by his words immediately.

"Here? How is that possible?" Aurae asked with genuine concern. "It seems Mideia, or perhaps *his subordinates*, have found a way to breach the protective magic of the *Hynafol Arboraneth*," Taegin replied, nearly sending her into a state of shock. "*Hera fy Angharad*," she said, putting a hand to her heart.

"Not all is lost, yet, as we still have a few ways to protect this realm. If we fail here, then this realm may not be the *only one* affected,"

Erumon said, raising a hand to calm her, but his words still held a weight that was difficult for Marte and Neko to comprehend.

Even Leona was still a little shaken, but she did her best to remain calm.

"What kind of *ways* are you talking about, Lord?" Thorsen asked. "Before I tell you, I would like you and Gwili to step forward," he said with a gesture that signaled for them to stand before him. The elf and the giant looked at each other with pure, unadulterated confusion, but they did as the Warden requested.

"While you may not be one of the Arwydus, your family has helped safeguard the Gwynnleaf for many generations," Erumon began, turning to Gwili, who swallowed dryly. "And *your* lineage, though heavily diluted now, is the same as my own; thus making *you* a guardian of this realm by birth and *Blodt*," he continued, turning to Thorsen.

The information he presented caused a slight stir in the small group, as they suddenly realized that these two, who'd loyally protected Leona and many others, were always *destined* to do so. The two before the warden were clearly the most shaken at this display of confidence from one so powerful, but neither of them could even say a word.

"On that note, I would like to give you something befitting of a guardian, one I have only given to *one other* person here," he said, giving Taegin a knowing nod. "W-What kind of gift might that be, Lord Erumon?" Gwili stammered, turning to see who he was looking at and shuddering in realization.

Erumon's expression softened as he produced a pair of bright, orange pearls from his bracelet. Everyone's eyes widened and focused on the pearls that glowed like twin suns in the palm of his hand, though none dared move toward it.

"This is known as *Shifting* mana. In my realm, this is a common power, though it has been lost to this realm since the time of the Great Partition. I have only deemed *one*, other than yourselves, worthy of this power in the past, though it was purely out of necessity," he explained, though it didn't seem like their words reached his audience.

"I-... *We're* honored, Lord Erumon," Thorsen stammered this time, shifting somewhat uncomfortably at the mention of being worthy. However, Gwili's eyes began to well with tears at the word, but he did his best not to break down entirely before the others.

He failed miserably, of course.

"It makes me glad to see you so moved, Gwili Gwynn, but please refrain from staining my boots with your tears," Erumon said with a hint of humor; the first time *anyone*, including Taegin, had seen him use such language. "Here, take them. I hope they will serve you, and the ones you seek to protect, well in the coming days," he continued, presenting each of them their pearls.

They gingerly took them, though Gwili nearly dropped his with the amount his hands were shaking, and washed them down with water from a skin handed to them by Leona. She stepped back with a prideful look and watched as the two began to glow brightly, like the last light of a setting sun. It didn't hurt their eyes to look at it, but there was a similar warmth as one might feel when standing next to a fire on a cold winter's day.

As the glow died down, Thorsen and Gwili looked at each other in silent contemplation as to what had just happened. "T-This is an incredible, and *humbling*, gift, Lord Erumon, but how are we supposed to learn it if it's been all but lost to this realm?" Thorsen asked, flexing his fingers momentarily, feeling the *Shifting* mana coursing through his veins and muscles.

"Taegin can assist with that, but as I said before, we *have* other options aside from our Wraithborn friends to help us fight against Mideia and his plans," Erumon began, causing nearly everyone to raise an eyebrow and emit a unified *huh* of confusion.

Has that much *information been lost to this realm?* Erumon asked himself with a soft chuckle before looking at the others.

"What do you know about *dragons*?" he asked in the same tone a professor would to a class of young students.

CHAPTER 91
WITH A VENGEANCE

"What do you know about *dragons*?" Erumon asked again, as if making sure his question was heard by everyone present.

"I've only heard about them in legends," Neko raised his hand skittishly, glancing at the others for support. "I think the situation is the same for *most* of us, at least," he added, lowering his hand slowly, getting a nod of acknowledgement from Erumon.

"I know there are a few *older* members of our group who've likely heard more about them, but to keep a long story short, they are incredibly powerful and have a deeply rooted hatred for *anyone* who's been corrupted by Mideia," he said loosely. However, his tone suggested there was *much more* to the story than he let on as he began to pace.

"After what I saw with the Dericoed, I concluded that if this is going to be a war of attrition, then we're going to need all the help we can get," he said, pausing to look up at the canopy far above him that caught the final rays of sunlight.

"Like I told Lady Kalia, I spent many years hunting down my former comrades, and you should know that they are *not* small in number by any means. When I reached my conclusion, I figured it would be in our best interest to call upon one of the ancients to come to our aid, since *our* realm is facing challenges of its own," Erumon said, the weight of his words heavy on everyone's shoulders, though they couldn't *begin* to comprehend what he meant.

"So, what would you have us do, Lord Erumon?" Bernar asked, taking a step forward. "For starters, all of you here should merely address me as *Erumon*. We're going to be brothers and sisters in arms shortly, and I don't think it would be wise to keep grades of status between us, much like Aurae and Leona have asked you all to do," he said with as warm a smile as his stoic complexion would allow.

He wouldn't do that unless he really meant it, Taegin realized, forcing himself to blink several times.

"Secondly, I would like Taegin, Ardrin, and Bernar to undertake the mission of waking him up. His *den*, as he likes to call it, lies at the foot of the Rhydian Mountains just north of Soule. I would accompany you, but I must return to *my master* with the unsettling news we discovered during our interaction with the Dericoed," Erumon said, getting a surprised look from Thorsen and Gwili.

It's just a shame we *weren't invited,* Gwili wordlessly sent Thorsen with a glance.

"In the meantime, the rest of you should continue your training as much as you can. Knowing his personality, he will likely be much more... *amicable*, if he sees you putting all your effort into training," Erumon continued, prompting Neko and Marte to swallow dryly. "We will abide by your advice, Lo-... *Erumon*," Thorsen stammered at the more casual use of the warden's name.

Ardrin placed a hand on his chin pensively, twitching his head as if working something out in the depths of his mind. "Something troubles you?" Erumon asked plainly. "A *lot*, actually, but right now, my focus is on what we would even say to him, given that he's been asleep for so long," Ardrin spread his arms, but the large man moved forward and put a large hand on his shoulder.

"When the time comes to wake him, be mindful of your thoughts and emotions, as with the Wraithborn and their connections to each other, *dragons* can see those *naturally*. As for what you will say, I'm sure the words will come to you when the time is right," Erumon said with confidence.

After bidding the others farewell, Erumon stepped through the portal that brought him back to Polarion. This time, the others nearby caught a brief glimpse of the realm beyond the bright, swirling portal, leaving them in almost as much awe as they had felt upon discovering a dragon.

"T-This is insane. What if he comes when we're *not* training?" Neko asked, prompting Bernar to chuckle. "That's why you're not going to stop until we return," he said with a wolfish grin and a pat on the young half-elf's shoulder. "*Aww*, come on. You can't be serious," Neko said with a nervous chuckle, but Bernar's smile never broke.

"How do you think Thoma went from being a base-level third-stage to a *high-level* fourth, *huh*?" Bernar asked, his smile never once dropping, sending a chill down Neko's spine. "It's fine, Bernar. I'll make sure he gets enough rest in between," Anwill chimed in. "While *I'll* make sure he gets as much value from it as possible. *Both* of them," Nenvalur stepped in with an equally wolfish grin aimed at Marte.

"We'll leave them in your care, then. We leave at dawn, so we should prepare anything we'll need and get some rest tonight," Taegin said, but Ardrin raised a hand to stop him. "We *could* leave tonight and reach Soule by dawn," Bernar suggested, even though they'd already traveled a considerable distance to the communion chamber earlier in the day.

"Ardrin, what do you think? We might as well get a head-start, right?" Taegin asked, but Ardrin began moving without more than a muffled grunt. "I guess that's that. Let's move, Bernar," Taegin said, following behind his twin brother.

Bidding the others farewell with a brief wave, their mana rapidly surged, and they disappeared with three massive, concussive blasts left in their wakes.

As they ran through the city gates, the guards were forced to hold onto their helmets as the strong winds swept past. It took them the better part of the night to reach their destination, though it was *much less* time than it would have taken them by horseback.

Moving as quickly as they were certainly took a toll on their stamina when they finally came to a halt, but even with the vague description from Erumon and the distant light of the setting full moon, they were astonished by what they found.

"Do you sense anything?" Bernar asked between battered breaths. "I'm not even going to hide the fact that I'm too fucking tired to sense anything, right now," he continued, breathing heavily. "It was *your* idea to run through the night, but I don't sense anything either," Ardrin said, spitting a wad of spit on the ground as he gasped for air.

"It's not that we're exhausted, since our mana is already replenishing our energy; it's that we *can't* sense anything," Taegin realized, looking up at the looming cave's mouth that gently hummed with a nearly invisible sheen of multi-colored mana.

It had the appearance of a broken lantern's oil spilling out onto the ground on a rainy day, but it constantly shifted and swirled depending on where one was observing it from. "What? That's impossible," Ardrin said, but after enhancing his vision a little more, he noticed what his brother had.

"It's not impossible as much as it is a *necessity*," Bernar added, getting a glance from the other two. "*What*? You two were in contact with Erumon *loooong* before I ever was, and I can tell you from first-hand experience: whatever mana's behind this barrier is going to *crush us*," he said with a heavy shrug.

"Now that I think about it, he's right," Taegin said, putting a finger to his chin. "The question is: how the *hells* do we get in? Did Erumon give either of you a hint?" he asked the others, still gazing up at the top of the cave. Ardrin's eyes squinted as he took a step forward, placing his hand on the barrier itself.

He closed his eyes and felt for the mana's response as he tried to push into it. The barrier rippled, but it wasn't enough to break it or let him through by any means.

"Damn it," he hissed, pulling his hand away as if he'd just touched a piece of hot coal. "I'm getting the feeling Bernar might be right about this dragon's mana," he said, showing the palm of his hand to the others.

"Let me try," Taegin said, placing his hand on the barrier the same way Ardrin had. The barrier rippled a little *more*, even going so far as to reach the outer edges of it, but like with Ardrin, Taegin was forced to pull his hand away.

"That was a bit more than Ardrin's," Bernar noted idly. "It's not a competition, *nephew*, but I suppose Ethereal mana *might* be more closely related to whatever this barrier is made of," Ardrin scowled, pouring mana into his still-smouldering hand. Bernar thought back as far as he could on his lessons, but no spell or barrier he could think of gave him any sort of answer.

Thoma, how would you get through this? Bernar thought, keeping it to himself.

"Wait a minute. Give me a hand, will you?" he asked after a few minutes of silence, moving up to the barrier and raising his hand. "We've already tried that," Ardrin groaned. "Just trust me, will you? I have an idea," Bernar sighed and shook his head, prompting the other two to share a glance and shrug before placing their hands at regular intervals beside his.

"We're going to have to push through it, since we don't know how it was put up to begin with," he said, getting raised eyebrows from the others. "Are you *insane?* This barrier's going to rip us apart, crush us into dust, and burn our remains before we even realize what's happened," Ardrin scoffed, removing his hand and using his head to gesture to their obstacle.

"I *know*, but Erumon wouldn't have sent *just us three* if he didn't think we could manage it. He must have known it was here, but that's *also* why he sent the three most powerful of us," Bernar began, getting an almost *prideful* look from Taegin.

"He's right, brother. Anwill couldn't be here since he's training the others, and we're running out of time," Taegin added, but Ardrin was hesitant to follow. "Fine. On your head be it," he sighed heavily.

"Taegin, you push into the barrier along with me, but don't use your *Ethereal* mana," Bernar said, causing Taegin to raise an eyebrow.

"How did you...?" he trailed off, but Bernar chuckled and shook his head.

"Do you know how many times I've heard Thoma talk about the night you came to get him? He always said your eyes *glowed like twin suns*, but I only put it together when Erumon produced the pearls yesterday. *You* were the one he was talking about regarding that *Shifting* mana, or whatever he called it," Bernar said, gauging Taegin's reaction and knowing he was right.

Ardrin, however, was taken aback.

"It seems you still hold secrets, even after all this time. A shame you didn't use it to fight me in Coltend," he said, shaking his head. "No one knew of the existence of other types of mana at the time. Why would I shatter their worldviews at what I considered to be such a *pivotal moment*?" Taegin shrugged.

"You know how Thoma is, and I'm sure he wouldn't have survived that fight with Irun if he were focused on me using *that*," Taegin sighed and shook his head. "I hate to admit it, but he's right. He even kept it from *me*, and I've been his right-hand man for *years* now," Bernar said with a hint of disappointment in his tone.

"I know *why* you couldn't use it, but right now we *have to* if we're going to get through this barrier. I'll ripple it; Ardrin, you provide the barrier to protect us if the mana really *does* crush us; Taegin, you find a way to take advantage of the ripples I create. Ready?" Bernar asked, turning his attention to the barrier as his mana began to surge.

"I admire his pragmatism, at least, but there's no guarantee I'll be able to protect us from the mana," Ardrin said with a single, internal chuckle. "We're ready whenever you are, *brother*," he continued with a single nod, putting his hand near the barrier once more.

How long has it been since then? Taegin wondered idly before his eyes began to glow like the twin suns on that fateful night.

As he changed his drawing of mana from the Ethereal to the Shifting realm, he created a small orb of sunset-colored mana in the palm of his hand, gently placing it on the barrier. A subtle ripple emanated from the barrier that continued to grow in strength as he increased his output of mana.

"It's working! Keep going," Bernar laughed, immediately increasing his output and digging his feet into the earth to push with all his might against the barrier. As Taegin's mana began to permeate the barrier, Ardrin's shield began to strain and bend against the weight of its mana.

"Not enough, we need more," Ardrin grunted, pushing even more mana into his spell. Taegin wordlessly followed his commands, his irises glowing even more brightly this time as his mana began to counter the mana flowing within the barrier.

The three of them began to push with all their might, feeling the barrier starting to give way like a needle trying to poke through a thick leather hide. Slowly but surely, they realized the small hole they'd made in it began to grow. "Just... a little... more," Bernar strained, his teeth bared and eyes widened.

Taegin let out a grunt of exertion that grew into a full-blown shout within moments. More of the shifting mana countered the barrier's flow, and with a final push, the three of them were through.

They nearly collapsed on the other side, hardly able to stand under the weight of the density of mana within the cave. Bernar chuckled and looked behind him incredulously, but realized that the barrier had *already* healed from their small hole.

"What... the *fuck*? How can... *anything* have... this much mana?" he barely managed through gritted teeth, forcing more mana into his muscles just to be able to *stand*. Taegin and Ardrin were both at a loss for an answer, doing their best to focus their attention on standing as well.

"I think, *urgh*... I think Erumon might have *oooverestimated* our... abilities a little," Ardrin said with a dry chuckle as he, too, was struggling to stand. "You're... not wrong," Bernar replied with a wry grin. "I think this must be similar to what Thoma trained in with Kalia," Taegin said, hardly struggling for words, prompting the others to look at his glowing form with utter confusion.

"*Oh*, my apologies," he said, raising a barrier of his own that immediately allowed their efforts of pushing against the stone to cause them to stumble when the pressure was released. As the other two regained their composure, they couldn't help but look directly above them, seeing only minor striations racing across the orange, translucent barrier.

"Nice trick. Again, you should have used that to save your shoulder back then," Ardrin scoffed in disbelief, his mouth slightly agape as he looked up. "Perhaps I should have, but finally seeing the two of you struggle beneath the mana's weight was rather satisfying, short-lived as it was," Taegin offered a dry chuckle.

"*Shifting* mana does exactly what its name suggests: it shifts things according to the will of the user, be they material or mana-based. Dragons don't bother fighting each other with spells, since they all have this ability innately," he said, reciting a shorter explanation than what he'd received from Erumon.

"Tha-... yeah, no. That makes sense," Bernar concluded with a few quick nods. "Well, now I'm worried we'll have to fight him. He's *not* going to be happy we've gotten through his ward," Ardrin said, straining his vision to see through the ward and into the depths of the massive cave that spanned nearly a hundred meters across.

"With any luck, he'll recognize this mana, but if not..." Taegin trailed off, not wanting to finish the thought. "That's comforting," Bernar said dryly with a curled eyebrow aimed at him.

The three began to move through the cave after Bernar conjured a small sphere of light. He struggled to keep it *outside* of Taegin's barrier, but quickly found that it was easier to keep it half-in, half-out. As their path became clearer, the cave walls became much more visible, revealing details they might not have noticed otherwise.

"This cave was *made* with mana. Look at the walls, you can almost see the rippling in the stone that would match a dragon's steps," Ardrin noted with utter fascination, prompting the others to look at him with surprised looks and raised eyebrows. "W-What? I've always sought knowledge, and *this* level of mana manipulation is unlike anything I've ever seen," he said with a defensive shrug.

"You're right, but have you noticed they're getting... *smaller*?" Bernar asked, unsure if he was right, prompting Ardrin to inspect them more closely. "They *are* getting smaller. Well, not *smaller*, rather less *spaced out*," Ardrin said, curiosity reigning over his tone as if he were a child seeing mana for the first time.

As they continued to walk, the rippling continued to decrease in spacing, though the cave walls kept the same width throughout. "Do you feel that?" Taegin asked, speaking curtly since it was taking nearly *all* his concentration just to keep the barrier up.

"Aside from the mana beginning to seep through your ward, I *think* I can sense it growing denser. Almost like it's condensing to a single *point*, much like the ripples on the walls," Bernar noted, getting a nod of agreement from Ardrin just before Bernar's light gave out. "What the...?" Bernar halted, trying to summon another one that hardly left his palm.

"*Who dares enter my domain?*" a voice resounded from deep within the cave, though how deep, they couldn't tell, as it felt like whoever, or *whatever*, was speaking was doing so aloud and in their minds. The voice was deep, like the rumble of a distant thunderclap rolling through a deep-cut valley.

It wasn't harsh, by any means, but to their minds and ears, it was *deafening*.

"We've come seeking your help, Great One, under the guidance of Warden Erumon," Taegin called out in response, since he was only *a little* less affected by the dragon's voice. "*And how can I know you're who you say you are? You might only be saying that to hide your true intentions,*" the voice said with obvious suspicion laced within it.

"You may read our minds and cores, Great One, but you will find no such guile within," Ardrin managed, knowing *all too well* what this being was going to do. "*It has been well over a millennium since anyone other than I has set foot in here, so how did you manage to break through my ward?*" the voice asked, its tone still suspicious.

"Have you been here so long that you've forgotten the mana used by your own kin?" Taegin asked, receiving a curt snarl from the voice before it spoke. "*Those traitors were also my kin, and yet you think that alone will bring me to trust you? If so, you are sorely mistaken,*" the voice's tone rose to almost a shout, increasing the mana pressure around them.

"Warden Erumon said that it would not be an easy task to convince you, and it seems he was right. Perhaps *this* will help you trust us," Taegin said, lowering his barrier immediately, nearly slamming him and the others into the stone beneath their feet. They couldn't bear to look in the direction of the mana's source, but they *could* feel a sense of curiosity permeating through it.

"*What sort of trickery is this? You would go so far as to rid yourselves of the only chance you might have had against me, slight as it may have been?*" the voice asked, pulsing mana momentarily.

I think it's moving toward us. Are you sure that was a good idea? Bernar sent Taegin with a pained look. *If this doesn't help, nothing will,* he replied, feeling the density of mana increasing, likely signifying that the dragon was coming their way.

However, instead of a heavy, rumbling footfall, they heard something more akin to the steps of a *man*, rather than a beast's. With concerned, yet curious looks, they peered into the darkness ahead of them and did their best to find out what was happening.

A *snap* came from the far end of the cave that echoed throughout it, repeating itself innumerable times before finally fading out. As soon as it did, the cave walls began to shift and move, creating various dimples that ran the length of them. Mana *spawned* in these dimples, gently illuminating the area as they lit up from back to front, revealing a tall, dark silhouette at the far end of the cave.

"*Who are you, really?*" the voice asked, taking a few steps closer, as the figure's broad shoulders rose and fell according to its breathing. "Great One, please. Look into our cores, and you will find no ill will coming from us. We're not here to fight you; we need *your help*," Ardrin struggled, doing his best to keep his speech calm and consistent with the others' demeanor.

Another pulse of mana came from the silhouette and ravenously entered their bodies through their chests, wrapping like a vice around their cores. Bernar and the others could not only *see* what the dragon was looking for, but it was like their entire lives were laid bare before him; from their happiest moments to their darkest secrets.

"One *of you has experienced this before, I see*," the voice said, its mana shifting ever-so-slightly to focus more on Ardrin. "*But it appears you* were *telling the truth. You may now raise your heads without fear of punishment*," it continued imperiously, prompting them to do just that in a calm and controlled fashion.

What the fuck *do we do now?* Bernar sent Taegin. "Such harsh language from one so young. Is that how they speak in this age?" the voice came, much less forcibly and without appearing in their minds as well as their ears. "M-My apologies, Great One. I meant no offense," Bernar immediately bowed again as his face flushed with embarrassment, since the other two were forced to follow his gesture.

Before they raised their heads again, there was an almost imperceptible movement in the residual mana in the cave that prompted the three of them to realize this figure was standing before them. Slowly, like the gentle flow of a river, a pale hand was outstretched and placed within their fields of view.

"There is no need to apologize for your habits, Bernar, as they are merely a byproduct of your environment. It is *I* who will likely have to adapt after being in here for so long," the voice said, subtly motioning for them to stand normally.

As their eyes traced along the figure's body, they realized that its boots were a pale white with red accents that swirled along their center, quickly followed by a white robe cut at the knees that split from the height of his waist. A solid belt of pure mana held his robe tightly to his body, swirling with multiple different colors, much like the ward at the entrance.

The multi-layered robe had folds of white and red near its mid-chest and clavicle, and broad shoulders to bear its weight, leading into a strong neck and sharp jaw. Piercing mismatched eyes met theirs, with one being a bright violet and the other a deep scarlet, beneath a scarred set of silver eyebrows.

His hair was cut reasonably short, though still long enough for a loose strand to hover over one of his scars while the rest were swept back neatly. At his temples, there was a slight hint of *scales* being hidden with mana, though they were hardly noticeable.

"We're honored to meet you, Great One," Taegin said, placing a hand across his chest and slightly tilting his head. "Likewise, Taegin. You three have done well to break the barrier, and I can see *why* Erumon chose you," the dragon said with a slow nod. "You know our names, Great One, but may we ask yours?" Ardrin asked with mild hesitation.

"*Ah*, yes. I apologize for my lack of manners, as I seem to have forgotten them. My name is Ryfon Ansuz, though you may simply call me *Ryfon*, since I can tell that Erumon has given you his blessing not to address him formally," Ryfon said with a subtle smile.

"Gre-... I mean, *Ryfon*, how much do you know of our situation here in Kavrass?" Bernar asked, curious as to how much he *truly* saw when he looked into their cores. "I would say that I know enough, but Erumon must have taken that into account, knowing I would see it and rise with a vengeance," Ryfon said, giving them a single nod as he sighed.

"Come, there is much work to be done," he continued after a brief pause, moving between them toward the cave's entrance. "That was almost *too* easy," Bernar muttered under his breath with a shrug.

"I heard that, but like I said, Erumon has placed great trust in you three to come and summon me. He wouldn't have done that if he thought I'd be difficult to deal with," Ryfon said, his language adapting by the second to reduce its formality and make it easier to converse with the three. "G-Good to know," Bernar chuckled nervously, rubbing the back of his neck with a smile while Taegin and Ardrin could only roll their eyes.

Ryfon led them to the cave's entrance, and with hardly a wave of his hand, the barrier was dispelled. "That took everything we had to get through it!" Taegin said in awe with a look of surprise that matched the others'.

"If *this* took everything you had, then we might be in a worse situation than I thought. When we return to the others, I will help guide you to become the strongest versions of yourselves, much like Kalia has done for Thoma," Ryfon said with a grin over his shoulder.

"H-How much do you know about Thoma?" Bernar asked cautiously, causing Ryfon to pause and choose his words carefully. "Thoma Fayren has the potential to grow more powerful than any of you. I'd dare say he's already almost as strong as *you are*, Bernar, though the only thing stopping him from being so is that he hasn't broken into the fifth stage yet," Ryfon said, though it was apparent he was leaving certain information out.

"That little *shit-bird*..." Bernar trailed off with a chuckle as he shook his head. "Don't worry. I understand competition between siblings, and while I *will* help you to surpass your limitations, it will be up to *you* to keep pushing those boundaries further," Ryfon said with a sly smile before raising a hand to halt the others, closing the mouth of the cave behind them.

"You might want to stand back for this," he said, his mana surging around him, weaving through his arms, legs, and chest as his size began to double, then triple. His robes underwent a smooth transition from a cloth-like material to scales, as the exposed skin around his face and hands began to change as well.

"Four legs, two wings; that's a *dragon*, alright. I still don't know how people confuse them for *wyverns*," Taegin chuckled in disbelief. "Only *uncultured swine* would confuse the two," Ardrin said, though he was a little less impressed than Taegin. "That would make most of the known *realm* uncultured, then," Bernar chuckled, interlocking his fingers atop his head in pure astonishment as he looked up at the titanic beast.

Within mere moments, the surge of mana was, once again, nearly causing the others to stumble beneath its weight, but once Ryfon had reached his full height of well over *fifty* meters tall, it subsided.

"Get on," his voice rumbled, shaking the very foundations of the Rhydian Mountains. He lowered a pale wing with scarlet accents along the scales that tightly wrapped around the bones supporting it. They did as he requested and found their footing was much more secure than they had anticipated, given the membrane's partially transparent nature.

"Hold onto these," Ryfon directed into their minds so as not to cause an accidental rockfall. He created three sets of handholds made of a material similar to the belt he had worn only moments ago. *"Ready to see the world through the eyes of a dragon?"* he sent them through a mental transmission.

They didn't even have to answer.

With a single beat of his wings, there was a blast of air beneath them that was a much more *powerful* version of the same blasts the three of them had left behind when they departed from Myrdin. Within a few seconds, however, they were far above the canopy, watching as the Rhydian Mountains sped by incomprehensibly quickly.

The morning sun was just coming over the horizon, casting a golden glow upon the land, and what had taken them hours to traverse the night before took mere *minutes* atop the dragon's back.

"This is *incredible!*" Bernar shouted over the sound of the wind rushing by his ears. "Shut up before he drops us!" Ardrin shouted back. "Just because you have Onyxe doesn't mean it's not an incredible experience, Ardrin. Let him enjoy the moment," Taegin snapped back with a light-hearted chuckle as the land of Caegwen sped by nearly a kilometer below them.

"I won't be able to maintain this form when we enter Myrdin, which means we'll have to stop a short distance away so I can return to a more humanoid *form,"* Ryfon sent them along with his feelings towards doing so.

Thankfully, they all understood without another word.

Nearly half an hour had gone by since they left the cave, but they were already on the outskirts of Myrdin's training area. Ryfon returned to his more *palpable* form, though Bernar and Ardrin led the way through the woods.

"I'm glad they took my advice, but I hadn't expected to return so quickly," Bernar said with audible relief at the sight of nearly *everyone*, including Leona and Aurae, going through multiple different training regimens. "I wager 50 Crescents that Neko shits himself," he continued hushedly to Ardrin, who gave him a wry grin in return. "I'll take that wager," he replied with a smirk.

As they broke through the line of dense trees that surrounded the training area, Aurae was the first to notice their presence, though she was closely followed by Anwill and Ren, who halted their instructions momentarily.

"We're *baaack*!" Bernar chirped, prompting the others to turn in their direction with visible surprise. "I thought you'd be gone for *at least* three days. How the *hells* did you return so quickly?" Gwili said, lowering his sword momentarily and dispelling a small orb of Shifting mana.

"We, *uh*, had some *help* getting back," Bernar replied, stepping aside to reveal Taegin and Ryfon, allowing them to move past with a respectful gesture. As Ryfon got closer, he realized that many of them were paralyzed. Whether that was out of fear or the intensity of his mana, he was unsure, but he reduced his aura even further, just in case. "Greetings," he said, giving them a nod of acknowledgement.

No one could move or speak.

That was, however, until Aurae stepped forward, garnering strange looks from the others as she moved, unburdened, toward him, with a gentle smile on her face.

"Hello, Father. It has been *too long*," she bowed reverently, prompting *everyone's* jaws to careen toward the ground.

CHAPTER 92
DENIAL

Ysevel, Athar, and I returned to Narin with Balgrim and his small scouting party.

We walked silently, considering the gravity of what we'd just observed, as well as the fact that Balgrim had seemingly *known* where it would show up.

How much do you think he really knows about that thing? I asked Ysevel with a subtle nod toward the druid. *It's hard to say. Athar doesn't trust him at all, and after seeing that, I don't blame him. I just don't know what to do about this,* she sent back with a mental sigh.

I couldn't have agreed with her more. On the one hand, he *was* acting very suspiciously, even without Athar's warning, but none of us truly felt we had any definitive proof. But on the other hand, it was almost like knowing something was wrong, but you had no way of proving it to anyone, or you'd look insane.

It was frustrating, to say the least.

Even with that at the forefront of our minds, we continued on our way back to Narin, where we found the others already waiting for us in the main hall.

"What are you all doing up this late?" I asked them, but Irun was the one to raise his hand. "In my defense, I thought Athar had disappeared again," he sighed. "It *also* doesn't help that no one here explained where *any* of you were," Mom added with a curled eye-brow, though I knew her comment wasn't *only* aimed at me.

"These two lads followed us out to investigate a creature that has been terrorizing the land to the north," Balgrim stepped forward in our defense, surprising the three of us who'd gone with him. "*Oh?* A shame *we* weren't informed," she replied, not believing his lie for a moment since I'd felt her tugging on our connection for information.

"Y-Yes, well, I simply didn't think it was going to be worth it to wake *everyone* up for that *thing*," Balgrim stammered under the weight of her gaze. She held it for a few moments, shifting her gaze to the rest of us briefly before landing her eyes on him. "*Nope*, I don't buy it, so you'd better spit it the fuck out," she said, taking a few steps toward him. "W-Wait, Siraye, I didn't me-..." his voice cut off as she grabbed him by the throat and lifted him into the air.

"Listen here, *shitling*, I've played this game long enough to know when someone is bullshitting me, and right now, my eyes are *stinging* at the stench. So, are you going to talk, or do I have to resort to more extreme measures?" she asked, her eyes flaring with mana as she lifted him a bit higher.

Don't kill him yet, he may be helpful to us, Kalia sent with a half-step forward. *I won't, but I need him to stop beating around the bush, and fear is always a good tool to use,* Mom sent back, though Ysevel and I already knew why she was doing that.

Balgrim's eyes darted around the room, searching for any way out of his predicament. However, since it was still so late at night, only a handful of guardsmen were in the hall, and *none* of them dared to get close to her. "A-Alright, you w-win," he managed weakly as he raised his hands in surrender, prompting her to drop him like a sack of potatoes.

He coughed and rubbed his neck when he landed, his lungs desperately reaching for any air they could. "Go on, then," Mom said, glaring at him imperiously. He coughed one last time before getting back on his feet, still rubbing his neck that had red finger marks near his trachea.

"You're still the same old *brute*, just like before, so I don't expect you to understand," he said venomously, but she maintained her composure much better than I would have, were it directed at me. "This creature we were investigating only shows up when the orbs of *Leech* mana are large enough for it to take notice of, though we've only ever seen them at night," he began, prompting Kalia to tilt her head and start prodding our connection.

"From what we've learned, it not only *consumes* the mana, but it takes it on as its own; almost as if it gained *a consciousness* from doing so," he continued, though Mom merely raised an eyebrow, while the others looked on in horror at the mere thought of it.

"What did it look like?" she asked plainly. "I think *he* can answer that," Balgrim said, jutting his thumb toward me, signaling he was done answering her questions. Everyone's attention turned to Ysevel, Athar, and I, prompting me to step forward.

"This creature was unlike anything I've ever seen or even *read about* in the bestiary at Codrean, with skin that seemingly melted into the darkness surrounding it, and a large, gaping maw in the middle of its stomach," I began, noticing Kalia *and* Devyr beginning to shift uncomfortably.

"Wait, are you saying that this is an entirely *new breed* of monster?" Ed asked, appearing out of one of the hallways that lined the main hall with Meliss right behind him. "I *think* so. Either that, or it's been here since long before the Great Partition, and these orbs have seemingly woken it up," I replied, though I wasn't sure of it myself.

"What happened when it consumed the orb, then?" he asked, walking up to the rest of the group. He, unlike everyone else, was still in sleeping attire, rather than his armor.

Who the hell woke him up and told him to come here? Athar sent me through a mental transmission, though he only did so whenever he *knew* he could control his alternate's thoughts. *Beats me, though I suspect Balgrim's guards had something to do with it,* I replied briefly, returning to Ed's question.

"It was like the creature was *made* for doing just that. When the orb was consumed, the mana flowed from its stomach up to its empty eye sockets, but somehow, it *saw* me and *grinned*," I said, seeing the creature's unnerving grin clearly in my head.

"That should be impossible," Kalia spoke, surprising everyone who *didn't* know she could. "W-What the...? I thought you took a vow to be mute until your vengeance was completed," Ed said, genuinely surprised, as both he *and* Meliss forcibly blinked a few times.

"If we find that creature, it *will* be, though it seems none of you here know what it is," she said, taking a few steps forward. "It's known as an *Obcasus*; a legendary creature that sits on riverbanks to feed on corpses, but they're usually no larger than a full-sized Thran, and they *don't eat mana*," she said with evident concern in her voice.

It was apparent she was trying to hide the fact that it came from Vareluth, but the fact that she *alone* knew the name was enough to draw some degree of suspicion from the others. Regardless, there were a few audible *gasps* and concerned glances from them, though I suspect many of those present were in denial at her statement.

"What if that creature decides to turn its gaze on Narin? Will we be safe here?" Meliss asked, but Kalia shook her head. "It isn't known to attack populated areas, but if it's as abnormally large as Thoma said it was and it *saw him*, then that could change, given its behavior," she said with a shrug, making Meliss' eyes widen at her nonchalance.

There was a short moment of silence as everyone considered her words, though no one seemingly had any proper response to the potential threat of the obcasus.

"Is there a way to kill this creature?" a voice came from the far end of the hall, prompting all the dwarves to kneel immediately as it reached their ears. "Great Calduran, you can't be serious! A creature like that needs to be *studied*, not *killed*. Please, consider the advancements we could make if we learned how it could do that," Balgrim pleaded hoarsely, his throat still red and sore from Mom's chokehold.

Calduran stepped toward us with a heavy gait and furrowed brows. "You've been studying it for *years*, and yet you have so little to show for it. With this major shift in its behavior, I don't think it would be wise to risk studying it further," he said in a low, rumbling voice that trembled the ground beneath our feet.

Balgrim was stunned at the comment and his lord's *vivid* display of a lack of confidence. "B-But Calduran, we don't ha-..." he began to stammer, but was cut off by a surge of mana that could have crushed an untrained human.

"Mind your *tone*, Balgrim. I will not have this creature running around our lands *freely* if it's using these orbs to gather its strength," Calduran burst out angrily, exerting his will over the mana to match his voice as he forced the druid to his knees.

"If it seemingly *absorbed* the mana, as Thoma described, and its behavior was unlike anything else we've observed, it stands to *reason*, not *emotion*, that it should be dealt with accordingly. I trusted that you once knew better than to forget your position here *required* that of you," he continued, stopping just before the subdued dwarf.

"M-My deepest a-apologies, Great Calduran," Balgrim wheezed, using all his strength to fight against the mana that wanted to crush him into the stone floor. Calduran paused for a moment as if considering his words and the honesty behind them. After a few tense heartbeats passed, Mom placed a hand on Calduran's shoulder and nodded her head, prompting him to release his mana.

While Balgrim found himself struggling to breathe for the second time that night, Calduran sighed heavily and shook his head disappointedly. "I'm sorry to ask this of you, Siraye, but it seems we will need your help yet again after all these years," he said with a pleading look hardly visible beneath his bushy eyebrows.

"Of course, Calduran. It's the least I could do for an *old friend*," she smiled, surprising the rest of us at the sheer amount of potential lore behind that statement. Naturally, no one said anything *aloud*, but we were all thinking it.

Just how long have you known him? I asked her. *Remember that crater Balgrim's always complaining about? Calduran used to live in the town that used to* be *there, but that's a story for another time,* she explained, forcing me to blink a few times.

"How soon can you and your *allies* move out?" he asked, glancing at the rest of us. "At your command, Great Calduran, though I think it would be a good idea for us to take Balgrim with us, since he seems to know more than he's letting on," she said, glaring down at the still-kneeling dwarf.

He returned the glare and either held back a spiteful comment or a wad of spit, I couldn't tell which.

"I'm going, too," Ed said, injecting himself into the situation, but Mom raised a hand to stop him. "I don't think that's a good idea. If this *obcasus* is unlike anything we've fought before, I don't want to put you at risk unnecessarily," she shook her head, causing his expression to drop.

"I'll vouch for him," I said, stepping forward, getting a look of concern from her. "I've known Ed all my life, and if there's anyone who can adapt to a creature's fighting style quickly, it's *him*," I continued with an approving nod aimed at him. "Are you sure?" Mom asked, meeting my gaze sternly.

"He killed an *addia* the first time he met one. I think he'll be alright, even if you would only take him for a supporting role," I said, knowing it wouldn't be easy to convince her. She thinned her lips and inhaled deeply through her nostrils, letting out a heavy sigh.

He knows Balgrim better than any of us. If something's off, he'll be the first to let us know, alongside Athar, I sent her, causing her concern to fade quickly when she realized what I was doing.

"Alright then. If you trust him, then I will, too. However, if anything happens to him, *you'll* have to take responsibility, do you understand?" she asked, not as my mother, but as a *commander*. "I understand the weight of my decision, and accept it entirely," I replied in a similar tone, giving her an elven salute, which caused Ed to pump his fist in excitement.

"What about me?" I heard Meliss ask him under her breath. "No. *That's* not a risk I think any of us want to take, no matter what *anyone* thinks," Mom said curtly, but I knew she was right. Meliss frowned, but ultimately seemed to understand the position we were all in.

Ed had been trained his entire *life* to fight monsters; *she* had not. There was a skill disparity that simply couldn't be avoided, and we were all sure that was the *only* thing Mom was taking into consideration. It wasn't that she didn't want all the help she could get, but it was also too risky because of her position with Edryd.

"Very well, Commander Siraye. I've heard about your combat prowess and, after having seen it for myself, I understand your judgment," Meliss replied with a slow nod, prompting Ed to turn to her. "Don't worry, we'll be back before you even realize we're gone," he said with a smile, kissing her forehead.

"*Might be a little longer than that, but...*" Athar's alternate muttered, getting a quick slap upside the head from Irun. "It's fine, Irun," Meliss said with a chuckle. "Do your best out there. *All* of you, and may whichever gods you believe in grant you swiftness in battle," she said, putting a hand across her chest and bowing; something she likely learned from Ren and Thorn during her training.

"Thank you, Meliss. We leave at dawn; get some rest until it's time to leave. We're going to need it," Mom said, excusing us with a bow to Calduran, who beat his chest twice at us with a solid *grunt*. Ed scurried up beside me, but noticed Mom raising an eyebrow at him before he could say anything.

"Make sure you have everything you'll need to take, Edryd Baelis. You're under *my* command for now, and I won't expect any less from *you* than I do my *own son*," she muttered, causing his eyes to widen and his throat to catch. "Yes, *she's* my mom. Sorry, I kept that from you," I sighed and nodded my head, while his head flicked between us with pure confusion. "B-But you don't have steel-colored hair; not to mention she's *stunning*, while you're, *uh...*" he trailed off, getting a raised eyebrow from Ysevel. "*Meh*, I guess you're *alright* if you've landed yourself a princess," he huffed, causing me to chuckle.

"Thanks, Ed," I said with a thin-lipped smile as I patted him on the shoulder. "I'm sorry I couldn't tell you earlier. There was just no good time to explain everything," I lied, but since she'd already spilled that secret, there wasn't much left I could do.

"It's fine. I'm sure it would have raised questions, many of which I *have*, by the way," he shrugged before elbowing me in the ribs. "When this is all over, I'll explain everything," I smiled as I gave him a shove.

Only a few hours had gone by, and even though I'd taken a nap in my armor, it wasn't as restful as I'd hoped. "Good morning, sleepy-head," Ysevel's voice reached my ears, followed by a gentle kiss. "Fuck me, is it time to go already?" I asked in a drowsy voice. "I *would*, but unfortunately, it's time to go," she chuckled and helped me to my feet. "Damn, foiled again," I groaned sarcastically, rubbing my eyes and shaking my head to wake up more quickly.

"Are you sure about Ed coming along?" she asked, to which I nodded my head. "He's exceptional at recognizing and analyzing attacks; always has been. I'm just hoping whatever relationship he seems to have with Balgrim won't interfere with anything," I said distantly. "I hope you're right," she replied gravely.

So am I, I thought, even though I knew she heard it.

Just as the words left my mind, I felt a mighty tug on my core. It was evident that Ysevel had felt it as well, as she, too, forced herself to catch her breath.

"What the hell was *that*?" I asked. "I-I don't know, at least not for *sure*, anyway," she said somewhat distractedly, as if an old memory stirred in her mind. Whatever image she had in her head, it was blurred to the point where I simply couldn't figure it out. "Come on, we should meet with the others and see if they felt it, too," I suggested, but she could only offer me a blank, confused nod.

We made our way downstairs and met up with the others. Balgrim was anything but pleased to have only gotten what might have been two or three hours of sleep, but we still needed him to lead us to where he'd tracked the creature. We followed him down to the courtyard, where Calduran was waiting for us, with a carriage prepared just behind him.

"Didn't expect you to see us off," Mom said with a grin, clasping his thick forearm tightly. "Well, if what your *friend* there said was true, you might be in for a good fight after all," he replied, nodding at Kalia. "She hasn't led us astray yet, after all, she was the one who taught us how to deal with the Thran, though I'm sure there are still some terrorizing your lands," she said with a sigh.

"I'm grateful for all the help you've given us so far, Siraye. When I saw you again the day you arrived with the others, I could hardly believe my eyes. I know Balgrim might have his reservations about you for what you did, but I trust that it was the best judgment call you could have made at the time. Just like then, I know you'll do whatever it takes to get the job done," Calduran replied, the corners of his beard around his mouth scrunched as he offered her a smile.

Mom bowed and signaled for us to come forward, and we did as requested, lining up around her and Calduran in an arc. "*The Order of Nightfall's Blade* will see this mission through, Great Calduran Lytehammer. I *promise*," she beat her chest twice, prompting us to do the same. While he tried to hide it, I could have sworn I saw a tear run down the side of his face, though I couldn't tell whether it was from pride or him having to say *goodbye* to her again.

He stepped aside and had his servant open the door for us to enter the armored carriage. This time, Mom decided she would sit up front to watch for any dangers and ensure Balgrim wasn't going to lead them astray. We waved at Calduran as he watched our carriage begin to move down the street that would lead to the northern gate.

"I wonder if we'll get the chance to come back here after this is all over," I thought idly, still impressed by the mana-stone infused architecture. "If we're successful in our mission, I'm sure he'll consider reforming his policy on foreigners," Ed said with a chuckle, prompting the rest of us to do the same.

"Thanks, by the way," he began again, forcing me to curl an eyebrow and scoff. "For what?" I asked. "For taking me along with you, and keeping Meliss here, where she'll be safer," he muttered, though I knew what he was trying to say. "Don't worry about it. Just make sure that *you* stay as safe as you can, alright? She needs *you* just as much as you need her, so don't do anything stupid," I said, tilting my head forward to let him know I was being serious.

He paused and looked at me for a moment, likely wondering what could have led me to say that. When Ysevel smiled and nodded at him, he seemingly figured it out.

Now all we have to do is kill this monster and find out what Balgrim was really *up to,* I sent her and the others, getting slow nods of agreement from them.

We rode off through the northern gate and headed roughly along the same path Athar, Ysevel, and I had taken the night prior. We reached the area where the orb once was, and found there was more of the same, dead ground beneath where it lay as the first one we'd seen.

"That can't be good," Ed said with widened eyes as he stared at the ashen ground that surrounded the crater it had made. "Look over here," Balgrim called out, gesturing to something in the ground a few meters away. There was a massive footprint in the earth that could have easily been mistaken for one of the valley's terrain features.

The others and I moved over to where he was, but Kalia examined it more closely, rubbing a pair of fingers in the dirt and bringing it up to the nostrils of her helmet. She instantly reeled backward, as if some *pungent* smell had riddled her senses.

"It's *sick,* or perhaps it's been so heavily influenced by *Leech* mana that it's *become* that way," she said plainly, but through our connection, I could feel her apprehension toward Balgrim beginning to grow. "Which way did it go last night?" Mom asked. "It went off to those north-western mountains, though I don't know *why,*" Kalia replied, raising a finger in the general direction she could trace with the residual mana and footsteps.

"Is there anything of note over there, Balgrim?" Mom asked, turning to face him. "N-Nothing *I'm* aware of," he replied, though the shakiness in his tone let us know he *was* telling the truth. To his credit, I wouldn't have wanted to be held by my throat again, either.

"Then let's go see what it's hiding," Mom said with a wolfish grin.

CHAPTER 93
RETURN TO FORM

"E-Erumon? What are you doing back here so soon?" Vauv asked, stepping aside as the large warden stepped through the gate with determination in his eyes.

"I need to speak with Karthus, it's urgent," he said, briskly making his way back to his master's tower. "Wait, wait, wait. You can't go in there right now," she cautioned, putting a hand on his shoulder, turning him around. His eyes searched hers questioningly, but the pleading look on her face made his own shift into one of genuine concern.

"Vauv, tell me what happened," Erumon asked calmly, placing his hands on her shoulders. As he tried to look into her eyes again, she averted her gaze and bit her lower lip as if to hold back a well of emotions.

I don't like the look of this. What could possibly have happened to him? Erumon thought, glancing over his shoulder toward the tower with a worried look.

"Please, just... You can't go in there. He wouldn't want you to see him like that," she said haltingly. "What do you mean? Is he injured?" Erumon asked urgently, but she shook her head. "Not *physically*, but he hasn't been the same since the day he dismissed us," she shook her head with a shrug, indicating she truly didn't understand what had happened.

Did anything happen between him and the dukes? Erumon immediately thought, but understood he wasn't likely to get an answer from her.

"Vauv, I still have to see him. I will bear whatever punishment he demands for my intrusion, but this *cannot* wait," he said, producing the pearl of Leech mana he'd spared the Dericoed from. Her eyes widened in surprise, and she flinched away the moment she realized what he had in his hand. "W-Where did you get that?" she asked, glaring at the small, pale orb that swirled with the sickly green mana within.

"One of Caegwen's guardians nearly succumbed to its influence. It seems our enemies have found a way to break through the magic of the *Hynafol Arboraneth*," he explained briefly, but his grave tone added plenty of weight to his reasons for wanting to see his master.

Vauv looked at it again, then to him, and finally, to the tower off in the distance, sighing heavily while she made her decision. "This pearl is bad news, but perhaps it might be part of the reason Father is *livid*," she shrugged, prompting him to blink several times. "He *already knows* about this?" Erumon asked with visible astonishment.

"Perhaps not that, specifically, but it might be one of the reasons he was forced to leave so abruptly," she shrugged, causing him to place a curled finger at the base of his chin. A few moments of silence passed between them, each considering the potentially dire circumstances they were likely to enter.

"Come with me, then. You know you can't stop me, but if he asks, I will take the blame for whatever happens," Erumon said, holding out an upturned palm for her to take. She glanced down at it and inhaled deeply, shifting her gaze from his hand to his eyes and furrowing her brow. "Don't say I didn't warn you," she answered firmly.

After traversing through the large gate, the guards immediately began to speak amongst themselves, though none dared to question Vauv's authority in bringing him there. However, as soon as they crossed the threshold of the gate, an incredible amount of mana burst out from the tower, nearly knocking them off their feet.

"What the...? Erumon, on me," Vauv urged with widened eyes, breaking into a sprint once the burst died down. He did as requested, though he noticed she hadn't drawn her weapon.

Perhaps he's in a fit of rage, he surmised, but didn't voice his thoughts aloud.

When they entered the tower, they found numerous signs of an altercation, with Karthus sitting on his throne and Sildyr right beside him, her hand softly rubbing his shoulder. "It's fine, my love. They will come to see reason soon enough," she said in a soothing voice. "They should have *seen reason* when Liagon's alternate reappeared in Kavrass," Karthus seethed as he balled his fist.

"Lord Karthus," Erumon called out from the entrance, prompting him to look up and immediately move toward him. There was a gentle shift in the mana as he appeared before his former pupil. "Erumon! I'm glad you've come. Any later and we might have had a worse situation on our hands," Karthus said, giving the warden a surprisingly tight embrace, catching Erumon entirely off guard.

"My apologies. I know how you are with physical contact, but I *am* grateful to see you," Karthus said, releasing his hold and taking a step back. "What happened? Vauv made it sound like you were in serious trouble. It appears she wasn't *entirely* wrong," Erumon replied, looking around the room.

"The *dukes* held a meeting that made it sound like some were beginning to side with the *traitors*. Though I must admit, we don't fully know how far their reach extends," Sildyr sighed, appearing just behind and beside Karthus. "Damn it, so it *has* come to that after all these years," Erumon sighed and shook his head. Sildyr approached him and put a hand on his shoulder, giving him a consoling look that only a mother could give.

"I know how much you have sacrificed to keep that realm safe, but you can rest assured that we *will* do everything in our power to ensure that it remains that way," she said comfortingly, giving Karthus and Vauv a glance as well.

"Thank you, Sildyr, but I feel that there are very few who can oppose the will of the dukes. I'm doing what I can to prepare those who *could*, but they need more time; particularly, Gwili Gwynn and Ser Magnar Thorsen, who have just now come into contact with *Shifting* mana," Erumon responded with a solemn nod, prompting Sildyr and Karthus to exchange a glance.

"*Time* is a fickle thing. While it is true that a *century* to us may pass in a single flap of our wings, to them, that could be numerous *generations*. Unfortunately, they're running out of the precious time they *do have*," Karthus said in a tone that sent a chill down Erumon's spine. "What do you mean?" he asked, genuinely shaken by the words.

"What do you know about Liagon's alternate in Caegwen?" Karthus asked, getting a confused look from the warden. "I know that the alternate we used as bait to try to trap Mideia escaped Valdis and made its way to Myrdin to try and attack Aurae, though none of the elves seem to know *why*," Erumon darted his gaze across the floor while he recalled the information.

"I see. It seems they don't know about Aurae's inheritance of the *Benevolent Ring* and what it contains, or perhaps, not *all of them* do," Karthus said, placing a curled finger on his sharp chin. "Wait, you can't mean tha-..." Erumon halted as Karthus's hand moved from his chin to his mouth in a silencing gesture.

Erumon's eyes widened in realization.

"*Oh*, I see," he began with an understanding nod. "However, is it *possible* that the *Scourge* was the one who brought it under his control?" Erumon asked, taking precautions not to use the name, though it was *Sildyr* who surprised him with a nod. "Unfortunately, it *is* possible, and what it implies is *far* worse than anything Kavrass is prepared for," she said gravely.

They let her words hang for a few moments, each trying their best to come up with a solution to their predicament, but nothing immediately came to mind.

"Well, at least the ring is in as good hands as it can be. I told Taegin, Ardrin, and Bernar to seek *him* out, given their current situation," Erumon broke the silence with a slight sigh, causing the others' eyes to widen in surprise. "They were able to *wake him*?" Vauv asked with genuine enthusiasm.

"I-I'm not sure, but out of those who remained in Caegwen, it would be those three who had the best chance of doing so, since Aurae is helping to train Queen Leona of Coltend in the ways of the Wraithborn," Erumon explained, getting a chirp of excitement from Vauv, and a look of genuine surprise from the others.

"What, ultimately, was the reason you had them wake him?" Karthus asked after having had a moment to consider the gravity of that request. Erumon produced the pearl he'd taken from his bracelet and held it out for the others to see. Their expressions shifted from hopeful to ones of pure disdain at the sight of it.

"One of the Dericoed tried to devour an orb of Leech mana laced with Tyrant mana. I was lucky to have gotten there when I did, since the poor creature seemed *out of control* when the orb grew enough to be cause for concern," Erumon explained, getting a shared look of worry and shock from the others.

"Then we're already too late, and our worst fears have been confirmed. Things have been set in motion now that will *not* allow that realm to return to form. Erumon, I'm sorry to ask this of you, but I need you to send *him* a message for me," Karthus said, lowering his tone to little more than a hush.

Are you trying to hide this from the other dukes? Erumon asked him, getting a nod of agreement. *Yes. Please inform Duke Ryfon that the other members of the council might be planning a coup, with Mideia as its herald,* Karthus said, prompting Erumon's eyes to flare angrily.

CHAPTER 94
ACCELERATED PLANS

A urae held her bow, while the others had their breath stolen away from them.

They could tell at a *glance* they were in the presence of someone incredulously powerful, but none of them dared to let a single word slip. Ryfon, however, could *feel* their nervousness through tiny tremors in the surrounding mana. He chuckled once through his nostrils and shook his head, allowing a warm smile to grow.

Did she just say Father? *Wait, no, that can't be right,* Bernar thought, suddenly realizing the weight of what that meant.

"Rise, my beloved daughter. You do not need to bow to me," he said warmly, immediately cutting through the nervous tremors in the mana like a scythe to blades of grass. Aurae looked up with tears welling in her eyes, but to everyone's surprise, she darted forward and embraced him tightly.

"I've missed you so much, and I've done my best to ensure this land was taken care of, just like you asked me to," she said, her voice slightly muffled by his robes. "I've missed you, as well, Aurae. I see you've not only kept your promise, but you've made some extraordinary allies recently," he said, holding her shoulders in his broad hands as he glanced at the others.

"Tell me, how is it that my *granddaughter* came to wield Wraith mana? I can sense her presence in the realm. Was that *your* doing?" he asked her, but it was Ren who raised his hand. "Great One, I believe that was partially *my* fault," he said with a bow, getting a look of pleasant surprise from Ryfon.

"*Ah*, so *you're* one of the others I felt here. Yes, I might have guessed as much, since you were the one who gave Bernar, Siraye, and Thoma that power as well. It's a pleasure to meet you, too, Rennyr Virie," he nodded, getting an even lower bow from Ren in return.

"To address your earlier question, Father, she's doing well. I've had Ren keeping an eye on her since they left for the Gramm Isles in search of information on the Great Partition, but it seems they may have discovered a *dark secret* in the land," Aurae furrowed her brow in worry. Ryfon's large hand went to her cheek and gently turned it back toward him.

"I *know* what they found, but if my understanding of Thoma and the others who are with him is correct, they'll be able to handle themselves for what's to come next," Ryfon said, allowing Bernar, Taegin, and Ardrin to breathe a sigh of relief.

"However, that doesn't mean it will be an *easy* task, by any means. They have a challenge they must face ahead of them, and I'm sure the enemy they'll face will *not* be beaten so easily," Ryfon added, but as the last word left his mouth, a portal appeared off to his right, prompting the others to turn and face it, as well.

As Erumon stepped through the portal, he immediately sensed Ryfon's mana, forcing him to place a hand on his chest and bow deeply. "Duke Ryfon," he said

"*My, my;* if it isn't Erumon Akkeri, Warden of Kavrass and the *Anchor of the Twilight Sea*. A true *pleasure* to see you again, old friend," Ryfon said, offering him a knowing nod. "Duke Ryfon Ansuz, the honor is mine," Erumon said, immediately bowing the moment he realized who was standing before him.

They shared a glance, though it was evident they were catching each other up on the situation until his arrival, since Ryfon gave a few, silent nods of understanding.

"Well, that makes my work here *much* easier, then. The rest of you can drop the formalities as we won't be needing them anymore, as in this coming war, *everyone* will need to carry their own weight," he said in a tone that sent shivers down nearly everyone's spines.

"However, to do that, you must all understand what it is we're up against, and who better to ask than the one who's been helping this realm keep them at bay for *over a millennium*," Ryfon said, gesturing to Erumon, prompting the others to turn and look at him in pure astonishment.

"I knew he'd been fighting his old comrades, but for over a *thousand years*?" Neko asked Marte hushedly. She couldn't offer him an answer, as she was just as surprised as he was. "It's true, Neko, but I'm afraid our situation has gotten *much* worse than it was back then," Erumon said, his head hanging a little lower than usual.

"There may be those in *my* realm who have succumbed to Mideia's influence as well. According to my master, Karthus, the last council meeting they had made it seem like there were more than a few who'd begun to side with him," he began to explain, but only got confused looks from the others.

"You haven't told them about the events of the Great Partition, have you?" Ryfon asked, realizing the source of their confusion. "I didn't know enough details myself," Erumon shrugged tiredly, feeling the weight of his words beginning to weigh on him. "I see. Well, then. Let's move somewhere a little more comfortable, shall we, daughter?" Ryfon asked with a warm smile aimed at Aurae.

She led them to the same meeting room they'd used when Erumon and Ardrin revealed their plan to stop Mideia. Within the hour or so that followed, the others began filling Ryfon in on everything *else* that had occurred until that point, leaving no detail behind.

"Of course, there *was* that matter with Liagon's alternate," Anwill said with a furrowed brow. "Tell me, what became of it after the attack?" Ryfon asked. "It's still being studied, but I haven't had time to look at it through the eyes of the *Authority* since we've been so busy training the others," Anwill admitted with a sigh.

"Bring it here so I can take a look at it," Ryfon said gravely. Within a few minutes, a pair of elves came through the door, using mana to levitate the examination table and gingerly placing it in front of him. The others, namely Trina and Wien, blanched at the sight of the grotesque figure split in half.

"Thank you, gentlemen," Ryfon said, giving the two elves a nod of appreciation before he leaned in to examine it. His eyes shifted from their mismatched colors into ones of the purest white light, causing everyone except for Erumon to shield their eyes. "W-What is that?" Wien stammered. "I've never seen anything like it, so I'm not sure either. All I can say is that it's both welcoming and *terrifying*," Trina added with a wince as she tried to get another look at it.

As the light from Ryfon dimmed, the others slowly lowered their hands and looked on in shock as the alternate's body was completely repaired, with clear, pale skin free of any runes or markings. "H-How did you...?" Ardrin asked with widened eyes, causing Ryfon to smile.

"*That* was what's known as *Meridian* mana. To explain it in full would take a dragon's lifetime, but to put it simply, it is the culmination of nearly *all* mana combined into one, singular power," he said, clearly pleased with his work on the corpse. "Of course, that doesn't mean it can bring someone back from the *dead*, but it *can* heal nearly any wound so long as the core remains intact," he continued to explain.

"After all this time, the answer was *so close* and yet so *far* out of reach," Ardrin chuckled in disbelief. "Indeed. Why do you think Erumon knew to tell you that combining Ethereal mana from the Gwynnleaf with Vexing mana would work the way it did?" Ryfon said with a smile.

Ardrin was, for the first time since childhood, too stunned to speak, though Erumon could only offer him a single nod of understanding. "But wait, what does this mean for Kavrass? If the alternate came here and attacked Aurae, what did it hope to gain from that?" Leona asked, but her question immediately caused Ryfon's smile to fade.

"To explain what that meant, I must first go over the events of the Great Partition. I will spare many of the details, as they are no longer important, but the fact remains that Mideia led a rebellion against his fellow dukes," Ryfon began solemnly, forcing everyone to lean in and listen intently.

"During his rebellion, he was able to influence many of the other Wardens to overlook what he had planned to do. He used Nexis as a sort of diversion, giving him information that would have otherwise been reserved for higher beings, eventually leading him to commit a taboo crime," he continued, making Ardrin shift uncomfortably. "Athar," he muttered, getting a nod from Ryfon in response.

"That was the moment we knew he had to be stopped. His goal was to be able to spread his influence as far as he could, reaching the far corners of the Twilight Sea by using that technique to *control* everything and everyone he needed to," Ryfon said gravely, getting a gasp from the others, particularly Wien, who'd never even heard of any of this.

"However, his power alone wasn't enough to do that, so he led the Wardens under his influence, as well as a handful of my own *kin*, to challenge the rest of us for control of the powers. We knew we couldn't hold them off forever, but we did what we could when we separated the *citadels* that contained relay conduits of those powers from the realm," he continued, though only a handful seemed to understand what he meant entirely.

"That's why Harut has those mana-storms between the Rhydian mountains and Escea, isn't it?" Bernar asked, getting a confirming nod from the dragon. "Indeed, though that wasn't the only scar we left upon the land. The Rhydian Mountains themselves are one, while the Gramm Isles are the other. Still, the latter was at the request of the then-dwarven ruler," Ryfon explained, letting his words hang for a moment before continuing to make sure everyone was keeping up.

"So, where are these *relays* now? Are there any still present in this realm?" Leona asked, getting a concerned look from Erumon. Ryfon saw the glance, but paused and gathered his thoughts before replying.

"That's... *difficult* to answer. We moved or destroyed the Ethereal, Leech, and Shifting relays that we knew of with the Wraithborn's help. It was Mideia's followers who nearly wiped them out because they quickly found that Tyrant mana simply *can't* affect Wraith mana in the same way Meridian mana can't, either," Ryfon explained, though instead of their eyes widening at his response, their gazes landed firmly on Ren and Aurae.

"If Mideia knew there were more Wraithborn who were enhanced with the *Authority*, regardless of whether it was synthetic or innate, he would stop at *nothing* to ensure they would *die* by his hands," Ryfon said, his gaze landing on the other two, as well.

"Thoma," Bernar muttered quietly with a worried expression. "Don't worry. He was still beneath Vareluth's barrier when he used and learned it. It's doubtful that Mideia was able to know he could use it to that degree," Erumon said, raising a hand to stop Bernar from worrying excessively.

"What of all the training we've done here?" Leona asked, mirroring Bernar's expression. "*Also* doubtful, since the power of the *Hynafol Arboraneth* still protects these lands. If it didn't, Caegwen would look much the same as Harut by now," Ryfon added, getting a sigh of relief from the others.

Well, everyone except for Taegin, that is.

"The *Hynafol* is one of those relays, isn't it?" he asked, prompting the others to freeze solid. "Yes, but it's the last known Ethereal relay in Kavrass," Aurae replied with a solemn nod. "I see," Taegin said, leaning back to process everything he thought he once knew.

"Alright, but what about this alternate? Why did it come here to attack Her Majesty?" Trina asked, still trying to piece it all together.

I have no idea how all of this has been hidden for so long, but I feel like I need to know as much about it while I still have a chance to get the answers, she thought through the cacophony of her mind.

Ryfon, having read them, smiled. "I appreciate you seeking knowledge, Trina Lande, and I apologize for this having been hidden from the realm. We figured that the fewer people here *knew* about it, the *less likely* they were to be influenced by Mideia; unfortunately, that was a poor assumption made on our part," he replied, though Trina blanched when she felt the dragon's mana leaving her core.

I hadn't noticed it, but did he just read all *of my memories?* Trina wondered, getting a warm smile and a nod from Ryfon. *I did,* he replied.

"To answer your question, however, the alternate's body was used as a form of bait, but the sealing runes Ardrin placed on it seemed not to be strong enough to contain him. It broke loose and made its way here looking for *something,* though for now, I *must* keep *what* that is a secret. If anyone here were to be captured and forced to speak, it could spell trouble not just for this realm, but for *all* realms," Ryfon said gravely, forcing a handful of them to swallow dryly.

His words hung heavily in the air, as each one of them did their best to understand the gravity of what he meant.

"So, then, what of the orb that showed up near the Dericoed? What does that mean for us?" Leona asked, causing Erumon to sigh. "It means that he's found a way to lace his mana with Tyrant mana, breaching the barrier around this land from the *Hynafol*. It's a tell-tale tactic of his, though he only uses it when he thinks he can *win*," he replied.

"That means an invasion is imminent, then," Bernar said, placing a curled finger to his chin. "If he can break through the barrier, that means he's going to send his minions to try aga-..." he trailed off, suddenly realizing something, as he turned to face Thorn. "When we first met, didn't you say they were studying Rivet mana in Soule?" he asked, trying to recall if he'd heard it correctly.

Shit, I'm right, aren't I? Bernar thought, gauging Thorn's wide-eyed expression of fear and worry beginning to grow more pronounced.

"Ryfon, Erumon; I think I know what's going on," Bernar said, standing up immediately, getting raised eyebrows from them in response. "Go ahead, then," Ryfon gestured to the table, prompting him to create a map of Caegwen by infusing his mana into it.

The Rhydian Mountains rippled across the table, as tiny ridges began to grow half a meter in height, while the trees and surrounding landscape details were like miniature sculptures crafted by an expert artisan. The *Hynafol Arboraneth* stood proudly at nearly the same height as the ridgeline of the mountains, and began to glow with a bright aura of Ethereal mana.

"Soule is over here to the west, while the *Hynafol* is here in Myrdin," he began, gesturing to each landmark on the table. "Now, watch this," he said, highlighting the location of the communion chamber where they'd found the orb of Leech mana.

Everyone's eyes widened in surprise at the revelation.

"Supposing he breached the barrier at *this* location, he would be located equidistantly from Myrdin *and* Soule, where, according to Thorn, they've been conducting experiments with Rivet mana. If I'm right, he could attack *both* places simultaneously, provided he has the forces to do so," Bernar continued, getting an approving nod from Trina.

"I agree. From a tactical standpoint, with enough forces, he could accomplish that *easily*. If *one* alternate under his influence was nearly enough to attain his goal, imagine what an *army* could do," she added, getting a smile from Bernar that she could see the same thing he could.

Ryfon and Erumon considered this with a single glance.

"*Heh*, it seems Thoma's view of you wasn't wrong after all," Ryfon said, making Bernar blush slightly. "Y-You talked to *shit-bi-*... I mean, Thoma?" he asked, rubbing the back of his neck. "Not directly, but he *is* a Wraithborn, and while none of you *here* aside from Erumon have gone *beyond* the fifth stage, it would be difficult for me to explain *how* I knew that," Ryfon chuckled.

Be-beyond the fifth stage? Wien wondered with a similar expression to Trina's. "Indeed," Ryfon grinned wryly. "However, now that we know his goal, we *also* know that he won't be bringing his corrupted allies here. It's most likely he will use a different force, with perhaps only *one* or *two* Wardens leading the way to not draw enough attention from the other dukes who *aren't* allied with him," Erumon said, moving closer to the table.

"After he prodded our defenses using our failed experiment, he must think we're much weaker than we are," Ardrin added. "I wouldn't say that. It took nearly everything *I* had to stop it, and that was just *one* creature under his influence," Anwill said, placing his spread fingers across his chest.

"He won't have that sort of opportunity again. It's more than likely he will use the *Thran* to his advantage," Erumon began, getting a few raised eyebrows from the others. "The *what* now?" Marte asked.

"They're powerful creatures, to be sure, but it's their *numbers* that usually give them the advantage. If *Kalia the Annihilator*, as they call her, were here, I'm sure more than a few of them would question their decisions to follow him," he continued, but immediately noticed Thorsen and Nenvalur had been silently fidgeting.

"Anxious for a fight, are we?" Bernar asked Thorsen hushedly. "I've been meaning to try out this *Shifting* mana, and I wonder what new kinds of abilities I can use with it," Thorsen admitted. "I already know what *you* want," Bernar chuckled and shook his head at Nenvalur, who'd been uncharacteristically quiet the whole time.

"Just point me in the direction of whatever it is I have to kill, and consider it done. You should know from the attack on Coltend that I don't really care for much outside of a good fight," Nenvalur chuckled, recrossing his arms and leaning back.

Fair enough, Bernar thought with an upturned lip.

"If they're as powerful as you say they are, we *definitely* won't have enough time to get stronger in such a short time," Neko said, getting a nod of agreement from Leona and Marte, who were still at the early stages of mana manipulation.

Can you help them? Erumon asked Ryfon with a slightly raised eyebrow. *Of course I can. Who do you take me for,* child? Ryfon asked with a tone that suggested mild offense taken at the question, getting a stifled giggle from Aurae with the exchange no one else had been able to hear in their minds.

"I believe *I* can help you with that. You there, come here," he said, gesturing to Thorsen, Gwili, Neko, Marte, and Leona. "*Hu-uuuuuh?*" Marte and Neko asked in unison as their faces paled. "Shut the fuck up and get over there already," Bernar hissed as he forcibly punted Neko's backside, forcing him to move forward.

As the five of them lined up before him, Leona felt a mixture of intimidation and an estranged sort of *fatherly* love emanating from Ryfon.

His presence really does *remind me of Aurae,* she thought as she smiled inwardly, though she immediately blanched when she realized the dragon had read her thoughts. *Don't worry, I won't tell her you feel that way,* he replied with a subtle wink.

"Thorsen, I will share with you and the others as much insight as needed for you to reach the *fifth stage,* though I must warn you *not to* overstep your boundaries, as you will still need to get used to it. Do you all understand me?" Ryfon asked. "Yes, sir!" the others replied in unison, though Leona could only offer him a firm nod.

I'll have to work with you last, but I think you know why, Ryfon sent her with yet another smile.

Her eyes shifted away in embarrassment, but she immediately felt his mana beginning to permeate the room, as well as the return of the bright white light. Through the small gaps between her fingers, she realized that he'd placed a hand on Thorsen's core, pouring his own mana into it.

That's Meridian mana again, she realized, astounded at the sheer purity of it just as she was the first time.

Thorsen's aura grew immensely, nearly twice the size it had been when Erumon had him and the others consume their pearls. Tendrils of Shifting and Ethereal mana licked the rooftop far overhead for a few moments, but were quickly brought back under control.

"Not bad for one so young. I hadn't expected you to manage all of that at once," Ryfon said with pleasant surprise. "I've had to hide my mana for many years as an outcast, as well as during my time in the Guild. Although I don't know if I can hide it any longer," Thorsen replied, putting a hand up to his face as he looked into the nearby mirror to see his eyes *glowing* like Bernar's.

"Quite right, but remember what I said earlier," Ryfon added, patting the giant on the shoulder and moving on to Gwili to conduct the same process. "You've been stagnant with your progress. Why?" Ryfon asked the elf while reaching into his core with his mana.

I can't lie to you, can I? Very well, then. I fear I'm going to fail to live up to others' expectations of me, and this gift you want to give me is far more *than I deserve,* Gwili took a breath, feeling the mana wrapped around and into his core.

Ryfon, hearing his unspoken reply, smiled warmly and nodded his head, as if he'd already expected that answer.

"*Ah,* I see. You don't need to *fear* your past shortcomings anymore, Gwili Gwynn. *Embrace them,* and understand that they've made you who you are today. In my eyes, you are worthy of this gift," Ryfon said, the strength of his voice changing to an almost other-worldly tone as he commanded the elf to do so.

Gwili's eyes were already glowing with mana, but he closed them once more and allowed whatever peace he felt internally to wash over him like a waterfall. His aura grew to a similar height as Thorsen's, though it took some time for it to die back down.

"You two might not feel like you deserve to reach it, but I've read your cores and know what you've gone through to get here," Ryfon began, darting his gaze between Marte and Neko. "T-Thank you, Ryfon," Marte said bashfully.

Did he read my core that quickly? No, I should consider everything *a possibility at this point,* Marte thought, getting a soft chuckle from him in response.

"You wouldn't be wrong to do so, but Neko, you should come closer, too. Marte shares many of the same traits as Thorsen, so I can do you both at once," he said with a gesture to call him over. Neko unquestioningly did as he requested and promptly stepped beside Marte, though it was apparent he was extremely nervous.

Even as far from Thorsen as I was, I could already feel it, but being this close to it is incredible, Leona thought as she watched in awe as Ryfon began to pour the pure, white mana into their cores.

Like the others, their auras rose high into the air, but *unlike* them, it took them nearly five *minutes* to get it back under control. During that time, however, Ryfon watched them closely and ensured that the two *less experienced* individuals had no adverse side effects. Once he was satisfied with their level of control, he moved on to Leona, who'd been patiently waiting for them to be done.

Ryfon stepped in front of her and placed his hand on her sternum just like the others, but he noticed her expression had shifted from only a few moments ago.

I wonder, Ryfon thought, gently pushing Meridian mana into her entire being, rather than just her core. *Oh, how marvelous!* Ryfon sent her with a bright smile. *W-What is it? I-Is there something wrong with me? Please, be honest,* she stammered fearfully, but the dragon smiled as he allowed himself a soft chuckle.

Does he *know yet? Rather, does* anyone *know yet?* Ryfon asked, causing her to raise an eyebrow in confusion. *Know* what, *exactly?* Leona asked, prompting him to chuckle again. *I see. Very well, then, if you wish to keep your* child *a secret, then I will oblige,* Ryfon said, giving her a slow nod.

"MY..." she caught herself, immediately putting a hand up to her mouth, prompting a handful of raised eyebrows. *My* what? *D-Did you just say what I think you said?* Leona reverted to their original form of communication.

Y-Yes? If you don't want to bear this child, I can handle *it for you without the others knowing. It's your choice, after all,* Ryfon said, mildly confused that she didn't know her own body well enough to notice the changes.

Leona froze, still feeling the mana circulating through her body. *W-Will this* augmentation *affect the child if I decide to keep it? I... don't want anything bad to happen to it, you see,* she explained, but Ryfon shook his head. *No, the child will not be affected by any sort of* ailment, *if that's what you're asking,* Ryfon shrugged, allowing her a few moments to consider his words.

Then I'd like to keep it. I think Bernar would be a wonderful *father in time,* she said with a determined nod, prompting him to return it in kind. "Very well, then," he said with a smile before pouring more mana into her core as gently as before.

A warm wave of mana raced through her veins from her core, reaching her extremities and pushing her aura outward. Like with the pearl, hers was intertwined with tendrils of gold and scarlet mana that nearly reached the ceiling. Like with Neko and Marte, it took her a few minutes to get it under control, but Ryfon observed her with *extra* care.

She reopened her eyes and looked in the mirror to find they'd gone from their sky blue to a deep scarlet. "It seems you favor Wraith mana more," Ryfon said with visible surprise. "Well, it's not that I prefer it, but since I'm here in Caegwen to learn it from Aurae, I might as well keep it that way for now. Thank you for this magnificent gift," Leona said brightly, as a single tear of joy streaked down her porcelain cheek.

The others bowed in gratitude, but Ryfon gestured for them to rise. "Now that we've brought *nearly* everyone up to the same standard, we shou-..." he halted, turning toward the door before it even opened.

A guardsman burst through it a few seconds later with bated breath. "P-Pardon the intrusion, but we've just received word from our scouts!" he shouted, prompting those who were seated to stand up, already fearing the worst.

"What is it, Captain Ense?" Aurae asked, briskly walking toward the man, who halted to catch his breath. "Your Majesty, Soule has reported the presence of a massive orb of mana in the south-western area of Caegwen," he said, causing the others to share a glance. "Has anything come out of it?" Erumon asked, doing his best to hide his anger.

"N-Nothing yet, my lord, but..." Ense stopped the moment Ryfon held up a hand. "There will be soon. There's no time to waste. Erumon, you'll lead a team to protect Myrdin. I'll take Taegin and

Bernar with me to Soule to help bolster their defenses. If it's the Rivet mana relay he wants, *I* won't let him or his *ilk* have it," Ryfon growled deeply as his mana began to flare.

"As you command," Erumon replied without a second thought.

They have no idea how long he's waited for a chance at revenge, do they? Erumon thought privately, watching the others leave at break-neck speed.

CHAPTER 95
INTO THE DEPTHS

A s we approached the foot of the mountain, there was a strange scent in the air.

The tracks Mom and Kalia had been following were growing increasingly pronounced and more frequent. Each one seemed to veer off in different directions, which was a clear indication that there was more than *one* of those mysterious creatures.

The obcasus could have also made multiple trips to find other orbs, Kalia added after having felt my consternation through our connection. *That's possible, too, but how likely is it that Mideia brought more than one?* I asked, scanning the surrounding area for any potential threats.

The heavy woodline near the base of the mountain made it challenging to see with eyesight alone, so we all resorted to sending out intermittent pulses of Ethereal mana through the ground at varying ranges.

I'm not going to say it's impossible, *as that was already disproven by its mere existence in this realm. However, I think it would be prudent of us to assume there* are *more of them,* she added, getting an approving nod from Mom.

"How much longer do you think it will take?" Balgrim whispered just behind me. "We're only moving as slowly as we are because of *you*, so it's difficult to say. You might be *exceptional* with earth-based mana, but relying on that for movement is *not* a good idea," Mom said over her shoulder with a glare, prompting the druid to swallow dryly.

We continued in contemplative silence for a few more minutes before Ed broke it with a question of his own. "Do you think there might be more than one?" he asked, leaning toward me. "*Always be prepared for there to be more of those bastards than you thought*," I said, giving my best imitation of Garett, which made him chuckle softly.

"It feels like forever ago since we were training there together, but I guess you're right. Besides, it's not like *The Masked One* would be here controlling them again, right?" Ed asked with a sarcastic chuckle.

The concept of that made me blanch.

"Why the *fuck* didn't I think of that?" I asked myself, feeling my eyes widen as I stared at the ground. "Think of *what*?" Ysevel asked with a curled eyebrow. I took a moment to gather my thoughts and immediately began picking up the pace. "We've got to move. If I'm right about this, we're in for one hell of a fight," I said, prompting the others, including Balgrim, to begin moving at a quicker trot.

"*Oooookay*, you're starting to freak me out now, Thoma," Ed chuckled dryly. "Think about it; If creatures like glicks and daemons can't coordinate attacks on their own, why haven't we considered the possibility that *those* creatures aren't under someone's thumb?" I asked, prompting everyone, including Mom, to look at me with genuine concern.

"I hate to think about that being a possibility, but I agree with you," Irun said with a furrowed brow. "If what we know about these creatures is *true*, and that they are, for lack of a better word, *necrophages*, then *why* would it want to consume an orb of Leech mana?" he continued.

Because someone *commanded them to,* Kalia sent the others and I, including Edryd, whose eyes could hardly fit in their sockets when he heard the gravity of her tone in his head. *W-What are you saying? You think Balgrim did this?* Ed asked, his confused emotions seeping through his words.

I'm not sure he would have the power to command one that large, but perhaps with the help of another, she trailed off, glaring back at him through the slit in her helmet and nearly causing him to trip.

"*Ho,* there. Are you alright, Ed?" Balgrim asked as he reached to steady him. "I-I'm fine, thanks," Ed replied with a bit of a stammer. There was an obvious sense of distrust in the way he looked at the dwarf, but I was grateful to see he shook it off quickly. "Come on. Let's keep moving," Irun said, patting Ed on the shoulder twice before returning to his original pace.

Balgrim gave Ed a weak smile before returning to a trot alongside the rest of us, but I could tell my friend wasn't done processing everything yet. *You might want to help him out. It seems he really doesn't know what we're up against,* Ysevel sent me with a nod. *Yeah, you're right. Go ahead, we'll catch up,* I sent back before walking over to him.

"Ed, are you alright?" I asked once the others had gotten well out of hearing range. Of course, I was still sending them whatever was being said, but it was good enough for me to be able to ask him more *serious* questions without Balgrim being able to listen in.

Ed didn't answer immediately. Instead, he began pacing back and forth, shaking his head and muttering something quietly I couldn't quite understand. "Hey," I said, snapping my fingers in front of his face to draw his attention. I'd always hated doing that, but it was the only way I could think of to get him to answer.

"What are you hiding from me, Thoma?" he asked, immediately turning on me with a scowl. "A *lot*, actually," I said with a sigh as I shook my head. "I thought I was your *best friend*; someone you could tell *anything*!" he raised his voice and arms simultaneously. "You still *are*, fuck-face, but there are reasons I couldn't tell you everything," I said, trying to keep my voice as even as possible, not to escalate things further.

"What the hell is *that* supposed to mean? What *reasons* could you have? I know you don't trust him, but that *shouldn't* mean you can't trust me, either," he gestured in the druid's direction, prompting me to shake my head. "I *do* trust you, Ed. Hells, I trust you with my *life*, but what we're dealing with is something *far beyond* what anyone we know of in this realm can handle," I said, allowing my emotions to show just enough so he knew I meant every word.

"W-What?" Ed asked breathlessly as his face paled. I took a deep breath and began to explain why we'd come to the Gramm Isles to seek out information on the Great Partition, the *real* reason. He listened intently, but didn't bother asking me any questions until after I was done explaining *nearly* everything that had happened until this point.

"Gods above and be-.... Well, I guess there *aren't* any below any-more," he said with a weak chuckle. "So you've suspected Balgrim of being under Mideia's influence since the day you met him? How the fuck haven't *I* noticed that?" Ed asked himself. "You didn't know him before coming here with Meliss, right?" I asked, but all he could give me was a shake of his head.

"Well, my mom *did*, and between her assessment of him, as well as Athar's, that's where we're at now. What we're trying to figure out is *why* he would be under Mideia's influence, and I have a sneaking suspicion we're getting close to finding that out," I said, already feeling Ysevel's tug on my core to let me know they'd arrived at the end of the trail.

Ed paused for a moment to absorb everything I'd just told him. After a few silent seconds, he gave me a firm nod. "How can I help? I know I'm not as strong as you or the others, but is there *anything* I can do?" he asked with grim determination, to which I allowed myself a weak chuckle and shook my head.

"Yeah, don't take your eyes off of him. If you think he's doing anything suspicious, call it out. Until we can figure out how to deal with the creature, you'll have to be on guard duty," I said, getting a groan of disappointment in response. "*Fiiiine.* I hope you know I *hate* guard duty," he sighed.

Thoma, we've found the creature's den. You're not going to believe this, Ysevel sent with an almost tangible amount of awe in her tone. *We'll be right there,* I sent back quickly.

"Ready to go, then? Just remember, he already knows we suspect him, but that doesn't mean he's not likely to try anything," I warned. "I know, I *know*. If he even *looks* at any of you the wrong way, I'll tell you," he said, offering a balled fist for me to pound with my own.

It was only a few minutes before we caught up to the others, but when we got there, we found them having a brief discussion and gesturing to the large, sealed door towering behind them at the foot of the mountain.

"What *is* that?" Ed asked with his jaw speeding toward the ground. "*That* is something we were hoping *you* could help with, actually," Mom said, jutting her thumb over her shoulder. "Me?" Ed's face paled. Mom nodded, prompting me to give him an encouraging push. "You'll be fine," I muttered, trailing behind him as we approached the others.

When we got closer, I noticed there was writing wrapped around a square slab of stone in a language I couldn't recognize at all. At the center of the slab, there was a fist-sized mana stone that looked dormant and dull, though it still held a small amount of its turquoise coloring.

Ed inspected it for a few moments, placing a hand on his chin and leaning toward the writing, while Mom stood directly behind him in a similar pose. "Do you recognize it at all? I can only read *some* of the words, but I don't recognize *these* ones," she said, pointing to a small cluster on the top-right corner.

"I can hardly read it myself, but I *do* recognize it. This is Markuss' writing," he said with a serious look in his eye. "Meliss' father? What in the deepest mine was that *lunatic* doing out here?" Balgrim's eyes widened as he took a half-step forward.

Athar didn't flinch, and he sounded just like he did when I offered him the Thran's head, I noted. "I don't know, but I recognize the shorthand he used in the notes he left behind for her. I can't *fully* understand it, but from what I gather, it says something about *blood of my blood, and curse of my curse,*" Ed replied cryptically.

"*Hmm.* Well, if I knew Markuss as much as I *think* I did, the *curse of my curse* part would likely be referring to his never-ending pursuit of knowledge. The *blood of my blood* could mean only someone of dwarven lineage, or perhaps his *bloodline* could open this," Balgrim replied, twirling a finger through his long beard.

"Well then, I think we just found our *volunteer*," Mom said with a wolfish grin. "*Bah*, of course you'd have *me* try it," Balgrim huffed. "Do you see anyone *else* cursed with the pursuit of knowledge or dwarven descent here? Didn't think so," Athar chimed in with a scoff. "F-Fair point, but being a dwarf isn't a *curse*," Balgrim admitted begrudgingly. "Never said it was," Athar shrugged indifferently.

Balgrim moved up to the slab and placed his hand over the dull stone, pushing some of his mana into it. Within a heartbeat of him doing so, it lit up like all the others we'd seen throughout Narin.

"*Hah!* It worked!" Balgrim exclaimed, visibly pleased with himself as the doors began to rumble. When we didn't quite share his enthusiasm, he turned back around and cleared his throat. "Well, then. Shall we *delve* into the depths of the mountain?" he asked, with an oddly bright smile.

Something's off, Athar sent me, prompting me to analyze the tone Balgrim had just used. Knowing his apprehension toward using mental communication, my guard was immediately up as we followed him in. I had to give Ed and the others as subtle a nod as I could, letting them know that we were probably walking into a trap. *There isn't much we can do for now, so just play along,* I sent back.

We could *kill him here and be done with it,* Ysevel sent with a mental shrug, making Athar and I stare at her with crooked eyebrows. *What? You can't tell me you haven't already considered that possibility,* she sent as she uncrossed her arms and cocked her head. *I think Kalia's rubbing off on you a bit too much,* I sent back with a chuckle as I shook my head. *Is that a bad thing?* Kalia chimed in with a tilted head. *Nope, not at all,* I smiled nervously before turning to see what lay behind the doors.

As we crossed the threshold, nearly a hundred mana-lanterns illuminated our path, revealing the actual size of what we had just walked into. A massive hall of black stone that could only have been carved by an incredibly talented druid or powerful craftsmen. The turquoise lights bathed the path before us, revealing a long, straight path to the heart of the mountain.

"This is incredible. I never would have thought something like *this* could have existed here," Ysevel said, pretending she hadn't noticed Balgrim's darkened expression. "Indeed! This place must be from around the time of the Great Partition, though *how* it wasn't in any of those records is beyond me," Balgrim said, immediately shifting his behavior to match hers as we continued down the hallway.

Devyr and Kalia were practically unfazed by the incredible architecture, given that their homeland had substantially larger structures made of pure *kataki*. Still, they *did* have mixed emotions about it, though it was difficult to parse between their feelings and mine due to the situation.

We continued down the hall for nearly fifteen minutes before we reached a new area. Before us lay something not even Kalia could hide her awe from. As we entered it, more of the same mana lanterns began revealing our surroundings, spiraling almost to the very top of the mountain from the inside.

It was an abandoned city carved directly into the stone and forgotten by time. Each building, while *very* reminiscent of those in Narin, had little more than the bones that held them aloft remaining, as many of the walls had crumbled or fallen. Before us was a crossroads containing *dozens*, if not *hundreds*, of paths to take that likely led to different sections of the abandoned city.

"What is this place?" Mom asked with visible astonishment. "I-I... I don't know. I can't even begin to fathom how *long* this must have been here, though perhaps Calduran might know," Balgrim replied with an almost dream-like tone to his voice.

"Shit. It'll take us *years* to figure out where this creature is," Mom spat, frustratedly. *No, it won't,* Kalia said, looking over the edge of the crossroads that revealed an almost *bottomless* chasm. "You think it's down there?" I asked, and she nodded in response.

"But how do we get down there? The roads leading that way are all destroyed," Irun pointed to the far side of the chasm. "I can think of *one* way, but Balgrim isn't going to like it *at all*," Mom said with a grin. "*Ooooh,* no! No, no, fuckity-fuck no!" Balgrim said, raising his hands defensively as she approached him. "*C'mere!*" she laughed manically, grabbing him by the nape and speeding off over the edge to the far side of the chasm.

We could only watch and stifle a laugh as we watched her bounce from side to side, all the while Balgrim's screams reverberated throughout the dead city. "Well, that answers *that* question," Ed chuckled with tears in his eyes, breathing heavily as if it had been the first time he'd laughed like that in a *while*.

"Do you think you can do it?" I asked between my own chuckles. Even though we were all sure something was up with the druid, it certainly eased our tension with that small stint of comic relief. Ed's chuckle halted immediately, as an evident chill ran down his spine.

"I-I'm not sure. I don't think I can, honestly. She's a fucking *monster*," he admitted. "I'll take him, then," Kalia said aloud now that Balgrim wasn't present. "W-Wait, *whaaaaat?*" his voice immediately grew distant as both he and Kalia disappeared in the blink of an eye.

"Guess it's our turn," Ysevel gave me a wry smile. "*Oh?* Is this a race?" Athar asked, prompting us all to share a look. Even Devyr was giddy with excitement at the prospect of a race, but I don't think any of us needed to really say anything. "Ready? Go!" I shouted, leaping headlong into the chasm.

Of course, Devyr beat us all to the bottom.

"How the *fuck* are you that fast?" Irun asked with bated breath. It was *much* deeper than I think any of us had expected, but since both Mom and Kalia had made it seem like it was *nothing* to them, I realized there was still a sizable gap between us.

Devyr, keeping up the charade now that Balgrim was around, shrugged and stifled a giggle. "Yeah, I guess that's fair," Athar said, having interpreted something Irun hadn't. "One day, Devyr. One day," Irun balled his fist and raised it to chest height. While I couldn't *see* her expression, the amount of time I'd spent understanding her through mine and Kalia's connection told me she would be waiting for him to catch up.

After gathering ourselves, we took a moment to look around and see if there were any signs of the creature. *Over here,* Kalia sent us a wave. Thankfully, the few mana lanterns that remained unbroken by time were illuminating yet another hall just ahead of us, but as we walked, I could tell Athar was beginning to grow restless.

"You feel it, too, *huh*?" I asked him, getting little more than a silent nod. "Stay focused. There are many worse things than *me* in the depths of the realm," Mom said with a warning, yet commanding tone.

As we continued in silence to carefully listen for any sign of danger, we continued the intermittent pulses of mana to search the area. Within a few moments, however, Kalia raised a fist to halt us and stared up at a mural. *This is the story of my people, but why is it here?* Kalia sent us with a mixture of both awe and frustration. Without a word, Mom summoned a dimmed sphere of directional light that was just enough to illuminate it.

The mural depicted the numerous battles that took place over the ages, along with all the bloodshed that ensued. "A-Are those... *dragons*?" I asked, looking up at a piece of the mural that was falling to pieces. All I could really see was what *I thought* was a wing, but I couldn't be sure.

"They are. They fought side by side with the inhabitants of this realm for *many* years," Ysevel said distantly, like she was lost in thought, though her words left me speechless. "I wonder if there are any left," Athar said idly, prompting Ysevel to chuckle. "Careful what you wish for. They're not known to have the best of tempers," she said with a chuckle.

How the hell would she know that? I wondered, not letting that thought slip out.

"But this mural... It seems to display *almost* the same information that we read about the Great Partition, only it seems to show the hegraphenes pushing someone *back*, rather than just laying down their lives," Mom said, bringing her light up a little closer to it.

"What in the seven hells? There's another kind of mana like that?" Ed asked, looking up in astonishment. There was still a faint hint of color that had survived over the years, and I instinctively knew that the mana the hegraphenes were using was *Wraith* mana. "That must be one of the ones we read about in the library, right?" he asked me, but Balgrim's presence forced me to feign ignorance.

It's probably best you didn't tell him about that. Without the Hynafol Arboraneth's protection, we'd only be exposing ourselves and painting a target on our backs, Mom sent me quickly. *If my understanding of what this mural means is correct, Siraye's assumption might be the most viable scenario,* Ysevel added, causing me to furrow my brow and sigh in frustration.

Just as my shoulders dropped again, we felt a pulse of Leech mana rippling through the air from the far end of the hall. "Shit, get behind me," Mom commanded, as both she *and* Kalia put up a barrier to block any other spells heading our way. After a few tense heartbeats, none came, but the Leech mana continued to grow in intensity.

"Let's go kill this fucking thing," Irun said, to which *none* of us, save Balgrim, needed any further encouragement. We sped down the hall, tracing the remaining tendrils of mana that still permeated the air around us until we reached another large door, much like the one at the entrance. With a mild amount of hesitation, Balgrim stepped forward and pressed the mana stone into the slab, causing the doors to open.

Nothing could have prepared us for what we saw next.

It was a massive hall, with towering stone pillars to support the weight of the high mountain ceiling. At its center was a large, sickly green orb, nearly forty meters in diameter, with three pairs of rings weaving into each other, wrapped around it. Within the orb, I could clearly see black streaks of Tyrant mana racing through the Leech mana, as if in perfect synchrony.

At its base was a platform, with another stone slab much like the doorway's, though this one was set between eight pillars that surrounded the entire platform. Each one held mana stones that lined them, emanating a sort of barrier around the orb itself.

Yet, even with the barrier in place, it was *still* emitting a hateful, crushing aura.

"W-What the...?" Ed asked breathlessly, but the rest of us knew what this was. "It's a relay for Leech mana. This might be the last one in the entire *realm*," Mom noted, but immediately searched the room for the obcasus. She sent out a thin pulse of mana throughout the room, gathering all the information she could about it, but it quickly cut off when it reached the other side of the orb. "There you are," she said, drawing her weapon immediately.

As if hearing her words, not one, but *five* of these titanic creatures spawned, each one with their bodies and eyes glowing with sickly green mana just like the one I'd seen that night. "Think we can take them?" I asked as they lumbered toward us, their heavy footfall causing the entire room to tremble.

She turned around to look at Balgrim, whose face was contorted with both excitement and *fear* at the sheer size of them. "Did you know there was more than one?" Mom asked coldly, but he didn't immediately reply.

Instead, he only moved his mouth silently as his eyes rolled into the back of his head before he was thrown to the wall by another large pulse of mana, but Ed quickly rushed to his side. "Balgrim!" he shouted, desperately trying to wake him up with a few slaps on his plump cheek.

While Ed was trying to wake him back up, the doors began to close behind us much more quickly than they had opened. "A-Are they closing because he's unconscious? Damn it, *wake up!*" Ed snarled, giving the dwarf a mana-infused slap.

He managed to get his eyes opened, but they were glassy and darting lazily around the cavern. "He's awake, but I can't tell what's wrong with him," Ed said over his shoulder, prompting Mom to click her tongue.

"Damn it. Athar, Irun; protect them from anything else that gets by. I have too many questions for him to die now, and we don't know if another one will come along," she urged, while the rest of us lined up beside her. "Kalia, any ideas on how to kill these things?" I asked, drawing my blade.

"Their regenerative abilities are incredible, but if you can cut them down quickly enough, they *will* die," she said, glaring back at the titanic maw in its belly that began to smile wickedly. *Just remember that you can't use your Wraithborn abilities yet. Not until we confirm what happened to Balgrim,* Mom reminded us.

Even if he's unconscious, if he really has *been corrupted by Mideia, there's no telling whether he could sense us using Wraith mana,* Ysevel noted. *Fair point. Let's handle these quickly, then,* Mom sent us with a nod.

The creatures had finished rising to their full heights and were gathered around the orb in a tight formation. "Are they *guarding* it?" Devyr asked with audible confusion. "*Heh,* not for long," Mom said, immediately dashing in, which prompted the rest of us to follow.

I approached my target quickly, dodging the massive, right-handed black fist that sought to crush me. The shockwave from its blow would have made me lose my footing if I hadn't dashed just before it put a crater in the ground. As I reared my blade over my right shoulder to make the most use of my momentum, I noticed its skin was writhing like a cluster of shadowy worms.

What the fuck is this thing made of? I wondered as I swung, feeling my blade bite and then slow down as the shadowy mass began to wrap around it.

With a grunt of exertion, I was able to pull my blade free from the back of its leg, just as soon as a hand with thick, stubby fingers tried to reach me. I leapt away, feeling the displaced air rush past my face. In the short time I had to reassess my situation, I'd noticed Kalia was putting in the work with her blade coated in mana, riding up the creature in a spiraling slash that traced from its feet to the base of its neck.

You'll have to do this repeatedly. The more encapsulating the damage, the less time they have to regenerate, she sent me and the others, but it gave me an idea that I traced back to my time in Codrean.

It made me chuckle in realization.

I coated my blade in a *Pyrus* spell, just like I had when I fought the ochelon in the cave, and waited for an opportunity to attack it. As the pair of balled fists tried to crush me, I slashed at the base of its left wrist as I dashed away, searing the wound and preventing the *skin* from growing back. The obcasus roared angrily, belching out a stream of pure Leech mana from the large mouth on its stomach.

I managed to dodge it with relative ease, but Irun and Athar, who were directly behind me, were forced to reinforce the barrier they'd put up around Balgrim and Ed. The beam of Leech mana crashed into their barrier, causing them to grit their teeth as they poured more mana into it. Once it dissipated, I could see them both breathing heavily. "*Watch where you're pointing that thing, asshole!*" Athar's alternate voice shouted at the obcasus I was fighting.

It halted mid swing and turned to look at them with the corners of its mouth turning upward in excitement, just like it had done to me that night. "Fuck, that's not good," I heard Irun mutter, though the barrier slightly muffled his voice.

An increasing amount of Leech mana began to gather in a sphere just before its mouth, causing the very air around me to reverberate with a pulsating sound as it readied its attack. Mom and the others seemed to notice the orb growing as well, and stared at it for a heart-beat with widened eyes.

Shit, what do I do? I thought, unsure of whether I could slice through it without using Wraith mana, sensing a loose blow that wasn't even aimed at me from Mom's opponent. *I hope this works,* I gritted my teeth, *drawing a copious amount of mana* and releasing my *Whip of Doom* technique. *So do I,* Ysevel sent, having understood what I wanted to do.

The jade tendril wrapped around my target's left ankle, and I pulled with as much strength as I could muster, even going so far as to use a mixture of wind and earth mana to help push me along. I could feel that the sphere of mana was nearing completion through the mana and reverberations in the air around me.

I gave one final push off the ground, and leaped into the air, drag-ging its leg behind me, and right into the path of the other obcasus' blow. The sweeping, balled fist from my mom's target slammed into my opponent's ankle, causing it to fall backward and release the mana sphere directly above us, creating a pillar of power that careened toward the ceiling. With a thunderous *boom*, it blew a hole directly through it, revealing a part of the chasm we'd come down from just above us.

Massive stone slabs fell around us, prompting Ysevel and I to reposition ourselves to avoid getting crushed as they, as well as flailing attacks from the obcasus I'd tripped as it scrambled to get to its feet. "That was *close*," Ysevel breathed with a sigh of relief. "Sorry, I didn't know what else to do," I said, dashing out of the way of another attack from behind me.

"Look out!" Irun shouted as my target was about to slam its fist down. Heeding his advice, I stepped out of the way, but I realized the burn I'd left from my attack still *hadn't healed*. "*Feathers, skin, or fur; let them burn,*" I muttered in realization, recalling a sing-song memory trick Roburn had taught me years ago to help me remember which spells to use.

Everyone, use fire on them! They can't heal from fire damage, I sent the others, getting a chuckle from my mother. "I was avoiding it with the lack of air-flow in here, but with that *fresh hole* in the ceiling..." she trailed off, immediately pouring an immense amount of mana into her blade before leaping off one of the nearby pillars to reach her target's nape.

I was forced to jump over another blow as the downed obcasus swiped wildly at me, but I could still see my mom forcefully driving her blade into its nape and pouring *even more* mana into the creature, burning it from the inside. As the beast reared in agony, I could see charred insides begin to pour out of its mouth like molten metal, and the sickly green hue of its mana-infused mouth began to dim.

I couldn't watch the rest, since I had *my own* target to deal with, but I had a plan. The creature got to its feet, and as it turned to face me again, I decided to use my *Flamebolt* spell, one that I'd created during my third-stage exam back in Caegwen. I *drew more mana* and began to condense it in my left hand, while carefully observing what the creature's next move would be.

Without much warning, it lurched at me with its maw wide open, like it was trying to eat me. Under normal circumstances, I might have felt a sense of *fear* of being eaten, but I felt a grin sneak onto my face as I waited for the maw to get closer. The heat from my spell had *also* grown white-hot, and I could feel it warming my exposed cheek, but I held my ground.

"Thoma!" I heard Ed shout just before the maw engulfed me, but with a burst off the ground, I raised my left hand, using my *Flamebolt* to punch a hole right through it, and came out the other end *mostly* unscathed. The Leech mana that it had gathered in its maw clung to my armor, but the farther away I moved from it, the more it dissipated.

Did that kill it? I thought as I stared into the meter-wide hole I'd left in its body. *I don't think so, look,* Kalia sent. Through our connection, I could tell she was talking about the large hand that covered its mouth, pouring its squirming skin into it to try to seal the wound. I *gathered more mana* into my left hand and used the mana in the air to send me barrelling toward it at a speed that might have rivaled my mother's.

I slammed the orb directly into the creature's side just below its shoulder and poured as much mana into it as I could. The portions of skin I'd landed on desperately tried to latch onto me, writhing and wriggling their way up my boots and legs. "Haven't had enough yet? *Good!*" I shouted, pouring *more* mana into it than I ever had in my life.

I could feel my connection to the Ethereal beginning to grow exponentially stronger, as if the mana was becoming *a part of me*, rather than simply channeling it. I continued to push mana into my spell, and I could feel the mana *inside* the creature's body just as well as I could my own; tendrils lashing out and *charring* everything they could reach.

Finally, the creature stopped moving.

Its body, steaming with a thick, black smoke, had finally ceased its writhing, and I let out a sigh of relief, but I knew that relief wouldn't last. As I turned to get a look at the others, Kalia was already done with killing hers; its body a macabre *tapestry* of seared cuts and missing limbs. Devyr and Ysevel had teamed up to take theirs down together, just as they had with so many other targets.

Each move was almost *surgical*, for lack of a better word. As their paths crossed each time, they kept up a steady stream of attacks on each of their targets, never *once* allowing them a moment to react. It took me a second to realize what they were doing, but it started to make sense.

The two of them raced up the titanic creatures' bodies, the streaks of burning, violet mana and cuts they left behind made it look like they'd covered their targets in a *fishing net* of pure, unadulterated violence. As one, their targets fell to the floor, prompting the mana in their maws and eye sockets to dim and fizzle out into nothing but black, dripping ichor.

To say I was merely *impressed* by their display of coordination and skill would be the understatement of the year.

Ysevel leapt off the back of her obcasus and flicked the remaining tissue from her blade with a single swipe, then resheathed it with a single, smooth motion and a satisfying click. "That's the last of them, I *think*," she said, walking over toward me while glancing around the area. "Yeah, that should be it, but we need to check on Balgrim. I don't think we can get through these doors without his help," I noted, tilting my head toward the sealed doors to my left as I resheathed my blade.

"How's *he* holding up?" she asked vaguely with a subtle head gesture, but I knew she was talking about Ed. I observed him closely for a moment, but when all I could see in his eyes was *pure awe* at what we had just accomplished, I figured he was unhurt. "He's fine, but let's regroup and figure out what to do about *that thing*," I said, glancing up at the large orb in the center of the room.

If I'm right, he'll have answers for us once we get him back on his feet, I sent her, prompting her to raise her eyebrows and widen her eyes as she breathed in through her nose. *Let's hope you are,* she replied with a determined look.

CHAPTER 96
The Best Defense

M yrdin's citadel quickly vanished from sight as Bernar, Taegin, and Ryfon made their way above the forest. It had only taken them the better part of an *hour* to reach their destination, but even with their rapid means of transportation, *none of them* could feel at ease.

They landed a few kilometers outside of Soule to ensure that if there *were* enemies already present, they would have had a difficult time seeing them through Caegwen's naturally tall canopy.

"The research chamber should be just beyond the eastern gate, but we haven't seen any sign of the creatures during our flight at all," Bernar noted, adjusting the blade on his hip with one of the pull-tabs Maikell had developed for his armor.

Mom would have loved to see me in this, Bernar allowed himself a mental chuckle.

"Just because you haven't *seen* them doesn't mean they're not already here. The Thran are notoriously good hunters in Vareluth, and it would be *wise* not to underestimate their capabilities for laying traps," Ryfon said, shrinking back into his human form. "W-Wait, really? I thought you said their *numbers* were their advantage," Bernar said between a few rapid blinks and shakes of his head.

"It's precisely *because* they're good hunters that makes their numbers so terrifying," Taegin added with a nod, as they began to sprint again. "*Ah*, I forgot about your past with Kalia. Do they really call her the *Annihilator*?" Bernar asked with a crooked eyebrow. "From what I've heard, yes, though there were never any of those Thran left alive to tell the tale personally," Taegin said with a grin, causing Bernar to whistle critically.

I really should have a duel with her someday. Get home safely, guys, Bernar thought momentarily.

As they approached Soule's outer walls, not even the birds were singing their customary songs. The woods were *silent*, almost lifeless, and not even a branch dared make noise as it swayed in the light breeze that always flowed through them. *Something's off,* Bernar sent Taegin and Ryfon, who nodded their agreement. *No more verbal communication from here on until we find out what the situation is,* Ryfon sent them in a grave tone before his eyes widened.

Incoming! Bernar sent the others, though Ryfon was already well aware of what moved toward them. There were three titanic dericoed simultaneously using their innate abilities to control the roots of the trees around them. Sharpened roots the size of castle pillars careened toward them, shearing and splintering the bark and wood of the trees in their path.

Bernar and Taegin both prepared to dodge and counterattack accordingly, but Ryfon held up a hand for them to stop. *If you do that now, our chances of bringing them back to* our side *will be slim. Let me handle this,* he said, having read their intent, causing both Bernar and Taegin to glance at each other worriedly.

As the trio of spears approached, Ryfon thrust his palm forward to put up a barrier of mana reminiscent of the one he'd had at the entrance to his cave. The spears *crashed* into his wall of mana, shattering as they did so, and creating a thunderous *boom* that echoed through the silent forest. The shockwave shook the very foundations of the titanic trees around them as the trio of dericoed struggled against Ryfon's might.

Both Bernar and Taegin could only stare in astonishment at the ease with which he held back not one, but *three* of these attacks. *One's bad enough, but to hold back* all of them *is pure fucking insanity,* Bernar chuckled to himself nervously. *I can't even disagree with that statement,* Taegin admitted, still trying to understand what he was seeing.

Listen to me very carefully: no matter what *or* whom *has infected these creatures, they are still guardians of Caegwen and the realm. They know who I am, and if they have forgotten, then I will remind them swiftly. Save your energy for the fight to come,* Ryfon sent the two of them, who nodded in silent agreement.

He turned his attention to the attack and slammed his hand on the ground, pouring his mana into the earth like a waterfall being fed by a *sea*. The dirt beneath their feet rippled like a stone thrown into a calm lake, but suddenly focused all of its energy into three, straight lines, each linking directly to one of the dericoed.

Within less time than it took to blink, the spears dissipated and returned to the earth, while the trio of creatures suddenly dropped to their knees. "*Hera fy, Dericoed,*" Ryfon said, staring at them imperiously. It wasn't a *shout* by any means, but the forcefulness of his voice carried through the forest like the sound of a falling tree.

Holy fuck. I don't think even Mom *can do that,* Bernar said, his eyes widening to their utmost limits. *This must be only a small portion of what someone* beyond *the fifth stage can do,* Taegin realized, holding a similar expression.

"L-Lord Ry-f-f-on," one of the creatures spoke, his voice much more distorted and shaky than the one who'd talked to Erumon. "W-We can-n-not h-hold it b-back," it said, struggling through each word through immense pain that was both audible *and* visible. Blackened, green sap poured from its mouth as it spoke, creating a small patch of disfigured flowers wherever its drops landed.

"I know, my friends. That is why I have come," Ryfon said gravely, balling his partially scaled fist tightly to where his knuckles turned white as he moved toward them. Bernar and Taegin followed closely behind, but with just enough caution to not be caught off-guard. "*S-Save usssss,*" one of the others hissed, but the sound of this one's voice prompted Ryfron to stop in his tracks as his features darkened and brow furrowed.

"You," he seethed through clenched teeth, while his aura of pure mana grew to an intensity neither of the other two had ever seen before. "*Welcome back,* lord. *It's been a while,*" the creature spoke again, rising to its feet shakily as it used Ryfon's title with *blatant* derision.

What... is... that? Bernar asked but received no answer, as they saw a being nearly twice Erumon's height reveal itself from behind a tree.

The man's eyes were glowing a bright, sickly green, with blackened tendrils swirling within their irises, hidden beneath matted blonde locks. Pale skin showed no signs of aging, save the dark circles beneath his eyes and the evident scars revealing missing scales where they were more prevalent. His undoubtedly muscular form was hardly concealed by his filthy, stone-gray robes that clung tightly to him.

In his right hand was a long, black spear with a single, blood-soaked cloth tied to the base of the tip, which he aimed in their direction. "We've been waiting for you," the man said, slamming the base of his spear into the ground and summoning a portal nearly the size of the cave's mouth just behind him.

We're in for one fuck of a fight, Bernar sent Taegin with a glance. *Indeed, we are, but we should leave the big one to Ryfon. As we are right now, we don't stand a chance against him,* Taegin replied grimly, to which Bernar agreed wordlessly. *After being cooped up for a thousand years, you think he's going to be alright?* Bernar asked, but Taegin could only chuckle through his nose and shake his head.

As Bernar returned his gaze toward the portal, he saw a whole legion of Thran exiting the portal in droves, gathering just behind the still-subdued dericoed, with many more likely on the way. "You can have your little *dericoed friends* back. After all, they've already served their purpose in being the channel for us to arrive," the man said, tightly gripping the back of one of their necks and hucking it in Ryfon's direction with a wolfish grin.

As if catching a precious artifact, Ryfon caught the titanic creature with a few tendrils of mana, gently placing it on the floor behind him. The other two were thrown in quick succession, and just as before, Ryfon gingerly took hold of them, but was nearly caught off guard by the large man's spear appearing just behind them.

"Move!" Ryfon commanded as he steeled himself to block the attack, prompting Bernar and Taegin to dash out of the way and begin moving toward the Thran. Ryfon caught the spear between the palms of his hands, sending a shockwave rippling through the massive trees once more. "Not bad for an *old wyrm*," the large man said with a curled eyebrow. Ryfon's eyes reduced to slits as he knocked the spear upward and kicked the large man in the stomach, sending him crashing through the edges of a few trees.

Take care of the others. I'll deal with this one, Ryfon sent the others. *Don't have to tell me twice, it's been a long time since I've had* this *many creatures to kill,* Bernar said with a mixture of excitement and ravenous hunger. *More like a few* weeks, *Bernar,* Taegin corrected with a slight grin of his own.

As soon as the two were clear of the area, Ryfon dashed toward his target, trusting the two with him to take care of the legion without so much as a second glance. He found the large, pale man already recovered and dusting himself off from a few woodchips as he cracked his neck nearly fifty meters from his new position.

"*Ah*, Ryfon. I really hope that wasn't your *best hit*, because if it was, this will not end well for you," the man said, getting into a fighting stance once again. "I have questions that need answering, *Halsek*. It wouldn't serve me well to kill you before then, would it?" Ryfon shrugged, prompting Halsek to click his tongue. "Are you really going to fight me without a weapon? You're at a disadvan-..." Halsek trailed off as Ryfon's knee instantly slammed into his nose.

Halsek did his best to recover for the next flurry of blows that came for him, rolling backwards then dashing forward in a fit of rage. He thrust the spear, aiming for Ryfon's core, but with a quick sidestep and a push from the back of his forearm, Ryfon managed to deflect the strike, leaving the remaining force of the blow to flow outward behind him.

He might be younger than I am, but there is no denying the strength of his attacks, Ryfon thought, feeling the mana in the uprooted grass, bushes, and smaller trees grow increasingly distant.

Halsek gritted his teeth in frustration, sending another series of attacks aimed for Ryfon's stomach, legs, shoulders, and head in rapid succession, forcing his opponent to block, dodge, or deflect accordingly. "You fight well for one so young, but tell me: *What did The Scourge promise you?*" Ryfon asked, infusing his voice with an impressive amount of mana.

"*Hah*, neither the *Voice* nor the *Words* will work on me anymore, *old wyrm*, but I'm glad to see my master wasn't lying about having found a way to get rid of your control over us," Halsek scoffed pridefully, leaping into the air and driving the tip of his spear directly toward Ryfon's forehead. Moving his head just a little to the side, he grabbed the haft and immediately spun to pull Halsek and slam him into the ground.

As he moved in for a heavy punch, Halsek rolled out of the way of the crater Ryfon left where his head had just been. Pushing off the base of his spear, he tried to use both legs to kick Ryfon squarely in the chest, but the shrewd dragon gave a spinning kick, hitting the base of the spear Halsek used as his support. As he fell to the ground, Ryfon caught him with a series of hard-hitting kicks and punches to keep him off the ground.

I haven't been able to land a single strike on him, and I can feel my ribs cracking with each punch. If this keeps up, he's going to kill me. But how? How is he still so strong? It's been over a thousand years since he last fought, and yet he's completely *overpowering me. Was my master wrong?* Halsek thought, doing his best to keep what little defenses he could.

"Who do you think *taught* your master?" Ryfon asked, having heard the thoughts Halsek had hoped would stay private.

Wha-...? Halsek's realization was cut short as Ryfon gave him a swift kick that sent him barrelling into a score of trees, landing flatly against one of them, and spilling blood from the corners of his mouth. As he gasped for air with a cough, he felt a gentle shift in the mana, only to find Ryfon standing before him with a pitiful look on his face.

"D-Don't give me that look," Halsek groaned, his eyes glowing a little less brightly than before. "I suppose it's not without good reason you're a *duke*, but why haven't you killed me yet? Are you here to gloat at your pupil's long-lost student, or are you simply not satisfied that I survived that?" Halsek asked, spitting a wad of dark blood from his mouth.

The forest around them grew eerily quiet, save for the distant sounds of dying Thran at the hands of Bernar and Taegin.

Ryfon didn't immediately say anything, but squatted down to be eye level with him as he was slumped against the tree. "I still have questions for you, but I'm more saddened by the fact that you've been driven so deeply into the delusion that you could've beaten me, Halsek," Ryfon shook his head with visible frustration.

"That's it? After all these years, that's all you have to say?" Halsek asked with a hint of venom in his tone. "No offer to bring me *home*, no proverbial olive branch, no redemption? I'm flattered, really," Halsek chuckled weakly at the ridiculousness of the situation.

"Why did he send *you*? Tell me what he offered you, and depending on your answer, I *may* spare your life, though I will utterly annihilate the others you've brought with you," Ryfon replied coldly with a furrowed brow and a glare as cold as stone.

"*There* he is. *Oh*, how I've missed that *disdainful,* disapproving look of yours. It seems I've already answered *one* of your questions, but like the other dukes, you're too blind to see it for yourself," Halsek began through a weakened cough. "The only things he offered me were *freedom* from the Voice and Words, but someone in *your position* could never understand what that's like," he said, lazily wiping away a streak of blood.

Ryfon cast his eyes downward, his hair falling in front of them to hide the sheer rage contained within them. "I'm sorry, Halsek," he began, lowering his voice to just above a whisper. "*Sorry*?" he scoffed, spurting a bit more blood onto his robes. "Yes. I'm sorry that you fell prey to his honeyed words and lies," Ryfon said, still not meeting Halsek's eyes.

"What *lie* did he tell? *Huh*? All I've seen, all I've ever *known* until *he* saved me from the oppressive heel I've been under since *birth* is that you have all lost your collective grasp on reality. You have no point of reference, no knowledge of what goes on beyond the council, and yet here you are after a thousand years trying to *lecture* me that *he's* the deceitful one," Halsek sneered and spat a wad of blood toward the ground.

Ryfon watched as it landed on the ground before him, and lifted his head to meet Halsek's eyes, who shuddered at the sight of the rage hidden just beneath the surface of his otherwise placid expression. "Thank you for the answers, Halsek. I will relay your words to the others and *ensure* that changes are made. I will let you live, but like I said before, those foul beasts you've brought with you will not see the sun set on this day," Ryfon rose and stared down at Halsek imperiously. "*Changes*," Halsek scoffed, hacking up another mouthful of blood.

Just as he did so, there was a ripple of ambient mana that tore through the forest from the portal the others were fighting at, prompting Ryfon to look in their direction momentarily. "Do not show your face before me as an enemy again. If you do, I will *erase* you from the annals of the Twilight Sea. I *swear it*," he said, sending a connecting tendril of pure white mana to Halsek's core.

Halsek, wounded as he was, couldn't resist the fear that latched onto him when he realized Ryfon had meant every word, as proven by the binding vow that writhed around his core. "D-Damn you," he hardly managed to say through his clenched teeth. "Go and tell your master that I'm *waiting* for him as well. When the time comes, I will meet him on the battlefield not as my pupil, but as a *mortal enemy*, and I will show no quarter," Ryfon said before leaving a broken Halsek, branches, and a cloud of dust in his wake.

As he approached the portal, the palpable smell of blood, entrails, and steel permeated the air before the portal, as hundreds of piled corpses nearly blocked the entrance entirely. Atop one of the piles was Taegin, wielding his blade and spells with expert precision and an efficient brutality that made it difficult for the other creatures to simply climb up to get him. Bernar, however, was little more than a bloody, lurching figure as he moved from target to target.

Even for all his ability, Bernar moved with such speed that even Ryfon found it a mild challenge to keep up with him.

Erumon wasn't lying when he said Bernar was like a young drake unleashed, but I want to give him the wings of a dragon, Ryfon thought with a mild look of surprise on his face.

Bernar moved to his next group of Thran, each one with a crude, yet massively oversized weapon raised in challenge toward him. With a wolfish grin, he watched as they all swung their weapons, each aiming for a different part of his body. He chuckled as his eyes shifted from their golden glow into that of a deep scarlet just before disappearing entirely.

The group's weapons struck the ground, kicking up an enormous cloud of dust, roots, and rocks high into the air. "Thanks for making that easy," Bernar jeered from behind them. As they turned to look at him, their heads collectively fell from their shoulders and landed on the ground with a unified *thud* in the blood-soaked earth.

They didn't even feel his strikes? I guess I'll have to pick up the pace as well, or my own grandson *will end up surpassing me,* Taegin thought, having watched the situation unfolding below out of the corner of his eye.

His eyes glowed more intensely than before as a group of over fifty Thran scrambled over their kinsfolk's corpses to reach him. In less time than it took to blink, he'd reached the bottom of his macabre high-ground, leaving a score of fresh corpses suspended in the air around him. With a stomp of his foot, he sent platforms of earth soaring into the air to launch several Thran high above him.

He jumped, reaching the first platform and severing one of the creatures in half before jumping through the freshly made mist to reach another platform. Each bound was a fatal strike against the airborne creatures, but when he reached the end of his platforms, he suspended himself in the air and began to bend mana to his will.

From his high point, the platforms broke and split to carry the airborne halves of the thran, but he wasn't going to stop there. He reached down with his left hand and *pulled* the earth beneath his pile of bodies, lifting it entirely. Many of the Thran at the entrance noticed the display, but had little time to react before the dismembered limbs, weapons, and stones from the earth pierced them at astonishing speeds.

How the fuck is he doing that? Bernar wondered momentarily, as each projectile left a sonic *boom* in its wake.

While only a handful of creatures weren't hit by the initial barrage, the ones that *did* manage to get out of the way were swiftly dispatched by Bernar, who slaughtered them with ease.

To answer your question, I've marked each one I've killed with earth and wind attribute mana. Why do you think I was staying in the same spot the whole time? The best defense is a good offense, after all, Taegin asked as he launched the last claw in his pile of corpses at another Thran, piercing its brain just before he landed back on the ground.

The portal was entirely congested with disfigured, bloodied bodies, which forced the incoming Thran to scramble over their fallen kin. "Back away from the portal. This has gone on long enough," Ryfon muttered, prompting Bernar and Taegin to look at him. "*Oh, you're back! I have more competition now,*" Bernar said over his shoulder with a grin.

"Competition?" Ryfon asked with a curled eyebrow as he watched Bernar ready himself for another round of attacks. He closed his eyes and began channeling an incomprehensible amount of mana that caused both Bernar *and* Taegin to flinch. He raised his hands out beside him and turned his palms upwards, bent his arms toward himself, and placed his hands on his chest at an angle.

The air surrounding them became entirely still, but a resonance flowed through it that could only be described as the bow of a violin tracing along the spine of a thin metal plate. The pitch reverberated through the forest at a low hum that gradually increased in volume to rumble the ground beneath their feet. Both Bernar and Taegin watched in awe as a hyperdense sphere of mana was being compressed at the height of Ryfon's mouth.

Move! Taegin sent Bernar urgently, dashing away on instinct as he gave him a warning glare.

As if time itself had come to a crawl, the creatures that still scrambled over their comrades' bodies some were even suspended in the air as Ryfon's gaze shifted from the orb in his hands to the mountain of corpses before the portal.

His mouth opened wordlessly as his elbows quickly tucked in at his sides when he leaned forward. A bright flash of light emitted from the orb a fraction of a second before a beam of pure, white mana, roughly as thick as a Myrdinian tree trunk, seemingly tore through the space between its origin and the portal.

The beam of light, coupled with the amplified bow-like sound, completely obliterated anything and everything in its path. The portal, however, collapsed in on itself to a point, then exploded outward with a blast of Leech mana that nearly reached the peaks of the Rhydian Mountains.

"What, and I cannot stress this enough, *the fuck*?" Bernar asked breathlessly, feeling a bead of sweat race down his cheek, and a fearful *chill* roll down his spine. "I thought you said it was *a competition*," Ryfon shrugged to Bernar, whose mouth would have buried itself in the dirt if it could have dropped any further. Bernar chuckled nervously, his eyes widened in astonishment.

"I said it was a *competition*, not that you were supposed to tear through the veil of the fucking *universe*," Bernar shouted, gesturing toward the town-sized crater in the earth. "You're right, and I had to defend my position as your superior, though I suppose *your mother* might put up at least a *decent* fight," Ryfon chuckled, leaving him even more befuddled than before.

"Are you saying Mom learned this technique? She never told me that," Bernar said with a decent amount of incredulity, prompting Ryfon to raise an eyebrow. "Did you forget who my *daughter* is?" he asked with a wry grin, prompting Bernar to look at Taegin, who could only shrug with an upturned lip.

"Thoma's going to throw a shit-fit when he hears about this," Bernar chuckled and shook his head. "I wouldn't be disinclined to teach it to you, but you'll have to promise me that you'll only use it in the circumstances I call for," Ryfon said, but as the words left his mouth, Bernar was already kneeling before him. "*I swear* on my life and *core* that I will follow your teachings and guidance," he said reverently.

"Get up; there's no need for showmanship," Ryfon said, picking him back up with a chuckle. "When this is over, I'll *personally* train both you *and* Thoma to use it. I wouldn't want my future *grandson-in-law* to feel left out," he continued with a toothy grin, causing Bernar to shudder.

Thoma, I swear on everything that if you end up breaking Ysevel's heart, I'll kill you myself, Bernar thought, using every ounce of his willpower to hide the thought, but to no avail.

"I already know he won't, and the same goes for her. In fact, once this situation is dealt with, there is someth-..." Ryfon trailed off, his head immediately flicking to the northeast with a worried look. Bernar and Taegin felt it as well, their eyes widening in astonishment at the dense ripple of Leech and Tyrant mana passing over them.

"H-How far is that from us?" Bernar asked, not that he couldn't tell, but he *needed* to confirm his suspicions. "It's coming from the Gramm Isles," Ryfon said, his voice immediately growing dark and grim. "What is the meaning of this?" Taegin asked, looking up and around to see if he'd accidentally missed anything.

Ryfon immediately backed away from them, his mana surging around him as he grew to his full size and extended his pale wing down toward them. "Get on, we have to go *now*," he said in his full voice. "Where?" Bernar asked.

Please don't be what I think it is, he hoped, swallowing dryly as he held on tightly to the shimmering handholds that formed when he got into a seated position.

"*He's here,*" Ryfon said, using his full strength to beat his wings and send them into the sky.

CHAPTER 97
EASY PREY

Ysevel and I turned toward Balgrim, who was still lying behind Athar and Irun entirely unconscious.

Ed was already trying to wake him back up, but none of us knew *why* he'd fainted to begin with. "Is he alright?" I asked, sheathing my blade as I walked over. "I feel like I should be asking *you* that. How the *fuck* did you pull that much mana?" Ed asked as he looked up at me from his kneeling position.

I can't tell him that the fight would have been much easier if I could use my Wraithborn abilities, I mentally sighed.

"I just did what I had to do," I shrugged, moving to kneel beside him. Mom walked over to us with a concerned look written clearly on her fine features, but I didn't have to ask *why*. She knew, just as well as the rest of us, that Balgrim *was* hiding something, but exactly *what* we couldn't tell.

"Wake him up," she began coldly. "W-What?" Ed stammered, the color flushing from his face. "Wake him up, or *I will*," she said, keeping the same tone and tightening her grip on the hilt of her blade. Ed blanched, but he did as she commanded. He started with a light shake, then gradually increased the force to where he was smacking him across the face. When nothing else seemed to work, he undid the latches on Balgrim's armor and rubbed his knuckles firmly along the dwarf's sternum.

"Wake up, you old fuck!" Ed shouted, drastically increasing the force of his rub. Still, Balgrim didn't wake up, and that was when I noticed it wasn't just *his* concern that was growing, but everyone else's as well.

If he doesn't wake up soon, we might have another *problem on our hands,* Kalia sent, looking over her shoulder. *What do you mean?* I asked, prompting Ysevel to turn to look at it as well. "It's becoming unstable. The aftershocks of our fight might have done that to the old device," she said, watching tendrils of Leech mana beginning to grow.

"If the device loses its hold on it any more than it already has, it might end up acting as a beacon for the others who are searching for it," she continued, but Ed could only offer her a worried look. "*Others?* What do you mean by that?" he asked, turning to me for an answer.

"Those *wardens* I told you about? Let's just say not *all of them* are on *our* side," I explained loosely, making his eyes widen. "*Oh*, fuck," he said, realizing the gravity of the situation. "If this device loses its grip on the orb, the explosion of mana will race out of that hole up there," I said, pointing to the circular hole in the ceiling from the attack the obcasus had initially aimed at Irun and Athar.

"If it hasn't done that already," Irun added with a shrug. "It's only a matter of time, but we need to do what we can to stop them from coming here. Athar and I can help protect Ed and Balgrim, but that's about all we can do at this point," he continued, giving Ed a subtle glance to gauge his reaction.

It was evident that Ed felt a slight amount of shame at the suggestion, but I knew Irun didn't mean anything derisive by his comment. "T-Thanks," he said, lowering his head a little.

"I'll be counting on you, then. I can try to hold it, but I don't think I can do that alone," Mom said, giving Kalia a concerned look. "I'll do my best to help you any way I can," Kalia said, giving her a firm nod.

"Devyr, we'll need you on standby to put up a barrier in case this goes to shit," Mom said, turning to face her. "I'll be honest, Commander, I don't know that my skills can hold up against *that*," she said with a tone that suggested she was being realistic.

"You survived ten thousand cycles with Nexis, didn't you? I think you'll be alright. I have full confidence in your abilities," Mom said with a cheeky smile. "Thoma, you and the others stay here. Use whatever means of protection that you can if this thing blows up," she said, turning to face the others and I. "Better not let it go to shit, then," I replied with a grin, prompting her to chuckle. "No promises," she said with a wink.

As the three of them moved into position, we cautiously awaited the signal to put up our barriers. Mom stared up at the massive orb floating a few meters above the platform in front of her and rubbed her hands together. "Are you ready, *battle-sister*?" Mom said, catching Kalia off guard at her use of the term. I felt a flush of relief, fear, and anxiousness flow through our connection.

I think she liked that, Ysevel sent me with a grin.

"O-Of course," Kalia said, regaining her composure much more quickly than I'd expected, though I could have chalked that up to her *ample* experience in hiding her emotions. "Good, then let's get this over with. The longer we wait, the easier prey we'll become," Mom said, furrowing her brow in concentration.

I could feel a swell of mana radiating from her position and noticed a glowing sphere of pure, golden light forming in the palms of her hands. I could see them working their way around the orb, as if meticulously laying each tendril or particle of mana individually. Kalia did something similar, though hers emitted a deep violet hue that pulsed around the room. Devyr stood just behind them, producing an ample amount of her own *kataki* in preparation.

"Ready?" Mom asked, her voice distorted by the sheer amount of mana. She got a nod from Kalia, and the two of them moved to cast their spells. Their spells shook the foundations of the chamber, causing a deep rumbling to resonate throughout it.

"*Waaaaait!*" a thin voice called out from *somewhere*, but it was too late. They'd cast their binding spells, supporting the structures already in place, and enveloping the orb entirely.

Meliss? I wondered, thinking I'd recognized the voice.

The sheen of Ethereal and Vexing mana clashed and mixed around it, dimming the green hue to a faint remnant of what it was before. "Hold it!" Mom said through gritted teeth, pouring an immense amount of mana into her spell, while holding the structure's pillars in place with her other hand. Devyr's quick thinking sent out a bit of her *kataki* to fill in the gaps of the now-cracking pillars.

"Stop, you're going to break it!" Meliss's voice came from behind us. *I hadn't even noticed the doors had opened again, when the hell did that happen?* I asked, but not even Ysevel had noticed them opening. "Meliss? What the fuck are you doing here?" Athar asked roughly. "Commander, please! I'm begging you to stop! You're all going to *die*," Meliss shouted, running into the chamber as fast as her abilities could carry her. There was something in her hands that I could only assume was a *scroll*, but what it said, I didn't know.

Mom glared at her with glowing eyes over her shoulder, but when she saw that there was seemingly no lie in her eyes or words, she signaled for Kalia and Devyr to release their spells. *Do you really trust her?* Kalia asked with an air of caution. *No, but we don't know enough about this device to know that our decision was the best one. Let's see what she has to say,* Mom returned, signaling to the rest of us to be on guard through our connection.

As the spells retracted, the sickly green glow filled the room once more. "I hope you have a good reason for this, Meliss," Mom said, her stare conveying the sheer lack of trust she still had. "I do, Commander. I apologize for disobeying your orders, but I knew *this* couldn't wait," she said with a low bow.

Mom looked at her and curled an eyebrow. "What's this?" she asked, gesturing to the rolled parchment in Meliss' hand. "It's the reason I disobeyed your order. Look here," she said, raising her head and unfurling the parchment. Ysevel and I moved in for a closer look after a subtle gesture from Mom, but what we saw on the page was unlike anything I'd ever seen.

It was a fully sketched diagram of the device that contained the orb, but beneath it, there were a few paragraphs of text that had scribbled translations between each line. Each translated sentence was a piece of a guide to what it called a *Relay Container*, including its location and how to operate it.

To each side of the parchment, there were letters that either weren't, or *couldn't*, be translated since they were written in an entirely different language. Each letter was glowing with a sickly green hue, much like the one coming from the orb, but it was hardly noticeable under the already present glow.

"These runes here, I've seen them before," Devyr said, tracing a finger along the side of the parchment nearest to her. "W-What? You have?" Meliss asked, visibly confused not only by the fact that Devyr spoke, but that she could recognize them.

Tell her not to translate them aloud. Words have power, especially in the old languages, Mom warned, to which Kalia relayed the information promptly. "I-I have, yes, but my betters have warned me not to speak them aloud," Devyr said, taking a step back.

"B-But you must know what they *mean*, right? Please, I need you to translate them however loosely you can without activating their power. If we can't use the knowledge in this scroll, we're *all* going to suffer for it," Meliss asked with a sense of urgency, trying to take a step forward, but Mom put a hand on her shoulder to stop her.

"Knowledge is learned through books, but *wisdom* is learned in blood, Meliss. I know you're trying to help, but if we don't contain it quickly, we'll be putting the entire *island* at risk," she said grimly, but still conveying a motherly tone to let her know that she *truly* understood that she was just trying to help.

Meliss's features shifted from hopeful to dejected in a heartbeat when she finally understood. "I guess I'll have to do it, after all," she muttered, lowering her head and turning to move toward the small panel at the front of the device.

"What are you doing?" Mom asked. "*Blood of my blood, and curse of my curse,*" Meliss said over her shoulder with a weak smile. "You can't mean..." Mom trailed off with widened eyes, but Meliss nodded once and began to explain. "I'd stand back, if I were you," she said weakly, turning to face the device while we did as she requested.

"My father was researching this device just before he died, and did his best to conceal its presence when he discovered it. He left what's known as a *blood bind* on it, meaning only members of his bloodline can use the machine properly, but I'm only *half-dwarf*," she said, reaching her hands out to touch the small dials on the panel.

A green tendril shot out from the panel and whipped against her arm, causing her to flinch and wince in pain. "Meliss, no!" Ed said, abandoning Balgrim and moving toward her in a heartbeat. "Edryd, don't fucking move!" Mom said in a mana-infused voice, pointing her finger directly at him. He froze solid, watching Meliss hopelessly struggle through the pain.

His emotional state won't help us at all right now, she sent us briefly.

"If you'd completed your spell, the rings on the outside would have disintegrated because of the unrecognized mana signature invading their purpose. *That* would have caused a complete meltdown of this system, ultimately leading to its self-destruction, and unmanageable containment of the mana within," she continued, turning one of the dials counterclockwise as she gritted her teeth for another whip of the tendrils.

She grunted in pain, but continued to adjust the dials as much as she could. "It's ironic, really. To think that something *Balgrim* coveted for so long could only be controlled by the offspring of his worst *enemy*," she said, overseeing the orb as she observed the tendrils' movements beginning to die down.

That's when the final gear *clicked* into place. I could feel it, like a misplaced puzzle piece found buried beneath the ashes of a past that didn't belong to me. It was a strange feeling, naturally, but everything about her, her father's death, and why she had to flee the Isles *finally* made complete sense. Ysevel, Mom, and Kalia all felt the same thing I had, and a collective mix of anger and *concern* began to grow.

That stumpy little fuck-nugget, Mom sent us along with the rest of her emotions. I couldn't find myself disagreeing with the name she gave him. He really was a slimy weasel shit after all.

But no matter how we felt, we knew we couldn't break Meliss's concentration. From where I stood, I could only see her making the most minute adjustments, though it was a testament to her willpower and Pyle's training that she managed to do so while in so much pain.

"There, that should keep it under control for the time being," Meliss said, but as she turned around to us, I could see her eyes were bloodshot and cloudy, like some of her life force had been taken as *payment* to adjust the machine. She managed to take a step forward before suddenly collapsing to the floor in a heap, losing consciousness entirely as blood began to pour from her nose.

"Shiiiit, pour your mana into her! She's going to die if you don't!" Athar shouted, rushing over to us to help, along with Irun. Each of us knew Athar, rather his *alternate*, had the most experience with Leech mana, so we instinctively took his word for it and began to cast every possible healing spell we knew, but nothing seemed to work.

"Is there anything we can do? Her pulse is fading as we speak!" Irun asked urgently, pouring a heap of Vexing mana into her. "I can think of *one* thing, but I don't know if I can handle it alone. I'd need your help to channel that mana into her," Mom said, tilting her head to the orb and giving Athar a serious look. *"Fuck no, that will kill* us both, *and I've already died once,*" Athar said, continuing to pour mana into her.

As his words sank into my mind, I knew there was really only one option left. *Her lifesigns are fading faster than we can pour mana into her safely,* Ysevel sent me with a subtle shake of her head. *I know, and I can't imagine what it will do to Ed if she dies in front of him,* I replied, feeling the air go still around me.

"*I can save her, or you can keep pouring mana into what is now little more than a corpse, though it will leave you* all *as easy prey,*" a familiar voice I'd buried in my memory sounded from the corner Ed was standing in. "What the *fuck* did you just s-..." I trailed off as I turned to look in his direction.

My eyes widened, since nothing could have prepared me for what I saw.

A single tendril of pure, green mana was gingerly touching Edryd's temple. His eyes were widened in fear and shock, his mouth quietly wording something I couldn't hear or read on his lips. But out from behind him was the bearded dwarf displaying a wicked smile, and eyes like black-green mana lanterns.

"It's been a long time, *Thoma,*" Balgrim mouthed, though it wasn't the voice I'd known him to have. Somewhere deep in the recesses of my mind, that same voice resurfaced, placing me back in that pantry, shirtless, and feeling like I'd been kicked in the chest by a mule.

The orb, seemingly reacting to his presence, began to shift and swirl viciously as I glared at him, though all I got in return was that same, wicked smile from the night my core was sealed.

"Mideia," I seethed, feeling my fist clench tightly, while I rose to my feet.

CHAPTER 98

KINSFOLK

E rumon stood atop the southwestern portion of the wall surrounding Myrdin. The trees gently swayed with the breeze that flowed through the forest, as if ignorant of the coming battle. Just below him, there were scores of soldiers all lined up and prepared for the eventual assault.

"Lord Erumon," Captain Ense began from his right, prompting the warden to look at him. "The citizens have all been accounted for and are each in their homes," he reported with a crisp salute. "Thank you, Captain. What about your family?" Erumon asked, causing Ense's eyes to widen.

"Her Majesty offered to protect them within the palace, and I was grateful to hear King Elhael agree with no hesitation. I could never repay her for such kindness, my lord," Ense said, lowering his head humbly, prompting Erumon to allow a slight grin that tugged at the corner of his mouth to show. "She *really is* a queen among queens," he said, glancing over at the palace briefly.

"In that case, I will see to the barrier myself. I'd suggest you stay up here, but if you wish to fight alongside your men, I won't stop you," Erumon said with a subtle nod. "I wouldn't have it any other way, lord," Ense said, offering him a firm nod, though Erumon's was much slower and filled with understanding.

Lifting his hand high above his head, he first muttered in a language Ense didn't understand, but could *feel* the power within the words he spoke. "*Clyw fi, un Hynafol,*" Erumon finally whispered in flawless Caegweni. His eyes burst open as power began to flow from his fingertips toward the ancient tree. It heard his command, and with a wave of mana strong enough to distort the air around its trunk, golden light flowed through all the roots that spanned the entire city.

Each house, regardless of how small, was encased in a barrier of the purest Ethereal mana Ense had ever seen. "*Hynafol mawr,*" Ense said in disbelief, dropping to a knee immediately in reverence to the sight of the entire *city* being protected.

This battle will be the first of many, but is this realm prepared for what comes next? Erumon wondered, observing a handful of guardsmen below him exchange worried looks. *With Nenvalur and Thorsen leading the defense, I'm confident in our ability to defend Myrdin, but for* how long *is another matter entirely,* he thought, shifting his gaze over to the Hjalfarian giant, who stood next to a frustrated-looking Nenvalur.

"*Bah,* where the fuck are they? If I weren't on direct orders from Erumon himself, I'd have gone out to look for them already," Nenvalur growled, fidgeting with the hilt of his blade. "If we did that, we would be putting all these men and women at risk. Would you really place your kinsfolk in such a position?" Thorsen asked, keeping his eyes straight ahead as he'd been trained to by the Guild.

Nenvalur sighed heavily and shook his head. "I wouldn't, but what good is it to throw their lives away by being out *here*? They would be much safer within the walls," he said with a shrug. "These brave warriors all volunteered to be here *instead of* hiding within the walls. I'm sure their sense of duty to their homeland *far* outweighs their desires to be safe," Thorsen said, giving him a quick glance.

"True, but the longer we wait, the more they'll begin to regret that decision. You know that just as well as I do," Nenvalur said quietly enough not to be heard by those directly behind him. "I do, unfortunately," Thorsen admitted with a subtle nod, recalling the first time he went out to hunt an ochelon with his fellow junior Synners.

While Thorsen was lost in thought, Nenvalur spared a glance up at Erumon, who looked out over the woodline with his eyes glowing brightly. "Can you feel it? There's a faint trace of him pushing his mana through the woods to sense their location. I've always prided myself on my combat abilities, but he's on an entirely *different* level," Nenvalur said, turning back to face the woodline once more with a shake of his head and a quiet chuckle.

"Thanks to the *Authority* he gave us, I can feel it, but it feels like I'm trying to feel for the edges of a long-lost thought," Thorsen said, slightly furrowing his brow, prompting Nenvalur to chuckle at his comparison. "I know what you mean, but you've only just been brought up to the fifth stage. It will take you some time to adjust to it, since you didn't gain it through progressive training," he said, clapping Thorsen on the shoulder.

"When this is all over, I'll *gladly* teach you as much as I can about it, though I won't be of much help with Shifting mana," Nenvalur said with a grin. "I'm looking forward to it," Thorsen replied with a slight grin that tugged at the corner of his beard. *They're closing in. Ready yourselves,* Erumon sent, immediately removing the grins from both their faces.

"Ready, *hen ellyll*?" Thorsen asked, using the term he'd learned from Bernar for *old elf*, taking Nenvalur by surprise. "Your pronunciation is brutish at best, but as your senior, I feel *I* should be the one asking *you* that question," he said, drawing his blade in a smooth motion as he backed away, letting it hang at his side with the point facing slightly away from his body.

Thorsen did the same, but never once took his eyes off the treeline. The guardsmen behind them saw their drawn weapons and readied their own in a unified draw, all holding the same pose as the next, finally prompting him to look over his shoulder and raise an eyebrow. "Impressive," he said, immediately returning his eyes to the trees, causing Nenvalur to feel a sense of *pride* come over him.

Wait, what's that? Thorsen wondered, thinking he'd seen something poke out for just a moment behind one of the trees.

A hissing sound gradually increased in pitch as it soared overhead. "Incoming!" he shouted over his shoulder as the massive arrow, nearly as thick as a man's forearm, careened toward its target. The guardsman it was aimed at managed to bring his shield up to deflect it, but the force of the arrow almost knocked him off his feet.

That was close, Thorsen breathed a sigh of relief, but set his jaw and exhaled firmly in preparation for the battle.

A cackling sound much like a barking wild dog came from the treeline as another arrow was sent their way. Nenvalur reached out and used a mild *Exar* spell to push it off-course. The thick arrow's broadhead sank deeply into the ground, leaving a small crater where it landed.

That could have taken a normal man's arm off. These elves really are *stronger than they look,* Thorsen realized.

Another few arrows came for them from the treeline, but none of them met their marks. "They're trying to lure us out and make us think there are fewer of them than we think," Nenvalur said with a snarl as he put up a *twenty-meter* barrier of pure mana to help protect the others behind him.

Don't rush them yet. I have a plan, Erumon sent them, having heard and understood what Nenvalur meant. *I wasn't going to, but how long are they going to keep hiding like that?* Nenvalur asked, clearly annoyed by their cowardly display.

As long as it takes to wear us down. According to Kalia, they're shrewd hunters who often wait for their prey to land in their traps before pouncing, Erumon said, his tone conveying just enough annoyance to let Nenvalur know he was feeling the same way, getting a mild grunt from the elf in return.

More and more arrows began to beat against the barrier, increasing in both frequency and power, much like the beginning of a rainstorm. One by one, the arrows clashed against the barrier, but there were no signs of any of the creatures who were attacking them.

Suddenly, the barrage of arrows halted, but in its place came a deep, low rumble in the ground. The canopies of the furthest visible trees began to shake and sway violently, some even going so far as tipping over with a thunderous *crash* onto the forest floor.

What devilry is this? Thorsen wondered, doing his best to see into the treeline, when a pair of bright green eyes in hollow, blackened sockets met his own. The towering creature was soon fully revealed, breaking out from behind a group of trees, followed closely by two others who began to spread out into a boar's head formation. Each one held the appearance of moving, swirling shadow, save for the bright eyes and gaping maw at its torso.

What the...? Thorsen half thought, but was interrupted by Erumon still atop the wall.

"Nenvalur, Thorsen; go!" Erumon boomed, though his face wasn't one of worry, but cold, calculating determination. "Finally," Nenvalur said with a wolfish grin, but even Thorsen had a hard time feeling confident against these new creatures. "Follow my lead; you'll be fine," the elf said, having felt his comrade's apprehension, before they darted into the woods at breakneck speeds.

The difference between a second stage and a fifth *is incredible,* Thorsen realized when the cones of air began to form around his torso and arms.

As they were going to meet their targets head-on, Nenvalur caught sight of a few of the archers who had been pelting them with arrows earlier. He quickly leapt off one of the massive trunks to his left and moved from tree to tree, slicing the Thran archers' heads cleanly from their shoulders.

Big fuckers aren't you? I can't wait to tell Siraye about this, he thought, trailing a mist of blood behind him as he moved.

Thorsen did the same, but was far more surprised by their size than Nenvalur was. His eyes widened when he found his first target, though due to his speed, it hadn't noticed he was even there. With a swing of his blade, the first of *many* Thran fell to his blade, as a diagonal slash carved cleanly through the beast's torso.

Before the two halves hit the ground, he'd already found another group of archers hiding in the trees to his left and proceeded to hunt them all down. Each swing *cracked* the air around it, sending bits of bone and trails of blood trailing in long arcs from the tip of his blade.

He decapitated one, ducked beneath an incoming blow from his right, and severed the legs of the as soon as spun, but one of the archers drew a dagger the size of a human longsword and swung downward in his direction. He deftly side-stepped the blow to the left, and brought his sword up through the midsection of the creature, infusing it with ample amounts of mana that caused it to explode.

Impressive. Where did you learn that one? Nenvalur asked, already working his way through another group of archers, scattering limbs and soaking the earth with their blood. *Bernar, actually,* Thorsen sent back briefly, finding it a bit difficult to keep his focus on the battle *and* talk. *I should've guessed as much. Clean up those on your side, and we'll meet up at those three charging at us,* Nenvalur sent with a mental nod.

As they each moved through their respective areas, the air quickly filled with the scent of blood, entrails, and the sounds of dying creatures. Erumon observed Thorsen carefully, making sure that he wasn't overstepping his limits as a new fifth stage.

He fights like he's been wielding a blade since birth. As expected of a descendant of my kind, he thought, seeing him crush the throat of a creature in one hand, while stabbing his blade through the skull of another.

Their enemies began to retreat in fear of their combined prowess, but Erumon could sense something much *darker* hiding behind the trio of obcasi that tore through the distant trees. As Thorsen and

Nenvalur met back up along their original path, Nenvalur raised an eyebrow at his comrade, who was drenched in a thick coat of blood.

"I'll have to teach you to move *out of the way* of the blood you spill," Nenvalur chuckled briefly. "I've never moved this quickly in my life. I feel I'm allowed to be covered in blood as I grow accustomed to it," Thorsen said, using the back of his gauntlet to wipe some blood off his brow. "So long as it's not your own," Nenvalur said casually, staring off toward the titanic creatures drawing closer during the lull in their fighting.

"What the fuck are we going to do about *them,* though? I've never seen one before," Thorsen sighed, flicking the blood from his sword. "Only one way to find out," Derion's voice came from behind them. "*Ah,* hello, old friend! I didn't know you would be in this fight," Nenvalur said with genuine surprise.

"We wouldn't be a part of the Commander's strike force if we just hid away at home, would we? I do apologize for our late appearance, but we had to ensure the other gates were secure first," Haldir said, spreading his arms widely. "*That,* and Derion keeps wanting to stop and *examine* the bodies you've left behind," Vyra said, pinching the bridge of her nose as Derion squatted over a large, severed arm.

"Who's this? Did you find Erumon's long-lost brother buried in something's remains?" Eirenne asked, pointing an arrow at Thorsen. "Not quite. It's just my brother-in-arms, Thorsen from Hjalfar," Nenvalur began proudly, patting his blood-soaked shoulder twice, assuming they hadn't already met. "Sarcasm flows right over your head sometimes, doesn't it?" she sighed.

Oh, he looks handsome, *even when covered in all that blood,* Vyra thought with a pair of raised eyebrows. *Don't you dare! I laid claim to him first,* Eirenne sent back with a glare, to which Vyra merely shrugged.

It would seem subtlety flows right past her. I wonder if she at least bid it farewell, Nenvalur thought, observing the brief exchange, though Thorsen could only offer a confused glance at Haldir, who sighed and raised his hands defeatedly.

"It's an honor to finally fight beside you all, but we need to figure out how to handle those *things*," Thorsen said, pointing over his shoulder, while Derion's ears perked up attentively. "Let me see," he quickly moved over to get a better look. His eyes flared with mana, allowing him to see the wicking tendrils of Leech mana seeping from their bodies. It also allowed him to see its swirling, writhing skin as its thick arm pushed another tree aside.

After a few brief moments of consideration and rubbing his chin as he paced back and forth, he finally turned to face the others. "Fire attribute spells will work the best on these creatures, but we can't really afford to get too close to them until we test that theory. Eirenne, Haldir; I'll need your support in hitting them with powerful ranged attacks," Derion said, surprising Thorsen at the speed with which he'd figured it out.

Is he always like this? Thorsen asked Nenvalur privately. *Has been since he was a child, but his word is as good as mine when it comes to oddities like those gigantic bastards,* the elf shrugged, prompting Thorsen to blink a few times.

"In the meantime, Vyra, Nenvalur, Thorsen, and I will do what we can to damage them, but we'll have to see how effective fire is against them first," Derion continued, entirely oblivious of Eirenne's frustrated sigh. "I'll go with Thorsen. I already *know* Nenvalur wants to take one of them on alone," Vyra said, rubbing salt in the wound. "Couldn't have said it better myself," Nenvalur grinned.

"In the meantime, keep an eye out for more archers. They hit harder than you'd think," he said, already turning in the direction of the incoming horde of Thran. "Let's move," Haldir said, getting a nod from the others as they rushed into their respective positions. Vyra gave Eirenne a wink and dashed off to Thorsen's side, prompting Eirenne to groan in disapproval.

As they made their approach to the first obcasus, they realized that by their feet were dozens, if not *hundreds*, of Thran spread throughout the trees, though many more trailed behind them. "Shit, that's a *lot more* than I thought they would have," Vyra said with a click of her tongue. "A few are going to get by us regardless, but we have to do what we can to protect your kinsfolk," Thorsen said, his voice calm and steady, as if he'd already taken this into account.

Vyra looked at him curiously for a moment. It certainly wasn't their first time meeting, though they hadn't interacted much since Leona's arrival in Caegwen.

Steadfast and *a realist? Oh, my,* she thought, feeling a smile tug at the corner of her mouth.

Derion and Nenvalur shared a glance and shook their heads just before darting off in different directions. "Thorsen, stay near Vyra; we'll cover you," Haldir shouted from somewhere *far* above the ground as a rain of arrows and spells began to strike the first line of Thran. Arrows sank into their skulls and spells charred, froze, or *buried* dozens of the massive creatures at a time. However, for each one that fell, another quickly took its place with a snarl.

Thorsen and Vyra dashed into the fray, each to their own clusters of creatures. Her speartip slashed across four of them at once, severing the hafts of their axes or arms that held their slab-like swords. Thorsen found himself quickly surrounded, but his experience in battle was *devastating* to those around him.

One of them tried to split him like a firewood log with its massive axe, but he quickly got the better of the creature and took up its weapon as his own. Dual-wielding a blade and an axe nearly as large as he was, he made quick, bloody work of those in his immediate vicinity with a combined spinning slash. Entrails soared through the air, as the screeching creatures fell to the earth in heaps.

Vyra, seeing the clearing he'd just made, used the base of her spear to launch herself over his head, jabbing her spear tip-first into the skull of an unsuspecting creature, only to leap off its shoulders and dive into a spinning attack that severed the heads of three others before she landed.

She's incredibly skilled, but how long can she fight like this? Thorsen wondered momentarily, ripping his newfound weapon out of the chest cavity of a fallen Thran.

As they left a trail of bodies in their wake, Derion and Nenvalur were fighting ferociously against the outer-lying formations, keeping as many stragglers from getting through as they could. In their wake lay not tens, but *hundreds* of corpses as they raced from side to side like a scythe to wheat.

They aren't as tough as I thought they would be, but they can certainly make up for it in numbers, Derion sent Nenvalur, carving his way through a trio of creatures with a rapid set of crossing slashes. *These creatures are hunters; their specialty lies in* trapping *their prey, not so much fighting head-on like this,* Nenvalur said, chaining a *Kyr* spell from the tip of his blade and forcing it to arc around him. *Then why were* they *sent here? Surely there were better options to pick from, right?* Derion asked, tossing a severed head at another creature, crushing its skull.

Whatever the case, Erumon has a plan and seems to know what's coming. We need to take care of these quickly if we're going to fight those large ones, Nenvalur added, spewing fire from his fingertips hot enough to melt right through a creature's chest.

Just as the corpse landed on the ground, a massive black hand smashed the ground before him, breaking the earth beneath his feet and sending him high into the air. "Son of a... Haldir!" Nenvalur shouted as more than a score of creatures raced beneath him.

Haldir leapt from branch to branch, sending arrows and spells at each of them, though there were too many for him to handle. Eirenne quickly took his spot in the tree, sending attacks at twice the speed she had earlier. "There are too many of them," Haldir shouted, already feeling frustrated at his own incompetence. However, he was immediately relieved when he saw Erumon leap down from the wall and dash at an incredible speed toward them.

Like a bolt of lightning, he moved from target to target, leaving little more than pink, static mist in his wake. The guardsmen, who remained behind a protective barrier he'd left behind, were utterly astonished at just how *easily* he defeated them. "That must have been over a *hundred* in the time it took me to *blink*," one of them said, his eyes wide and mouth agape.

"It's not for nothing that he bears the title of *Warden*," Ense said with a proud look on his fine features. His braided blonde hair swayed in the wind left in Erumon's wake as he returned to his post above the wall in a flash. "No harm will come to you while I'm here, but soon I will have to fight *my own* enemy, so reserve your strength for when I have to go," Erumon said, his hand steaming as the blood evaporated from his fists.

As he looked out onto the battlefield before him, he could tell his vanguard was starting their assault on the first obcasus, raining fire, arrows, and mana-infused slashes across its body.

Where are you? Erumon thought, sending a pulse of mana out beyond the reaches of their battle.

Suddenly, a violent pulse of Leech mana rippled through the land, causing his eyes to widen. As if heard from the bottom of the lake, a *boom* resonated through the forest, prompting him to look into the sky through the small gaps in the canopy far above.

Thank you, Lord Ryfon, Erumon dipped his head slightly as he saw the dragon's silhouette flying through the air at an incredible speed.

As he raised his head, he felt the presence of *another* whom he'd expected would arrive. "I see you wasted no time once your master revealed himself," Erumon said without looking to his right, where a woman roughly his height and pale skin stood. Immediately, the air surrounding them became incredibly dense with mana, so much so that the guardsmen below could feel it through his barrier. They staggered momentarily, prompting Erumon to pour more mana into the barrier he'd created to protect them from further harm.

Her bright green eyes flashed with delight beneath long, black bangs, as she put her hands behind her back, idly fiddling with the pale gray tunic she wore. "My *sweet, caring* Erumon. Do you think that barrier will protect them from my mission?" she asked, her voice calm and silky, while reaching her hand out to trace a finger along his shoulder. It was flicked away faster than it took her to blink, and her surprised look was met with one of pure, unadulterated *hate*.

"Don't you *dare* call me that again, *Nevesh*. You have long-since forsaken the right to do so," he said, his voice low and commanding. She raised an eyebrow doubtfully, then pursed her lower lip as if to show she didn't care. "But *I* think I will *always* have that right, won't I, *sweetheart*? Regardless of what I've done, or how many of our former comrades I've *slain*, you never *could* forget me, could you?" Nevesh asked coyly, placing her spread fingers across her ample, almost-bare chest.

Erumon held his glare and tilted his head forward. "If you're here to kill *me* next, I promise you won't find it an easy task," he growled, but she burst into a brief, manic fit of laughter. "No, no, no. I'm not here to *fight you*, though I *am* disappointed by the fact that you're here defending *them*," she gestured to the city beyond the wall.

"It's a shame, honestly. I thought that you would be in some far-off realm dealing with *the others* who walk the realms. Tell me, when was the last time you were able to stretch your wings, *eh*? Was it in Nayara that you failed to save those poor creatures from us? Or, could it have been that one time on E-..." her voice cut off the moment Erumon grabbed her by the throat.

"Do not speak of the fallen as if they are lost *forever*, Nevesh. You know just as well as I do that once *he* falls, so too will his control over them," he seethed, bringing his face closer to hers than he'd initially intended. She stuck out her long, forked tongue and licked his cheek, then smiled wickedly. "*Ah*, I've missed the taste of *regret*," she said wryly, placing both her hands on his wrist and slowly lowering his hand, prompting him to take a step back.

"Unfortunately, you're wrong about that. His plan is coming to fruition right before your eyes, and yet you still think *killing* him would be enough to stop *that*? *Hah,* you've grown even *more* delusional than when we spent that night together in Malfurst," she put a hand to the corner of her mouth in an attempt to stifle her laughter.

Erumon scowled at her, forcing himself not to take his eyes off her. "In any case, *my dear*, I've already told you that I'm not here to fight you, as I know I would likely *die* trying, but I *do* have a mission to complete. If you'd be so kind as to *step aside*," she said forcefully, causing the ones below her to drop to a knee. Erumon reinforced the barrier again, but noticed it wasn't doing much.

How is she doing this? I need to find out what she's doing before I can..., his thoughts trailed off the moment he risked his eyes to flick away from her toward the ground.

Several sickly green tendrils raced along the floor down into the earth beneath the gate, filling the dome with mana. Recognizing this, he immediately dispelled the barrier and created a second, thinner one at the center of their formation and expanded it. It pushed the Leech mana out of and away from the formation, allowing the Caegweni soldiers to breathe clean air again.

"Not bad. I thought that would have worked a lot better," Nevesh sighed with a shrug. "But no matter, I *will* complete my mission, and you know that just as well as I do," she teased, twirling her finger in a circular motion at the height of her nose. "Not this time," Erumon snarled, reaching for her neck once more to slam her into the ground, but his hand gripped nothing but the distorted image made with pure Leech mana.

As his eyes widened in confusion, she began to chuckle lightly as the image of Nevesh reformed and shook her head. "My, my. I never would have thought that would work on the ever-vigilant *Anchor*," she said through a bright smile. "You were *so close*, though I might recommend you go and check on *Her Majesty*. Maybe you'll get the chance to see me take what belongs to *me*," she spat the title wickedly, prompting him to glance over at the citadel.

In a flash of light, Erumon left behind another barrier for the guardsmen as he sped toward the Myrdinian palace. The world around him became a blur for only a moment, but when he crossed through the barrier at the main entrance, he saw the wake of what her handiwork could accomplish.

The main hall was in complete disarray. The shattered pillars and broken flooring pieces made it evident that a fierce battle had been fought here. Neko and Marte were unconscious on the floor with gaping wounds across their chest, faces, and arms. Both Anwil and Gwili were wounded as well, though Gwili was pouring his mana into his old master, shouting and shaking him with his good arm. Blood flicked from his mouth, and his left arm hung loosely at his side as he did so.

In the corner to the right of the throne was a severely wounded Trina, dragging Wien to lean against the wall with a hand to his side, nursing a handful of broken ribs, cuts, and a swollen jaw. Meanwhile, Ardrin, battered and bruised, stood between Nevesh and the queens with his arms spread widely.

"You cannot pass!" he shouted, slamming his hands together to form a barrier around them. Nevesh sneered, but as she raised her hand to strike at him, Erumon caught her wrist, her *real* wrist, and jerked it to where it bent unnaturally. She screeched in agony for a moment, but used the loosened skin of her wrist to twist and attempt to stab Erumon with a dagger of pure Leech mana.

Erumon deftly pulled at her broken bones and cast her into the far wall, placing individual healing spells over each final defender. "Thank you, Erumon," Ardrin breathed heavily as he slumped to his knees. Leona and Aurae rushed over to his aid, but when he waved them off, they moved to Anwill and the others who were severely wounded.

"Damn you, *my love*. I didn't think you'd make it in time," Nevesh snickered, digging herself out of the crater in the wall. With a wave of her good hand, she healed her broken wrist in *seconds*, making it appear like it had never broken in the first place.

"Like I said, Nevesh, *this* will be the first mission you fail," Erumon said, his eyes glowing much more intensely than before as his balled fist crackled with pure, golden lightning. "Perhaps I've failed *today*, but I promise you this: there are *plenty* of other days I can complete my mission. I always do, after all," she smiled wickedly, just before vanishing like a wisp of smoke before their eyes.

Erumon waited a few moments before releasing the spell he'd prepared, just in case she returned. When there was no longer any hint of her presence, he relented and turned to heal the others alongside Aurae and Leona.

"Who, or rather, *what* was that?" Leona asked, her keen blue eyes digging into Erumon's as he knelt across from her over Anwill. "*She* is the kind of warrior we'll be up against in the future. I'm glad that neither of you used your Wraithborn abilities, since it would be extremely *unwise* to reveal that hand now. Thank you, Aurae, for your prudence," he sighed and lowered his head deferentially.

"I'm just glad you arrived when you did; otherwise, I might not have had any choice," Aurae said distantly, weaving her mana into Neko's and Marte's chests to heal their wounds. "You mean to tell me there are *more* of them? By the Graces, how are we supposed to defend against *that*? She hardly even *struggled* against them, like they were mere *children* in her eyes," Leona said with no small amount of fear in her tone and features.

She looked at him, then to Gwili, who winced when his shoulder popped back into place. "Sorry, it's my first time," she said, but he put a consoling hand on hers and gave her a pained smile. "It's fine, but I have to agree with Leona here. We hardly stood a chance against her, and if she comes back any time soon..." he trailed off.

"I know, but she *won't*, now that she knows I'm helping you. As a result of her attack, we might need to consider more *drastic* measures to take to keep you all safe," Erumon said, already weighing his own words in his mind. "I-I see," Gwili said, wincing again while Leona worked on his arm.

Anwill's wounds healed, though there were still more than a few scars left behind on his chest and near his neck. Off to their right, under Aurae's talented hand, Marte coughed up a mouthful of drying blood and hardly managed to tilt her head to look at Neko, who was still being treated.

"N-Neko... will he, *ugh*... will he be alright?" she hardly managed to say, immediately reaching for his hand to take it in hers. "He'll live, but I'm sure his pride might be a little hurt," Aurae said in a calm and soothing voice. "*Ah*, good..." Marte smiled weakly before falling unconscious again. Gwili flinched to move toward her, but Aurae gave him a glance to stay where he was. As he shrank back into Leona's care, Aurae shifted her gaze back over to the warden, whose expression was, even now, hard to read.

"Erumon, what do you have in mind?" she asked in a tone that all but *forced* him to answer right then and there.

CHAPTER 99

INCHOATION

I could feel my heart beginning to race as I stared into the bright green eyes laced with dark tendrils of mana. His name had left my mouth venomously, though it could hardly *begin* to express the deep-rooted anger I was feeling.

Whether Balgrim had merely been possessed by Mideia, or perhaps had become his form-incarnate, I didn't know. There was, however, a stillness in the air that I couldn't ignore. It vaguely reminded me of that night in the storage room, and regardless of how I felt at that moment, I knew I couldn't act rashly.

Thoma, how are you sure it's him? Kalia asked me through our connection, her worry, as well as Ysevel's and Mom's, pouring through our connection while they helped Meliss. *I'd know that voice anywhere after that night, but I don't know why he chose to show himself now,* I replied, never once taking my eyes off him.

We began to circle each other with matching steps, with him moving toward the orb while Ed was held hostage, and I carefully watched every minute movement of his. If I had to compare it to anything, I would say it was akin to a predator stalking its prey, which had noticed it doing so.

But who's the predator in this case? I thought, adjusting my grip on my blade.

"What are you doing here, Mideia?" I asked through gritted teeth as clearly as I could over the deep *humming* of the orb behind him. "Am I not allowed to see an *old friend*? I thought you'd be pleased with the gift I left you last time when I inhabited that broken farmer's body," he spoke in a smoother voice than he'd used before, though I suspect it was due to him getting used to inhabiting Balgrim's body.

"*Friend*? What kind of friend seals a young boy's core, or possesses an old farmer who had nothing to do with *anything*?" I scoffed. "The kind who didn't want you to be used for a purpose you know nothing about," he replied with a knowing smile aimed at Kalia.

I felt a sinking feeling in my gut that I couldn't entirely ignore, one that caused my eyes to widen ever so slightly. "*Ah*, I see you haven't been told anything *at all*. I suppose I should congratulate your mentors for keeping such a *precious* secret from you," he said, giving her a glance that forced me to look at Kalia momentarily.

He's trying to turn you against us, Thoma, and this *is how he does it. He doesn't know your core is unsealed, so you should use that to your advantage,* she sent me with a subtle nod. I knew I had to play along to get as much information out of him as I could, but it took me a few moments to gather and order them properly. To avoid giving him any indication she'd communicated with me, I simply blinked and turned my gaze back to him.

I trusted Kalia with my life, and even more than that. I also knew that whatever warnings she would give me were *not* done so lightly, and so I figured feigning ignorance was the best move I could make until I got what I wanted.

"What are you trying to say then, *friend*?" I asked with a loose and begrudging use of the word, but he *clicked* his tongue a few times and shook his head. "Take that back, Thoma. It's not a good idea to *lie*," he scowled, nearly causing me to lose my focus on protecting my thoughts.

"I don't believe you would see me as a friend so easily, not after all the years you've spent *hating me* and wondering *why* that happened to you in the first place," he shook a finger on the hand that still held the dagger to Ed's temple, forcing me to set my jaw and sigh through my nostrils.

"Fine, then. What do you want to tell me?" I asked flatly, but my question seemed to confuse him. "You're not going to *demand* I let your best friend go first? My, my. Your pragmatism rivals that of even *Duke Karthus*," he said, though I had *no idea* who he was talking about at the time.

"To answer your question, there is only *one* thing I want from you, Thoma, but I believe you already *know* what it is," he said with a wicked smile, sending a dozen tendrils of Leech mana that raced through my body like lightning. I shielded my core with as much Ethereal mana as I could bear, but that left the rest of my body vulnerable to his power.

I felt my brow furrow as memories of that fateful night returned in full force, making me *re-live* that piece of my past, and the years of pain I endured thereafter flowed through my entire body. I could smell the salted pork hanging above me, see the flicker of candlelight dancing across the cloth that covered his face, and the taste of *blood* in my mouth as I struggled against his will.

Once the memory was nearing its end, I forced myself to blink and shake my head to push the memory from my mind. I didn't realize it immediately, but I was breathing much more heavily than before.

That fact was only accented by the *horrified* looks on my mother's, Kalia's, and Ysevel's faces.

They must have seen and felt everything I had that night as the re-lived memory flashed through my mind, but I couldn't bear to look at them for much longer than a glance, lest it give away my innermost thoughts.

"Y-You wanted my a-allegiance," I said with no small amount of difficulty as the air in my lungs *pained* me to escape, prompting his shoulders to tremble as my words reached his ears.

"*Mhm-hm-hm-hm...　　hahahahaha.... HAHAHAHA! AAAAAAAAH, YES!* Yes, Thoma! *Oh,* you cannot even begin to *fathom* how *excited* I am to hear that you *finally* remember that! What a little bit of *pain* won't get you, *huh*? To listen to you say those words is like music from the halls of *Polarion* to my ears!" he shouted with the purest elation I'd ever seen, while I tried to steady my breathing.

"*Ye-he-hessss*, Thoma. Yes, yes, yes. This is *good*! Just look at us! A step closer to the *end* at last!" he continued, tilting his head back and raising a hand to grasp at some invisible hope far beyond this realm. After taking a second to breathe in deeply, the skin around his eyes *darkened* into a deep-set black that only accentuated the sickly green glow of his irises.

He looked at me with a ravenous glare, as if his prey had just walked into his den. "But do you know *why* I'm as pleased as I am?" he asked, his tone carrying the curiosity of an instructor quizzing a pupil, but I could only weakly shake my head.

"Because since that fateful night, I, too, have *dreamed* about the day we would meet again, so that I may *guide* you on the path to *greatness*," he said, hardly able to keep a manic grin from showing. "What *path to greatness*?" I asked, doing my best to let him speak as much as possible so I could regain my strength, recalling a lesson I'd learned from Aurae during my first attempt at using mana to detect people's intentions.

She'd told me that one of the best ways to force your enemy to make a mistake whenever I was at a disadvantage was to *let them talk*, as it would often lead to them spilling information they would have otherwise kept to themselves.

There's no way she knew this would happen even back then, right? I wondered idly, coating my thoughts in as much protection as I could.

"I'm glad you asked, Thoma. After all, you *are* an essential sign at the crossroads," he began, twirling the dagger at Ed's temple ever so slightly. "You see, the powers that be have grown *complacent*. They sit on their thrones and hold counsel with each other about what's best for the realms," he began, stepping backward toward the orb's controlling device, prompting me to take a half-step forward as well.

"Unfortunately for *them*, I exist to *challenge* what they view to be best, and believe that *all realms* should be given the power to rule over themselves, and not be subjugated to the will of a *few*," he said with a halfhearted shrug.

"They would *never* agree to that," I said, taking another step forward as he took another back. "You would find yourself pleasantly surprised at how *incorrect* that statement is," he tilted his head forward, the wolfish grin returning to his features.

"These beings hold the fates of *infinite realms* in their hands without allowing those who reside in them to have any *real* control over their own lives, but don't you think that's *unfair*? You experienced it for yourself when I sealed your core. You *know* what the inability to have a say in how you live your life feels like first-hand," he continued, forcing his eyebrows upward to seem almost *pleading*.

"And you think giving power to *all* the realms is the way to make that happen? What of those that have creatures that could potentially *challenge* that *liberation* you're trying to give them and seize control for themselves?" I asked, hoping to find a flaw in his argument I could exploit.

He took a moment to pause and think about the question, pushing his bottom lip outward just a little. "Well, I suppose there *are* those who would be affected by the paradigm shift in power. After Nexis' *untimely* death by the *wardens'* hands, I wonder if any others might try to take up his mantle as my disciple," he began lightly, tilting his head side to side in consideration.

"Out of all the species I can think of, usually the more intelligent, *human-like* species are the greediest and most evil, often requiring the *harshest* means of *control*. However, their resistance will be of little consequence against the might of a *true* bearer of the Autarchica Primaria," he said, with a shrug, but apparently hadn't noticed the fact that I picked up on what he was implying.

Got you, I bit down a grin.

"That statement *alone* is why your plan would never work, Mideia," I began with a shake of my head. "*Oh?* Why do you think so?" he asked with genuine confusion. "Your version of *liberation* is nothing but a medium for you to step in and take control for yourself. In your case, you would end up subjugating these realms to a freedom only *you* have a say in, which, to me, sounds a lot more like *slavery*; a promise of power in exchange for *undying* servitude,"

I said, my tone growing dark with the last word, but much to my surprise, he *grinned*.

"*Ah*, I see. A *minor* slip of the tongue to a keen mind is like a loose scale on the mightiest dragon," he nodded slowly. "Well done, Thoma. Well done *indeed*, but regardless of your personal feelings toward the matter, it *doesn't* change the facts," he halted just before the panel Meliss had adjusted only a few minutes prior.

"You're right about that, but sadly, that doesn't make me want to take your side. Maybe in another life, I'd truly believe in your ideals, but this is not the one," I let out a heavy sigh, hoping to get him to let his guard down even for a split second, since I noticed Mom and the others growing restless, their hands gripping their hilts tightly.

To say I was genuinely surprised they'd held off on attacking for *that* long would be an understatement, but since they could *sense* my intentions of getting him to talk, they'd avoided it for as long as possible. Unfortunately, he'd already noticed what I was trying to do and chuckled lightly again.

"*Oh*, I understand, but you cannot say later that you weren't warned," he said with a dismissive wave. "You really would do *well* among *them*. You're as cunning as ever, but I *pity* you for thinking your little stall for time would succeed," he said, aiming a hand a Meliss and lifting it in one, smooth motion.

Leech mana exploded around her, forcing those surrounding her to protect themselves any way they could. Irun was nearly sent flying back into the wall. Thankfully, he was able to dig his daemonic claws into the ground beneath, then put up a barrier of violet mana hardly big enough to shield him under the forceful weight of the mana.

Mom, Kalia, and Ysevel each did their best to protect against the blast, but even *they* found it difficult to bear.

Athar, however, looked like his mind was tearing itself in half, prompting Devyr to pick him up and lead him away from the source of his discomfort and shielding him as far away as she could.

I was also forced to shield myself from the blast, but in the split second of deviated attention, Mideia pinned Edryd to the ground by sickly green chains tethering him to the ground beneath the orb. "Ed!" I shouted through gritted teeth as the full brunt of Mideia's power suddenly engulfed the room.

Meliss suddenly disappeared from sight, only to reappear directly beside Balgrim's possessed form, her eyes glowing with Leech mana. "Damn you! How *dare* you use her body so carelessly, you mangy *fuck*?" I heard Mom seethe. I knew she didn't like Meliss very much, but even I was surprised to see he would stoop that low.

"Test me and *find out*," he grinned, his words tinged in the purest malice I'd ever seen. With a grunt of exertion, Mom dashed toward him with everything she had, her first strike taking them to the far side of the chamber, with Kalia following close behind, leaving Ysevel, Irun, and I to handle Meliss.

"Be careful, she's completely under his control, so it will be no different than if we were fighting Mideia himself," Ysevel warned us, drawing her weapon. Meliss held an emotionless, shadow-cast expression, but the look of both despair and acceptance in her eyes was only highlighted by the memory I had of her back when I told her the truth of how I felt that night on the balcony.

To be honest, I'd never wanted to see that look again, not even on the *worst* of my enemies' faces, but a single, mana-ridden tear streamed down her face that shed just enough light to burn it into memory with the might of the *sun*.

"I never would have thought I'd be fighting your ex, Thoma. At this point, it's *really* making me never want to date," Irun sighed and shook his head, forming his jagged *kataki* blade.

I know he's just trying to lighten my mood about this, and even though I know it's Mideia inhabiting her body, I never would have guessed it would come to this, *either,* I sent Ysevel, slowly drawing my blade. *I know. Will you be alright? If you need to step away from this, just let me know,* she offered, but I shook my head.

No, I can't walk away from this now. It would be a disservice to the sacrifice she made for us earlier. The least we can do is give her a quick death to put an end to Mideia's control. I'm sure that's what she would've wanted, I sent back, taking a deep breath and setting my jaw once more.

Just behind her, I saw the orb of Leech mana beginning to react, but to *what* was something I couldn't pinpoint with it being as saturated in the chamber as it was. However, my focus was drawn back to Meliss immediately as her mouth moved silently. I couldn't hear or *understand* what it was she'd said, but I felt my anger and hatred toward Mideia grow that much stronger.

I didn't need to tell the others it was time to begin our assault, but they followed my lead as I led the charge, *drawing* as much Ethereal mana as my body could handle.

I'm so sorry, I thought privately, gripping my blade as the stones beneath my feet crumbled into little more than dust.

CHAPTER 100
PATH OF THE WRAITHBORN

I felt the stale air of the chamber rush past me as I moved in to strike. Meliss stood perfectly still until I got close enough, but the moment I did, a tendril of Leech mana lashed out of her back and formed a spear-like point to counter my blade.

There was no change in her expression from before, no soft-spoken words or even any sign of her having some semblance of control over what she was doing. The only thing I knew for *sure* was that this would *not* be an easily won battle.

Ysevel and Irun moved in as well, each aiming their strikes at different parts of her body, but like with my attack, more tendrils spawned to counter them. Ysevel spun low, aiming an attack at her legs while Irun and I struck from above.

"These fucking tendrils have a mind of their own," Irun grunted as he landed just a few meters away. "Thoma, we need to find a way around them," he said with a firm nod before we both dashed in for another set of attacks. We were hoping that Ysevel could provide enough of a distraction, but even that proved futile as she was sent flying past us and into the wall.

Ysevel! Are you alright? I asked, ducking beneath a tendril and launching an uppercut that nearly met its mark. *I'm fine, but this is a much worse situation than we had with Nexis,* she grunted briefly.

I don't know how we're going to get past this without using Wraith mana, she said, but I could feel the hesitation in her words.

I know, and I definitely agree with your hesitation, but we might not have a choice soon, I replied, deflecting a triple strike aimed at my head, neck, and chest, then dashing to the side to find an opening. Irun was preparing another attack with an ample amount of Vexing mana infused into his blade. The overhead strike slammed into a pair of daggers, sending a rippling shockwave that prompted Meliss to steady herself.

Her now-sickly green eyes looked at him, and with a flick of her wrist, she sent him barreling into the pillar behind him. However, during her moment of distraction, Ysevel managed to slide beneath the tendrils and slice at Meliss's ankle. She staggered momentarily, losing only a split second of her iron-clad focus, but a split second was all we needed.

I knew Mideia's focus was, at that time, heavily placed on me, as was evident by the fact that Meliss had hardly even bothered to look away any time she needed to deflect a strike. Still, I could tell there was much more to this fight than just taking over hers and Balgrim's bodies, but what *exactly* was still a bit of a mystery to me.

I'll follow your lead, I sent Ysevel, closing the gap between us, as she and I fell into a dance of strikes, dodging and parrying each blow that was aimed at the other. A sharp tendril tried to slash us both, but I caught it on my blade just long enough for Ysevel to land a perfectly placed slash across Meliss' chest.

With a grunt of pain, she staggered backward for a moment, putting a hand to her chest and pouring Leech mana into the wound to seal it.

That's an absurdly quick healing technique. Think we can keep up? I asked Ysevel, who dodged an overhead blow that cracked the stones beneath us. *I'm learning her attack patterns. It looks like while Mideia is offering her* power, *he's not doing much in the way of focusing on our fight, but instead on you* alone, she replied, deflecting another tendril that aimed a strike at her shoulder.

What she said began to make sense to me. There was only so much one person, no matter *how powerful,* could focus on, which likely meant that there was *some way* to overload them with information.

Mom and Kalia are definitely giving him a run for his money, then, I sent, risking a glance over to where their battle was taking place. While I didn't focus on it for long, I could see the two of them using the openings the other left behind to try to strike him. Balgrim, rather *Mideia*, had a wicked smile plastered across his face the entire time, as if he were taking *pleasure* in our struggle.

As I watched their combined and successive attacks wreaking havoc on his defenses and the structural soundness of the chamber, it gave me an idea. *Mom, Kalia, lure him over here. I think I figured out how to beat them,* I sent briefly, dashing in for another attack. *What do you mean?* Mom asked, her sword cracking through the air.

His focus is too split between Meliss and Balgrim's bodies, so neither body is at full strength. We can use that to our advantage, I sent, deflecting a rapid succession of strikes that were a bit slower than the ones when we'd first begun our battle. *I know what you're doing, Thoma, but it's risky. You can't hope to bring him down that easily without Wraith mana,* Kalia sent, having recognized the plan that was forming in my mind.

Risky or not, we'll need to attack as quickly as possible, and who better to do that than two of the quickest people I know? I asked wryly. I felt a slight tug on my core from Mom, who impressively read my memories mid strike. *I like the way you think. We'll follow your lead, son,* she sent back with a sense of pride seeping through her words.

With a nod from Ysevel, she and I distracted Meliss, forcing her to keep the entirety of her attention on the two of us. I saw Irun's eyes widen out of the corner of my eye momentarily, since another set of tendrils aimed to keep him in place.

Thoma, I'm pinned down over here. What can I do to help? Irun asked through a grunt of exertion. "Nothing," Mideia's voice spat from Meliss' mouth, whipping the cluster of tendrils as one to send him careening into the far wall.

Even from where I stood, I could hear his ribs being crushed against the stone, and the sound of the air in his lungs releasing in a burst, while his eyes rolled backward. "Irun!" I shouted, but was immediately halted from going to help him as those tendrils rapidly turned on *me*.

This is about to hurt, isn't it? I thought, bringing my blade up and infusing my body with more mana to withstand the attack's crushing power.

Just before the attack landed, I saw Mom's blurry figure appear before me to block them. The shockwave ripped through my torso along with the wave of agony she was feeling through our cores' connection. I heard her grunt, but that was all, as she pushed through the pain and gave me an opening to strike. *Fuck, that hurt, but let's make it count,* she sent plainly, but I could tell she *really was* injured from the tone she used.

I noticed Kalia and Ysevel were both on the offensive, but I realized that *this* was the opportunity I was looking for. *Now!* I sent urgently, *pushing* mana into my legs and arms to get enough power that would allow me to dash around Mom and leap into the air. Ysevel and Kalia feinted their attacks and used their momentum to carry them upward toward Balgrim's possessed form.

His eyes widened in surprise when he saw me leap toward him, but that was the *point* of Kalia and Ysevel's feint. I'd assumed that he would account for Meliss's downfall and prioritized trying to take *me* out instead. In my head, it would be like him sacrificing a limb to land a killing blow, though it was clear he hadn't accounted for losing *more than one*.

I made a show of charging up an attack, coating my blade in an ample amount of Ethereal mana, and allowing some of it within my body to leak out like an aura. "*Mideiaaaaa!*" I shouted, doing everything I could to keep his attention on me.

I can honestly say I was *relieved* to see how well that worked.

His nauseating grin widened, and I watched as tendrils of Tyrant mana overcame the pale green in his eyes. I paid it no mind, as again, I needed him to fully believe I would attack. I raised my blade high above my head, using all of my momentum to bring it down onto him. It clashed with the tendrils he brought up in his defense, sending a large shockwave out from the point of origin.

I gritted my teeth, using all my might to drive him downward as best I could, but he simply wouldn't *budge*. I pressed down harder, pouring mana into my already struggling arms, and feeling my muscles and tendons begin to strain to their absolute limits.

"Not bad, Thoma. To think you can do all of this with the sea-..." his voice cut out as we struggled against each other. His eyes shifted downward to his severed legs, and an armored, violet-glowing hand that pierced through his torso, holding a small, green orb in its hands, covered in trailing spinal fluid and tissue from his heart.

Thin tendrils of Leech mana still connected it to where it once was in his chest, but with a sudden jerk back the way it came, they frayed like a rope bearing too much weight, and eventually snapped with a blast of mana that sent me flying in the opposite direction.

Balgrim's eyes slowly returned to their standard color, and I could see there was a sense of relief in them as they watched me move in the opposite direction. *I'm sorry, Balgrim. This was the only way,* I thought, not knowing whether he could hear me without mana.

Thank ye... lad, he sent with the last bit of mana that flowed through his body. My eyes widened when I noticed there was a peaceful smile barely hidden beneath his thick beard.

His body slammed into the floor with a wet *thud*, cracking his skull wide open to spill brain matter and blood in a wide arc across the floor. At the same time, my back slammed into the far wall, nearly knocking me unconscious when the crater formed around my point of impact. I felt the air flee from my lungs, but rather than allow myself to succumb to the pain, there was one last thing I had to check.

I managed to get a look at Meliss before my eyes shut entirely, and it seemed Mideia's influence over her had *also* dissipated, though it seemed her body was *mostly* intact. The wounds we had inflicted hadn't *fully* healed due to the lingering presence of Leech mana in her body, but it was evident she wasn't in a life-threatening state.

I couldn't feel much relief, however, since I felt my mind slip a little as I began to slump off the crater I'd made in the wall, hardly conscious enough to do anything about it.

Yse...vel, I thought weakly through blurred, darkening vision.

Thankfully, instead of dropping to the floor like a sack of potatoes off the back of a wagon, Ysevel caught me in mid-air and landed safely on the ground with a minor grunt of exertion. I felt my eyes drift to hers weakly, but I was quickly met with a reassuring smile. "You called, *Prince of Caegwen?*" she asked in a playful, mocking tone, though I could hardly bear to laugh with the pain in my fractured ribs.

"I did. Thank you," I managed weakly, feeling immediately reassured by the warm smile she gave me. "How are the others?" I asked, unable to look around. "They're alright. Devyr is tending to Athar, but I think we need to help Irun quickly. Can you stand?" she asked. I sucked in as much air as I could and nodded.

She helped me to my feet, steadying me as my head spun enough to make me lose my balance, but she put my arm over her shoulder and made sure I was stable. I managed to look up, seeing Devyr rush over to Irun and begin to tend to his wounds. Athar was entirely unconscious, but thankfully, he showed no signs of possession in any way.

Mom had a hand to her side, wincing as she poured mana into it, but regardless of the pain she was in, she was amazed at Kalia's skill in enveloping it in a solid casing of her *kataki.* Meliss, however, stirred slightly, prompting all of us to give her a worried look. Kalia left Balgrim's sealed core in Mom's free hand and rushed over to help her.

She was battered, bruised, and scarred, but the still-healing wounds were a cause for concern. *It doesn't look like she's under his influence anymore, but I don't really know how to explain what's happening,* Kalia sent us this while giving her a brief examination.

That's good, but we need to keep an eye on her. Bring her to Devyr. We need to consolidate our injuries so we can heal them, Mom said with a tone that suggested she'd done this *hundreds* of times before. "That means you, too, Thoma," Ysevel noted wryly. "I know. I wouldn't mind a bit of a break from all of tha-...." I felt my throat catch under the weight of the mana flowing from the orb.

By the time I realized what was happening, it was too late. "Tho -...!" Mom's voice cut off as she was sent flying into the wall by yet *another* green tendril, leaving a crater just like Irun had, but *much* deeper. Ysevel gave me a worried glance. *Help Mom, I'll be fine,* I said, but her eyes begged me not to let go of her.

She shook her head, but with a reassuring smile and nod from me, she rushed over to help my mother. Kalia took Meliss into her arms and brought her over to Devyr, where they shielded everyone who was injured with a thick wall of *kataki* and mana.

I turned to face what I'd hoped wouldn't be true, feeling my stomach turn and my mouth grimace when I realized who was standing there. "*Hullo,* Thoma. I'm *baaaack,*" Ed's voice was muddled with Mideia's as he spoke.

I could only offer my best friend a pained look. His eyes were the same sickly green, but they had a much *deeper* presence of Tyrant mana swirling within them. His skin began to crack near his eyes and mouth, as if his body were a clay pot left too long in its oven.

Out of the cracks that formed were countless streams of Leech mana, gently flowing through the air like tall blades of grass on a spring morning. However, the eerie persona of my best friend was viciously cut through by the grin of a *starving wolf*.

"You shouldn't have done that," I seethed, gripping my blade and *drawing* as much mana as I could to support my battered body.

Shit, I'm in no shape to fight him right now. None of us are, I thought, feeling and *hearing* my fractured ribs grinding together as I tried to breathe.

"And *you* shouldn't have ripped that dwarf's core out of his *chest*," Mideia spat and glared at me. "I was *so* content to have a body that could wield nearly a *third* of my power, but now, you've left me no choice," he snarled, prompting my eyes to widen.

"You *knew* we were going to win that fight. Rather, you *let us* win," I realized, feeling the weight of the decision to kill Balgrim beginning to weigh down on my consciousness. Mideia snickered and spread his arms. "Of course I did. You didn't want to listen to me before, but now that I've left you *no choice*..." he trailed off, giving me a smug look as if he'd already won.

"You know, I really must admit I *was* surprised to see how much you've grown. That seal on your core must have been no simple thing to overcome, and I can say, without a *shadow* of a doubt, that you would make a *great* addition to my cause," he said, putting one of his arms behind his back and pointing at my torso with the other.

He began to pace back and forth, staring at the ground and furrowing his brow. "You know, for all you've told *him*, there's just *one* thing that doesn't make sense to me," he said, gesturing to himself.

"And what's that?" I asked tiredly, still finding it challenging to stand as I wiped some blood away from my brow.

"The fact that you *lied*," he halted with a severe glare. "There's no way you could have gotten *that* strong without having broken the seal on your core. I took *extra* care in putting it there that night on your weak, little body, and I *don't* make mistakes. So tell me, *why* did you lie to him, *eh*? How could you do that to your *very best friend*?" he asked, mimicking a whimper with the last few words.

I took in as deep a breath as I could and let it out with a sigh.

No point in hiding it now, is there? So be it, I thought, doing my best to gather the only words I could through the fog of my mind.

"Part of me *wanted* to tell him, and I knew I would at *some point*, but I didn't think he would hear it through the murky veil you've placed over his mind," I shook my head, but he barked a mocking laugh that shook the very foundations of the chamber.

"You're a good liar, Thoma, *almost* as good as *I* am. I should congratulate you for being able to hold your ground in a battle of wits, let alone being able to stand after such a blow," he smirked. "I don't give a flying *fuck* what you think," I managed a shrug, prompting him to place a hand over his chest in pure disgust.

"Such *vulgarity*! And here I thought you were at least a gentleman enough to *avoid* using such harsh language. Then again, I should have expected as much from a *half-breed* who has not only the *gall* to lie to his friends, but has also never learned his *place*," he snarled, spawning well over a dozen whips of Leech mana laced with the blackened tendrils of Tyrant mana in my direction.

I hardly managed to dodge them all, knowing full well more than a handful had traced deep scarlet lines across my arms, legs, and torso.

I sucked in air through my teeth, feeling their sting like pouring lime juice over an open wound, but instead of the sting dissipating quickly, I could feel it beginning to eat into my *flesh*.

I tried forcing Ethereal mana toward the wounds, but due to the presence of the Tyrant mana, it quickly dissipated, even going so far as to *strengthen* the burn. I couldn't hold my screams any longer. The pain of my ribs, coupled with the burning cuts, was simply too much for me to bear. Again and again, he launched his attacks, scoring marks across my entire body as his blades cut cleanly through the weak points in my armor.

I was losing blood, and at an alarming rate, but I didn't know just *how much* until one of the tendrils cut at my leg just above my knee, forcing me to the ground in a heap.

Thoma, I'm almost done healing Siraye. I will join you the moment I finish here, Kalia sent, though I could tell she was nowhere *near* done by the tone of her voice alone. *No, I'll go,* Ysevel interjected, but I knew it wasn't a good idea for *anyone* to be out of their protective dome right now.

No, don't. If he gets his hands on either of you, I could never forgive myself. It's me he wants, and I promise I'll find a way out of this, one way or another, I said, doing my best to project as much confidence as I could, since I knew they couldn't *visibly* see the state I was in.

I could feel their worry bleeding through our connection, but the sensation I got from my mother was something *else* entirely. It was a feeling of grim acceptance, much like what one would feel when they *know* the answer to a question they've avoided asking their entire lives.

It's alright, Mom, I'm okay. You've always taught me to face any challenge I meet head-on. You taught me the value of being honest with myself and ensuring that those I care about don't needlessly suffer because I feared what came next. You taught me always to hold my head high, no matter what it might cost me, and be proud of how far I've come. Just know that, if I don't walk away from this, please don't blame yourself, I said in as calming a voice as I could, trying to keep my tone even as another barrage of attacks scored my skin.

There was no immediate, verbal answer, but the violent torrent of rage, anger, sadness, and regret flowed through me like a waterfall. While I embraced her feelings, time seemed to slow the incoming attacks to the point where it looked like they'd been *frozen* in mid-air.

Make. Him. Bleed, she finally answered in a tone that could easily have been mistaken for an enraged *empress. As you wish,* I replied, gritting my teeth for what came next.

The attacks lurched back into motion, each one stinging, stabbing, or slicing me to no end. I hissed through the pain as I got back to my feet, feeling my arms shake as I fought against the weight of his attacks. Cuts began to dash across my face, pouring more blood than I could afford to lose into my eyes.

I set my jaw and glared at Mideia, at *Edryd,* and while I couldn't afford to dodge all of the attacks, the one aimed at my eye was one I could only afford to tilt my head to dodge, but to *him,* it must have seemed like I was beginning to see through *all* of his attacks.

His eyes widened in surprise as that disturbing grin of his returned to his face. "What's this? Have you somehow *stumbled* upon the will to fight me again? Come now, you *know* how this ends, right?" he asked, halting his barrage momentarily, though the other tendrils still floated in the air around him, poised and ready to strike at the slightest movement.

I slowly, *painfully*, brought my hand up to the pendant around my neck, allowing a wolfish grin to show ever-so-slightly. "Time to find out," I said, ripping the pendant from my neck and allowing my Wraith mana to flow freely in and around me. The burst of scarlet mana caused him to stagger not by force, but with the slightest bit of *fear*. "N-No, that's impossible," he stammered and shook his head slightly.

I suspected that, for the first time since the Great Partition, *this* was the first time he'd felt *fear* creep into his mind, eating away at him like a parasite he couldn't be rid of. I held his gaze for a few moments, allowing the Wraith mana to course through me as it began to heal the wounds he'd caused.

He watched with a growing sense of discomfort as my wounds began to shut, entirely disregarding the Tyrant mana he'd laced his attacks with. "You little..." he seethed, causing sickly green spittle to drip onto the floor. "What's the matter, *friend*? You look like you've seen a *phantom*," I said wryly, forming the *kataki* blade I'd kept on my wrist and coating it in mana.

He scoffed and shook his head. "Fine. Have it your way, then. Just know that *he* will suffer the consequences of your actions," he jutted a thumb toward himself. I nodded, feeling the last of my superficial wounds close shut.

Ed, I don't know if you can hear me, but I hope you know that I don't want to do this to you, but I don't have a choice, I sent, not knowing whether his consciousness was still present to understand my meaning.

"Very well. My turn," Mideia said coldly, suddenly bursting with an amount of Leech mana that created a pressure in the chamber that reminded me a lot of the first time I met Erumon. The sheer weight of it made me feel like I weighed over *three times* my normal weight, but it only brought a smile to my face.

Just like old times, right? I asked Kalia and Ysevel. I could feel their worry mixed with encouragement, but the former was a bit stronger. *Just like old times. Do your best, my love,* Ysevel said reassuringly.

The moment her words reached me, the binding rings that wrapped around the orb began to disintegrate, being absorbed into the orb itself as Mideia rose to about half the chamber's height. The surge of power contorted Ed's body, as a guttural scream left his mouth. I would have chosen that moment to attack, but since I needed to bide my time to heal my ribs, I knew it would be a dumb idea to do so.

Another pulse of mana, this time one *much* stronger than the last, burst out from the *orb*, not Mideia. I watched curiously as I tried to figure out what was happening.

He couldn't absorb all of it, but he's still much stronger than Nexis was when you fought him. Be on your guard, Kalia sent warningly. *I'll do what I can,* I said, gripping my *kataki* blade tightly.

Mideia's burst of power came to an end shortly after, and he glared down at me like I was still an insect to him. "I should thank you, Toma. It's been a *very* long time since I've felt this *free*," he said, running his fingers through his hair that seemed to float around him like the tendrils.

"Now, then. Shall we begin our *honorable* duel?" he asked with a raised eyebrow. Before I could even answer, he appeared in front of me in a flash, driving a clawed hand directly toward my core. I side-stepped the blow, and regretted it almost immediately as I felt my still-healing rib crack a little more. I winced in pain, but I didn't have any time to nurse the wound.

He swung his left arm in a diagonal arc, hoping to carve into my torso. I caught the claw on my sword and deflected as much of his momentum as I could.

It's taking almost everything I have not to pass out right now, I thought, parrying and deflecting another rapid succession of blows aimed at my neck, chest, and stomach.

The moment I parried another one of his strikes, he used the redirected momentum to launch into a spinning kick, sending me careening toward the wall. I used the *odoruki* technique to get out of it and appeared behind him, slashing at his back. He caught my blade with his bare hand and shook his head with a wry smile before *crushing* it in his fist.

The chunk of my blade dropped toward the ground, but if I'd learned anything from Kalia, it was that *kataki* could only respond to the bearer's intent, but I was sure he didn't know that. I caught the piece with my left hand and reshaped *both* pieces into daggers.

Using a technique I'd learned a long time ago from Derion, I tore the remaining piece away from his hand, slicing off a finger in the process, then rapidly counterattacking with a quick succession of slashes in an attempt to push him back.

He grunted from the pain of a lost finger, but quickly regenerated it and began to counter my blows, redirecting each one away from him with *undeniable* precision and accuracy. I could feel my ribs *weeping* in agony, but I knew I had to press on. With one of his deflected attacks, I mimicked the same move he had and used my momentum to kick him square in the gut, sending him back a decent way.

By the time he recovered, I was already behind him, having re-formed my daggers into a long spear and using the techniques I'd learned from Vyra. Quick jabbing movements allowed me to gain some distance, but he was able to dodge or deflect each of *those* as well.

"Someone's been *busy* these past few years, but it's not enough to *stop* me right now," Mideia snickered, but his use of the word *stop*, not *kill* told me everything I had been missing during this entire fight.

That means his real *body is somewhere else,* I realized, but I was still unsure of what that meant for this battle.

I shook the thought from my mind and returned my focus, almost a little too late to the task at hand. A heavy punch that I barely managed to block *slammed* into the middle of my reformed spear. With one piece longer than the other, I decided a *different* tactic would be necessary to give me time to devise a proper plan.

I formed the *kataki* into a bow, breaking the smaller part into arrow shafts, and enveloped them with my scarlet mana. I dashed away, giving myself enough room to fire off an arrow without risking him being able to grab it so quickly. As the first arrow soared, I recalled how Taegin had shown me the arrow moving through the living room of my old house.

Taking that idea into consideration, as well as Eirenne and Haldir's training, I *curved* the arrow, bending its trajectory to match my intent. The first one nearly struck its mark after he tried to block it with his mana, but being the shrewd warrior he was, he resorted to deflecting them with punches and kicks alone. Arrow after arrow, it was *my turn* to hit him with a barrage of attacks.

"Petty tricks will only take you so far, Thoma. You'll have to do better than that," he said, deflecting another arrow I'd sent toward the back of his head. "I know," I grinned, immediately vanishing and bringing the arrows back together with the piece I was using with the bow to form a *scythe* like the one I'd used on Nexis.

Before I could bring the weapon down, however, I noticed a grin tugging at the corner of his mouth. He turned more quickly than I could process and grabbed the haft with a single hand. The sudden halt in momentum caused my ribs to protest, but I gritted my teeth and did my best to push the tip of the scythe into his skull.

"It was an impressive fight, Thoma, but this ends here. You, and your little *group* along with it," he scowled before punching my solar plexus with a mana-infused punch. I crossed the chamber in the blink of an eye, slamming into the wall much the same way as before, but I didn't *just* lose consciousness.

To say that I *died* would be an exaggeration, but the feeling I had was much the same as the one when I first tried to step into the fourth stage. My mind was blank. I couldn't hear, see, taste, or smell. There was nothing but a blank void, dark as the deepest night.

I don't know how much time had passed before I *felt* anything. Yes, I *felt* something first, quickly followed by the muffled sounds of someone's voice calling out my name. It wasn't a panicked voice; instead, it was *soothing*, like a mother making *cooing* noises to calm a baby down.

"There, there. *Shhhh*, it's alright. There's no need to panic," a soothing, female voice said. While I couldn't attribute it to anyone *I* knew, it *did* feel familiar in a way that a warm blanket feels on a cold day. "Welcome back, Thoma," the voice said before I could register what I was looking at.

It *was* a woman, but she was unlike anything I'd ever seen before. Her skin was like freshly polished porcelain, glistening and without so much as a single blemish to be found. Her deep, scarlet eyes swirled with life and held a sense of caring that immediately made me feel at ease.

"W-Where am I?" I asked, my voice sounding distant to my own ears. "My *home*, or rather, I should say that this is now *your* home, as well," she said, brushing a lock of deep, scarlet hair behind her ear. "S-Sorry, I'm a little confused," I blinked a few times, trying to clear my vision. "*Oh*, I don't doubt that at all. You're in the middle of an *exciting* battle, after all," she chuckled as lightly as a feather landing on my face.

"I'm sorry, but I don't know if I'm going to win this one," I frowned, feeling the memories of the battle flood back into my mind. "*Perhaps*, but that battle means a lot more than you realize. Not just to you, Mideia, or your family, but to *all* realms," she said, helping me to sit up.

The bed was soft and warm, making me feel genuinely at home. "Wait a minute, this is..." I trailed off, recognizing the rest of the room. "Indeed. I replicated your room in Myrdin to help you feel more at ease. Besides, what sort of host would I be if I didn't make you feel comfortable?" she asked with a playful tone.

"*Oh*, I-I see..." I trailed off, rubbing the back of my neck in embarrassment. "There's no need to feel bashful, but there *is* something I'm going to need you to do for me. Do you think you're up to the challenge?" she asked with a smile. "I-If I can, but I still have to go back at some point, right? I mean, I can't just *leave* them there like that," I said, guessing at the fact that she knew the whole situation already.

"You're right. You can't. Which is *why* I'm going to help you, just like I did all those years ago," she said plainly, as if I was supposed to know what she was talking about.

Obviously, I had no clue.

"Here, take my hand. Let me show you something," she said, standing up from the side of my bed, revealing a long, scarlet dress that clung tightly to her body, revealing a strong, yet slender form that loosely reminded me of Aurae and Ysevel combined. I did as she requested and took her hand in mine. It was soft, not too warm or too cold, as well as sleek and slender, just like the rest of her.

She led me to the door to my room and halted before it. Before she could say another word, I reached for the doorknob and pulled the door open. "A gentleman through and through," she smiled warmly, taking my arm in hers. "Mom would kill me if she ever heard I'd failed to open a door for a lady," I chuckled, earning one from her as well. "Believe me, I *know*," she winked, gesturing outside the door's frame.

Before me was the Wraith realm, much like I'd seen it so many times before, but something felt *different*. It felt more alive, and like I was more a part of *it* as it was of *me*. "You're well acquainted with this realm after all that training with Kerre Kalia, so I'm sure you know how things are here," she began loosely, staring off into the distance.

Matching her gaze, I could see her, Mom, and Ysevel's forms, somewhere off in the distance, but I didn't see them with my eyes; rather, I *felt* them. "You see, Thoma, every realm must have its own set of rules. I couldn't perform half the miracles that the Ethereal or Meridian realms could, but there are things I can do that they *could only dream of*," she said, turning to face me.

"You mean like countering Tyrant mana?" I asked loosely, earning me a light chuckle. "A *primitive* example, but yes. I suppose that will suffice for now," she said, using her free hand to cover her mouth demurely.

"In any case, each realm has its own path to take. Some choose their own, while others are fated into it. Mideia, for example, is one such creature who only *thought* he was choosing the right path, but the reality is *far* from it," she began, her porcelain features creasing slightly as she seemed to recall a past no one else knew.

"Your path is different, however. Where Mideia failed, you will succeed, though there isn't much more I can tell you than that for now, lest you stray from it," she regarded me searchingly, nearly causing me to flinch away.

I couldn't have even if I really wanted to, I realized.

"Then what must I do, my lady?" I asked, not knowing what else to do. She paused, as if considering the weight of her words seriously. "Unfortunately, there are things I cannot tell you at the present moment. It's not that I don't *want* to, but it just wouldn't make sense to you right *now*," she said cryptically, but I knew better than to prod any further.

"It's alright. I understand. It's not the first time I've had to figure things out on my own," I shrugged, but instead of laughing, she grimaced a little. "I wish that weren't so. If it were up to me, I would give you the secrets of the Twilight Sea myself, but it is not my place to do so," she said with a tinge of regret.

"I understand," I nodded solemnly, already knowing she meant everything she'd said. "So young, and yet so *wise*. I'm sorry you've had to live like that for so long, but bear with it a little longer, and I will make it worthwhile. I promise," she said, gripping my hand a little more tightly.

"I'll bear it as long as you need me to, my lady," I gave a half-bow, placing my free hand across my chest. She looked at me searchingly to see if I was joking or lying, but after a few heartbeats, she smiled and chuckled through her nostrils.

"In that case, the Path of the Wraithborn is open to you. I will always be here to guide you and ensure that you do not stray from it," she said with a smile that reminded me of Ysevel. It took me a few moments to understand what she said, my mind racing with a million different questions when I finally realized her pupils were *slits* rather than circular.

"Not now. We will have *ample* time to discuss things at a later date. The reason I brought you here *now* is that I wanted to be the first to *welcome* you to the *fifth stage*. You've certainly earned your place along the Path, one that you've been walking for quite some time now without even realizing it," she said with a bright smile as she raised a hand to halt my questions.

Ah, so that's what this is about, I realized, feeling a sense of humility that I could never put into words.

"To whom do I owe the pleasure, then? I just realized my rudeness and that I never asked your name," I said, feeling my face flush somehow, getting a light chuckle from her. "My name is *Essentia*, and I look forward to seeing you again, Thoma," she said, offering me a Caegweni greeting.

"It's both a pleasure and an *honor* to meet you, Essentia," I said, returning the greeting. "The honor is *mine*, Thoma," she said warmly before turning to face the door we'd stepped a short way from.

"That door will take you back to your realm. Well, your consciousness, anyway. You're currently passed out in a crater, but I promise I will do everything in my power to help you grow into the man I *know* you can be," she smiled, placing a hand on my shoulder. "I just hope I can live up to your expectations," I said lightly, matching her tone. "You *will*," she said confidently, gesturing toward the door.

I approached it and grabbed the doorknob once more, giving her a final look before returning to Kavrass. "Go on, then. I'll *always* be here waiting," she smiled, offering me a delicate wave of her hand. "Be sure to visit me sometime, and bring Ysevel with you!" she called out as I was crossing the threshold.

She knows Ysevel? I thought in the heartbeat before my world went dark again.

Dust and rubble bounced off my face, and I woke with the horrifying realization that I *was* in a crater. *Thoma! Are you alright?* Ysevel's voice came through in a panicked scream. *I'm fine, I think,* I said, unsure of my body's current condition. I looked down to find a piece of Mideia's sickly green claw sticking out of my chest.

"*Fuuuuck*," I hissed, gripping it tightly as I began to tug. The strength in my arms was waning, but I poured every ounce of my might into *ripping* that piece of shit from my chest. "You're still awake after that? I suppose I underestimated you," Mideia's voice came from somewhere beyond the dust cloud in front of me. I could neither sense nor hear him while I pulled at the claw buried in my chest, but I did everything I could to get it out.

"Your struggle is futile, Thoma. You won't be rid of *that* as quickly as you think. You're just a half-breed whose body is *broken* beyond repair," he cackled. I could hear his footsteps approaching through the dust, but I had no clue just how far he was.

As if half-remembering a dream, I *reached for the Wraith realm and lifted my hand to the sky. The tendrils of mana didn't only move toward my hand, but enveloped me entirely, encasing me in its mana faster than I could process.*

"*I'm always with you,*" Essentia's voice resounded in my mind. With a final pull, I returned my consciousness to my body. Mana exploded around me, as scarlet blades followed a growing sphere of the purest mana I'd ever seen. I didn't have time to acknowledge what had just happened because I soon landed on my own two feet and felt a power within me I'd only ever dreamed of.

The dust cleared before me, and I could see that on the other side of the room, Mom, Kalia, Ysevel, and even Irun's faces were peering through a small hole in their *kataki* dome. Their eyes were wide with a mixture of awe, fear, and *relief*, but it was Mideia's face that made it more *real* to me.

"*Noooooo,*" he hissed through gritted teeth, immediately launching attack after attack, hoping to hit me *even once*. I disappeared from his line of sight, appearing to his right and landing a cut with my reformed *kataki* blade clean across his face. His eyes widened at the sight of red-green blood trickling down his face.

He tried to swing at me, but I was far faster than he was, reacting to every blow with enhanced precision. A claw came for my face to try to grab me, but I caught it in my hand, feeling my ribs healing as quickly as they were breaking.

"You were right, Mideia. *This* fight ends *here,* but I'll promise you something many others might have," I said, snapping his wrist, causing him to reel in pain. "You'll only be hurting poor *Edryd* if you keep hurting him like this," Mideia said with a derisive sneer.

"I'm sure he knows there's no other way, but there's something *he* knows about *me* that you don't," I said, still holding his wrist. Mideia looked into my eyes for a moment and saw *no sign* of remorse or hesitation. "I mean *every word* of what I promise, and I *promised* I would make you *bleed,*" I scowled, tightening my grip on his wrist as I leaned my face in toward his.

For the second time, I saw *genuine* fear in his eyes just before I launched him into the air.

Drawing out the *kataki* to match my intent, I formed the scythe once more and leaped into the air, severing one of his limbs in the process. Before his voice could register the pain, I sliced off another, then another. As quickly as I cut them, I could tell they would regenerate almost just as soon as before.

I have to keep the pressure up, I thought, doing my best to mentally stave off the pain in my chest.

I gritted my teeth once more, forcing myself to move from one point to another and keep him suspended in the air as I hacked away at his floating body. It got to the point where I nearly crashed into a streak of my own scarlet mana that was still performing a cut across his torso. From the outside, it must have looked like a pane of scarlet glass was shattering before even touching the ground.

Strike after strike, slash after bloody slash, I carved into every single nook and cranny that I could, the air around us both becoming a mist of blood and entrails. Just as I moved in for what *would* be the final strike, there was a split second of *Ed*, not Mideia, looking at me with a similar look that Balgrim had given me.

His eyes widened in the heartbeat it took for him to take in my different colored hair and eyes, but I could tell at a glance that he knew I was only doing what I could to save him. I felt bile rise in my mouth as both the physical *and* emotional pain I was in were beginning to be too much to bear.

Seeing him like that, with no limbs and minimal blood remaining in his body to speak of, was a *gut punch* worse than the one Mideia had given me only a few moments prior. My heart and core *ached*, but the look of acceptance on his face reminded me of something I'd nearly forgotten.

He was my oldest friend, and I trusted him with my life, just like he trusted me with his. The weak smile he gave me told me everything I needed to know, and the courage to land the final blow.

"Sunder," I said, my final swing carefully carving around his core as the other slashes finally caught up to what I was doing. Each one was carefully aligned so as not to harm his core with a slash or the impending explosion, like what had happened with Balgrim, but I knew that the most challenging part came after the final cut landed.

Through the misty remains of my best friend, I grabbed his core and encased it in Wraith mana, much like I'd heard from Mom that Ren had done with the dericoed's. There was no sound of his remains hitting the floor, not a whisper of his cry for help echoing throughout the chamber.

There was nothing but silence, both in my mind and in the air around me.

I landed back on the floor as gently as I could, given my current state, but the weight of the core in my hands was *far heavier* than anything I'd ever felt before. I stood there, in motionless silence for a few moments, mourning the loss of my best friend. My ears were ringing, my entire body was a scarred, bloody mess, but none of that mattered to me in that moment. I just stood there, blankly staring at what I'd done, what I'd been *forced* to do, and felt the tears stream down my face.

I heard the gentle *crumbling* of Devyr's *kataki* shield as it was drawn back into her, but I couldn't bear to look. I couldn't look them in the eyes after what had just happened, and so I did the only thing I *could* do.

I dropped to my knees and wept tears of anger, regret, and sadness all at once.

Kavrass itself had allowed me a few moments of solace before the brutal reality settled back in. Through the sound of my sniffling, I heard a faint humming growing louder and louder right in front of me, and I realized what had happened.

"The bindings... they're gone," I said, the sinking realization that there was nothing left to keep the giant orb stable anymore. "I know," Ysevel's voice came from behind me, her hand in the middle of my back, using her mana to heal my wounds as best she could. "Just like old times, right?" she said idly, as we watched the orb grow increasingly unstable.

"No, not this time," I said, struggling to get to my feet, tripping more than once along the way. "What are you doing?" she asked, catching me just before I tripped over my left foot. "We're not getting lucky a second time; it's time to make our own luck," I said, clutching Ed's core tightly to my side.

"Will you help me?" I said, sharing my intent through our connection. "*Always*, my love," she smiled weakly, giving me a knowing look. "Thanks," I said, turning to look at the orb as she helped me hobble toward it.

Mom and Kalia came as well, following just behind the two of us. I could feel their eyes burning into the back of my skull with their questions, but those could wait, and they knew that just as well as I did.

We reached the base of the platform, and I found it challenging to get up onto it so I could put my hand to my core. Mom gingerly stomped her foot on the ground, creating a platform to lift me. *Thanks, Mom,* I sent her with a pained smile, earning me a solemn nod.

With Ysevel's help, I approached the unstable orb and reached out my hand. My hand and fingers, for the most part, were still a bloody mess, but they were now only *tired*, rather than slashed. My hand shook as I *drew more mana than I could mentally bear* into me, and then out into the surrounding area. The others followed my lead, supplementing my spell with their own mana, but we were all exhausted from having used so much.

My spell wavered a little as it began to envelop the orb, but as it spread nearly halfway over the orb, I heard the sound of *massive* beating wings.

Fucking give me a break, I sighed, not knowing what sort of creature was heading our way, but it somehow *felt* like I knew who it was.

I couldn't attribute the feeling to anyone I could think of in my injured state, but I knew I had to accept whatever or *whoever it was*, with caution.

As the sound grew louder, the air suddenly grew close, as if the realm was waiting to bend to whatever will drove that creature here. "*Oh*, shit. Move!" Mom said, grabbing me by the waist, while Kalia pulled Ysevel to safety. As we fell backward, I saw a bright beam of white light descend like the brightest morning sun on top of the orb.

Time, once again, flowed strangely as I watched the bright white beam entirely *consume* the orb.

Is that...mana? I thought, before the sound of shattering earth and crushing rocks bore down on all my senses. It lasted, perhaps, the entire time it took me to perform an *odoruki* technique, but I could hardly tell with my eyes burning from the light. The shockwave blew us back a reasonable distance from the platform, which, in turn, made us slam into the ground, sending pain through my entire body.

I nearly lost consciousness, but I wanted to know who could have *possibly* had enough power to do that. I blinked slowly, and when I reopened my eyes, I saw the silhouettes of three figures where the Orb once was. While I could roughly make out two of them, there was *one* I couldn't *visually* place, but I knew they were *extremely* powerful.

I didn't know what they were saying since my ears were ringing and my vision was extremely blurry, but I could have sworn I heard Ysevel say something. She had a surprised look on her face, and while I wish I'd heard what it was, my mind was just too foggy to understand what was happening.

From what I could tell, given the others' reactions, they were allies, but the pain in my ribs raced through my body now that my adrenaline was wearing off. I knew I wouldn't be conscious much longer, but when I saw Bernar's worried expression drawing nearer, I offered him a weak, confused smile.

I have no idea how *he's here, but I guess I'll figure that out later,* I remember thinking before allowing myself to sink into darkness.

EPILOGUE
A Vow and a Promise

I heard the sounds of hushed voices around me, their movements causing slight gusts of air to rush past my exposed chest.

Where the fuck am I? I wondered with my eyes still shut.

I wanted to open them, but try as I might, nothing I did would work. That's when I realized it was because my *face* was covered by a thick piece of cloth. I tried to say something, but it came out as little more than a muffled grunt. My voice was weak, my ribs still hurt, and I had no idea where I was, or what *physical state* I was in.

All I knew was that I could feel mana circulating within my body as easily as it was to *breathe*. I recalled my conversation with Essentia, and everything that happened after, but the few moments of consciousness I had before I blacked out were still a little fuzzy.

"H-Hello?" I managed weakly, feeling my voice scratching in my throat. "*Oh*, he's awake!" I heard a strong, unfamiliar voice exclaim from somewhere to my left with a quick rustle of clothing. I tried to move my hand up to pull the cloth from my face, but I was quickly met with some form of resistance, like I'd just smacked my arm on a plate of *steel*.

Huh? Am I a prisoner or something? I thought I saw my brother *running toward me, but if I've somehow been captured, then I'm in a much worse situation than I initially thought,* I wondered, trying to figure out what was going on.

I knew I was still in the fifth stage of Wraith mana and was about to use a spell to break out of my predicament, but just before I cast anything, I heard Mom's voice coming from a few meters away. "Welcome back to the land of the *living*," she said wryly before helping me get the cloth off my face. My eyes burned with the sunlight that bore through the open balcony to my right.

I flinched away from it, but when I was able to see again, I saw Mom and Ysevel standing beside me wearing strange clothing that I didn't immediately recognize as being Caegweni, though it *was* rather similar. "Mom? Ysevel? Wha...?" I was cut off, my voice immediately muffled by Ysevel's shoulder. I smiled weakly and pressed my face into her neck, allowing the moment to last as long as I could.

"I'm so glad you're alright," she said with a light sniffle as she pulled away. Her eyes were filled with tears, but there was no denying the look of relief she had. Mom's eyes welled with tears as well, and I could tell at a glance that she'd used the wry comment from earlier to try and fight them back.

"Me, too. What happened after I blacked out? Better yet, where in Kavrass are we?" I asked, using my limited ability to look around the room. It wasn't Caegwen, that much I was sure of, and it most *definitely* wasn't the dark, stoney complex of Narin. No matter where I'd tried to place the location in my mind, I simply *couldn't.*

"About that, I believe it would be best if we let *him* explain," Mom said, stepping aside as a tall, pale man with mismatched eyes and long, flowing robes of red and white stepped into view. His hair was neatly swept back, save for a handful of strands, but his features were sharp and his slitted-pupil gaze *piercing*.

"H-Hello... *sir*? I'd offer you a proper greeting, but I'm a little *stuck* right now," I said, trying to lift my hands again, only to hear them *knock* against the metal plate with intricate, geometric designs inlaid with gold that I noticed reached the middle of my chest. "*Ah*, yes. My apologies, but it was all we could to make sure you *didn't* die during treatment," the man said with a voice that reminded me of the one from earlier.

"I was *that* close, *huh*? Well, sir, I, *uh*... I don't know how to thank you for everything you did," I said awkwardly, but I was relieved to hear a low rumbling chuckle coming from him. "To say that you were *close* would be an understatement, but I'm sure that being in the fifth stage was what saved you," he smiled, giving a brief gesture to my chest.

I struggled to look down, but when I tried to, the metal plate that was covering my body suddenly retracted, reminding me of the slits on Kalia's face. I realized, *very quickly* I might add, that the only clothing I had on me was a tight-fitting piece of fabric that I couldn't identify. My eyes widened at the sight of it, but as my eyes shifted to the rest of my body, I realized what he'd meant.

"*Oh*," I said, somewhat disappointedly. My body was *riddled* with scars, some nearly as deep as the first one I had on my back, while others were already fading into thin, white lines. There was one, large scar from where I'd pulled Mideia's claw from my chest, and I realized he'd only missed my heart by about a *centimeter*.

"You'd lost a lot of blood, and without the medical advancements we've made here, you might have *actually* died. Your friends' wounds weren't as severe, but I did leave them in Aurae's capable hands," he continued gravely.

"I-I see. I'm forever in your debt, sir," I said with as much humility as I could muster, but he held up a hand to stop me. "Nonsense. If anything, *we* owe *you* a great debt," he said, offering me a slight dip of his head.

That slight dip is something I've only ever seen Aurae do when she thanks my mother for something. It must mean he's of a much higher status than he's letting on, I thought idly as I returned the gesture.

When I realized that wasn't enough, I tried to sit up. Ysevel stepped forward again to help me, but I was pleasantly surprised to see my ribs now merely felt *bruised* rather than *shattered*. As I looked around the room, I realized that this place really was *far more* advanced than anything I'd ever seen.

It even makes Narin seem primitive by comparison, I chuckled internally in disbelief. "I'm glad you're impressed," the man said, obviously having read my thoughts, getting a weak chuckle out of me. "I should have assumed you could read my thoughts, and for that, I apologize if I was rude to you earlier, sir," I said, offering him as much of a bow as I could in my seated position.

"Nonsense. You've only just woken up from a terrible ordeal that you shouldn't have had to be the one to deal with," the man shook his head. As the words left his mouth, my mind suddenly flashed with the memory of Edryd's death, and everything that happened in between. I felt my features drop a little, as the guilt quickly filled me once more.

"Thoma," Ysevel said, putting a hand on my shoulder, knowing *exactly* what was going through my mind. I reached up to gently take her hand and nodded. "I know..." I trailed off, not being able to find any words to say. "At least I was able to encase his core in Wraith mana," I felt the words go hollow even though I knew that was the only option I *had* at the time.

"*Oh*? If he was able to do that, then he's smarter than you said he was, Bernar," he said over his shoulder just as my brother was walking in. "Hey *shit-bean*, glad to see you're awake, but not as glad to see you almost causing a full-blown riot," Bernar said, gesturing to a group of what I thought were medical personnel in the corner of the room with their jaws dropped to the floor, but I had no idea *why*.

The use of the term *shit-bean* prompted Ryfon to raise an eyebrow at him, but Bernar merely shrugged as if it were normal. I suddenly felt a minute pulse of Wraith mana in the air, but since my mind was still a little fuzzy, I couldn't tell if it had been between Bernar and the strange man, or my mother who stood right beside him. "*I should have guessed as much,*" the man said with a light chuckle. "Guessed *what*, sir?" I raised an eyebrow in confusion. "Please, you can drop the *sir*. My name is Ryfon Ansuz, but feel free to address me simply as *Ryfon*," he said with a warm smile that radiated a sense of unease throughout the other medical staff.

"V-Very well, *Ryfon*. I'll do as you ask, but what should you have guessed at?" I repeated my question from before with an extra layer of humility, just in case. "When you entered the fifth stage, who was there to greet you on the other side?" Ryfon asked plaintively, though the question took me by complete surprise.

"Lady Essentia. She was kind to me, and said that she wanted to *be the first to welcome me*, whatever *that's* supposed to mean," I shook my head as I struggled to piece my thoughts together. Ryfon's eyes widened in genuine surprise, but after a few, searching moments, he chuckled softly to himself.

It left everyone, including *me*, in a state of pure befuddlement.

"So she's chosen *you*, then? I must say, I'm impressed you caught the eye of the *Wraithlord* herself. I'm not sure if even my *grand-daughter* would be much in the way of competition," he chuckled loosely, but the horrified look on Ysevel's face gave me chills.

Did I just fuck up? What did I say that was so wrong? I paused, feeling my face blanche as he chuckled.

"You didn't *say* anything wrong, I'm only joking. I'm *glad* you two are together. She's told me a lot about you, after all," Ryfon said, giving the tomato-red Ysevel a knowing look.

That's when it hit me.

"*Wha-ha-ha-hat* the fuck...?" I muttered, piecing together the fact that Ryfon was *actually* her grandfather. "I'm surprised she didn't tell you earlier, though it wasn't for a lack of trying," he said play-fully, wrapping his arm around her with a bright grin. "Although, to be fair, I haven't been around much the past *thousand* years," his expression suddenly shifted into mild dejection.

"I-It wasn't your fau-..." Ysevel cut herself off as a deafening screech and a heavy wave of mana came from just beyond the balcony. Without thinking, I used the *odoruki* technique and formed the *kataki* blade as I leaned into the space between the balcony's edge and I.

Even though I was in a decent amount of pain from how quickly I'd moved, I realized that I had no idea *what* I was looking for, let alone what I was looking *at*. Below me there was a busy courtyard lined with high-arched walls that shimmered with the purest mana I'd ever felt outside of when I'd draw from a realm.

There were a number of buildings with domed roofs of a deep blue that reflected the triple-sun's light. Far above me, I could see what I *thought* was a moon, but it was over *twenty times* as large, and had a strange ring around it like a belt on an over-fed knight.

The streets that connected the nearby buildings shimmered with the same mana as the walls, and I couldn't help but feel a strange sense that we were no longer on *Kavrass*, but somewhere *else* entirely.

My eyes widened at the sight and I struggled to take it all in, though I couldn't help but notice a titanic shadow of a winged creature circling around the courtyard.

"Damn it, I *told* them not to fly too close to the medical ward," Ryfon snarled, suddenly appearing beside me with the faintest shift in the ambient mana. "R-Ryfon, wh-where are we?" I asked shakily, reforming my blade into the band on my wrist. "This is my *home*. Welcome to Polarion, Thoma," he leaned on the railing, tracing a line with his eyes from the sky to an open area of the courtyard far below us.

Trying to see what he was looking at, I realized that the great, winged-creature was, in fact, a massive, white and blue *dragon*. I felt my eyes go wide as a half-chuckle escaped my mouth in genuine astonishment. "Well, *that's* not something you see every day. I can feel the weight of his mana from here," I swallowed dryly, but was immediately comforted by the feeling of Ysevel's arm wrapping in mine.

Ryfon gave us an amused look, but said nothing about the gesture. "This is your home, too, now," he said, still looking off in the distance. "Sorry?" I shook my head in surprised confusion.

"Generally speaking, we can only allow those with the blood of a *dragon* into Polarion. Given the fact that both you *and* your mother had lost a vast amount of blood during the fight with Mideia, I had no choice but to bring you two here for treatment," he began to explain, prompting me to nod slowly.

"I see, but if I don't have *dragon's blood*, how was I allowed into this place?" I asked, getting a light-hearted chuckle out of him. "Who said that you *didn't*? When we were treating you, we had no choice *but* to give you some of our blood. Granted, only the blood of one at the level of a *duke* can bring someone back from the brink of death, but since you're my granddaughter's mate, I had to *call in a favor* for you, Siraye, *and* your brother. That stubborn brat wouldn't leave your side," he said with a wry grin.

What the fuck am I supposed to say to that? I asked Ysevel, while my jaw dropped to the floor in astonishment, fear, and surprise that he'd gone through so much trouble to bring me back. *Just thank him for now. We'll deal with the details later,* she smiled, tightening her grip on my arm gently.

"Th-Thank you, Ryfon. I don't know what to say," I offered him as low a bow as I could. "Don't thank *me*, thank *her*," he said, turning around to face the entrance of the medical ward. In the doorway stood a woman with sharp features, flowing black robes and pearlescent hair, with calm sapphire eyes that swirled with power.

"It's a pleasure to see you awake, Thoma. I've heard many great things about you from *Duke Ryfon*," the woman said with an elegance that rivaled even Aurae's.

D-Did she just say Duke Ryfon? I felt my eyes widen in surprise. *She did, but don't read too much into it for now,* Ysevel said with a nervous, but charming smile. *R-Right, yeah. Of course I won't*, I sent back nervously.

The woman smiled, but said nothing during our brief exchange.

As she approached, she had a presence around her that I found difficult to ignore. Her eyes were *sapphire*, which, to my limited knowledge, had no designated realm for it, but they were entirely *unavoidable*. She moved with the grace of a feather, stepping more lightly than the most highly-trained Synner, but there was a power that emanated from her that I felt could crush *realms* with a snap of her fingers.

Even with the flood of information my mind was receiving, there was an underlying sense of familiarity toward her that I couldn't explain. It felt like seeing a long-lost family member, but one I was *wildly* estranged from. "Lady Syldir," I said and bowed without thinking. "*Oh*, so you *do* know who I am. I'm impressed that you could sense that so quickly," she said with a tone that suggested mild surprise.

"My apologies, I don't know why I said that," I winced at my own stupidity. A soft, melodic chuckle came from her as she outstretched her hand toward me. "We are bound by *blood*, Thoma. I consider you as much my family as I do my own *daughter*," she smiled warmly. Not knowing what else to do, I took her hand in mine as she helped me back up.

"I see my blood has healed you well, but you'll still need some time to learn our ways," she said, though I was evidently confused by what she meant. "*Learn our ways*," I muttered to myself accidentally. "If you and your family are going to stay here a while, there are things you must learn about bearing the blood of a dragon, as well as a number of *other* things that I'm *anxious* to see you try," she gave me a knowing smile.

"*Oh*, I-I see," I smiled nervously, though I was hardly able to constrain my excitement. However, as excited as I was, I knew that I couldn't just stay here without checking in on the others, training in the fifth stage, and figuring out what to do with Ed's core.

Speaking of which, I realized shifting my eyes from Syldir to my bedside.

There was no sign of the core anywhere I looked, not near the bed, desk, or even on the floor. A mild panic began to set in as I began to fear that it had been destroyed when Ryfon and the others had made their entrance. "It's alright, Thoma. Ed's core is about as safe as it could ever be," Ysevel said in a calm, soothing voice. Even without knowing where it was, I knew Ysevel wouldn't lie about something like that, so I could only breathe a sigh of relief and gently squeeze her hand.

"Thank you. Thank *all* of you for everything you've done for us," I said weakly, giving both Ryfon and Syldir my most humble bow.

"As I'm sure Ryfon already told you, it is *us* who owe you a great debt. If Mideia had been successful in unleashing the full power of that relay, I fear we would have been in a much more *difficult* position were it not for your and your friends' sacrifices," Syldir placed a gentle hand on my shoulder to comfort me.

I hadn't even realized it, but the effect her blood had on me allowed us to share emotions freely, much like the connection I had to the others through the Wraith realm, though *this* was *far more* intense. The only reason I *did* notice was when I saw a single tear crawling down the side of her face as her emotions mirrored my own at the mention of *sacrifices*.

Guilt, anger, rage, and sorrow filled me to my core, and while I tried my best to bury it all deep down, it wasn't *entirely* possible. I looked back up at Syldir with bloodshot eyes, only able to offer her a solemn nod and a quiet whisper to those who had passed on to the next stage of their lives.

However, whether it was my own thoughts or Syldir's, I couldn't help but notice there was a silver lining to it all. Like a distant thought clawing at the entrance to my mind that was too far to hear or see, *something* was telling me it wasn't over.

"Is there a way to bring him back?" I asked, unsure of my own question. My experience with Athar had taught me that it *was* at least *possible*, but how that was going to play out would be another story entirely. Syldir's eyes widened at the feeling I'd passed to her, the slight tinge of hope at the edge of thought.

"I-It might be, but..." she trailed off, looking at Ryfon for guidance. I turned to look at him as well, and he raised an eyebrow at me. "Are you suggesting you do what was done to that boy Athar?" he asked me with a serious tone. I wasn't sure if I'd just said something they considered blasphemous or even *taboo*, but I needed an answer.

"I'm only asking if it's *possible*. Nexis, my ancestor, knew the way to do it using a strange combination of Vexing, Leech, and the power of the Nethersong Mask, according to Athar, at least," I said, trying to deflect the weight of his stare. Ryfon looked at me, then to Syldir and the others.

"I can vouch for Athar. He might be a little disturbed, but he's honest and a strong warrior. Even Kerre Kalia of the Iron Plume clan has accepted him, and from what I know about them, that was *no easy feat*," Mom spoke up, coming to my rescue. "Bernar?" Ryfon asked with a raised eyebrow. "Like my mother said: he's a weird little *fucker*, but I've never seen him as an enemy," Bernar shrugged, prompting Ryfon to nod and slowly turn to Ysevel.

"He's the founding member of *The Order of Nightfall's Blade*, and I would trust him with my *life*," Ysevel added with a solemn, respectful bow. I could sense Ryfon's apprehension even without a direct connection to him. He stroked his chin and began to pace, as if considering the weight of the decision to be made.

"I can't allow you to do this..." he finally sighed.

W-What? I felt my stomach *plummet* like a stone in a lake.

"I can't let you do this *without a guide* and a *promise*, I meant to say," he added with a wry grin. "Th-Thank you, Ryfon," I bowed quickly, reveling in the wave of relief that washed over me. I held it for a few moments, then found his pale hand outstretched toward me. "And by a promise, I mean a *vow*, from one Wraithborn to another, and from an *absent grandfather* to my future *son-in-law*," he said, his right eye *flaring* with scarlet mana.

I'd come to know the value of such a bond through my experience with Kalia, but I had *no idea* he would be the one to offer *me* that. As I rose, I did my best to hold his gaze and clasped his forearm.

This time, however, no words needed to be spoken. I felt his mana racing through my arm and into my core, as well as a secondary binding that I assumed was due to my new relation to Lady Syldir. As we exchanged our intent through the scarlet mana, Syldir placed her hand on ours, and gave me a knowing smile.

"You two, come as well," she said, gesturing with her still-free hand to Mom and Bernar. "A-Are you certain, Lady Syldir?" Mom asked as if she knew the weight of what was happening. "Of course, *child*. You *both* already have my *blood* flowing through your veins," she said with a warm smile.

Are we getting adopted by a dragon? Bernar asked me with no small amount of concern, prompting both Syldir and even *Ryfon* to chuckle. *I guess so?* I shrugged, earning me a smile from Syldir.

"You may come as well, child. You *are* the granddaughter of a *Duke*, after all," she spoke plainly and evenly to Ysevel. I saw a flash of hesitation come over her, but with a nod from her grandfather, and some *other* form of unspoken communication, she stepped in toward us, placing her hand on ours.

Mom and Bernar quickly followed her example, though it was blatantly obvious that they were both just as confused as I was. However, before *any* of us could say anything, her power surged through me like a bolt of lightning, and I thought my *skin* had caught fire for a moment, but it wasn't *painful*.

There was a brief flash of light that faded quickly between us, and when it was over, I felt an immediate wave of relief and warmth coming from her that radiated out from around us in the form of *pure* white mana.

As we stepped away from each other, I hadn't realized just how much more *connected* to the realm I was. It was like her power, coupled with mine and Ryfon's vow heightened every sense I had, nearly *doubling* what I already felt in the fifth stage, which was already nearly more than I could bear.

"So *that's* what it feels like," Mom said half-distractedly, taking a deep breath through her nose, earning her a nod from Syldir. "I can hardly believe it. I thought my senses were already at their limits but *this*," Bernar looked at his hands, then rapidly shifted his eyes around the room.

"There will be plenty of time to test your powers later," Ryfon waved dismissively. "Right now, Thoma's friend will take priority until that mission is complete, and while I don't know *where* the one who will help us is *now*, I do know his last known *title* after the Great Partition," he continued, prompting the four of us to raise an eyebrow in unison.

"What might that be?" I asked, but it wasn't Ryfon who answered. "*The Mouth of the Twilight Sea*," Bernar said with a knowing nod.

Author's Notes

Hello there!

So, now that we've kicked off the second trilogy of *The Synner Saga*, there are a few things I want you to bear in mind moving forward, as well as things I want to talk about that happened in the book.

First, I'm sure you've noticed a major formatting change to the series. After I finished college, I lost access to Adobe InDesign (which is what I was using to format the first trilogy), and I figured that was probably a sign for me to change things up. I was lucky enough to have finished the first three in the same style, but now... Well, I guess we'll see how this goes with Atticus.

With that said, let's get into the characters of *Path of the Wraith-born*.

Regarding Mideia, the next "big bad" of the saga, he's an interesting character. His unpredictable nature allows me to write him almost any way I want to, but at his core, he's a vehement manipulator. I won't spoil much else for the coming books, but as I'm sure you've noticed, I never once mentioned what he *actually* looks like. To be fair, that's mostly because I haven't decided on a design, but I'll certainly have one for *Cry of the Voiceless* (Book 5) coming out Q1 of 2026. That said, I think he'll prove to be a fascinating villain who isn't evil just for evil's sake.

Like everyone else, he has a role to play and goals to achieve, but whether he'll reach them is entirely up to Thoma and the others.

Next, let's talk about the dragons and their home, Polarion.

Polarion is an interesting place enough as it is, and while won't spoil much here, just know that it's a highly important place in the following books. There's a hierarchical structure to the place, and while it may seem that they've all got their roles to play, some are far more important than others, such as the *dukes*. Putting it simply, Wardens serve the Dukes, who ultimately serve the Council (Dukes who are a bit higher up on the chain, like the difference between a junior and a senior position, as I'm sure you've noticed).

That dynamic will be important to keep in mind later, I promise, but I wanted to clarify that now *juuuust* in case there was any confusion. That said, I'm glad I finally get to talk about them in a bit more detail, since they played a massive role during the Great Partition. Ryfon was definitely one of my favorite dragons to introduce to the series, as his mere presence alone has a much deeper significance than I let on throughout *Path of the Wraithborn*.

Oh, right. I almost forgot about Ed and Meliss.

Anyone who's been paying attention since *Echoes in the Snow* could've seen this coming from lightyears away. However, I both wanted and *needed* Thoma to find a way to deal with it. For those of you who felt *that scene* on the balcony hit a little too close to home: trust me, it took me 3 days and 4 different iterations of that conversation to get it right. I don't normally share much about my personal life in these, but that entire situation was difficult to write, since I had to go through something *extremely* similar in my own life, but felt I could help Thoma navigate the situation in a way that I wish I would have.

But no one wants to hear *that* sob story, so I'll leave it at that.

As for Kalia's, and the rest of the hegraphene's troubled past, I won't get into it here, but I'm pretty sure that if you've been paying attention, you'll see the breadcrumbs I've left behind to help paint the picture. The idea of leaving breadcrumbs without telling the full story of certain things is something I've come to enjoy doing since hearing the term *moldy worldbuilding* (the idea that there's a story to be told, but it's one that's been lost to time). Either way, not *all of it* will come to light, but there will be enough to satisfy the more curious readers.

All in all, I'm both gladdened and humbled by the fact that I've made it this far, and cannot thank you all enough for accompanying me on this journey.

Stay safe, be kind to one another, and I hope to see you all again in *The Synner: Cry of the Voiceless.*

www.ingramcontent.com/pod-product-compliance
Lightning Source LLC
Chambersburg PA
CBHW031212050726
47495CB00017B/218